THE ANCIENT GAME OF CASTLEDOWN

When played on a board, with Players carved from shell and stone, you stand to win honest gold, or lose your purse. When played between nations, with Players of flesh and blood, you stand to win a kingdom— or lose your soul.

These are the Players of Castledown:

Leron the True King; Ddiskeard the False King and his cruel, beautiful bride. Clerowan the outlaw; Dzild-zil the Treacherous, chieftain of the desert tribes. Arrod of the deep sea; and Sibyl Barron, a college student, who is about to step from the world of Boston, Massachusetts, into the magical Otherworld that has haunted her dreams...

Ace Fantasy Books by
Joyce Ballou Gregorian

THE BROKEN CITADEL
CASTLEDOWN

CASTLEDOWN

JOYCE BALLOU GREGORIAN

WITH DECORATIONS BY THE AUTHOR

ACE FANTASY BOOKS
NEW YORK

CASTLEDOWN
An Ace Fantasy Book/published by arrangement with
Atheneum

PRINTING HISTORY
Atheneum edition/1977
Ace edition/May 1983

ISBN: 0-441-09240-3

Ace Fantasy Books are published
by Charter Communications, Inc.,
200 Madison Avenue, New York, N.Y. 10016.
PRINTED IN THE UNITED STATES OF AMERICA

This book is for Shirin
Worthy namesake of Khosrow's Queen

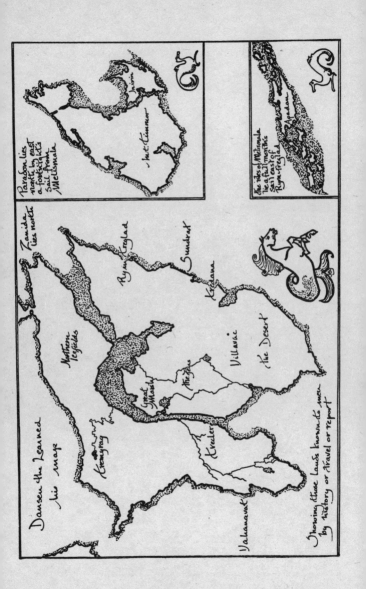

Dousen the Learned
his map

Tanida lies north

Kramyng 5

Northern Icefields

Great Marsh

Mejus

Kvellen

Villania

The Desert

Yahanava

Ryme-Tryfod

Sundvat

Kitlana

Showing those lands known to men
by history or travel or report

Paradon lies
north by east
a fortnight let's
sail from
Melismala

Auct Sinamar

Paramin

The isles of Melismala
lie a full month's
sail east of
Ryme-Tryfod

Contents

CASTLEDOWN PERSONAE

ADABA TAYYIB	Mekrif or leader of the Tayyib tribe of the Karabdu.
AJJIBAWR	The Karif, head of all Karabdin tribes.
ARBYTIS	Undying High Priest of Ornat, the temple of ancient Treglad.
ARLEON	A prince of Treglad and the legendary founder of Tredana.
ARMON	Twin to Leriel, Leron's mother: the father of Sibyl.
ARROD	Spokeswoman for the Dylalyr.
BODRUM	The Master of Vahn.
CLEROWAN	Legendary outlaw and hero; the poor man's friend.
DANSEN	Surnamed the Learned, the chief scholar of his age.
DASTRA	The supposed daughter of Simirimia, married to Ddiskeard.
DDISKEARD	Leron's cousin and the usurper of the Tredanan throne.
DELGAR	Vahnian Captain of the ship *Damar*.
THE DOUBLE GODDESS	*Rianna* and *Simirimia*, worshipped at Ornat.
THE DYLALYR	The people of the undersea.
DZILDZIL	The Holy Reader, a fanatic and tyrant of the Karabdu.

THE FOOTSMEN	Thieves and beggars, people dispossessed by Ddiskeard's rule.
GANNOC	Steward of Rym Treglad, Leron's chief counsellor.
GINAS	Headwoman of the Players; a reader of the future using the ancient Book of Ornat.
GIZMIR	An emissary from Vahn to Tredana.
GLISSER	A wealthy provincial farmer, faithful to Leron.
GORGA	Shirkah's brother, usurper of the Zanidan throne.
GWILLAM	A loyal captain of Ddiskeard's.
HAKMA	A noble of Zanida, loyal to Shirkah.
HALILA	Karive of the Karabdu, wife to Ajjibawr.
HERRARD	A wandering scholar, Dansen's friend; known to the Karabdu as Rassam, and Ajjibawr's blood-brother.
HUFFING DICK	The Footsmen's leader, a poet and thief.
THE KARABDU	Horse-breeders and warriors, tribespeople of the desert.
KERYS	Bodrum's son, a prince of Vahn.
LERON	Rightful prince of Tredana, in exile the lord of Rym Treglad.
LINIRIS	The granddaughter of Ginas.
THE MAHIVA	Dolphins, companions to the Dylalyr.
MASALA	Son of Mubassa, and like him, Horse Master to the Karif.
MARA	The wife of Gannoc.
MARITI	Young daughter of Gannoc and Mara.

MATHON BREAD-GIVER	True King of Tredana, father of Leron.
MEDDOCK	Chief of the people inhabiting the ruins of ancient Treglad.
MELADIN	A footsman and a seaman, enslaved aboard the *Damar*.
MICHAEL ARLEON	Sybil's boyfriend at Harvard, later First Lord under Bodrum.
THE MORAGANAS	Monstrous winged servants of Vazdz.
MUBASSA	Late Horse Master to the Karif.
THE NAQRA	Most ancient and powerful monster of the deep.
ODRIC	A minstrel, disinherited son of Bodrum and lord of Treclere.
OSMIN	Ajjibawr's sword-brother.
THE PLAYERS	Traveling actors, tumblers, fortune-tellers: exiled years past by the fall of ancient Treglad.
RASSAM	Herrard's name among the Karabdu.
RIANNA	A Goddess left to fade in the ruins of Treglad.
RICHARD	A friend of Sibyl's at Harvard.
RUAVE	A lesser Goddess, ruler of the tempest.
SHADITH	Adaba's twenty-ninth and final wife.
SHIRKAH	True King of Zanida, sold into slavery.
SIBYL BARRON (SIBBY)	Born in Massachusetts, she later returned to the Otherworld and found it her own.
SIMIRIMIA	She broke from Rianna to rule alone in Treclere, the Goddess of the Moon and Sibyl's mother.

TALYAS	Spokesman for Melismala.
TAMARIS	Sibyl's infant daughter.
VARYS	Bodrum's son and brother to Kerys, a prince of Vahn.
VAZDZ	Most powerful of the Gods, invoked by four false kings.

CASTLEDOWN LOCI

APADAN	Chief city of Melismala.
INIVIN	The land of Vazdz, on Paradon.
MELISMALA	A pleasant group of islands, east of the mainland.
MINDO'ILA	The estate of Madame Letha, Bodrum's sister.
ORNAT	The great Temple of ancient Treglad.
PARADON	An island north of Melismala, inhabited by Vazdz and ruled by Seven Warlords.
RYM TREGLAD	The new Treglad built by Leron in his exile.
SUNDRAT	A provincial capital north of Tredana.
TRECLERE	Simirimia's city, later ruled by Odric.
TREDANA	A city-state on the eastern coast.
TREGLAD	The continent's most ancient city, overthrown by Vazdz.
VAHANAVAT	Chief city of Vahn.
VAHN	A land of seafarers and traders on the western coast.

VALLEY OF THE DEAD KINGS	Ancient desert capital, rebuilt by Dzildzil.
VILLAVAC	A provincial capital west of Tredana.
ZANIDA	An icy northern land.

CONCERNING CASTLEDOWN
(from Milecta's *PASTIMES, FEATS OF SKILL AND GAMES OF CHANCE)*

The Popular and Ancient Game of Castledown combines both Skill and Chance. Two Armies, each of Eighteen Men, engage upon a Board of Eighty-One Squares. Attempting to make *Castledown,* the Player follows Age-old Order. First, *Attack:* wherein each Player sets out his Men as best he can, in hopes of the Advantage of Surprise. Second, *Capture:* wherein Men are lost and Advancement gained through the workings of Skill and Subtlety. Third, *Widegame:* a Time of Peril ruled by the Roll of the Dice, (called *Casting a Fate),* wherein many a man may be lost on the Outer Board, (called *Feeding the Naqra).* Fourth, *Siege:* a Weary Time, which leads at length to *Castledown.* Certain Ancient Sets are known, the Property of Kings and Princes, which bear many a Fanciful Ornament. Some show the Great Naqra himself coiled about the Board, while the Skill with which the Men are carved from Shell and Stone delights the most Particular Eye. That the game is of Great Antiquity can be seen from such Early Writers as Skotla, who often in his discourses used the Game as Symbol for the Intricate and Hidden Nature of Fate.

CASTLEDOWN

Prologue

I

Sibby walked by the river with her shoes in her hand, enjoying the short tired grass of September, still almost green under her feet. All day it had been very hot in Cambridge, but now in the dark with a cold breeze lifting off the water, she felt more comfortable. There was a round orange moon in the sky, doubled in the quiet Charles and framed by the gentle curve of Weeks bridge; she raised her hands, shoes dangling, and began to sing.

"I asked my love, to take a walk..."

Mike scrambled down the bank towards her, tearing the ground with his heavy boots. "Hey, Sib, c'mon, we're gonna be late..."

"A little walk, just a little walk..." She gestured towards the river with her shoes. "Down by the banks, where the waters..."

He had her by the hand as she finished the line. "C'mon, Sib, don't start goofing off. You know it starts at eight. Put on your shoes."

Sibby sat down obediently and began fitting one shoe on, carefully. She had missed her chance to speak. The song continued in her head, softly, as she did the leather lacing. "She said True Love, don't murder me, I'm not prepared for eternity..."

1

II

In the inner garden of his mud brick palace, Leron walked
restlessly, unable to enjoy the cool blue quiet of early morning.
It was their eighth year of exile in the north, and the second
one of drought. In a few hours it would be hot again, and the
bright sun would show how cracked the ground was and how
dry the grass; the sunny day would fill with dust and darken.
Leron sat down heavily on a stone bench and looked into the
dry bottom of a small ornamental pool. Soon after dawn the
people would be arriving at the palace with their problems,
and he would have to be ready.

He slumped farther forward, his face in his hands, and
dreamily watching through his fingers, he could see the pool
full again, deep and brown, the color of late summer. As he
half slept in the growing light of sunrise, shapes and shadows
altered quietly. There in the pool was his own dark reflection,
and above his head a ripple of water streaky with light. The
moon itself was deeper still, large and round, and the path it
made across the water was interrupted by a smooth round arch
of brick bridge. Now nearly asleep, Leron watched the girl
who walked singing by the river. The man who interrupted her
was an intrusion, and Leron angrily raised his head to order
him away. With that movement he awoke, and rising, stretched,
the dream breaking apart and disappearing in his memory. He
went inside to join his father the old King and Dansen the
Learned for breakfast.

DANSEN THE LEARNED
The History of the Kings of Tredana: Mathon Breadgiver an
extract

*. . . Prince Leron and his party journeyed safely to the island
in the frozen lake where Dastra had been imprisoned by her
most unnatural mother. There by good hap she was rescued
in safety and made one of our party, and little then did any of
us think that time would make us bitter enemies. But shortly
thereafter the power of Simirimia and the forces of nature drove*

our party asunder, and Leron the prince was lost to us, and the child Sibby and I left in the desert. We returned safely to Tredana bringing Dastra with us, chiefly through the most noble aid of Ajjibawr, the Karif of all the Karabdu, and in Tredana we greeted with joy Gannoc and Mara, safely returned their separate way. But the loss of the Prince and our other companions was heavy on us. And here one may see how deeply laid were the schemes of Ddiskeard, for it was he first urged that Leron be declared dead, the better (he said) to avert any cause for battle between Tredana and Treclere. To this we agreed, though heavily; but the child Sibby did not agree and left to rescue the Prince herself, quitting the city by good fortune on the very day Ddiskeard took his first step towards the throne, when he caused the King to be crazed with drugs and thus assumed the Regency.

When the child returned the following autumn, the Prince was with her, and they brought news of the destruction in Treclere of Simirimia and all her works, and the founding of a new order under the kindly leadership of Odric, disinherited son of Bodrum, master of Vahn and once the Great Queen's loyal vassal. Also they brought the truth of Sibby's lineage, revealing her to be the Prince's own close cousin, daughter to his uncle Armon. The King was released from his painful state, although in a sadly altered condition, and we set out to build again, as the forthcoming chronicle will show. And it was on our second journey north that the child Sibby was taken away as abruptly as she was sent, nigh to the spot where she first appeared.

I: ATTACK

Chapter One

Audiences had lasted all morning, and now as Leron walked in the garden with Mariti he began to relax for the first time that day. He sat on a bench under a dying, drought-killed tree and idly fingered the pieces on a Castledown board set up in its shade. Little Mariti had run off down the path; now she returned with three drooping blue walistas in her hand. "For you," she said triumphantly. "From Mariti."

Leron took her on his knee and examined the fading blossoms. "My thanks, sweetheart. No gentleman or prince had ever a better intended gift."

He set the flowers down on one side and picked up a shell-carved knight. "What is this called?" he asked, and Mariti hid her face against his arm.

"Horse," came the muffled reply, and Leron squeezed her approvingly.

"Almost," he said. "And this?"

She peeked at the quartz king and a big smile transformed her face. "Mathon!"

"No, Mathon is the real king. This one is only stone." He set the piece down on the painted board, and Mariti correctly named the castles at the four corners and the squares as he pointed them out. There was a fancifully drawn sea monster twisting through the ocean that encircled the playing area, and Mariti refused to name it, burying her face against his arm again. She did not look up until she heard her father's step on the path, and then jumped down and went rushing up to him.

Gannoc stooped and picked her up, then strode over to where
Leron sat, nodding respectfully while Mariti pulled at his beard.

"I sent the maid to fetch you, and when you did not come,
I was certain she had lured you into the garden instead. A ship
is approaching and should be in harbor by nightfall. The vessel
is a curious one and not of Vahn. Dansen believes she may
come from Melismala. In truth, that is a ship for which he has
waited long."

"And shall for longer, I fear. Dear Dansen, I believe he
expects the sea folk and the winged company to send us embassies."

Gannoc smiled and stroked his abused black beard. "Until
we know whether or not the vessel be friendly, I have posted
archers in your father's name commanding the harbor entrance,
and have issued orders that boats be ready to escort her as she
comes in."

"Well done. Gannoc, you manage so well I feel unnecessary."

"Sir!"

"Never mind my words. I am in a melancholy humor. It
will pass."

"May I speak freely? This melancholy might pass more
quickly, were you a little kinder with yourself. Is there so much
to be done here you can not take time to ride or hunt or dance
of an evening? Is this how you intend to spend your youth?"

"What would you have me do?" Leron spoke so loudly
Mariti looked up in surprise. "If people make the journey here
to settle in exile, do they not deserve to fare better than they
did in Tredana? How should it look for me to go riding off a-
hunting while the farmers struggle to save a living from the
drought?"

"The drought is not your fault."

"There is no drought in Tredana: and being here in the north
is, in a sense, my fault."

"Sir, we are here of our choice as well you know. And
since we are alone in exile, why do you cut yourself off from
those who would be your friends?"

"It is not like you to speak so indirectly. Friends? I suppose
you mean one of those young girls that you and Mara have so
unsubtly brought to my attention."

Gannoc shifted Mariti's weight against his arm and stood
up. "Perhaps you have waited long enough. You must know

she will not return." He cleared his throat. "Dansen has a plan for irrigation, difficult and costly he says, but sure of success. He desires to wait upon you at your convenience."

Leron stood also and touched Mariti's cheek. "I will go to him. He is in the library? Very well—I shall meet you at the quayside this evening." He went back toward the palace quickly, and Gannoc followed with Mariti on his shoulder, shaking his head.

In the library Dansen was making careful notes in the margins of a manuscript. Despite the warm weather, he wore his usual gown of brown velvet, the wide embroidered cuffs turned back so as not to smudge the parchment. A breeze ruffled the hair that stood out around his small tight cap. Leron closed the door softly behind him and watched a moment, then spoke. Dansen started to his feet.

"My lord, forgive me. I did not hear you come in."

Leron waved his hand and sat down. "Continue, please. Gannoc brought your message to me. Have you new thoughts concerning our lack of water?"

"In this very paper, a copy made in your grandfather's time of a document written in the reign of Arleon himself. Yes, Arleon, my lord, I make no doubt of its antiquity. You know he gathered in Tredana many skilled persons, homeless after the fall of Treglad."

Leron looked over Dansen's shoulder at the drawing and description before him. "I see this tunnel angling down from the mountains, but how is it to be constructed?"

"It is difficult but not unreasonably so. You see, there are these pits, sunk at regular intervals . . ." as Dansen pointed to the diagram, Leron's attention was drawn to another page of notes, written in Dansen's hand, and illustrated with cryptic circles and lines. He listened with half an ear to Dansen's scheme for irrigation, then pointed to the other page.

"Is this a part of the system?"

Dansen started nervously. "No, no, my lord, an experiment merely. A toy now, but possibly a weapon."

"A weapon? I see no edge, nor any mechanism."

"But that is the beauty of it! So simple! Of course, it may not work!" Dansen smiled, and covered the page with his other notes. "When I have finished the experiments, I will show you, but not before. I cannot have you laughing at me. But if it works, I will show you how a handful of sand, formed by fire into a circle of glass, can itself make fire and with no other help than that of the sun. Sand into fire."

"Very well, I shall wait to see your proof. But you know I would not laugh at you, Dansen. I have faith in your judgment."

Dansen nodded and smiled at this, then shook his head. "No, my lord, you do not. You would not sit here talking in the library if you belived this ship to come from Melismala."

"Dansen, I trust your judgment. Fantasies are something else."

"Fantasies, my lord? I am a man of science, of rationality. You know that even Arbytis respected the skill of Ginas. When last the Players were here, she read for me, and I saw a true picture of what will be. These are no fantasies."

"Dansen, for how many years have you looked to see Erlandus vindicated, with his tales of men that live beneath the sea or go winged through the air? Is it not possible that you saw, not a picture of what will be, but what you wish will be? When we set out on our journey nine years past, you had my head and that of Gannoc so filled with tales we took little Sibby to be some sort of foreign creature when we found her on the beach." He laughed, sadly. "You may be right. Hold to your beliefs. I will laugh no more. Mayhap the ship from the far country will sail at last to us here." Leron stood up. "Whatever the case, we shall meet at the harbor tonight. If you have need of me sooner, I will be with my father."

That evening, Leron stood on a small headland overlooking the harbor with Gannoc and a few men-at-arms. Minutes later Dansen joined them, with a young scribe following, in case there should occur some noteworthy event.

Leron had persuaded his father to stay within, for Mathon had never fully recovered from his great ordeal at the hands of the usurper Ddiskeard and his doctors, and his years in exile had been marked by a progressive weakening.

As they watched the ship, it sparkled plainly against the blue summer twilight. Sea and sky made an unmarked backdrop for its tall white sail. The ship was long, riding low in the water, and all hung round with flickering lanterns. As Gannoc had said, it was quite unlike the high-sterned ships of Vahn and drew far less water, coming in quite close to shore before it anchored. The escort boats went up to it without incident, and soon the first few were returning with the visitors on board.

Gannoc went slowly down the hill, but he came hurrying back moments later, almost breathless. Before he spoke to Leron, he bowed deeply to Dansen, with a look of humorous apology. "Dansen, write me down in your history as a fool. This ship has come direct from Apadan, which is the chief city of Melismala, and brings us an embassy in peace from the council there."

Leron raised an eyebrow and looked at Dansen. "My dear, I shall apologize anon. For now it will be more to the purpose to greet these guests."

On the small jetty the first landed party stood motionless, heads proudly raised. In the gathering dusk they were partially obscured, but Leron could make out strong-featured faces, dark hair and pale skin. The leader was a man of middle age named Talyas, who rapidly introduced the rest of his party in accurate but lightly accented speech. Leron greeted them all in peace and conducted them back towards the city.

In the main hall, high-ceilinged and torchlit, Leron had his guests sit, and Gannoc went to procure refreshments. Near Leron's chair Dansen sat at his special table, pens and parchment ready, his head at an alert angle. Talyas stepped forward and gestured to his hooded companion. "Here," he said, "safe from the ignorant and the curious, I present to you an emissary from the ancient ones, the Dylalyr. Friendship has existed ever between our two races, and our blood has mingled for numberless generations. Arrod will speak for her people as I will for mine."

Arrod threw back her cloak with a gesture of distaste so it fell in folds around her narrow feet, and Dansen drew in his breath with a gasp and half rose from the table: for the Dylalyr were the sea people written of years past by the great scholar Erlandus. Arrod stood with arrogant eyes looking directly into Leron's, naked, her body whiter than milk or marble and obviously a woman's, though less developed than a human child's of twelve. The hair hanging about her shoulders was so deep a green as to seem black, and her eyes also: the only mark on her body was a green line on her shoulders where the seam of her linen cloak had pressed too heavily, and the narrow slits at the base of her neck, which fluttered with her breathing. Leron nodded gravely, his pulse racing.

"Lady, you are welcome. I did not think ever to behold with my own eyes one of your noble and ancient race."

Arrod nodded slowly in return, gracefully, and her colorless mouth curved in a faint and lovely smile. "We are glad to have arrived, though we regret the necessity that has driven us thither." She looked at Talyas. "But of that we shall speak anon." Talyas nodded.

As she spoke, Gannoc returned, followed by kitchen servants, and the table was spread with various delicacies. Gannoc started at the sight of Arrod but controlled his features well and spoke in the servant's ear. In moments the man had returned with a platter of freshly caught fish, as skillfully arranged as though raw fish were the usual food of Treglad. This was placed with the other dishes, and Arrod smiled at the sight, making a small pleased gesture with her hand. Leron could not resist Dansen's pleading face any longer, and taking him by the sleeve led him over to where Arrod was delicately swallowing the small fishes whole, with evident delight.

"Lady," he said, "allow me to make known to you the chief man of learning in our realm, one who is personally dear to me. For long he has studied concerning your people, and to speak with you I know is all his desire."

Arrod looked from Leron to Dansen with remote friendliness. "I will be pleased to speak with you," she said. "What would you know of us?" Dansen opened his mouth to speak, but no sound came out: for perhaps the first time in his life, he was at a complete loss of words.

The news that the embassy brought gave Leron much to consider. Overseas as well as on the continent the servants of Vazdz had been growing in power, and many lands had seen the overthrow of ancient forms of rule. First Leron told the Melismalans of the establishment of false rule in his own city of Tredana and in the desert among the Karabdu, and also of how his friend Odric in Treclere was isolated from any practical alliance by distance and enemy forces. To all this, the Melismalans listened gravely, and then Talyas spoke for them, remarking that their history was more closely linked with the mainland than had been supposed.

Dansen took copious notes as Talyas spoke. "We are a group of close-knit islands, with many pleasant harbors and small bays, mild-weathered the year around. Life with us developed an easy pace; and from the earliest days, the sea folk have not feared to come up out of the water and from time to time mingle with the heavy-footed people of the land. Some of us, more adventuresome perhaps, long ago built boats and sailed to find adventure, and many made landfall upon the great island of Paradon, five hundred miles or more directly north. On Paradon they found a less friendly land, more rough and hostile, and there built cities and fought battles one group with the other. One part of the island they never did subdue, a part shrouded with fogs and mystery, and it was to this land Vazdz came perhaps three thousand years ago, when first he found the mainland inimical to his aims. He took hold of that region, called by us Inivin, and grew great in power there, sending forth from time to time his servants the Moraganas to frighten and subdue. The people of Paradon came then to worship him, first from fear and later from liking. And thus Vazdz prospered in his kingdom of Inivin until that day a thousand years past when the Double Goddess of Treglad was split in two, and the goddess Simirimia called upon Vazdz to return in power and help her to destroy the goddess Rianna, and all who worshipped at the Temple of Ornat. Since that time he has grown a little greater each year, until now he is acclaimed not only by the three tyrannical princes of the mainland, as you have explained, but also by the seven cruel warlords of Paradon. What he does here, you have told us: what he does in our lands, we shall now tell you.

"In Melismala we were famous for our honey: Vazdz has called away the bees and they return no more to swarm upon our island. In Melismala we were famous for our wines: Vazdz has caused the grapes to shrivel on the vine, so they are hard and green, good for no use at all. In Melismala we were famous for our oil: but now the hardy olive tree no longer flourishes. Each year they come from Paradon to burn our villages, lay waste our fields. And when they have despoiled us, they send embassies, saying, 'Admit Vazdz, join with us, and we shall sweep the world.' We do not wish to sweep the world: we only wish to live our lives in peace."

Talyas finished speaking, and Arrod rose to stand beside him, her slight breasts rising and falling with emotion, the narrow slits in her throat flaring slightly with anger and despair. "As Talyas says it is so, for I have seen with my own eyes what happens each spring: they sail from Paradon to despoil the shores of Melismala. In the name of Vazdz they wage war also on my people, the Dylalyr, and on our servants and friends, the Mahiva, the fish that breathe. From their ships they cast

spears at the Mahiva as they play, and stay not their hand for
any pity: when by evil chance one of my people has fallen into
their hands, him they put to terrible tortures, mercifully coming
to death at the end, for they say Vazdz has told them the Dylalyr
are not people and should be treated as beasts. This he has said
for he knows so ancient a race as ours can never be deluded
to his worship. I have seen myself how they use us, for my
own brother fell victim to their cruelties. They captured him
as he lay on the beach, asleep in the moonlight, and they stuck
him with their daggers to see the color of his blood and burned
him to see if he would cry out; and when at last he died, they
laughed and wondered if he would rot quickly, like a fish."

As she spoke, her mouth trembled, and she pressed her hand
against her throbbing neck. "So we have sworn implacable
enmity to all who proclaim Vazdz, and we will oppose his
people alone or together with you landsmen should you so
decide." She was not alone in her emotion as she spoke: Leron
saw that Dansen's hand faltered as he wrote, and his mouth
was tight with indignation.

That night, Leron called Gannoc and Dansen to meet with him,
bidding them speak freely what came into their minds. Dansen
held his goblet loosely in his hands, staring into the blood-red
liquid; Gannoc set his aside and spoke briskly. "Sir, I think
there can be no question that our sympathy lies entirely with
the Melismalans. Their purpose, and ours, and that of our allies,
all run counter to the plans of Vazdz and those who claim his
name. Motives are not at question. The trick lies in the how,
not the why, and here we are baffled. How do men, even kings,
nay, even an alliance of kings, destroy a god?"

Leron sighed. "This war, if war there be, will not be one
that can be marked out with flags and counters. A fortunate
roll of the dice is as likely to bring us victory as any force of
arms."

Dansen looked at them consideringly. "Think again, my
lord. It is the arms of Vazdz, or rather of his allies, that trouble
us. His chief power is in men, not monsters. We cannot discount the Morganas or the Naqra but neither should we let them
trouble us overmuch."

Gannoc looked up. "What do you know of the Moraganas?
Today was the first I ever heard the name."

Leron nodded. "I, too."

Dansen smiled. "I feared to mention them before lest you discount all my advice as fantastic. If you could not believe in the Dylalyr, what hope had I of explaining the Moraganas to you?"

"Peace, Dansen." Leron held up his hand. "Forgive us. We will not doubt again."

"I shall hold you to that. Very well. My reading did indeed speak of the Moraganas, and without wishing to seem credulous or easily dismayed, I have come to fear more and more that this great drought we suffer is their handiwork. Heat is their chief weapon. They are among the most ancient servants of Vazdz, birdlike, monstrous, bronze-bodied and copper-winged. They do not stoop except to strike or strike except to kill. Where they are, the earth is parched and no thing grows, no waters run: they are heat and corruption and utter devastation. They range the air as freely as the Great Naqra rules the undersea."

Leron shook his head. "This has been a day for stretching beliefs. The Dylalyr arrive from Melismala, the air is filled with bronze and copper monsters, and now the Naqra come swimming up out of childhood terrors to menace us. I have often rolled the dice in Castledown and lost a man to the Naqra, but never thought that sea-monster would come to claim its prizes in the flesh. Perhaps our next visitors will come from Zanida, where it is said there is no sun and the men are black and eat only ice and snow."

Gannoc laughed, but Dansen shook his head. "There is truth in most of these old legends, if one but knew where to look for it. I only hope that legend has made the monstrous servants of Vazdz more terrible than the reality." Under his breath, he recited softly,

> "Water harrier, armored warrior,
> sea-floor walker, landsmen stalker
> fins and feet, teeth and wings,
> Name the one has all these things."

Leron interrupted briskly. "Let us leave the monsters to games and nursery songs, then, and hope they do not trouble us. What of the military aspect? I love Odric like a brother, and could ally myself with him, but for the little matter of distance and enemy forces between us. We cannot aid each other."

"Not now, perhaps. But if you were to have a navy, and he should capture a port city north of Vahanavat, much could be accomplished."

"Indeed. But I do not think our boats will sail so far, and there is no timber here to construct a larger vessel."

"My Lord, I am surprised with you!" Dansen spoke impatiently, and Leron felt himself once more the student of ten years past. "The ships exist already, the merchantmen and slavers of Vahn. It needs only that they be captured. I suggest that such a feat should lie well within Clerowan's ability and liking. Through him and his outlaws, amass your fleet: by Herrard when next he comes, send messages to Odric with your plan. Then you may defeat Bodrum in his own city, land men secretly at the great desert port, attack Tredana from the sea as well as by the land, and even sail to Melismala to aid the gentle people there. I had not thought to find you so wanting in imagination."

Leron considered a moment, swishing the wine about in his goblet until some slopped over onto the edge of his sleeve. He looked at the dull red stain, bleeding out through the coarse linen cloth, and finally spoke. "Dansen shames me with his breadth of vision. These months past, I have narrowed my concerns too much to this city alone. I think, however, it were best if we promise no aid to either to Melismala or the sea folk for a while. Peace, Dansen. But we shall further say that when we have ships, one shall sail to their aid. For truly, without ships we might promise the world and give not as much as a handful of dust. The pirating of vessels should certainly lie within the talents and liking of Clerowan." To this they agreed and shortly after retired to their separate quarters.

Next morning Leron breakfasted with his father and with Dansen, whose custom it was to read to the old king while he ate, stories and poems from the early days of Tredana, or the last days of ancient Treglad. As Dansen read, the imagery brought back a dream to Leron's mind, and he stared over his father's bent shoulders to where the sun lay on the window ledge.

There had been a river, moonlit, at night. On either side black buildings fantastic in their height and density, lit with a

thousand tiny lights. Sibby had stood by the water's edge with
her shoes in her hand, singing, and he had watched her, feeling
so close he might almost have touched her. But she turned,
and he could not follow: the need to make her stay and speak
startled Leron with its desperate intensity.

"Damn fine!" said Mathon loudly. The old king wiped his
mouth and white beard briskly with his napkin and hit the table
for emphasis. "Damn fine bit of verse. Almost like old times,
eh, what? Dansen, damn me if I ever knew anyone could make
so much of them old stories. Give us that chorus again, now.
You know, 'coral walls, de-dum, de-dum.'"

Dansen dutifully went back to the section indicated, and
Mathon listened with his head on one side, his beard heaving
on his massive chest as his hands and breathing kept time with
the rhythm of the lines. Leron watched his father fondly, then
as Dansen reached the end, asked innocently, "Are there not
verses that refer to the Dylalyr? You should read us one, for
my father is to meet the embassy today, and it would be most
pertinent."

Dansen flushed. "Indeed, there are verses, now most happily
proven true by recent events. There is one here translated by
Brydeni, which I happened on last night, an heroic verse concerning warfare in the old time, when the Dylalyr were a more
violent people than now."

As Dansen read, Leron watched him closely and read the
changing emotions on his face. He had never thought of Dansen
as being any particular age, but now he realized that he was a
man not much into middle age, still gravely susceptible in
matters of the heart. As Dansen finished, Leron arose, and
taking his father's hand, pressed it briefly to his lips. "You
must excuse me now. I am promised to Mariti for an hour in
the garden. I shall see you both in the council chamber at the
appointed hour." As he closed the door, he could hear Dansen
once more declaiming, "Coral walls . . ." with Mathon's deeper
voice echoing him.

from THE PROPHECIES OF THE ZANIDAI
spoken by Shirkah, King of Zanida, in the year he was taken
treacherously by his brother Gorga and sent in chains to Vahn

The False King on the Eastern shore
will find the True King at his door

The False King of the South is sure
until the True King plays his wooer

The False King of the North will reign
until the True King breaks his chain

The False King of the West will rule
until the True King plays the fool

The False King of the homeless men
will help the false turn true again.

Chapter Two

Four days before the Melismalan embassy was due to return home, Leron, unable to sleep, walked at dawn on the hill above the city, looking down on his small town so beautifully planned by Dansen. All was quiet in the early morning. As Leron stood there, he saw a man wandering up the harbor road, and as the man came closer, he saw that it was Dansen. The scholar's face was pale from lack of sleep, and there were deep shadows under his eyes, but his face was dreamy with delight and the hem of his gown wet with sea water. Past him in the harbor Leron saw a flash of white against the rough green water. He looked down at Dansen's slowly moving figure, pitying him the separation ahead.

But soon all other concerns were driven away. Gannoc came up to him as Leron entered the palace, with word that Herrard had just returned in haste, with messages. "He was too hungry to wait for your arrival, and is at your command in the small dining chamber."

Herrard half rose as they entered the room, but Leron waved him back to his breakfast. He was a big man, and the meal Gannoc had set before him would have been too much for two of more ordinary size. Although his clothes showed signs of travel and hard wear, Herrard himself as usual looked fit and relaxed; his old friend Dansen had already joined him at breakfast.

While they finished eating, Leron read over the official messages from Odric in Treclere. Then, over a tankard of ale, while Herrard stretched out his saddle-cramped legs and settled himself more comfortably in his chair, Leron pried the details from him. "How goes it in Treclere? Are the people still content with their chosen lord?"

"Content enough for the most part. The city is strong and of good temper. Ever and anon informers are found, doubtless in the pay of Bodrum, and with these Odric ever deals too gently, sending them back to Vahn with stern messages. You know that Bodrum straightly refuses to recognize Odric as his son; well, as to that, there is an intriguing new development not mentioned in these papers." He smiled ironically and paused for effect. "You know that Odric leads a somewhat outlawish existence; and when I visit him, we ride now and again on various sorties, for amusement. But six months past we captured a merchant train, and took prisoner the men as well as capturing the goods. Picture then our surprise when youths traveling in the guise of journeymen proved to be the two young princes of Vahn, Kerys and Varys. You met them I think in Mindo'ila when they were children. They were returning thence to Vahnanavat at their father's orders. Odric would have sent them on, but no, they had had a taste of adventure and liked it well enough and were dismal at the thought of court life again. So they threatened Odric with the exposure of certain secrets should they be returned, knowing full well he loves them too much to cause them harm, and thus they dwell in Treclere also. It is rumored Bodrum has declared them dead already, fearing betrayal."

Leron looked back at Odric's letter. "He only writes of crops. I wish that trade were possible. There will be a poor harvest here: another winter spent on rabbit and fish, and I fear there will be more weakness and sickness than last year."

Herrard nodded. "As I entered the city this morning I was hailed of a rogue who told me I should stay in the north only if I learned to give up eating, else it were better I went home again. He spoke like a footsman."

"That would be Alwyn. He had his ears cut off for sedition in Sundrat, and says it would have been his hand next. Since this would have spoiled his trade in the south, as a pickpocket, he works honestly here out of preference. What is this I read of a navy?"

"Odric captured a boat some months ago and keeps it in a northern harbor, easily defended. It was a slave ship and put

ashore for water, when Odric and some men happened to be
in the hills above. One of his men got through to the prisoners
and with their aid the ship was taken. It is sweetly beamed and
nearly a hundred feet long."

"So, Treclere has its first ship. This fits in well with our
hopes and plans. What of the slaves?"

"Glad to be free men and settled in Treclere. Three of them
are from Zanida, captured there in a time of civil war: their
skins are so dark a brown as to seem black."

Dansen looked up alertly. "Is it truly so dark? Erlandus is
vague in his descriptions."

"They are as much darker than ourselves as a brown horse
is of a chestnut, and they manage to live in an icy land where
any race less skillful would soon perish utterly. There are no
trees there, but they build great halls of ice and dress in furs;
the cold is so intense that a fire can burn in the hall and yet
the walls remain frozen. Despite the bitterness of the land, they
are a learned people, famed for skills and enchantments; I hope
to hear more of their history when I return to Treclere. Recently
their land has suffered as ours have, for the rightful king was
betrayed by his brother and sent to Vahn a prisoner, in chains
made unbreakable through sorcery. The Zanidans dare not return while Gorga rules in place of their true lord, Shikah. Now
tell me of your seafaring plans."

"We planned to counsel Odric to try for a harbor and a ship
if possible. We further intended to set Clerowan the task of
turning pirate for us, to gather from the fleet of Vahn certain
choice ships and thus make us a navy."

"I believe that Clerowan has outstripped you in this, even
as Odric has. I have heard from the Players that he intends to
come to Rym Treglad by water, and is presently in Sundrat
securing a ship to suit his purpose."

"In truth? Then he has read our minds. When last he came,
he brought us twenty horses from the farms that were once my
father's, outside of Sundrat. He spoke only of horseraids and
certain small skirmishes with Ddiskeard's men, whom he has
made to look ridiculous."

Herrard laughed. "Clearly he has not changed so very much.
I have a message for him, which I will leave with you, should
he arrive soon by ship as intended. Adaba Tayyib, a great
chieftain among the Karabdu, who renounced the late Karif in
a fit of passion, has now rejected the Holy Reader Dzildzil. It

was because of his raiding he fell out with Dzildzil, for orders were sent to him that he must observe the treaty between Vahn and the desert, and treat the subjects of Bodrum with courtesy. He felt that by courteously requiring tolls, rather than robbing outright, he was obeying Dzildzil's command. The Holy Reader felt otherwise. Of course the Tayyib was ever a scoundrel, but the late Karif knew how to handle him."

"And this Tayyib now sends messages to Clerowan?"

"Yes, an offer of renewed friendship. I will leave it with you as I said."

"I wonder how he will receive it."

Herrard shrugged. "On this I cannot speculate. I am the bearer only. And I bear another message for you, Prince, one that is both urgent and private." He looked at Gannoc and Dansen, who both excused themselves. "It comes from Ginas." Leron looked enquiringly at him. "A few weeks past," he said, "I met with the Players unintended, I on my way here from Treclere, and they on the road to Sundrat and Tredana, where they intend to entertain a season. Ginas was most pleased to see me, for she had been about to send a messenger to you and knew I could travel here with more speed and certainty than one of her own people."

"Why so urgent? The Players were here in Rym Treglad not more than two months ago."

Herrard looked into his tankard and spoke slowly. "It is a matter of some delicacy. Ginas tells the Book of Ornat more often now that the true cards are in her hands. Often she asks for news of you and your fortune, or how it goes in Tredana. Particularly she has looked into the matter of succession."

"Ddiskeard is childless."

"And fortunately, too, since any child of his would inherit under your own laws, if born before your own."

"I can still in good conscience defeat the usurping father and make a cleaner realm for my young cousin."

"True, but nevertheless the coldness that lies between the lady Dastra and Ddiskeard has been of great service to you. There is however a rumor that she still thinks of you, and it has been said you do not marry for desire of her."

Leron looked up in anger and was relieved to see the humorous crinkle around Herrard's eyes. "My cousin and Dastra are perfectly suited."

Herrard nodded. "As I say, you have been fortunate and

benefited from their coldness. But no longer. Ginas sees in the cards that this year Dastra will be delivered of a child. She has seen further that some will call it yours."

"By what enchantment? We are happily far apart."

"I do not know. But Ginas, looking to aid you in this and other matters, has seen more. Your other cousin, lost to us for so long, is now close."

"Sibby?" Leron felt the blood rush into his face. "Close? Explain yourself."

"I cannot. Ginas says only that she is close and can be summoned. This she has already prepared to do. You are charged to meet the Players in a certain glade in the forest north of Sundrat, known to you but secret from most eyes. There Sibby will be brought back, and as you cherish your future happiness and that of your realm, you are to meet them there the night of the next full moon."

"Herrard, as you know, nothing could make me happier than the return of my sweet cousin. But why should such a happiness wear so grave a face? And how can I reach Sundrat so quickly?"

"Ginas said you would come by water, and did not explain herself further to me."

"Herrard, how could she have known? There is an unexpected embassy here, from Melismala. A large ship in port for the first time since the settlement of Rym Treglad. Just in time to bring me to my meeting in Sundrat."

Herrard was startled, but he shook his head warningly. "Prince, I would put in a word of caution, which is not from any ruler, chieftain or seer, but from one who has traveled widely, seen much and been your loyal friend—that is, myself. It is clear that Ginas expects an alliance between you and your cousin Sibby. No, let me continue. You have cherished a sentimental affection for many years, understandably; you, like the Players, seem to think life will arrange itself as neatly as a drama on the stage. But if Sibby does return, she will be a child no longer. A woman, and more than that, the daughter as much of Simirimia as of your uncle Armon. I have seen the power move in her when she was only a child. I do not think she will tamely submit to Ginas's arrangements, however well she likes you. The Players are too fond of fate, I think." Leron nodded, but inattentively.

The following day, Leron spoke with Gannoc, who was

amazed that Leron should consider traveling to Sundrat for no better reason than the intended magic of a Player. Leron's own doubt made him all the more deaf to Gannoc's arguments. The steward had barely gone when Dansen came into the room and excitedly took Leron by the arm.

"The Lady Arrod tells me you intend to journey with them down the coast. Can this be true?"

Leron frowned. "Are my plans already spoken of over town?"

Dansen flushed. "No, no, my lord. She spoke to me in all privacy. But if this is true—I see it is time, and I must tell you something I have kept secret these past few months."

"Which is?"

"Some words that Ginas spoke for me, last time the Players were in Rym Treglad." He looked away and carefully smoothed one velvet sleeve. "She spoke of me to the Dylalyr, though guardedly; and then she spoke further what seemed so unlikely I put all thought of it from my mind. She held a leaf from the Book of Ornat before my eyes and spoke these words. . . ." His voice faltered slightly.

> *"Dansen the Learned learns at length*
> *wherein lies the greatest strength,*
> *Dansen the Learned to his cost*
> *learns for what all might be lost,*
> *never a lesson of his own choosing*
> *but wisdom lies beyond its closing:*
> *to burn as fire, as water flow,*
> *and to the farthest islands go.*

And the picture was a blue circle on a yellow ground, that signifies the wisdom of the closed circle, the Temple Ornat."

"She did not explain?"

"She only said it would be all clear, shortly after the prince left the city. And now you are leaving, and we have met the people from the islands and promised them aid if possible. Do you remember those drawings of mine that you saw? I believe now my weapon will work. Used from a ship it could devastate any port city; used from port, it could burn up ships at sea. It may be the saving of Melismala as well as of our Tredana."

"It sounds most terrible. When will you know that it works?"

"By the time you return from Sundrat, surely."

Leron looked up sharply. "You know why I am going, then?"

"No, no. Only that you must to Sundrat, in answer to a message."

"The message was from Ginas. She says that my cousin Sibby will be in Sundrat at the next full moon. She says she will call her back."

Dansen smiled with delight. "If she says so, then I believe her, for she has spoken most truly for me. My lord, I am very happy for you. And it will be good to see the child again—child no longer!—before I go."

"Go? I do not understand."

"My lord—when the weapon is perfected, I will take it to the eastern islands myself, as it was spoken in my future by Ginas. We told them we would send a ship."

"Yes, but Dansen! You are not some silly youth to challenge death for amusement. You are most loved and needed here."

Dansen looked up with a twinkle in his eyes. "May I venture, sir, that you are repeating words but lately spoken to you by Gannoc?"

Leron laughed. "The gist, yes."

"My lord, as Milecta has so concisely put it in his *Maxims,* 'The clever man stores knowledge, the wise man seeks it out.' There is much in life I never cared to know until recently."

"And now?"

"Now, I fairly burn to learn." Dansen looked up and Leron smiled and put his arm around the other's shoulders. "Dansen, my dear, you must of course do as pleases you. I entreat you, however, that you make from the 'farthest islands' a happy return to us."

"My dear lord, I shall endeavor so."

The next three days were a blur of hurried preparations. On Gannoc's advice Leron decided against telling his father of his journey, for Mathon worried easily in his weakness. Gannoc felt they could put him off, with some tale of a hunting trip. How Leron would return was another matter, and Gannoc was not pleased by what he considered to be an irresponsible confidence in fate to provide transportation.

"Clerowan is in Sundrat now. If all else fails I can return safely with his raiders."

"Or be caught and strung up with them," Gannoc replied sourly.

But later on the quay Gannoc was quiet and reserved, accepting from Leron the ring of office with complete composure. He kissed the prince's hand then hugged him warmly, reminding him to return home soon. Leron answered him as warmly, but he was increasingly alert to the sharp smell of salt in the air, and the way the sea stretched so invitingly flat to the horizon. The messages and ritual farewells were finally done, and then at long last came the moment he could look back at his city from the sea. It was small, unimportant seeming, but he felt a keen love for it now that he was leaving.

It was not until Leron stood alone on shore, a few miles north of Sundrat, watching the receding vessel, that he realized how very foolish this venture was. But there was no sense in a half-hearted recklessness; Sundrat was less than an hour away. He threw his small pack over his shoulder and started out.

The day appointed by Ginas for their meeting in the woods was the morrow. To while away his waiting, Leron made for the old inn built outside the city walls, a place he felt would be safely crowded, and one that had a fine overview of the harbor. He was curious to see how many ships of Vahn might be in port. Partway up the hill, he stopped to look down, watching the fishermen handling their nets, dark against the blue water, the little fishes silver in the sun. Two or three large ships were anchored far out by the harbor mouth, slavers and merchantmen. One in particular he fancied, a tall-sided ship with crimson sails and green painted carvings he could not quite make out. That would be a fine ship for Clerowan to capture. He would rename her *Rianna* and she would be the flagship of his fleet. He laughed at his vainglory and went on up the hill.

The inn was as busy as ever, despite hard times. Three boards of Castledown were set up in the yard; onlookers as well as players betting small sums noisily, and the great oak casks of ale were flowing freely. No one remarked Leron as he quietly ordered a tankard and settled against the wall overlooking the harbor. The players at the nearest board were dressed in fantastic rags, shredded silk velvet mixed with patched stained

cotton. One was a young pale man with a bandaged hand; the
other had a fierce black patch across his eye. He was darker
than the boy and powerfully built with huge shoulders and a
fleshy, humorous face; his tunic was ludicrously pieced with
velvet, and there were flowers embroidered over the rips of
his cloak. A friend with a bandaged foot watched over his
shoulder, leaning on a twisted crutch, surveying the board with
a dubious expression. Casually Leron listened to them talk, his
face buried in his tankard. Apart from Alwyn, they were the
first footsmen he had seen.

"Five more silver dunyas on Dick. He'll have the castledown
and soon, ye'll see." Two more footsmen had joined the first
three and were assessing the board.

"Ar, that'll be the day. Thorns will turn to butter, and the
king will come back too: footsmen will ride horses and turn
kingsmen outadoors. Five dunyas on the Fambler."

The man with the patch, clearly Dick, looked up mock
angrily. "I'll see you rowing a windcar from Vahn for that
disloyalty. 'That'll be the day,' says he. Now when have you
lost money for the following of Huffing Dick?"

"No more recent than yesterday."

"I cast the chance too soon, is all. Mind to Huffing Dick,
m'lads, lay out your money mimpsily, and you'll not fear the
rope to your pipes, the chain to your pinchers, the metals to
your hobblers or the emptiness to your pocket." The lame
beggar behind him laughed. "I'm as true-bitten a bully boy as
any here, but I'll trust my sword to you before I'll lay down
silver." Huffing Dick laughed, but the lame beggar suddenly
froze, looking past the board towards the inn-yard entrance.

Two kingsmen stood there, mailed and helmeted. They surveyed the crowd and then strode in, loudly calling for ale. The
noisy group of footsmen went suddenly silent as two more
kingsmen entered and joined the first at a nearby table. The
servant girl hurried to serve them, two tankards in each strong
hand, and they took their ale without a word or any sign of
payment.

The silence was broken by Huffing Dick, who raised his
hand to call the girl as she left the kingsmen's table.

"Uncamber the cask, lass, fill our slings with floods of sweet
brown ale. The coin is good at this table." She brought them

their drinks, and he paid her from the coins on the table, then picked out another and added it to the handful. "I'll pay for the King, too, since his servants seem to be running short today."

She smiled nervously and hurried back inside. The kingsmen looked up slowly from their tankards and then at each other. The lame beggar tried to hush his friend, but Huffing Dick shook his hand from his shoulder, drinking deeply. Then he put down his tankard and lifted one of the pieces from the board holding it up to the light. It was the king. "Did I tell you my newest verses?" he asked conversationally. "They lack refinement, which suits them to their subject.

> *I went to Tredana t'uncamber a cask*
> *and saw the black king in his bloody black mask."*

He smiled sweetly at his friends, and Leron belatedly realized that Huffing Dick was extremely drunk.

There was a small commotion at the kingsmen's table as Huffing Dick went on,

> *"I went to Tredana to skimble a crowd*
> *and saw the black king in his bloody black shroud."*

One of the kingsmen hurried to his feet, drawing his sword. "Here's a prize indeed. That's Huffing Dick behind that patch!" The others drew their swords also, and Huffing Dick sat back in his chair. He pushed the patch up onto his forehead, blinked his uncovered eye and nodded pleasantly, while the other footsmen, except for the Fambler and the lame one, withdrew discreetly into the crowd.

"So the kingsmen are fanciers of literature." Huffing Dick smiled at his lame friend. "You're a liar, Hoppler, you told me they could not read. Perhaps one of them will teach the king. Then he can read me for himself and see the poems that so upset his ministers." He smiled benignly on the kingsmen. "Perhaps this time you will let me finish it in public. You know, the one which goes,

> *Tell me where's that goodly king*
> *who wore so well the golden crown*

*and made the birds of fortune sing
ennobling the Tredanan throne
with a peculiar . . ."*

One of the footsmen stepped forward with his sword, and Dick
with surprising grace scrambled up onto the table, crushing the
fragile playing pieces under foot. He spread his arms. "I never
have the chance to recite the refrain, and that's my favorite
part." He declaimed loudly,

*"Princes everyone are doomed to death.
Of course, that's true of any who draws breath.
Angry or annoyed? Curse, cry or crawl,
in any case the wind will take us all."*

"The kingsmen will take you sooner!"

The leader sprang forward, and Huffing Dick clumsily accepted a weapon from the Hoppler, parrying awkwardly but
effectively. As he fought, he took up his tankard and drank,
the sweat running down his pink face, the sweet smile un-
changing. "My epitaph is all prepared, my friends, so you will
put me to extra work if you do not save me for the rope. I
might not have time to rewrite it." He pinked the man in the
shoulder and whirled as the other three kingsmen came on him
with their swords.

*"I, Huffing Dick, learned luck too late.
Born in Sundrat, it's my fate
to let some donkey kingsmen state
with rope and noose this ass's weight. . . ."*

The Fambler had a dagger in his hands but was hanging
back, waiting possibly for some signal Huffing Dick was too
drunk to give. The Hoppler had given up his weapon already.
Bleeding from his shoulder, the first kingsmen took up his
dropped sword and circled round to get him in the back. Before
the Fambler saw the danger, Leron had moved without thinking. He grabbed the kingsman in his arms, and the Fambler
struck the sword away with his dagger. The Hoppler threw
aside his crutch and taking the fallen sword went to Huffing
Dick's aid. When they had disarmed a second man, once more

Leron and the Fambler managed to remove him from the fight. Now Dick and the Hoppler were evenly matched with an opponent apiece, and the fight was a short one. Soon four kingsmen sprawled unconscious on the ground.

Huffing Dick swung clumsily down from the table, wiping his forehead. He accepted the ale the girl brought with a deep bow and drained it, then resettled the patch across his eye. "Time to foot it again, boys, before the lads awake." He turned to Leron and held out his hand. Leron took it and involuntarily grimaced at the strength of the clasp. Huffing Dick laughed and clapped him on the shoulder. "Not bad, m'boy, not bad. Huffing Dick will not forget the favor. Just tell him who it is he owes it to."

A wild idea began to take form in Leron's mind as he grinned in answer. "Our sleeping friends here won't forget me either," he said. "May I come along with you and speak in private?"

Huffing Dick shrugged and pushed him towards the gate. "Mimpsy now and foot it prettily. We'll find some better music you can sing to." The other footsmen fell in around them, and they hurried out onto the road, towards the hovels built against the lower walls, the slums of Sundrat. Huffing Dick was humming unconcernedly, fitting verses together as they went, and Leron shook his head in wonder.

THE GLORIOUS HISTORY OF THE BENEVOLENT REIGN OF DDISKEARD, KING OF TREDANA, GOVERNOR OF VILLAVAC, LORD OF THE EASTERN SEAS AND PROTECTOR OF THE TRUE FAITH... an extract

When in order to conserve the wealth of the realm, King Ddiskeard in his wisdom closed the public charities, which leech-like had been sucking at the noble blood of the Treasury, and showed for cause how these same hospitals, wards, infirmaries and other dens of idleness had become the breeding places of dissatisfaction and rebelliousness against the Kingsrule, certain of those rogues who had their livings thus rudely sundered fell to plotting against the life of our gracious lord, rogues given to fantastic costumes for the begetting of pity in the breasts of honest citizens and to even more fantastic speech for the purpose of privacy and intrigue, and soon they were like to overrun the Kingdom sowing discord and ruin in their rapacious wake, had it not been that our King in his sublime wisdom put down the chief of them, one "King Crookneck," thereby averting many from their treasonous ways for fear of a like fate, that is, death by rope or axe or the least a lifetime rowing on a merchantman.

Of late however we have seen the rise of another manifold traitor; and the numbers of the footsmen also increase, increasing in consequence their ability to create turmoil and call down on their heads once more an even more complete and terrible retribution.

Chapter Three

The music finished its storm passage and died down. The Captain spoke, Viola answered.

> *"And what should I do in Illyria?*
> *My brother he is in Elysium.*
> *Perchance he is not drowned.*
> *What think you, sailors?"*

Sibyl swallowed, hot in her awkward mask, and squinted out into the dark theater. "Did that come through okay?" Somewhere in the dark the manager must have nodded, because the technical rehearsal suddenly broke up. "Sound levels okay back here. Just remember those places we marked—don't drop your voice tomorrow." Sibyl nodded.

Richard pulled off his Malvolio mask and sauntered over, dropping his long arm around her shoulders. "Want to go out for a bite, love? Or have you got a date with Caliban?"

Sibyl laughed reluctantly as she undid her own mask. "Yeh. We're going over to Alan's. Aren't you coming? I thought we could petition him to drop this fool mask idea."

Richard shook his head as the low growl of Mike's cycle outside roared, barked sharply and cut off. "Speak of the devil. 'Growls without.' You'd better hurry. Who knows, if he found us together he might knock me down." He grinned at her and turned to help roll up a line of flex that snaked across the stage.

Sibyl jumped down, picked up her denim jacket from the front seats, then turned impatiently.

"Richard . . ."

He looked down at her and his face softened. "All right, love, I'll be there."

The smiled died on Sibyl's face as she stumbled down the awkwardly shallow brick steps outside the theater. Mike was jiggling impatiently on his bike; he kicked it back into life as she climbed on behind, careful not to touch the exhaust where her jeans were already scorched. She bent her head for him to fasten on her helmet. It had stars and a picture of Super Chicken. He stuffed her hair in roughly and gave her a dry little kiss. "How's my girl?" he asked and she smiled quickly.

They roared through the tunnels towards Broadway, the long fast way to Central Square. Mike raced a succession of almost red lights the entire way, screaming through the last intersection just ahead of the cross traffic. Sibyl tightened her hold and Mike laughed. "That's right, hang on, baby." He took a sharp swooping corner that brought them down to Central Square, slowing with short caressing touches on the throttle, then whipped across in front of a silver MBTA bus and stopped with a jerk in front of the three-decker where Alan was having his party.

While Mike chained his bike to the porch, Sibyl went in. She could tell they were already pretty high because they had the same Doors album on two different players, out of synch and loud. Everybody who didn't have to go to the tech rehearsal had come to the party early. The door on the third floor landing was open and the smoke made patterns around the weak light bulb in the windowless hall.

There were a lot of people in the room, enough to make it too hot. And there were still plenty to come. Lynn, Sibyl's roommate, was on the couch with Alan sharing a joint and giggling. Sibyl took a plastic glass of sour red wine punch and drifted towards the window, leaning her forehead against the cool glass pane. The words and music from the stereos were beating against her head in intolerable syncopation. "Bre-break o-on thr-through t-to th-the oth-other si-side . . ."

In the dark window the reflected party was tiny and remote. She hurriedly closed her eyes, for fear of their tricking her again. She'd only been a month at school and already things were as bad as ever. Even the heavy class load and endless rehearsals were no protection. Let her guard down for one moment, let her mind wander, and snap! Another crazy vision would flicker into focus, like a movie badly spliced. This morning in Sanders it had caught her, the hall had shifted sideways and for a moment she was somewhere else. First the lecture tuned itself down into silence. Then as she looked up, the ribbed high ceiling broadened out and darkened with shadows of irregular torchlight. All around her were strange people dressed in robes, strange yet familiar. But before she could really look at them they wavered out of focus again and the lecture was once more droning in her ears. No wonder she was behind in two courses. She'd probably blow it right on stage and make a mess of the play. Then she'd be sorry for cutting off her hair to play Viola.

Sibyl sighed and drank the last of her punch. Why worry about crazy visions when she was crazy enough to be going with Mike. There he was at the door, talking about carburetors with two friends. She turned her head so he wouldn't catch her eye. She didn't want to have to stand with him and smile as he continued to discuss carburetors. It was so stupid being a girl friend. On the other side of window it was dark and peaceful. That must be why people threw themselves out, from time to time, on the off chance it might be a door. Break on through to the other side, break on through to the other side . . .

"Where's Caliban, love? Drop him in a pit somewhere?"

"It would have to be a grease-pit. No, he's over by the bar somewhere."

Richard removed the plastic glass from her hand, produced a bowl of unsalted cashews and raw cauliflower sections from one of the side tables, and sat down beside her on the window seat. He placed a leather-bound notebook on her knee. "A book of gibberish underneath the bough, a plate of cauliflower, nuts and thou . . ."

Sibyl picked up the book with delight. "Where'd I lose this? I thought it was in my jacket pocket."

"It was on the floor by the stage. When I opened it up and saw all the Sanskrit, I knew it had to be yours."

"I don't get Sanskrit 'til next year. This is just an old journal I found at the book sale today. It was in with a bunch of poetry. I was going to throw it out, but then I started reading it."

She stroked the pebbled calf binding with her fingers. "It

reminded me of something that happened when I was a kid."

Richard looked at her curiously. "How did you read it?"

She laughed. "Left to right, just like Sanskrit."

He smoothed back his hair with an exasperated gesture, and Sibyl spoke again, more seriously. "The handwriting's funny, but I think it's just some kind of copperplate. You probably couldn't see it well in the theater. Here, take another look."

Richard shook his head. "What did you mean when you said it reminded you of something?"

Sibyl touched the blue glass ring that hung from a thong around her neck. "You know how I always wear this ring for rehearsals and exams and stuff like that? It's part of a fantasy I started when I was a kid. With a special country. I gave it the name of a place I saw once in an old travel book. Tredana. This is my Tredana ring. I made up lots of things about it, but I never saw the name in print again, until I read this book. That's why the book made me feel funny. When I get home tonight, I'm going to start copying it all out on the typewriter. I'd begun to think that maybe I made up the name, too."

They bent over the notebook cheek to cheek, but in the dim room the crabbed round letters in feathery brown ink barely stood out at all from the musty smelling, discolored pages. A darker shadow fell over them, and Richard spoke without looking up. "Michael Arleon, I presume?"

Mike took her by the upper arm in a hard grip. "C'mon into the kitchen. Alan's reading palms. Wants to do yours."

At the kitchen table Mike stood behind her, his hands on her shoulders, while Alan took her hand with his usual line about sensitivity and vibrations. "I might be crazy," she thought, "but at least I'm not stupid." Then she felt Mike's hands on her shoulders and she wasn't so sure.

"Viola, my dear. Or is it Sebastian?" Alan peered at her right hand, then her left, tracing the lines with his forefinger. "Now this is outasight. Talk about typecasting. Two lifelines, fantastic. Bet you're crazy." Sibyl looked at him in astonishment, and the blood rushed to her face. Alan went on unconcerned. "Look, see here?" He pointed to where the lines started on each hand, circling the thumb. "First it's single, then for a little stretch it's double, then single, then double, then single and finally double all the way to the end. That first line dies out."

Mike leaned over her shoulder, breathing down the open

neck of her shirt. "What's the good word? Dead at the age of
18? You've got a lot to live . . ."

Sibyl pulled her hands away and tossed her head. "Just blew
my cover, that's all. No more double identity. Outwardly a
simple peasant, secretly the nemesis of the Sheriff of Not-
tingham." Mike laughed vaguely, his hands still on her shoulders, and Sibyl controlled a savage impulse to hit him. "Look,
Alan, I know you try harder, but you're still not number one.
Don't we have a date with a real fortune teller?"

"A witch, honey, accept no substitutes. But that's not until
ten-thirty."

Sibyl looked at her watch. "I know what she'll say when
we get there. 'You are unpunctual and cred—oo-lous!'"

Alan looked at his own watch and swore. "We can make it
if we hurry." Sibyl looked at the living room as Mike pulled
her through but Richard had disappeared. They collected Lynn
and hurried downstairs, crowding into Alan's old VW.

They were not too late when they got to Kenmore Square.
Dame Carrie lived on the first floor of a brick townhouse, and
as they waited for her door to open, the old smell of onions in
the hallway made Sibyl wrinkle her nose. They had all learned
to be wary of Alan's new enthusiasms, but still the thought of
a witch was exciting.

A large dark man opened the mahogany door a crack, then
swung it open, sweeping back a curtain of plastic beads that
was in the way. In a soft West Indian accent, he welcomed
them, tall and impressive despite his bright green satin robes
covered with sequins and glitter. "I am the Warlock Emerald
Lord. Be welcome tonight."

The inner room was comfortably tawdry, with worn-out
flowered carpeting and ruffled lampshades done up in plastic
shrouds. The tall, old, marble fireplace stood stark and white
in a clutter of posters and bright-colored clippings. On the
mirror above it danced a row of five-and-dime cutout Hallow-
een skeletons. There was a small fire burning, and in a low
chair by the hearth Dame Carrie huddled, wrapped in a long
fringed shawl. The little cat by her feet wore a yellow plastic
flea collar.

Emerald Lord showed them to a group of folding wooden
chairs, arranged in a semi-circle, and went to stand by his wife
with a hand on her shoulder. She was very old and tiny, white-
haired and pink-cheeked, with bright blue eyes. She smiled

and nodded as they cautiously sat. Lynn and Alan were suddenly very sober.

"Well, my dears," she said briskly. "how curious we are tonight, to be sure. Emerald Lord, turn down the lights, there's a dear. Pass the saucer, love, and let us see their silver." They each contributed a quarter to the little mound, and Dame Carrie shook her head sadly. "It's not the same, you know. Now that they've changed the coins it's not the same. There's not as much silver in these coins as I had in my teeth. Ah me, we do what we can."

Emerald Lord placed the saucer on her knees and she clasped her hands over the dish, concentrating a brief moment with closed eyes. She nodded and muttered. "Yes, yes, some power here too, more than one would think. The moon of course explains some of it, but still..." She opened her eyes and smiled again. "Emerald Lord, show them some fire magic. I think it best if I prepare the board."

She pushed some papers off the little low table next to her chair, revealing a brightly painted Ouija board. It was marked in red and black like a backgammon set. Sibyl's interest turned to irritation as Dame Carrie carefully polished the platen, inlaid with a design in abalone shell. Why on earth had she come? Answers indeed. Now they'd probably hear from the soul of some nineteenth century bunko artist doing time as a control at second-rate seances.

While Dame Carrie fussed with her implements, Emerald Lord picked up a brand from the fire in his bare hands and began running it over his arms and face. As he caressed the fire, he talked quietly with a soft lilt. "Now I know what you thinking. You thinking, what that young man doing, getting married to that old lady there?" He laughed and shook his head at their foolishness. "But you don't know warlocks, any more you understand fire. I three times as old as Dame Carrie. But I lucky. I grow up with magic. My daddy was a warlock. Dame Carrie, she grow up here, in Cambridge, Massachusetts, no one know about magic here. She get old, then find she is witch. Too late, you see? But she learn a lot, very smart lady." He laughed and tossed the ember back into the fire.

Sibyl looked sideways at Mike. He was sitting forward, watching closely. He was determined to figure out their tricks, though it sure looked real. Suddenly Dame Carrie interrupted Sibyl's train of thought, moaning. Her head was tilted back

and her hands lay loosely on the platen. Emerald Lord pointed
to Alan and had him come and put his own hands on it also,
in proof of good faith. A few moments they were motionless,
the old witch quiet with her head hanging back. Then the marker
began to move. First it made wide circles, elegant loops like
a practice sheet for penmanship. Then it began pausing, stopping at letters, jerking rapidly back and forth so quickly Emerald Lord could barely keep track of the message.

"Come home come come moon's daughter hurry come Ginas here Ginas come..."

Emerald Lord looked at Alan. "This Ginas. You know him?"
But Alan shook his head. Emerald Lord turned to the rest.
"Anyone here know Ginas? Maybe he got wrong number." He
laughed and his teeth were very white. Then the pointer began
again, in little irritable swoops and stabs.

"Full moon full moon come now home Ginas, Ginas, Ginas...."

"Don't know any Ginas here. Who you want?"

"Come Tredana Tredana come come..." Sibyl looked at
Emerald Lord in amazement, her pulse thumping in her throat.
How did he know about Tredana? Mind-reading? Or more?
She looked at Alan and the witch, and tried to think what to
ask.

But Alan was impatient. "Let's try something else. This
isn't working. Couldn't you read cards or something?"

Emerald Lord smiled but Dame Carrie was still entranced,
her eyes closed, her hands limp. Emerald Lord leaned over
and yelled in her ear, "Ask who they want. Who this Ginas?
Who he want?" The pointer began to move once more, with
short determined stabs. He watched it move, they turned to the
rest, smiling. "Three times, same name. Anyone named Sibby
here?" Sibyl looked angrily at Alan, but he seemed as surprised
as anyone.

When they got back to Alan's, the party had moved on. His
rooms were cold and dark, smelly with leftover wine and food
and smoke. There was also a soft sound of Mozart's *Night
Music* on the stereo, and Richard was curled up in the window
seat, reading *The Tempest*. He looked up pleasantly as they
entered. "There you are. Alan, what about this for spring term?"
He smiled at Mike. "I've got some great casting ideas."

Lynn turned on the lights, and Alan covered his eyes. "Why
don't you all do me a favor and forswear your magic until

tomorrow. If *Twelfth Night* works we can try another." Mike
took Sibyl by the arm. It was beginning to hurt, and she pulled
away more strongly than before.

"Cool it, Mike, I want some coffee."

Alan pressed his head again. "My home is yours. Just don't
make too much noise. Sibyl, it'll be a long day tomorrow.
Early to bed and remember, boys sap your strength." He went
into his room and shut the door.

In the kitchen Sibyl lit the jet under a saucepan of water
and found Alan's instant coffee in an old mayonnaise jar. When
she brought the mugs back into the living room, Lynn was
sitting straight up between a glowering Mike and an affable
Richard. She sat down opposite. Richard took his mug then
handed her the notebook for a second time, shaking his head.
"It still doesn't make sense to me."

Sibyl opened it to the light. The pages were thin and worn,
and the inside cover was filled with scratchy columns of figures
and some calculations done in pencil. She looked at the cryptic
opening page, and read aloud.

> *"27th Inst. We have seen a matter of much power in the
> Book of fallen Ornat. The Moonlit City that is Treclere
> stood high, triumphant over the Broken Citadel that is
> Treglad, and also the Round Sun that is Tredana was
> inferior in its placement. Then the truth of Lord Vazdz
> spoke through the mouth of our Sister Anne, telling of
> the Moraganas and the Naqra and how they stand to
> help all who believe in Him. There is no help for us
> however, lost beyond recovering out of our own world.
> How long, O Vazdz, must we remain in exile? When will
> the door to home be opened once more?*

Mike looked up suspicious. "What is this anyway? Tredana.
That's what the old lady was spelling out on her board.

Richard ignored him, speaking to Sibyl. "You're sure Tredana is the word you saw as a kid?"

Sibyl nodded. "In a travel book. It said Treclere also. I
remember that now. I don't know why it stuck in my mind.
Probably because I never saw anything else about it."

Lynn touched the book gently. "Maybe it was a country that
doesn't exist, now. An African colony or someplace on the
Indian coast. That book looks a hundred years old, anyway."

Mike plucked the notebook from her hand and flipped it open. "Lemme see." Something was stamped in faint blue ink on the inside back cover. He maneuvered it under the light and whistled with surprise. "Lookit that. This came from my uncle Harris's place, up on the hill. Near where you used to live, Sib. See?" He pointed at the mark and they all could see it was a name and an address, partially obscured. "That says Orleon Lodge, Otis Street, West Newton. Lots of our books have the same stamp. He had more books'n Widener Library. Sib's father helped my father sell the place when Harris died—five, six years ago. Made a bundle on condominiums when he tore the place down. Most of his books were real weird—they had some kinda occult group there. And then those people disappeared from the house, and never were found again. All the kids hung around when they brought in the 'dozers—thought for sure there'd be skeletons or something. But there was just a lot of plaster. Jeez, the dust was incredible. Covered the whole hill."

Sibyl nodded. "I remember. The cellar hole looked too little to have held such a big house. So this book came from there." She shook her head and smiled at Richard. "That's where I saw the other book. I broke into the house once when it was empty. I guess it must just be some stupid spiritualist stuff. No magic at all, really." She dropped the notebook on the table and pulled out her ring, frowning at it.

Richard touched her knee sympathetically. "Forget about Tredana. Tomorrow you have to be in Illyria. Won't help to sit up all night. Another cup of coffee, and we should all go home." He helped her to her feet and steered her towards the kitchen, where he lit the jet with his free hand and supported her with the other, shaking his head. "You look absolutely beat. Why do you stay on with that cretinous lout?" Sibyl made a little helpless gesture and Richard shook his head. "Now, now. You're tired but you're not helpless. You weren't such a doormat last year."

"I wasn't crazy last year. Mike's so ordinary. So normal. I thought it might rub off on me."

"God forbid. He's about as normal as I am, and not nearly so nice. Now sit down and listen to uncle." Richard paused, the mayonnaise jar half-opened in his hands. When he spoke it was quite seriously, his affectations forgotten. "Let me put it to you directly. What is in it for you?" Sibyl twitched her

shoulders, unable to answer. Richard carefully measured the
coffee and poured the water. "I know why you hang around
Mike. He doesn't give you time to think. But that's one thing
you're never going to get done by proxy." Sibyl took up the
steaming mugs and went back into the living room, avoiding
Richard's eyes.

It was late when they left Alan's. Richard quietly lifted a
hand in farewell as he helped Lynn into his wretched little Fiat
to give her a lift back to the dorm. Mike was also silent, and
in a dream Sibyl settled herself behind him on the cycle, clasp-
ing her arms around his muscular body as lightly as possible.
He was such a pig and yet so attractive. She turned her head
and closed her eyes against the slipstream. Why did Richard
always have to speak the truth? And just before opening night.
"O time you must untangle this not I, it is too hard a knot for
me t'untie . . ."

The cycle stopped with a jerk and Sibyl shook her head to
clear it. They were outside Mike's apartment building on Mass.
Ave.

"Mike, no! I'm going home tonight. I have to get some rest.
Tomorrow the critics will be there and everything." Mike unwound the chain from around his waist and began locking up
his bike, the muscle in his cheek flexing. "See here, Mike, I
said I'm going home." She started away, briskly awake now:
it was not quite a mile to the dorm, ten maybe fifteen minutes.
Mike caught up with her and grabbed her arm. It was bruised
now from his grip, and the slight pain angered her unreasonably. She tore herself loose. "Don't you ever do that again!"
She found herself backed up against a lamppost, forced to look
up, despite her height, into Mike's angry face.

"What's the matter with you, Sib?"

"I just wanta cool it, that's all. I'll talk about it tomorrow."

"Well, I don't wanta cool it. So where do we go from here?"

"I go from here, that's what. What a fool I've been, patching
your jeans and mending your jacket and making your coffee
and riding around on your bike. We might as well be married!"

Mike suddenly relaxed. "That it? You want to get married?
Why didn't you say so?"

"No! I . . ." she floundered, appalled at his presumption, yet
for some reason unwilling to make her rejection too brutal. She
recovered her courage. "No. I just want to be left alone." She
pulled away and saw him reach for her from the corner of her

eye. She whirled and raised her fist between them. "You touch me now, Michael Arleon, and I'll make you regret it for the rest of your life. This is no time for muscle." She turned on her heel and sprinted off down Mass. Ave., blinded by furious crying.

Free at last, free at last, O my God, I'm free at last. She shook her head and wiped her face with the back of her hand. Why couldn't she have written him a nice polite letter? He couldn't help what he was. It was her fault anyway. She'd always known what he was like.

Well, it was over. No more Sibby Barron and her crazy personal relationships. Just crazy Sibby Barron, period. She drew a deep breath and turned down a side street, to cut across to Garden Street.

Her footsteps made crisp little echoes in the quiet night. Idly she watched her shadow chase itself past the street lights shooting out ahead, shrinking in again, then once more scurrying forward, vague but determined in the diffuse moonlight. Then her shadow had company, and she heard a hurried step behind her, and a man's voice telling her to stop. Mike? No, he wore boots. This step was lighter and more rapid.

Not even turning to look, she began running, out into the middle of the narrow back street towards the faraway main intersection. She was sure there would be a policeman out there, because a man had been stabbed nearby a week ago. Stabbed. She ran faster and tried to call out but had no extra breath. Although she knew it was a foolish thing to do, she doubled into a small alley, one she knew that made a right-angled turn around some houses and out onto the main street. As she ran into the shadow, she could hear a faint voice calling. "Come here, come." Turning into its dark depths, she hit her foot against a box sticking out from a pile of rubbish and she stumbled and fell onto her hands and knees on the gritty pavement. She shut her eyes and waited. No one touched her. But a cold wind whistled down the road and she shivered and opened her eyes.

This was a different alley. Somehow she had gotten completely lost. The moon was riding lower in the sky, and everything seemed much brighter and clearer than before, the air sharper and the wind more cold. Under her jeans her knee was bleeding and she had skinned her palm. How had she come here? She touched the unwindowed wall beside her, and it was made of mud brick, crumbling under her fingers; the road where she had fallen was unpaved and deeply rutted.

It was terribly quiet. She could hear crickets. And surely that smell was chickens? She walked down to the end of the alley hesitantly, trying to understand what was happening. Then she heard running footsteps in the dark behind her and loud voices. "Which way did she go?" "Down here. Come quickly."

She did not dare to wait and see if they were looking for her. Still lost and confused, she ran out into the road and turned to her right, towards a group of buildings in the distance that she hoped would offer a hiding place. As she ran across the moonlit open ground, a voice behind her called, "Halt in the name of Ddiskeard, Lord of Tredana."

She ran faster. Tredana. How on earth could she ever have forgotten?

THE MAGICIAN AS SURREALIST
A Poem
by Sibyl Barron
(reprinted from the Harvard-Radcliffe *Literary Agent*)

*Four Kings: Cups, Swords, Coins, Spears, continuously
ride through my readings, teaching me reversal.
These dooms and warnings are a long rehearsal
the cards tell for themselves, and not for me.
See the Surrealist point his baton
to North, South, East and West: his eyes are closed.
Don't worry, Gypsy Lady; I supposed
you knew which road it is, these four ride on.*

*They ride across the sands to their own doom
crying, Seek not for whom the cards foretell,
they tell for thee: but Alice-like I scatter
your Tarot in the air. There is no room
for Gypsy-cant, here on the shores of Hell.
Go call your cards, impress them with your patter:
Return, O Kings, each lord to his own quarter;
There's knocking at the gate where fate stands porter.*

Chapter Four

From close at hand, the buildings ahead proved to be large and square, set on either side of the road Sibyl was following. Between the first two, she stopped and shrank against the nearest wall, for voices were speaking just ahead of her, in piercing whispers.

"What was that?" "The brigsmen are out tonight. As long as the nimbleshanks be in town, there'll be brigsmen all a-litter to help us keep the sundowning." "Not that, not that. I thought I skint a nosepoke on the kingsway." "I doubt they'll send another, now we cracked one's skull to match the other three. You'd think a nosepoke would know better than to come to footsmen town, at shuttertime and all. Our Huffing Dick won't fall like old Crookneck."

The two whisperers turned down a small opening between two buildings. Baffled and wary, Sibyl waited a moment longer before venturing on. She had never heard anything like that before, in Tredana or Treclere or Vahn. A few steps farther on she stopped again, all thought of pursuit by the guardsmen gone from her mind. There was breathing in the dark around her. Quiet breathing.

Looking closely with slowly adjusting eyes, she began to see the people huddled in the shadows. By the edges of the road, under walls and against the buildings they slept, so bundled in their clothes and rags and bits of blanket that only their breathing and murmurs and restless movements betrayed them. A baby whimpered somewhere and fell silent. Nervously Sibyl walked carefully along the road, seeing ahead the city walls, massive and dark in the moonlight, while around her the air thickened with unpleasant odors.

The tall city walls were broken by a small oblong of light, coming from an open postern near the large closed wooden gates. The guardsmen had been careless. Sibyl paused a moment, then hurried through, wincing for fear of discovery as she ducked past the flaring torch set in the archway. Inside, the streets were cobbled, high in the center with drainage ditches along either side, and the buildings were large and close together, stone-built. The huddled groups of poor and distressed seemed strangely remote from these dignified sleeping streets. Sibyl was suddenly very tired, and she wondered where she might sleep in safety.

A horse whinnied somewhere to her left, and for lack of a better omen she turned down a narrow way leading in that direction. A stable would offer concealment for the night, and warm straw or hay.

The square she reached was filled with carts and wagons, pushed close together, with horses picketed along a rope on the farther side. Suddenly she was wide awake and filled with relief. She had known she would not be lost forever. Ginas had called, just as the witch had read. And here she was, at the wagons of the Players. In one small curtained window there was a light, and she walked to that wagon. Only a moment she hesitated, looking up at the painted doorway, then she stepped up and lightly knocked against the wooden frame.

"You may enter."

Sibyl pushed back the velvet hanging and looked in. This was indeed the wagon of the headwoman Ginas. Her legs were suddenly limp with relief, but the old woman looked at her unmoved. The lamp flame glowed on her long white hair and filled her crystal ring with blue light. "You have come," she said. "But where is Liniris?"

"Liniris?" Sibyl's puzzlement was clear, and Ginas got suddenly to her feet and took Sibyl's hand in both of hers.

"If you have found us unaided, then assuredly this is a good sign. But I fear for Liniris. It was she called you and was to have led you thither."

Sibyl closed her eyes a moment, reflecting. She was very tired and easily let herself be pushed back onto a bench. "I don't know how I got here," she said slowly. "I mean from the Otherworld. I had a message from you, saying come, but I didn't understand. I had forgotten everything about here. Then I stumbled, in my own world, and I found myself here. I heard a voice calling that time, too. Perhaps it was Liniris. I was outside the gates, and there were soldiers around, so I ran away and found my way here. Wherever this is."

"You are in Sundrat. No doubt those soldiers scared Liniris to flight, and she will presently come home by a secret route. We are not allowed out at night, and it goes hard on those who break a kingsrule. I doubt Liniris knew she had been successful."

"Why did you call me here? How did you do it? And what's been happening, anyway? Things are terrible out there. How long has Ddiskeard been king? Where's Leron? And Mathon?"

"Since you left us, eight years have passed. Many bitter things have occurred. Leron and his father are safe, in exile still. You were called because you are needed. But explanations must wait. You cannot be seen dressed as you are. I have clothes for you such as we wear, and you must change even if it is only to sleep. The kingsmen will rouse us from our beds if it please them."

Ginas lifted the lid of a wooden chest and pulled out a long green robe with a low neck and dangling sleeves. Sibyl's jeans and flannel shirt were bundled out of sight, and Ginas helped her pull the other over her head, remarking on the shortness of Sibyl's hair. As she tugged the dress into place, Sibyl stumbled with weariness. Ginas spoke more kindly. "You have traveled far and must sleep now. I shall wait up for Liniris. Your questions can keep a few hours longer. Here in the back is room for you."

A curtain across the end of the wagon concealed a wide painted box filled with sweet straw and covered with quilts. Too tired to wash or ask questions, Sibyl lay down gratefully and was almost asleep before Ginas could throw a cover across her. She lay curled on her side, her hand clasped over her blue glass ring. She remembered now that Ajjibawr the Karif had given it to her, in the desert. She would find out about him tomorrow. And the others.

When she awoke next morning, the bedding next to her was comfortably warm although she was alone. She sat up and began picking the straw out of her hair when the curtain was pulled back and a dark, pretty girl dressed in gold-embroidered

red smiled in at her. "Good, you are awake. Our meal is prepared."

"Are you Liniris?"

"Yes."

"I'm glad you got back safely."

"It is more to be wondered at that you found your way here alone. Here, I will help you." Expertly she laced the waist of Sibyl's disarranged dress and straightened it about the shoulders. "You truly appear to be one of us. Except for your hair. This morning I will teach you some skills; but food first."

There was warm milk in bowls on the table, bread and cheese. The sight and smell brought back pleasant memories to Sibyl, and she sat down with delight. But as they ate, there was a commotion in the square outside, and the sound of tramping feet. A heavy tread on the wagon's step made the room shake, then there came a knock on the door frame and a deep voice cried, "In the King's name!" The curtains were thrust aside, and two men stepped up into the room, stooping because of the low doorway. They wore chain mail and were armed: the captain looked them over with narrowed eyes.

"Ha! One of your skulking coven has been disobeying the kingsrule. She led my men a fine chase in the moonlight. Do you know what this could mean?"

Ginas nodded quietly. "We have been told. But where is the lawbreaker?"

"Through craft and darkness she evaded our pursuit and well for her that she did so. But remember this, old woman: your kind may not come into our cities and ply your trade unless you abide by the kingsrule. We cannot afford to be easy on those found wandering the streets by night, with brigands such as Clerowan the White on the prowl. This is no light matter."

"We seek only to entertain, and value our own skins. We have no wish to see our heads on spears above the city gates. We shall obey your rules."

"It would take little enough to change the rule, and then you could look to spend your nights outside the gates with all the pickpokes, slit-throats and others who inhabit that plague-sink."

"I have said we shall obey your rules."

"See to it then. We shall be watching."

They turned and left, and as their steps sounded away across the square Liniris laughed lightly. "A fine chase indeed. I doubt they shall ache today. And they puffed so as they ran!"

"Do not forget that they hold our lives in their clumsy grasp. Your parents are no more because of them. You must live, to continue our line; as must the daughter of Simirimia and Armon, the true foreteller, who was summoned here to fulfill her destiny."

Sibyl interrupted. "What destiny? You still haven't explained. And what about my friends? What has happened to them?"

"So much has happened—how to tell it? Ddiskeard whom you met before is King, a short step from the Regency he assumed eight years ago when you were here. Mathon Breadgiver he has declared to be dead, as Leron was before. The true King and his son hold court in exile at Rym Treglad, and with them are Dansen the Learned, Gannoc and Mara, and others whom you knew."

"What is Rym Treglad?"

"The city Leron caused to be built in the ruins of the ancient citadel. Many champions have joined them there, but he is not yet strong enough to strike. And the people of Meddock who lived there before have gone farther north and do not care to be involved any more with outsiders. Their true friend and guide and ours, Arbytis, sleeps still."

"Is Odric still in Treclere?"

"He maintains order there, but under constant seige and distress, for his father Bodrum has made an alliance with Ddiskeard and Dzildzil against him, as against Leron. It is the navy of Vahn brings wealth to Sundrat and Tredana and fills those warehouses through which you passed entering the city. Sundrat was not always as you see it now. Beyond the walls stretched a fair grassy plain, the fields of the King's Farm filled with fat sleek horses, and beyond the noble woods. Now there is the bear pit, and in the shadow of stuffed and barricaded warehouses sleep the dispossessed farmers, the cast-out servants, the branded thieves and traitors, maimed and blinded felons, the diseased turned out-of-doors from hospitals and other wards shut down by order of the close-handed King."

"Who is this Dzildzil? Why can't the Karabdu help Odric?"

"This Dzildzil now leads the Karabdu; they are tools to Vahn and as fanatical as ever they were in ancient days. There is no help for us in the desert."

Music suddenly began to play outside. Liniris jumped to
her feet. "They're starting! And I haven't shown you your part!
Come along now, your disguise won't be any good unless you
know what to do."

Ginas nodded. "There is much more to be said, but no time
now. Go with Liniris."

Sibyl paused in the doorway, her hand on the blue glass
ring. "But I don't understand about the Karabdu. How can
Dzildzil rule? What happened to the Karif?"

Ginas smiled sadly. "In the year you left us the Karif was
set upon by his own people and slain, his faithful sword brothers
with him."

Sibyl held up the ring. "He was my friend. Ajjibawr—the
Karif. He gave me my horse. And this. I thought—I thought
I would see him again."

"Not in this world, child. He is one with the desert again."

Sibyl let Liniris take her by the hand. She was pulled down
the stairs into the square and around behind the high wooden
stage, where the Players were preparing for their first performance. There were no more questions she cared to ask.

Her two worlds merged as Sibyl listened to Liniris's instructions. Here as in Cambridge she had a mask and a costume
to wear, a role to learn and words to say. The dialogue was
unfamiliar, but the plots were not. The play they were per-
forming was a traditional one for autumn, the *Dance at the
Crossroads Inn*. It was a sort of Harlequinade with King and
Queen, man and maid, and a wandering knight called the Clerowan. There were only a few verses to learn, but the staging
was tricky and Sibyl had to concentrate on the thickly plotted
exits and entrances. There was no time to think about the news
she had heard; but today she was glad for the mask, which
protected her grieving face from the crowd.

Between performances, street-singers entertained the crowd.
By noon she had heard at least three ballads about the outlaw
who called himself Clerowan the White, after the traditional
figure in their play. The ballads made him to sound like a
mixture of Robin Hood, Lancelot and the Lone Ranger. He
was a champion of Rym Treglad; the singers called him the
"right arm of the true prince" whenever the kingsmen were out
of earshot. When they stood near he was a thief and outlaw.

The Players' skill was great. Those times Sibyl was allowed
to rest and watch, she forgot everything but the play. They

were adept at all sorts of invention, and could turn any incident to their own advantage. That morning a table, weakened from much use, collapsed as the Queen sat down by it, whereupon the actors spent a good ten minutes in a silly diversion, trying to sneak dancers onto the stage to repair it before the Queen should notice. That scene ended with one dancer crouched beneath the board, silently screaming in distress, as the Queen—for no apparent reason—absentmindedly piled the entire furnishings of the set upon the table. She finally left, and as her skirt swept through the curtains the precarious arrangement collapsed, to the delight of Sibyl and the rest of the audience.

As for the play itself, the events at the Crossroads Inn made Shakespeare's Illyria a tame, quiet place by contrast. The final chorus stayed in her mind all day.

> *Within the inn we change our place*
> *as all must dance a little space*
> *between the rising of the sun*
> *and evening when each dance is done:*
> *Queen to King and Maid to Man*
> *returns each to the proper one;*
> *only the Knight who stands alone*
> *is partnerless at dance's end.*

That afternoon the crowds in the square were increased by twenty or so sailors from a merchant ship. The Vahniyan dress was familiar to Sibyl, and the Captain when he strode up to the stage reminded her so of Odric she watched him covertly for several minutes. He had the same stocky build, long chestnut beard and heavy-lidded eyes; but there was no humor in his face, and his men, tough as they were, fell back respectfully out of his way. In addition to the usual gold earrings, he wore two heavy silver wristlets, each a handspan wide.

For some moments he stood watching the Player's performance, his hands clasped behind his back and his legs planted widely apart. A tumbler drew his interest and surprisingly, he drew off one bracelet and threw it to the young acrobat, instead of the customary few coins. Then his interest wandered and he went in search of drink, but later that afternoon he reappeared and after watching the play a few moments turned abruptly on his heel and strode to Ginas's cart. After a few moments inside he came back out, followed by Ginas herself. She stood a moment blinking in the light, then motioned to Sibyl and Liniris with her hand.

"We are honored," she said in a strange tone. "Captain Delgar is pleased with your performance. He has commanded your presence at dinner tonight, when he entertains certain merchants of this city on board the *Lady Damar*. His sailors shall escort you thence and back."

Sibyl bowed humbly with Liniris, and Captain Delgar nodded in return, looking at them with dark, expressionless eyes. "Perform well and you shall we rewarded. Tonight, then." He turned and left, his sailors obediently following in two lines.

Ginas took Sibyl's wrist and drew her inside the wagon. "Something·in me mislikes this assignation. Yet to refuse is impossible; Delgar is the guest of the Governor at whose sufferance we remain in Sundrat."

Sibyl loosened the tight laces at her waist and sat down. "We aren't going far. It will probably be all right."

"Watch and weigh your words carefully. Your accent is still strange. Do not speak except to answer, and then say little. Tomorrow we will be safely away, and we will meet a friend of yours if he has had my message in time."

"What friend?"

"He for whom you were summoned. Your cousin, the prince."

Sibyl stiffened at the phrasing. "And what do you mean by that?"

Ginas looked past her and did not answer directly. "Soon we will be safe in Rym Treglad, but I feared to wait even that long. There are ill omens in the cards. So I sent Herrard the Traveler, whom well you know, north to Rym Treglad with a message for Leron. The sooner you two are joined, the better it will be."

Sibyl looked at her suspiciously. "When I last saw Leron I was twelve years old. I'll be very glad to see him again. But I don't plan on joining with anyone just yet—not if you mean what I think you mean."

Ginas raised her eyebrows. "The time of your alliance is at hand. The stars cannot be stayed. If an heir is born to Ddiskeard first, then Leron is dispossessed forever."

Sibyl stood up, too amazed to speak at first. "You could

have saved yourself a lot of trouble," she said at last, "if you
had checked with me before you brought me back here. I'm
afraid you are going to have a few surprises."

Ginas shrugged. "It is your destiny as well you know. You
are of the race of true dreamers."

Sibyl laughed. "There are some things, Ginas, I wouldn't
dream of doing, and your little arrangement is one of them.
You'll see."

Ginas nodded. "Yes, I will."

The sailors came for them before dusk, to escort them to
the ship. In the gathering dark they could see the kingsmen at
work, clearing the streets of people before the gates closed,
pushing them roughly out with blows and curses. Even the
kingsmen respected the sailors of Vahn, however, and they
passed safely through to the harborside. There at a line of
wooden piers was a small boat from the *Damar*, long and
narrow, propelled by six impassive rowers. The boat pushed
quietly out into the calm lapping water, following the slow
outgoing tide. They were already some hundred feet from shore
when Sibyl noticed, with her first real sensation of disquiet,
that the rowers were chained to their benches.

Liniris noted her surprise. "Did you not know? All these
merchantmen are slave ships as well. It is their most profitable
cargo." Sibyl looked from the closed faces of the rowers to the
shoreline glowing pink, now far distant. She was suddenly hot
despite the cool sea breeze.

The words of the sailor who met them at the ship did not
reassure her. The *Lady Damar* was tall-sided with crimson
sails, and he lowered a rope ladder down to them from the
deck. Sibyl looked first at the thick, taut anchor rope, green
and slimy, rising past them from the dark water, then up into
the sailor's face. He was smiling down into the boat, and his
words were for his companions. "Safe across the water, I see.
Perhaps their powers are not so great as some men fear." And
the other sailors laughed.

On deck Salama, the ship's mate, met them. Sibyl saw with
surprise that he was one of the Karabdu, pale-skinned, blue-
eyed and sandy-haired, although sun and sea had burned his
face red and whitened his hair. He welcomed them aboard with
unexpected courtesy and proudly pointed out the ship's finer
features.

Cabins lined both sides of the ship, with the Captain's suite

across the high carved stern; a small private deck roofed his
rooms. From these Salama led them down a narrow hatchway
into the wide shallow cargo hold. It was sweet and dusty smelling, filled with barrels and boxes and jars, great clay urns sealed
with wax, and piles of carpets, bolts of fine fabric. Salama
gestured about him with real pride. "Here you may see the
riches of Vahn and her allies, the produce of this continent and
other far places and secret islands. There are tissues of gold
cloth thin as a spider's web yet heavier than chain mail, carpets
intricately detailed, so fine they might pass through the eye of
a needle yet hard enough for a hundred years' use, silk cloth
from the desert, wines from far Loresta, oil from Mindo'ila.
Precious, precious all of these, and yet most precious is the
cargo that lies under our feet. Have you heard of a black man?
Or a yellow?"

Liniris's eyes widened with surprise, and Salama smiled
affably as he gestured to the sailors who escorted them. "Open
the hatch forward," he said, and two of them went to obey.
They were stripped to the waist and the muscles bunched in
their backs as they heaved at the heavy wooden trapdoor. As
it fell back, the stench from below decks filled the storeroom
like a poison gas and Sibyl felt faint, recalling descriptions of
slave ships from her own world. Obeying Salama's gesture,
she and Liniris came forward and peered down into the rowing
deck and slavehold.

The men below were chained naked to their benches, and
a few were indeed black or yellow as Salama had said, though
most had the familiar features of Tredana or Vahn or of the
desert. They had terrible sores where the irons rubbed, and
their arms and backs were knotted painfully from the rowing.
Some had marks of dried blood on their backs, and one at least
who looked up slowly when the hatch opened had been branded
on the forehead. They were thin and filthy.

"Here our cargo is tamed as a horse is broken to the plow,
at the same time powering our ship in calm weather. Some are
felons, others we purchase abroad. The strong survive and fetch
high prices at market in Tredana or Vahanavat. See that black
giant there? Once he was a lord in the frozen north, but the
new king sold him to us in chains. Yes, Hakma, we talk of
you."

The man to whom Salama pointed sat upright despite his
chains, his handsome face impassive, the eyes turned inward

and the mouth steady, making no response to Salama's taunting voice.

A moment longer Salama savored the view, then they left the hold behind them, and he conducted them upstairs to their dressing room. It was a small, stuffy cabin, but there were water and towels laid out. As they washed away the smell of the hold, Liniris said, "I will not draw an easy breath until we are safe on shore."

Sibyl nodded. "If only there were some way of freeing those people down there."

Liniris shook her head. "There is not. And this is only one ship of many. The Vahniya have a great fleet, and now they build for Tredana's use as well." As Sibyl arranged Liniris's silk mask, her fingers trembled with anger and impotence.

Salama conducted them to the Captain's dining room and left them at the door. It was a wide, low room with windows on three sides open to the cool sea breeze, and they entered from a private passage separating his other two chambers. The many swinging lanterns gave the room a festive air. Ten or twelve guests sat at Delgar's table, close against the farthest wall, with space in front for the entertainment. They were still eating. The table was laden with silver dishes, casks of wine, and all manner of foods. A monkey, chained by his silver collar, climbed among the dishes chattering and snatching; the guests ate freely, using their hands, and drank deeply, laughing and wiping their mouths and belching with satisfaction.

Delgar waved his hand. "Proceed, proceed. We shall be watching, never fear." He was quite unlike his dour self of that afternoon, and he spoke the truth, for although he and his guests continued eating and drinking, they followed the performance carefully. Sibyl as the Queen spoke the first verse, and the Captain's intent eye embarrassed her so she stumbled on the words and looked away.

> *"The inn was dark and silent*
> *where all things come to rest*
> *and I must lay my royal head*
> *upon his somber breast . . ."*

Delgar wet his lips; hot-faced behind her mask Sibyl turned towards the far end of the table. There one man stood out, and as the play progressed her eyes strayed back a second and a

third time. He was watching her no less covertly; again she
blushed behind her mask and looked away. His face was thin
and somehow familiar, with high cheekbones and a narrow
mouth. His eyes were a startling blue in contrast to his dark,
clean-shaven face and black hair. She could not think of whom
he reminded her.

When he spoke, sometime later in the evening, his voice
gave her another unplaceable shock of recognition. He suggested softly that the performers be given a few moment's rest
and some refreshment, and with this idea Delgar jovially com-
plied. Sibyl was glad for Liniris's sake, for she had stumbled
several times from the motion of the ship and was hot despite
the breeze from the windows. As Liniris came to sit by Sibyl,
she stumbled again, and Sibyl where she sat was rocked in her
seat. There came another lurch, and Liniris suddenly raised her
head, listening, a wild expression on her face. Sibyl listened
also, and the silk mask twisted in her fingers as her ears reluctantly identified the sound they were hearing. She looked
to see Delgar sitting pushed back from the table, laughing
hugely with one hand to his eyes.

"Friends, friends," he cried. "Our birds have heard the hunter's step, but too late, I fear." Outside the window the splash
of rowing came in clearly on the breeze.

THE SLAVE'S A B & T
as sung on the slaveships of Vahn

A is the anchor we heave away
B is the bilge we do drink every day
T is the torment to which we are bound
and C is the Captain who orders us on.

Wearily, wearily so weary row we
No one on shore like a slave on the sea
Chained to his bench as he's chained to the oar
Have pity, O Slaver, and set him ashore.

D is the doublequick time we do row
Dd is the ddimry shows which way to go

R is the rope we would set to their necks
And F is the fever we catch below decks.

(chorus)

V is for Vahn in whose chains we now be
G is the galewind that sets our oars free
H is the helmsman, how fast he do beat
and K is the kennels wash over our feet

(chorus)

L is the lash they do lay to our backs
M is the metals in which we relax
P is the pintle that holds each chain fast
and Z is the zerif that flies from the mast.

(chorus)

S is for slave, the which we now be
Sh is for ship, now our coffin at sea
N is the Naqra who's waiting below
when W's wave lays our prisonship low.

(chorus)

So now I have sung you my A B & T
No one on shore like a slave on the sea
If you want any more, E I O Y & U
You must sing it yourself for I've nothing will do.

Wearily, wearily so weary row we
No one on shore like a slave on the sea
Chained to his bench as he's chained to the oar
Have pity, O Slaver, and set him ashore

Chapter Five

Leron sat uncomfortably in the small, low alehouse, surrounded by footsmen speaking their incomprehensible cant. The light was poor and the atmosphere fetid; Huffing Dick was drinking as his companions told the story of the fight; one of them had pressed a metal tankard into Leron's hand but it was so scummy and crusted he could barely touch it politely to his lips. There were several women in the group, dressed as fantastically in rags and cast-offs as the men.

As the story came to an end one plump girl in a low-cut blouse pressed herself against Leron's arm and smiled invitingly into his face. He smiled back uncertainly. Then Huffing Dick shook his head and rubbed his eyes, setting down his tankard with a thud. "Mulsie, sweet, we have a need for your room." The plump girl left Leron's side and Huffing Dick gestured for Leron to follow. Together with the Fambler and the Hoppler they went up a crooked flight of stairs built next to the fireplace. Mulsie's room was simply furnished, with a mattress and a ragged blanket: Huffing Dick dropped the wooden bolt into place behind them. He was still red-faced, but his eyes were shrewd and his speech precise and unblurred. The narrow window behind him gave on a dark space between two buildings. Huffing Dick gestured encouragingly. "Speak up, boy. If these walls ever had ears they were all cut off long since."

"I know a man who lost his ears. The only footsman I ever knew before today. His name is Alwyn."

"He lost his ears, all right. They were cut off in the main square of Sundrat. I was there. But Alwyn's far from Sundrat now."

"He is in Rym Treglad."

"And how would you know that?"

"I came from Rym Treglad. Perhaps I should say I was sent. We knew there were dangers here in the south, but not how difficult things really are. I can see I will have trouble completing my mission—I am too much the stranger, and strangers are too readily noticed."

Huffing Dick picked at his front teeth with his thumbnail and looked out the window. "Now what kind of mission would be coming from Rym Treglad?"

"I travel for the prince. More than that I cannot say."

Huffing Dick spat on the floor. "That for your prince! Warm by his fire in the north while we starve in the streets of Sundrat."

Leron felt his face go red. "That is one reason I am here. There is talk of a return. You would not welcome it?"

"Eight years ago I might have, six years ago or four. What does your prince wait for then? Does he so fear his cousin that Ddiskeard must rot away entirely before he dare leave the shelter of his little city in the north?"

"We did not know the pretender was ill."

"Ill? He's rotting on his feet! It's common knowledge in Sundrat. Your prince had best send a few more spies before he makes that return. But he needn't fear overmuch loyalty to Ddiskeard." The Hoppler laughed at this, and the Fambler smiled. Huffing Dick regretfully examined the empty tankard he had carried upstairs and set it down on the narrow window ledge. "Why did you mention Alwyn now?"

"Because is my friend and I thought he might be yours."

"And what did this friend call you?"

Leron puzzled a minute, then understood what Huffing Dick was asking. "He used to call me wingsman: I thought he made it up. Does the name signify anything?"

The Fambler laughed at this, but Huffing Dick silenced him with a look. "It has a meaning. He gave you a name, but no sign?"

"No sign."

Huffing Dick belched and looked off into space a moment. Then he quickly recited.

"Three feathers mark a friend,
two fingers name a stranger,
wheat marks a lodging house,
berries for danger."

He coughed and wiped his mouth with his hand. "I had to translate for you: we do not drop the fancy speech except for strangers like yourself." He pulled off his cap and straightened the bent little feathers sewn to it. "We'll give you three before you go. Hold your fingers like this when you're unsure. Any part of the wheat is good, stalk, kernal or chaff, on a door or a window or low down by the steps out of sight. And berries in the same place will make a wise man stay away." He nodded to the Fambler. "See the wingsman gets his feathers. And he might want to change his clothes a little before he ventures nigh to Sundrat city again." He saluted Leron with the special sign of the footsmen and went out, leaving him with the other two.

Not an hour later Leron entered the city of Sundrat; limping from a bandage knotted under the instep inside his boot. It was an old trick of the Hoppler's and made the limp convincing. His clothes had been artistically treated by the Fambler and a sailcloth cape given him in trade for his good wool cloak. Three draggled feathers drooped from a copper brooch pinned to his shoulder.

Ginas did not expect him until that night in the safety of the woods outside the walls of Sundrat, but Leron could not resist working his way slowly into the center of town, where the Players' carts were assembled and the stage set up. As he walked slowly along, pausing to rest his leg and lean convincingly on the rough staff he had cut, he noted the plainness of dress and the poorness of the stalls set up for market; even the vegetable sellers seemed short of merchandise.

Despite the precarious nature of his visit, Leron could not help laughing at the Players' skill. He had always enjoyed their performances since he was a small boy; today a table collapsed on stage and their antics to keep the Queen from noticing were superb. But there were armed men all about, kingsmen and ship's officers, and Leron soon wandered away, as inconspicuously a part of the crowd as possible.

By noon Leron had had enough of Sundrat. Outside the

gates he followed the main road a little way to where a path
led downhill to the harbor through a rough pasture where some
sheep were grazing. All the long afternoon he sat there with
his back propped against a wall, low out of the wind and out
of sight, basking in the sun.

Below, a boat put into harbor from the ship he had fancied
that morning. If only Clerowan were in town and could be
directed to that prize. The miserable rowers below decks would
be freed, and the ship would make a fine start to a fleet. Down
at the jetty the boat tied up, and the captain slowly started up
the hill towards the town, his sailors tramping around him,
hands resting on their sword hilts. Leron smiled to himself as
he imagined running down to the boat, rowing out to the ship,
and making away with it. Best leave that to adventurers like
Clerowan. He had an appointment tonight that he did not want
to miss, even for the prize of such a ship.

Before Leron left, at dusk, the boat had gone back and forth
from his ship another three times, taking at last a small party
from shore out to the ship on the retreating tide. As Leron
lazily pulled himself to his feet, the ship bowed into the current,
and long oars winked in the water as she turned to catch the
tide. At the hill's foot, Leron watched it go, then turned away
towards the woods, stabbed by a sudden and inexplicable sense
of loss.

It was much dimmer under the trees, and before Leron had
reached the grove, it was full dark. A little way from the open
space, he sat down in a sheltered spot, behind some bushes,
and took out some bread and cheese the footsmen had given
him. The moon would not rise for another few hours.

The bread was dry, and he chewed it slowly. Excitement
was rising now, as the appointed meeting time drew near, and
it was hard to swallow. The moon had still not fully risen when
he heard a loud blundering in the bushes, followed by cursing.
Leron stood up very slowly and pressed back against the tree,
tight against its trunk. There was a faint glow in the grove,
and Leron could see that the newcomer was tall and massively
built. He seemed to be dressed all in leather but it was hard to
see clearly.

"Blast it all anyway. Where in hell am I?"

Leron drew in his breath sharply. The stranger's accent was
as familiar as his words were strange. Alone in the grove the
other heard some sound and whirled to face it. There was

suddenly hanging from his hand a length of chain, which had apparently been around his waist. The moonlight had increased a little, and Leron could see he was dressed in black leather with heavy boots. There were no other sounds, and the stranger laughed a little in relief, clipping the chain back in place. Leron loosened his instinctive hold on his dagger.

"Damnation! How did I ever get here? How did that stinking river turn into a whole blasted ocean? And where in hell am I?"

The stranger went up to a tree and put his hand on the trunk, staring up into the boughs as though he had never seen one before. Then he shrugged and crossed the clearing rapidly, disappearing into the bushes. For several minutes after he had disappeared, Leron did not move. He was beginning to feel that all would not go as smoothly as Ginas intended. He knew now why the other's accent had seemed familiar. It was the accent of Sibby. Surely Ginas had not called more than one from Sibby's world?

A little more time passed, and the grove was now much brighter. In the small opening overhead he could just see an edge of the moon, very white. Soon it would fill that small bit of sky. As he impatiently waited, there was a faint rustling sound and another dark-clothed figure entered the grove. But this was no stranger, and Leron stepped out from the trees eagerly.

"Ginas!"

She turned slowly and gravely, the black hood thrown back from her white head, her ring glowing on her hand.

"You are here, my prince—I thank you for your trust."

Leron bent his head briefly before her. "I came, I think, more out of hope than trust. I did not dare believe in your success."

"Prince, there was no doubt of success. Easily she was summoned." Leron looked past Ginas, but she was alone. He looked at her in bewilderment.

"Yes, too easily, she came last night as my powers suddenly told me she would, a little sooner than my plans intended."

"Sibby is here? Where?" He steadied himself against a tree, suddenly dizzy, his heart pounding.

"She is with us in town, dressed as one of us, and she will leave with us tomorrow and meet you here."

"I thought she would be here tonight."

"That was my intention, but she danced today with my granddaughter Liniris, and they were asked to perform for certain nobles tonight. We could not refuse."

"I see." He laughed. "And perhaps I saw. I ventured into Sundrat this morning and saw part of the masking. She is taller than Liniris, dressed in green?"

Ginas nodded, and Leron grinned. "I can hardly believe it. She is here, I saw her and I did not know."

"It is not so simple, my prince. That is why I wished to talk to you, why I asked you to hurry here and not wait for our journey to Rym Treglad. I have been successful, yes, but there is much to worry me."

Ginas walked over to a heap of felled trees and sat down, silently choosing her words. Leron sat down lightly at her feet. "The stars do not fit, my prince, the cards do not speak of good fortune. Oh, there is an alliance for you, soon, but the joy is clouded. And all about, such deception, so much disappointment, treachery within and without. In every suit the kings are shown reversed, and I cannot see which kings are meant, the true ones or the false. And the unbroken circle, Ornat itself, stands also reversed."

"Ginas, I do not understand. I do not know the cards."

She placed her hand on his shoulder. "Nor need to. But there are words I have held in my heart for many years, which speak most clearly of danger. *The Moraganas in the air, the Naqra in the water, the race of man upon the land, challenge the moon's daughter . . .*" As she recited the words softly she shook her head. "It is a long and ancient prophecy, and none of it is good. Prince, there are many obstacles before us." She laughed, for the first time that evening. "And not the least is your cousin. She is a grown woman now, and perhaps she will listen to your arguments with a better grace than to mine."

Leron flushed. "Where does she perform tonight?"

"On board a merchantman from Vahn, for a Captain Delgar and his guests. They will not return from shipboard until late and have a special pass to reenter the city. I have my own routes."

Leron looked up, suddenly tight in the stomach. "From shipboard, did you say? There was only one great ship in harbor today."

"That is the ship, the *Lady Damar*. They left at dusk."

Leron stood up, and turned his face away so Ginas could

not see. "Then it is no wonder your cards went all awry. I watched that great slaver put out on the tide tonight. By now they are far at sea."

GANNOC
to his JOURNAL, privately

Our Prince had been gone but ten days when in the afternoon, I was dismayed to see smoke arising from the Palace, and also the fearful cry, Fire. I marshalled the servants to bring water from the cistern and also wetted therein a portion of our heaviest quilts and bedding. The fire proved to be in Dansen's private rooms and was most happily confined to a single area, where I found the scholar endeavoring to protect certain of his notes and instruments, the while disregarding any danger to his own person. I forcibly removed him and rolled him on the ground in a wet quilt, thereby extinguishing the flames in his robes and hair, and was surprised to see upon his face the look not of surprise or of dismay, but rather triumph.

Later he showed me amid the ashes a lump of glass, in shape like a shallow cup, saying that with this instrument alone he had caused the fire, never expecting it to burn so quickly and so hot. Picture, he said, a glass of similar property, but so large as to concentrate the sun's heat at great distance. Why one might strike down ships at sea or cities from afar. Even so, I questioned, where might such a glass be made? Look to the sands for glass, he said, and settle matters among the Karabdu. The Prince being away we left matters so, I admonishing him to spare the Palace in his further researches, but now as I reflect upon this matter I grow fearful when I think upon the use of so terrible and so remote a weapon.

II: CAPTURE

Chapter One

Sibyl was furious. She got up and walked to the window, seeing, as she had expected, the harbor much farther away than before. Clenching her teeth and her fists, she turned on the captain. "What stupid trick is this? Tell your men to turn the ship around."

Delgar had been caressing the monkey with one hand. He winked at the sailor next to him and laughed again. "You will have to ask me more sweetly. Come here," he patted his knee, "come here and ask me again."

"You can hear well enough from here." As always, her hand found the glass ring hidden in her bodice, and she twisted the thong around her fingers as she spoke, in her mind searching desperately for some weapon. She had known he was a slaver. What had she expected, anyway? She saw the thin-faced man's blue eyes fixed on her, and her anger exploded. "Beware," she cried. "The wrath of the Players will lie heavy on you! Would you die before your time?"

She had the satisfaction of seeing the captain and his men draw back in momentary superstition, then the captain's heavy eyes narrowed and he made as though to rise. "The Players will have to manage better than that," he remarked. "I have seen better tricks from this babioun." He tossed the monkey a bit of food. "And now, come here. I will not ask softly again."

Sibyl's fists tightened until she could feel the nails biting into her palms. No weapon, no way out, no help—the force of her fury made her sick. Burn in hell, she thought slowly, may you all burn in hell. She stood her ground, one shaking fist half-raised, and as she cursed them in her mind, the ship gave a little lurch to one side. The heavy lantern above the table swung wide despite the cunning counterweight, and a startling stream of flaring oil slopped onto the table, leapt up in flame, and died. The Captain drew back with an angry curse, holding his burned wrist to his mouth, while the thin-faced man silently touched his fingers to the hurt spot on his face.

There was silence, then the captain spoke again. "The revenge of the Players is dramatic, but lacking in force." He signalled to two sailors who stood by the door and they came up behind Sibyl and Liniris, who was standing by in tears. "Have them approach." One of the sailors tentatively touched Sibyl on the back, to push her forward. She could feel the fear in his hand, and a sudden wave of power swept through her. She raised her hand once more, gesturing with her outer fingers as she had once seen Simirimia do, and in her mind she called the powers of fire and revenge down upon the captain's head.

The fire did her bidding. The lamps flared up in a hot smoky roar, charring the gaily painted ceiling; the candles on the table spread wide and red, and all their small tongues flamed together in a sudden wall of light and heat. The captain and his sailors stepped back as the flames pressed against them.

Sibyl felt as though she had stopped breathing. The pressure on her heart and throat was intense as she held the flames stretched out against her enemies.

Then the thin-faced man stepped forward past the flames and came up to Sibyl. He took her by the arm in a hard grip and looked her in the eyes. "A pretty trick, my dear, but more suited to the stage than here." Her attention wavered with surprise, and the flames lessened. He smiled and nodded. "Now that is better. Come quietly." He pulled on her arm, and arrogant of her new powers, she blasted him contemptuously in her mind. He winced slightly but did not loosen his grip. When he spoke, it was more quietly than before, as though they were alone together. "Save this power for your enemies." He turned to speak with Delgar as Sibyl looked at him more closely.

"Captain," he said in his dry voice, "you owe my friend Mindra and myself something on the game we played last night. Let us see if these wild ones can be brought to hand, and we shall call the accounts cleared. Then if any further wrath come

from the Players, it shall be upon our own heads and not yours."
He looked down at Sibyl and smiled a little cruelly. "I do not
think this task will require any lighted lamps or candles."

The Captain laughed at this despite his recent fear, then
shook his head. "But Mindra lies sick below."

"Do you know a better medicine?"

The Captain answered consideringly, "Truly I am tempted,
friend Ziliman. I am a reasonable man, and last night's losses
at Castledown were heavy on my pocket. But these girls do
not seem reasonable; and you know they must be in good
condition when delivered to Tredana, or my purchaser will
forfeit his contract."

"Captain, Captain, do I appear a violent man?"

"No, no." He looked at Sibyl and then at Liniris, still shaken
with tears. "Take them tonight and we shall call it quits. But
one night only. This has been a weary voyage and I long—I
long for port."

Ziliman bowed his head with a small smile. "One night
should do me well, and cure Mindra also of any fancied ail-
ments." He motioned with his hand to the sailors standing
behind them, and Sibyl could not help but recognize that proud
gesture. She looked at him with rising wonder as he took both
her wrists in his hard clasp and bent forward. The thin lips
barely touched her own rigid mouth, and she felt a trickle of
breath as he spoke softly. "It is time for you to fight."

"Take your hands off me," she said loudly and as his grip
slackened she pulled one hand free and hit him across the face.
He flinched, a faint amusement in his eyes, as he called to the
sailors for help.

"Bring these two below," he said, and Sibyl was taken by
the arms, followed by Liniris who was half-fainting with terror.
Ziliman nodded a last time to the Captain and followed them
out.

Pushed through the dark swaying passages, Sibyl was aware
of little until a door opened before her, and she was roughly
shoved across the raised threshold into a small cabin, and the
door bolted behind her. She was left alone for some moments,
then the door opened and closed once more.

Her captor paused in the doorway, then brought a small box
from his belt and flicked it open. He drew the snuff in deeply,
sneezed, then rubbed one finger against his nose in the old

familiar gesture. As he replaced the box, he shrugged and raised an eyebrow. "It is easier to relinquish a kingdom than tobacco. Did you know I was on this ship?"

Sibyl shook her head, unable to speak.

"Well for you, then, that I played the captain and won last night. Do not fear for your friend. I have left her with Osmin, who just now is far too weak to cause her any alarm. I have instructed her to knock him on the head if he seems overmuch recovered and annoys her." He looked at her keenly.

"Why so pale?"

"I—they told me you were dead."

"You heard this from the prince?"

"No, Ginas of the Players. I—I just arrived."

He nodded. "Ginas was not entirely wrong. Ajjibawr the Karif is dead indeed, these many years." Sibyl suddenly sat down on the bunk, exhausted, as he stepped over to the table and poured wine from a beaker. He closed her fingers over the goblet and smiled. "Let us drink, then, to an unexpected reunion. I thought it must be you, but could not be certain until I saw the ring. It moved me that you have kept that trifling token."

"I felt stupid not to have recognized you. The dye doesn't change you that much."

He glanced into the small brass mirror on the wall and rubbed his chin with one hand. "Nevertheless, I hope it will come off. Otherwise you will arrive in Rym Treglad with Clerowan the Brown, not the White."

"Clerowan? . . ."

"As I said, Ajjibawr no longer. Clerowan the White at your service, and better me than the captain. Your being here forces my hand somewhat. I am on this ship with a few friends to turn it around and bring it safe to Rym Treglad. Now we must act a little sooner than we had planned."

"And free the slaves?"

"Of course. I have made friends in the hold already. There is a Zanidan who wishes to return to the north and avenge his fallen King. You would like to help us?" Sibyl nodded, and Clerowan said musingly, "Naturally, this ship will be an important prize for the Prince."

Sibyl looked at him suspiciously. "I'm surprised that Ginas didn't know you were still alive. You both have similiar ideas." He raised an inquiring eyebrow. "You all seem very eager to

reunite me with Leron. Ginas even had him come to Sundrat.
If he got her message, he's there by now."

Clerowan shook his head. "Foolhardy but not surprising.
Why do you not wish to see him?"

Angry tears came into Sibyl's eyes, and she banged down
her goblet. "It's not that I don't want to see him. But I'm
treated more like a child than when I was twelve. Why was I
able to make my own decisions then?"

Clerowan shrugged. "You were not then a woman."

Sibyl rose to her feet. "I'm sorry. I thought we could still
be friends. But maybe that's impossible now that I'm just a
woman and not a child."

He lifted his hand gently. "I was explaining the thoughts of
others. I am no longer the Karif, arranging the lives of others;
I have learned the pleasures of independence. I would not deny
them to you. Shall we then be friends?" The tight skin crinkled
at his temples as he smiled at her, and Sibyl hurriedly looked
away, feeling her heart thump. She nodded, and Clerowan
laughed. "Now for the small problem of the ship. It is too bad
you do not have more of the goddess Simirimia's power. How
great is the force at your command?"

"I'm not sure. I don't even know how it happens."

"If this were the captain's cabin, and he had you here, how
do you think it would be?"

Sibyl laughed. "On fire."

"Could you hold the captain's attention some few minutes,
an hour at the most, while I arrange matters below decks?"

"Sure. What's your plan?"

"I have been voyaging on this pestilent slaver some four
months and have already made my plans. The rowers in the
hold are ready and brave with desperation. I do not think the
sailors will offer much resistance without the captain to bully
them. To strike now requires only a few keys and some weapons: Hakma the Zanidan is waiting for my word. But the Captain must be treated with and he is never alone, save when
there is a woman in his cabin. So I ask again, how well do
you trust your powers?"

Sibyl shrugged. "I'm sure I can hold his attention. I just
hope I don't burn up the whole ship."

Clerowan looked up at her seriously. "It will be well if you
have as much of the goddess's power as you do her pride. We
had best strike tonight. If I take you to the captain now, he

will be sleepy, drunk, pleased and surprised—a help to you in your task and to us in ours." He looked at her critically. "I cannot bring you as you are; you are too unmarked, and he will be suspicious." Without warning he closed his hand on her shoulder, digging his fingers in deeply. Involuntarily she pulled away, and the fabric tore a little. "Good," he said, as he loosened his shirt at the throat. "Reknot your laces." In the corridor he took her wrists in a bruisingly painful grasp and jerked her along. "Loathing and fear," he whispered as they approached the captain's door.

The sailor standing guard looked at them with surprise. "A present for the captain," said Clerowan with an evil twist to his mouth. The sailor went inside, then returned to motion them in, discreetly withdrawing to the outer passageway.

Delgar sat on his bed, propped up on cushions, a flask in his hand and a red flush on his face. Sibyl was jerked forward with such force she fell realistically to her knees on the floor. "A present," repeated Clerowan, closing the door behind him with one hand. "We have had an entertaining time but not to the value of three hundred krahs. The fire trickery was the limit of her resistance, I fear. Would you have her tonight, in consideration of only a partial remittance?"

Delgar breathed heavily, looking at Sibyl's bare bruised shoulder. Then he began to laugh and put by his flask. "Thank Valdz I'm not so tight a merchant. I'll pay you half the debt remitted earlier. Agreed?"

Clerowan nodded and took up the flask to drink a seal on the bargain. "Agreed. As I said, there is little to fear, but I caution you'll need a firm hand." He nodded and left without a backward glance. As the door shut behind him, Sibyl suddenly felt a wave of apprehension. Then Delgar stood up and she had no more time to think.

Sibyl backed against the farther wall, but Delgar was in no hurry. He merely took another swallow from his flask and laughed when she refused his offer of it. "Tell me," he said at last, "will the wrath of the Players fall on Ziliman's head or mine? Both, perhaps?" He took a step forward, staggering a little, and steadied himself with one hand. "Come, tell me how you will have your revenge on us." He reached out with his hand, but she easily avoided him. They slowly circled each other in the small room, a step at a time. Sibyl felt strangely calm; no fiery anger had yet overtaken her.

Delgar made an unexpectedly sudden lunge and caught her
by the hair. Before she could pull free he had slobbered a few
open-mouthed kisses against her neck and the anger she awaited
leaped up in disgust at the smell and touch of him. She shoved
him back with her knee and a curse, and he staggered back to
sit heavily on the edge of the bed. For a moment there was a
pounding silence and uneven breathing, then Delgar made another lunge. She jerked out of his way, but he had caught the
hem of her sleeve in his hand and with a mighty heave split
the velvet apart and tore the sleeve partly loose. She was surprised to find how much she disliked his eyes on her bare skin.

As they once more circled each other, there came sudden
noises from outside and a man's loud warning shout. Delgar
turned to listen and quickly, Sibyl pretended to stumble as she
dodged away. Delgar forgot the noises and threw himself on
her. She rolled over, winded and bruised, and tried to heave
herself up, but he was too heavy. There was an increasing
commotion in the corridor beyond, shouts and thumps and
scuffling noises, but Delgar did not notice, trying clumsily to
get his arms around her. As she struggled to rise from under
his weight, she felt the power return to her and she blasted him
back with her mind as she pushed with her arms. The cabin
grew bright and hot, and Delgar fell back with his hands to his
head. Sibyl stumbled to her feet and looked down at him in
contemptuous anger; as he reached forward to catch at her
dress, she leaned over, caught up his heavy silver wristlet from
off the table and hit him once, hard, behind the ear. His head
fell limply back, and he sprawled on the floor, rolling a little
to the motion of the ship. Sibyl's breathing quieted, and the
lamps died down.

Once she was sure he would not get up, she laughed a little
with relief and sat on the edge of the bed, rubbing her sore
neck and arms and wiping her neck clean. There were still
some muffled sounds from outside, but not so many as before.
She went to the door and looked out. No sailor stood outside.
She hesitated, then looked back at Delgar on the floor. He
might awaken. She found some lengths of clothing in his chest
and tied his hands as best she could, with many knots. Also
in the chest was a small sharp dagger, and with this in her
hand she went out into the corridor.

All seemed quiet on the main deck. A tall figure rose up
out of the darkness, black and enormous, and Sibyl shrank

back against the wall. Then it smiled at her, and she saw it
was Hakma the Zanidan, holding a dagger in each hand, broken
chains hanging from his wrists and ankles. "I was sent to find
you," he said in a deep rich voice. "Our friend Clerowan told
me where you were. How does the captain?"

"I tried to tie him up but I don't think it will last long. Is
the ship ours?"

"They could not prevail against us. Many are slain, and our
prisoners lie below in a cage they made for us. Delgar shall
join them there for future reckoning. Wait."

He moved silently past Sibyl and reappeared with Delgar
slung over his massive shoulder. "Come greet our other friends;
tonight we rejoice."

Sibyl followed him along the passage and down into the
cargo hold. Lanterns had been lit along the walls, and sprawled
among the bales were the slaves of a few hours since, some
wounded, some sick, some weary, but all relaxed and laughing,
draped with cloth of gold and bolts of velvet. The wine casks
had been broached, and there was food scattered everywhere
about.

The Captain's monkey, collarless, was running about with
food stuffed in his mouth. At the sight of Delgar, much good
humor vanished, but the Zanidan pushed through unmoved,
and opening the hatchway easily, let the Captain drop from his
shoulder down through. He turned to the others with a smile.
"If he breaks his neck in the fall, it will save us the trouble.
But where is my sword brother?"

An old man spoke up worriedly. "After you left us, when
we thought ourselves finished here, Salama struck him with a
small knife he held concealed. Salama he slew in return, but
the wound he took is black and strange. He has gone to the
Player maid to see if she has any knowledge in herbs." Hakma
swore, then turned to Sibyl with a reassuring look. "It would
take more than such as Salama to cause him hurt. But we must
see to him. My brothers, eat and be glad; but those of you who
were sailors, be prepared to help us set a course to Rym Treglad
and freedom. We dare not wander back too close to shore."
He looked at several men in particular as he spoke, and they
nodded. Then he took Sibyl's hand and led her back towards
Clerowan's cabin.

Liniris was bent over the bed, pressing down hard with a

torn bit of cloth in her hand; many crumpled rags, red and wet, were littered about her feet. She looked up distractedly, and as the pressure of her fingers relaxed, some blood spurted out from a tear high in Clerowan's side, under the arm. His eyes were closed and his lips were bloodless. Sibyl looked a moment hopelessly, then pressed the cloth down herself while Liniris pulled the torn tunic apart better to expose the wound. It was not large but the edges were black and hard and would not join. There was no place for a tourniquet she could see, and whenever she lifted the rag, fresh blood spurted out.

"Why is it black?"

Liniris shook her head. "It is not natural. I fear poison."

Sibyl looked down on Clerowan's face, pale under the dark stain, and saw how he struggled for his breath. The lamplight shadowing his features gave her an idea. "Can we burn it clean?"

Liniris put a fresh rag into her hand and pulled away the soaked one. "With what?" she asked, but Hakma had already taken his dagger and was holding the blade in the lamp flame.

"There is a chance," he said, then shook his head. "But the lamp is not hot enough."

Sibyl looked at the flame calmly, trying to summon up by will alone the powers she knew were hers in anger. The muscles in her jaw clenched tight. For a long moment nothing: only the troubled sound of Clerowan's gasping breaths. Then the flame welled up, brighter and hotter, not towering out of control but smooth and steady, until the dagger within glowed clear and orange. She put out her hand. "I will do it," she said, and he handed her the dagger without comment.

As Liniris moved out of her way, the blood spurted up once more. Sibyl bit her lip and pressed the blade down hard on the blackened wound. There was a sizzling sound and a smell of burning, and as Clerowan cried out in pain, tears ran from her own eyes. But she held it down a moment longer, and when the dagger was lifted away, there was only a leaf-shaped burn where all had been hard and discolored before. She turned to Liniris. "It is soft now. Can you do what must be done?"

Liniris nodded, trembling. "I will need silk and needles."

The Zanidan nodded, and as the door shut behind him, Sibyl sank onto the bed beside Clerowan, suddenly weak. But she stayed to help hold him steady as Liniris skillfully stitched the wound, and after Liniris had fallen asleep, she continued awake throughout the night, still sitting on the bed, changing the cold cloth on Clerowan's forehead from time to time.

It must have been nearly dawn when Sibyl finally fell asleep, and she had not slept long when the ship unexpectedly listed far over and threw her to the floor. In a daze she tried to sit up as the ship leaped and rolled far over the other way, slamming her back against the wall. All the ship's timbers seemed to shift apart, creaking loudly about them, then came a roar of wind and the small window was violently lit. The entire cabin snapped with a fierce white light; and the thunder following after rumbled over the length of the ship.

Sibyl pulled herself over to the bed and tried to keep Clerowan's inert body from rolling onto the floor. Even with the help of Liniris it was almost impossible. The ship threw them from side to side, and soon a rolling wave of water seeped in under the door, chilling their legs as they knelt. Between the splitting sheets of lightning, the cabin was dark and the noise of the storm roared confusingly all about them. Time passed, and Sibyl would rather have let herself be thrown about, but for Clerowan. In lulls they could hear the men shouting on deck, but there were no frightening sounds of damage, splitting wood or crashing masts. Nothing but the terrible fury of the wind, the crack of lightning, and the deafening explosions of thunder. The water continued to roll in and out of the room, but it was never more than a few inches deep.

At last the lightning came less often and less bright, and the thunder murmured at a greater distance. Shuddering, the ship slowed its race before the wind, and the waves began to slap against its sides rather than break furiously over. Sibyl smiled at Liniris as the cabin filled with grey dawn light. "I guess we made it."

Liniris stumbled to her feet. "But to where?"

Sibyl shrugged. "I don't know. Will you stay with him, Liniris? I'll go out on deck and see what I can find out."

Sibyl's long skirts trailed uncomfortably through the swamped dark corridor: but at the end of the deck she saw the sun's edge above the low sweeping clouds. There was a tangle of sail and rope on deck, weighted with axe-cut wooden crosspieces, for the sails had been cut down when the storm sprang on them. Now some men were busy lashing up new supports, while others bailed out water.

The Zanidan smiled at Sibyl's approach and steadied her as she stumbled over her skirts. "Truly these are strange storms Rauve brews up for these waters. So much light and noise and yet no rain. And we have been driven north north east as truly as though it were not the autumn of the year when winds blow southward. How does Clerowan?"

"Still asleep. Is there any way of knowing where we are?"

He gestured to the captain's deck, where a man stood with a gleaming brass ddimry, sighting the new sun. "Meladin, once a navigator for Vahn, will attempt to set our course. But for how fast and how far we were driven, who but Vazdz or Ruave could say?"

The sail began to rise on its new supports, flapping wetly. Sibyl watched it a moment, and then asked, "Who is Ruave?"

Hakma looked surprised. "Ruave is of the race of the Great Mother, and holds the tempests as her own property. It is a thing well known in my land, if not in Tredana."

Later that day as Sibyl sat with Clerowan, who still slept heavily and unmoving, Osmin, who had traveled under the name of Mindra, visited the cabin. When last she saw him, he had been a proud young warrior, with five wives and twelve horses, one of the Karif's most trusted bodyguards. Now his long braided hair had been cut short and was streaked with grey. His face was thin and lined with his eyes bright blue in their shadowed pouches. His hands clasped nervously together, and his eyes not moving from Clerowan's quiet face, he added to what Sibyl had already learned, telling how the Karif had summoned a council to deal with the new fanaticism, eight years past. As he described the cowardly attack upon the Karif, by those he had thought faithful, tears came to his eyes; for it was then his sword brother had been killed, defending the Karif with his own body, Ab'Bakr who had also been Sibyl's friend. At this point in his story, Osmin paused and shook his head as he looked at Clerowan. "That time he also took a deadly hurt, for a sword passed through his body, and I carried him away to safety slung like a corpse across my own saddle. But he did not lie so still as he lies now. I fear there was a poison in the blade that fire could not kill."

The second day dawned very calm and clear. As they proceeded slowly on, not knowing where they lay on the flat and featureless ocean, Meladin sighted a tiny smudge on the horizon, which soon proved to be another ship of the Vahnian type, approaching swiftly. Nervously, the newly freed men armed themselves. The oncoming ship was not larger than the *Damar*, but she carried more sail, and it was clear they would not be able to outrun or outmaneuver her. Sibyl left Liniris with Clerowan in the cabin, and resolutely went on deck to join the others, rigid with apprehension.

The prow of the other ship was carved in the likeness of a grinning monster, and as its painted jaws came cutting through the green waves, they could all see plainly what dangled from a rope in the open mouth: a human skull. Beside her, the Zanidan, his hand on his sword, gave a great cry and dropped to his knees so suddenly Sibyl looked to see a spear or arrow between his shoulders. But his cry had been one of joy, not pain, and it was echoed on the farther deck, for there were no Vahnians there. Freed slaves like themselves stood there, still showing the marks of chains and abuse, and at their head a mighty dark figure even taller than Hakma, who was wearing a gold circlet in his curly black hair. Beside her the Zanidan had gotten to his feet again, laughing with delight. "It is Shirkah," he said at last, and there were tears in his eyes despite his laughter. "It is Shirkah our king, and he is in chains no longer."

The ships drew alongside each other, and Shirkah came across in his boat. He embraced Hakma, lifting him off the deck in his enthusiasm, then turned and bowed courteously to Sibyl, extending a large yet carefully gentle hand. Only a few words had been exchanged when Hakma took his king by the arm. "This is a more fortunate meeting than you might suppose," he said. "We will hear of your exploits later. But first you are needed as a healer. Clerowan the White lies wounded below, poisoned by an enemy blade. It was through his help we won this ship." Shirkah spoke to the men who had accompanied him aboard, then followed Hakma and Sibyl to the cabin, stooping a little to get under the six-foot-high doorframe.

Liniris looked up at them in amazement, then stood away from the bed as Shirkah fell to his knees by the bedside. Under the touch of Shirkah's black-skinned hand, Clerowan looked too pale to be alive and still have blood flowing through his veins, despite the veil of dark stain on his face. Shirkah shook his head. "Leave us alone," he said. "I will do what I can." His voice was deep and comforting. Sibyl let herself be drawn out, and they waited in the corridor as minutes passed silently. Then the door opened and Shirkah stooped to come out, his face shiny with sweat. "He will awake tonight," he said. "Do not disturb him now." Sibyl forced herself to follow them back on deck, Liniris's cold grasp on her hand giving her courage.

Outside a fresh wind was blowing, and Shirkah spoke, his hand on Hakma's shoulder. "The Lady Ruave is true to her word," he said. "She will hurry us westward to home." He smiled at Hakma's expression. "There can be ho doubt, for I spoke with her myself. It happened not long after our sailors turned on their own captain, hanging his head as you may see from the front of the ship as a warning to those who might follow him. In their bloody quarreling we were run aground on an island, and those who went ashore did not return. In the absence of any guard, we freed ourselves, pulling the staples from the walls and looping our chains around our waists. How strange and quiet it was on deck, no sailors to be seen. And the island looked so very peaceful, showing no sign that it was the home of Ruave, and her a prisoner to Vazdz, cruelly beset by the Moraganas."

Hakma shook his head in wonder. "I do not think I would believe this if I heard it from any other man."

"Nor I," said Shirkah. "I will not tire you with the whole tale now. Enough that Ruave is free again, able to send hèr storms to the coast and relieve the long drought there. And in freeing her I lost the chains with which my brother bound me. Will you accompany me back to Zanida? There is a crown to be regained." Hakma bent on one knee, and Shirkah smiled as he touched his shoulder.

All day the ships kept close company, and Shirkah remained aboard, talking with Hakma and planning their return to Rym Treglad and thence to Zanida. Sibyl, restless, paid scant attention to Shirkah's story, stange and exciting though it was. He had foiled the Moraganas as they attacked by deflecting their sunlike eyes with brightly polished mirrors from his ship: the heat of their attack had melted the bronze mirrors in his hands and also the chains from off his wrists, while the blinding reflection had sent them screaming back to their master Vazdz with news of their defeat. It was an exciting tale, told with impressive simplicity, but Sibyl listened without responding, and before nightfall she was back in the cabin where Clerowan

still slept. Despite Shirkah's words, he seemed unchanged.
Moved by his continuing helplessness, she lightly touched his
face with one hand. The closed eyes opened slowly, and she
drew back nervously. He seemed to want to speak, but after a
moment his eyes closed wearily again. She was bent over
listening, close to his face, as Liniris entered the room. Sibyl
smiled at her. "His eyes opened. I know he saw me. Now I
am sure everything will be all right." Liniris smiled doubtfully.

SONG OF SHIRKAH
composed, after he had been sold into slavery, by HAKMA the
Faithful

Shirkah King of Zanida dressed for hunting
strong bent bow in his hand and straight bone arrow
sharp knife sure by his side his spear well-sharpened
eager for hunting

Shirkah King of Zanida killed the grey seal
Shirkah King of Zanida killed the walrus
Shirkah King of Zanida killed the brown elk
feeding his people

Shirkah King of Zanida skillful hunter
he is hunted and he is trapped and taken
sharp pains sharper than arrows pierced his strong heart
treachery took him

There is never a wolf would so have torn him
There is never a bear would so have slashed him
There is never an owl would so have struck him
Lord of Zanida

Far the Bear of the Mountains has been taken
Lost the land of Zanida waits to welcome
home with fire and with song the noble Shirkah
King of Zanida

Chapter Two

Late that night, as Sibyl sat on the floor with her back against the bed, Liniris rapped softly on the door. She had a covered goblet in her hands, and when Sibyl removed the lid, a delicious odor filled the small room. Liniris smiled nervously. "There are flowers and herbs in it. I found them in the ship's stores. My grandmother taught me how to make this drink. It will make you feel much better."

Sibyl sipped and nodded. "I can tell." She stretched. "Now I don't feel so stiff."

"Would you like me to take your place?"

Sibyl shook her head. "Tomorrow will be soon enough. I don't mind watching through the night. I only hope Shirkah was right. I don't really see how he could have made any difference."

"The Zanidai are famous for their skill."

"I hope their fame's well-founded."

After Liniris had gone, Sibyl let her head lean back against the bed, finally falling into a light slumber. She awoke in the dark to a light touch on her face. "Sibby." The whisper was light and hoarse. "No, leave the light. My eyes are as weak as the rest of me. How long has it been?"

She got up to her knees and bent over his face. "Just a few days. You were poisoned. But everything will be all right now. We're on our way to Rym Treglad. Drink this, it will make you feel better." She held Liniris's drink to his lips and he drank thirstily. Then he lay back against her arm and listened as she softly explained about the fight, his wound and the arrival of Shirkah and his ship.

"The wound was black, black and hard?"

"Yes, and we could not stop the bleeding."

"That is a poison from the desert. Fletcher's root, we call it, for it can also be a gum for fixing feathers to an arrow. Salama was of a tribe of weapon makers. One of the first to turn. How did you treat it? The poison is fatal."

"I burned it clean, and Liniris stitched the wound. Then you slept, until tonight. Shirkah visited you this afternoon and said you would recover. I don't know what he did."

In the dim cabin she could make out his smile as he answered her. "The craft of the Zanidans is a secret. But if their King says I will recover, then I will believe him, however unlikely it seems to my other senses." Soon after he was once more asleep, his unguarded face fallen back against Sibyl's arm.

She was tired and longing for sleep herself, but it was impossible. Impossible because he lay next to her. At first she was drowsy enough not to notice the drift of her thoughts. Then awareness of the longing that was rapidly spreading through her body jerked her fully awake, startled and upset. One of his hands lay limply against her hip, and she could feel its weight burning through her hipbone all the way to her spine. She turned her head away, towards the cabin, and forced herself to breathe slowly and evenly. You will go to sleep, she said silently and firmly, you are a stupid idiot and you will go to sleep. But the torment of trying to keep still, and keep separate, to breathe evenly, not to press more closely against his body made it impossible. Finally she gently disengaged her arm from under his head and pulled away. Her arms and legs ached, and she was giddy when she stood up. It was impossible for her even to stay in the same room; she slipped out and sat down in the corridor, leaning against the door. She dropped her head back at an uncomfortable angle and finally slept again.

Liniris stumbled over her at sunrise and helped her stiffly to her feet. The longing to go back into the cabin was still so strong that she resolutely turned away and left Clerowan to Liniris's competent ministrations. Alone in Liniris's room she slept deeply for several hours. As she washed and dressed, she tried to remember exactly what had happened the night before. Try as she might she could find no reason for her sudden passion. What if she had hugged him last night, and he had awakened? What could she have said? What would he have thought of her? She looked morosely at her reflection as she brushed her short black curls. Watch your step, she said to Sibyl in the mirror, or you are going to make a very big fool of yourself and lose a friend.

She took over from Liniris that evening, and Liniris reported that Clerowan's recovery was progressing rapidly. The wound was closed and natural looking; he had eaten heartily and even walked out on deck, supported by Osmin. Liniris was concerned with Sibyl's pallor and made her once more the special drink of the Players. Sibyl drank deeply and found herself greatly refreshed as before. She ate the supper set out for her, then taking Liniris's cup with her went down to Clerowan's cabin, sensing in her tight stomach difficulties ahead.

He was sitting up against the cushions, a lamp on the table beside him and charts spread out on the covers over his hunched up knees. He greeted her pleasantly, but there was such a closed look on his face that Sibyl blushed guiltily, wondering if he somehow knew her secret. The feelings of the night before were back as strong as ever, but easier to control in the light and standing up. "I have brought you some of Liniris's potion again," she said, and he looked up briefly, then back at the charts, thanking her.

Sibyl saw how the color rose in his own face, and she backed up a step, startled and confused. Nonsense, she told herself, it's the lamplight, then aloud, "It's good to see you so much recovered. I felt bad about leaving you last night, but I was so—so tired, and I didn't think you would need anything. Liniris says you've been up on deck." Heavens, she thought, why am I babbling on like this? Go away and leave him in peace. Fool.

But as she babbled, his color rose again, and she could see it was not the lamplight or her imagination. He folded the charts slowly, meticulously matching the order and direction of all the varied creases, slow to meet her eyes. "I was not sure if you had gone or not. It must be one of the effects of the poison in the wound. I dream so vividly." He pushed the charts onto the leather case, laid them down, and took up the cup to drink. There was no chair, and Sibyl folded herself awkwardly against the chest.

"I have not thanked you yet for helping to save my life. It

is not worth what it once was, yet neither am I ready to quit
it." Sibyl said nothing. He tapped the charts. "We are off course
considerably to the southwest, but Shirkah thinks we may make
Rym Treglad in two weeks. The crew is enthusiastic but lacking
a little in experience. What do you plan to do in Rym Treglad?"

Sibyl made a shrugging gesture with her hands. She was so
nervous, a pulse was beginning to tick in her eyelid, and her
breathing was growing ragged. He's babbling too, she thought.
Why? Clerowan went on, "I want you to know that whatever
happens, I will be your friend. You need not feel you have
nowhere to turn, should Ginas or any others seek to coerce
you. Yet I feel you will find stronger and more useful friends
in Gannoc and Mara and Dansen the Learned than in Clerowan
the Wanderer."

His humility seemed unfeigned and Sibyl looked at him
sharply. "Just tell me one thing," she asked and was relieved
to hear that her voice sounded quite normal. "Why do you play
at Clerowan like this? So, so humble? Ajjibawr the Karif was
the least humble man I ever met."

He looked at her in surprise, then slowly and reluctantly
began to laugh. "A death thrust, that. You are the first who
ever dared to ask me. Do you truly want to know?" Sibyl
nodded. "Tell me, how old are you now?"

"Eighteen."

"Eighteen. I was eighteen the year I became Karif. That
was more than twenty years ago. I defeated the old Karif, who
was my cousin, in single combat. He was in trade with Vahn
and had made it his custom to sell his enemies in chains to
Bodrum. It was not a practice that I liked, and it was stopped
while I was Karif. After I had killed him, I took his wife under
my protection and married her later that year. She was nearly
forty then, and a very wise woman." He reached for his little
snuff box, took a pinch, and continued. "It was perhaps two
years later that Halila came to see me one day, when I was
breaking young colts in the spring. I was then furious with a
grey colt. He would be the sire of the colt I gave you. Ah, he
was a proud one and very foolish. I could hardly put a rope to
him. Touch him and he would stand up straight in the air or
dance around the pen, kicking and calling. Halila loved to watch
him, and she asked me why I was so set on mastering him.
There were other horses more suited to the saddle. Why not

enjoy him and leave him free, she asked me. I remember to this day how I glared at the colt with my back as stiff as his and my teeth clenched. 'Yes, he is beautiful,' I told her, 'but he will be more beautiful when he learns to bend his neck a little.' Halila looked at me and laughed and spoke as sweetly as always. 'He is the perfect horse for you, my lord,' she said, and it was not until evening I understood her meaning. . . ." he laughed at the memory, then looked at Sibyl with one eyebrow slightly raised. "The grey horse learned to bend his neck, and when I became Clerowan I resolved to learn to bend mine; though I fear the success has been more in my head than in my heart."

Sibyl smiled. "I've never understood why humility is supposed to be so attractive."

"Nevertheless, it is commonly held to be a virtue. And speaking of virtue, I think perhaps you should leave." He carefully placed the snuff box on the table, not meeting her eyes. "No, it is not your fault. But I am not quite myself tonight." As he spoke the ship swayed gently, and the little box skittered across the table and onto the floor. His fingers and Sibyl's closed over it at the same moment and their faces were inches apart. She felt him shudder and dimly considered pulling away; but instead she closed her eyes, and as his lips touched hers she clung on his arm for the shaky minutes that followed. Her heart was still lurching uncontrollably when they pulled away from each other with meaningless embarrassed excuses that lapsed into awkward silence.

He spoke first. "You are sure that you left last night?"

"I was afraid—not of you, but of the way I was feeling."

"If you say so, I believe you. But I too was surprised by my feeling, and I was not quite sure what had happened. I still think you should leave. On land we may feel most differently."

Sibyl nodded and stood up, unable to think clearly, but instead of moving to the door she found herself sitting down on the edge of the bed, putting her hand over his. He was not looking at her but his hand shook under hers; her own heart was hammering painfully, and the moment of indecision seemed very long. She sighed sharply and turned her own face away, feeling tears rising in her eyes, still unable to speak. He reached past her and turned down the lamp a little, then put his arms around her. For a while they clung together, gently rocking in motion with the ship, then kissed; and when she called him Ajjibawr, later in the night, he made no objection.

Next morning Sibyl went lazily out on deck. The captain's cabin was roofed with a small private area railed on three sides and lined with benches; here Sibyl sat and dreamed with closed eyes in the sun. The air was extraordinarily soft and gentle on her face, and the breeze on her bare arms was a pleasure. She did not open her eyes or speak when Liniris came quietly up the stairs to sit down by her, until a sudden upsurge of delight set her to singing, very softly.

"Sibyl, aren't you anxious to arrive in Rym Treglad?"

Sibyl considered the question gravely, then lay back against the bulwark and spread her arms out to the sun. "As far as I am concerned, this ship can sail on forever," she said quite truthfully. Then, once more singing, "Come all you fair maids, and learn by me."

"Sibyl, you must listen to me! Are you not anxious to see the prince?"

"Liniris, I am not in the mood to feel anxious about anything. Yes, I will be glad to see him. Okay?" She closed her eyes, humming.

"I'm sorry. But I thought that perhaps—perhaps you were in love now. I'm sorry."

"Sorry? Don't be sorry. You are absolutely right and one hundred percent correct. And to think that only a few days ago I had it all planned out to start living alone. Some other time, I guess."

Liniris jumped to her feet. "It's impossible. I mean, you are fooling, are you not? You're teasing me." She spoke so vehemently Sibyl opened her eyes.

"No, I'm not teasing," she said more seriously than before. "And what's impossible?"

"Nothing, but I thought I thought that after last night—oh, I know I put in all the right things, meadowsweet, oakgall, broom—my grandmother couldn't be wrong!"

Sibyl suddenly laughed with understanding. "O Liniris! You tried to drug me! That's it, isn't it? A special drink to make me see reason? Am I right?"

Liniris sat down again, her face in her hands. "I knew it was wrong. But my grandmother explained it to me. She said it would make everything all right, so you wouldn't be angry with your destiny. It was for your own happiness."

Sibyl shook with laughter. "Oh Liniris, Liniris. Didn't it ever occur to you that even if the drink did work, it would have to be when Leron was around? I'll bet your grandmother meant it for both of us."

Liniris looked at her doubtfully. "Perhaps, but she said it would make you a good wife to Leron, so I tried—"

"Liniris, I shared your drink both times with Ajjibawr!" She stood up and stretched, luxuriating in the sun. "Don't cry. Whether it changed things or not, it's too late now." But Liniris had her face in her hands and did not look up when she left.

That day she and Ajjibawr were gravely polite to each other in public, taking care not to touch so much as a hand. But at supper with Hakma and Osmin in the Captain's dining room their eyes met over the wine, and Ajjibawr's mouth quirked a little as he set down his goblet. "Perhaps you will indulge me later tonight," he said, a slightly wicked look in his eyes, "in a set of Castledown? It is time you learned." Sibyl nodded and looked up to see Hakma and Osmin smiling in perfect understanding. They said nothing however, apart from courteously bidding them good-night when they later left the table, turning to talk with a suddenly white-faced Liniris.

The thick glass window in Ajjibawr's cabin was open to the breeze, and Sibyl stood by it looking out at the sunset as he set up the board and discussed the basic movements. Brassy streaks of sunlight made a road above the waters from horizon to ship; the sun had bellied out into a bloated sack of fiery color that suddenly extinguished in the sea leaving the sky dark. As many times as she had recently seen the sun set in the sea, it still surprised her that it was so different from sunset on shore. Now in the dark she felt colder and turned away from the window. The lamp made a warm yellow circle around the table; Ajjibawr stood beyond a little in the shadows.

"There is a problem," Sibyl said at last.

"Yes?"

"I do not know who moves first."

"In the game it is simple: shell over stone."

"And apart from the game?"

"As you say, a problem." He waited while Sibyl pushed a shining shell warrior forward two spaces, then brought up a

quartz spearman on one side. As she considered her next move
he remarked conversationally, "I am not often so astonished
as I was last night."

Sibyl bit her lip, and pushed forward a second warrior. "If
you want an excuse, I think I found one today."

He sent his spearman farther into enemy territory, then looked
up. "Excuse?"

She explained about Liniris, and his mouth twitched a little
in amusement. He took a pinch of snuff and surveyed the board.
"Of course," he said. "I should have realized that we were
compelled. What other reason could there be?" He watched
her deploy her men and brought in a knight on the left. "Furthermore," he continued, "it strikes me that this potion is remarkably long-lasting in its effect."

The small tension that had been building under Sibyl's heart
relaxed, and she began to smile. She looked up into his bright
blue eyes, so curiously ringed with yellow about the pupil.
"Yes, Castledown is an intriguing game. But I know a better
one, where both can win."

Ajjibawr stood up and leaned over to take her hand. "So
do I. Shall we see if it is the same one?"

She leaned against him and put up her face to be kissed.
"There are differences," she said, "but they are compensatory."

Later in the night Sibyl awoke. The strange sea glow of reflected starlight filled the cabin, rippling overhead as though
they were under the water, not on it. She could see her shell
warriors standing in their unfinished advance. Ajjibawr's knight
stood alone at the far edge of the circle and her little carved
admiral lay on his side, carelessly knocked over. She turned
her face towards Ajjibawr's. His head lay heavy on her shoulder
though she would not have moved it for the world. Clerowan
the White: pale indeed, his face glimmering in the light against
her dark tanned skin. Half-hoping to wake him she pulled
herself in more closely under his heavy arm, but he only murmured and lay still again. She slept; and before the sun rose it
was he woke her.

Later in the morning they arose and dressed, in no great
hurry. They washed each other, and for once Sibyl did not
shrink from the cold water in the cabin's copper urn. Ajjibawr
kissed the nape of her neck tenderly and then in mischief
squeezed the sponge out down her bare back; she jumped a

little, and when he reached to catch her, they fell against the table, scattering playing pieces on the floor. Sibyl helped him scoop them back up, then exclaimed in dismay at the little stone knight, whose head had broken off. Ajjibawr made light of it. "The stone pieces often break, for they are brittle. The shell is not as hard, but stronger, for it only chips." It seemed a bad omen however, and bothered her more than she would have admitted.

The next few days passed all too quickly. But following two weeks of calm weather, a little breeze sprang up, increasing until by nightfall there were gusts of irregular force filling the sails. The creak of rope above them grew loud, and the sheets boomed and flapped. Hakma looked uneasily at the sky. "Ruave is overgenerous with her wind. If she drives us aground here, we will be many a long day's journey south of Rym Treglad."

Sibyl squinted westwards. "Aground?"

"Yes, there are signs that show us not many miles off shore. If it were not for the wind, I would put farther out, for fear of shoals. But the wind and tide prevent us."

An hour before sunset the sky was a deep black and they lost sight of the other ship; it rained so heavily the sea was beaten flat. The canvas ripped, and it was all the sailors could do to stand upright. For a while the ship drove furiously along, plummeting into the storm. The blackness was the most frightening part of the storm, to run along so terribly fast before the wind, utterly blind. Sibyl and Liniris were within, out of the way of the scrambling sailors, when the ship fell suddenly forward on its prow in a crunching stop that hurled them to the floor and threw the loose contents of the cabin after them. Then it began a violent heaving and rolling as the sea following after caught it and tried to roll it over.

Ajjibawr appeared in the doorway, dark and dripping, hanging onto the frame for balance. "We are aground. A sandbar, not the rocks. The ship is uninjured, but soon may break apart if the storm does not lessen." He pulled Sibyl to her feet, then Liniris. "Have Liniris dress as you are, quickly. Cloaks also. We are lowering a boat." He shut the door, and Sibyl forced Liniris, protesting, out of her draggled gown and into a belted tunic. She grabbed two cloaks from out of the chest and also a dagger, then opened the door again with difficulty, fighting the sickening plunges of the stranded ship. Ajjibawr took them each by the arm and together they stumbled out through the

swimming passageways. The rain on the deck fell so thickly
it seemed a solid wall of water, and the cold wind threw it
across their path in waves as fierce as those that rolled up out
of the sea.

At the rail Sibyl looked down helplessly at the wildly whipping ladder. Ajjibawr shouted in her ear, barely making himself
heard above the storm. "I will lower you first, then Liniris.
There are oars lashed within, and the boat is tied up with a
long rope. If the ship heels over or starts to break apart, cut
loose and push away. There are other boats aboard; fear not."

She started to protest, but he pulled her against him and
kissed her violently: his face was as cold and wet as the sea
and she could only taste salt water. Then he roughly turned
her around and fastened a rope below her arms. He staggered
a bit as he lifted her over the rail, hugged her once more briefly,
and let her drop a few feet. She steadied her descent by clutching at the rope ladder, and once in the wildly tossing boat, she
slipped the noose off over her head and he jerked it back out
of sight. Liniris descended moments later, a dark shape in the
blackness. Sibyl helped her out of the rope and it once more
pulled up out of sight.

Now their only link with the ship was a heavy hawser running up to the deck: as she tested it with her hand, she felt it
loosen as they paid out the rope from above. The ship was, all
at once, much farther away. Sibyl drew out her dagger, ready
to cut free, but she could hardly see the ship to judge its
condition. They tossed about sickeningly, the hawser pulling
taut and slacking loose. As fast as they bailed, the low boat
filled again with rain and seawater.

Now the boat was across the sandbar, inland from the
grounded ship, and pulling to be free and race with the waves
towards land. Sibyl strained to see what was happening on the
ship. Above the noise of wind and sea a great cracking noise
rose from the ship, and she set her blade resolutely to the thickly
plaited hawser. Wet as it was, it seemed almost impossible to
cut. As she sawed away, crying and cursing with impotence,
the rope suddenly went slack in her hand and the section of
the *Damar*'s railing to which it had been tied loomed up out
of the dark, the released cable all tangled about it. There was
no other sign of wreckage but little chance to look for any as
the boat sprang free and began its tumultuous race with the
wind.

Sibyl and Liniris clung to the sides desperately, unable to do more than hold themselves aboard. The rain was now less and the sea higher; the boat ran up great hills of water and skidded down into valleys, impossibly deep. Then gradually the hills were a little less high, the gullies shallower; the wind dropped and the rain thinned to a mist. The sun was rising now above the storm, a pale diffuse light in the east. Sibyl ached from the strain of holding on. She tried to straighten a little, and as she did a violent shock threw her down into the boat's watery bottom. Once more they were aground, this time on rock; their boat was split apart and filling fast. But even in the thick mist Sibyl could see that the stones were dressed in squares, laid evenly; a man-made seawall.

Thrown into the water, she kicked her way up to the rocks and threw the heavy cloaks up over, then turned for Liniris, who obviously could not swim. Sibyl struggled over through the choppy water, awkward in her clothes, and cautiously grabbed at Liniris's floating hair, avoiding her flailing arms. It was only a few feet to the wall, but she was exhausted when they reached it, and Liniris was too far gone to climb to safety. Sibyl coughed and choked, treading water desperately. She was too tired now to try to heave Liniris up out of the water. Letting her own head bob below the water, she struggled to undo her wet belt with one hand, still holding Liniris's hair with the other. An eternity, then it came apart. Now completely under water, she knotted it through Liniris's belt and then, holding it by the extreme end, she called on her last strength and forced herself up, out of the water against the stones. A handhold, a place for her foot, and she was atop the wall. There was no time to rest. She braced her legs and hauled on the belt until the muscles in her shoulders seemed to crack apart, pulling the limp body up. Finally Liniris lay across her knees, vomiting seawater and shaking.

For many minutes they clung there to the rocks, hugging each other tightly in relief. In the growing light, white shapes appeared to the east. In the sheltered bay beyond the breakwater, a fishing fleet rode safely at anchor, many small boats painted white and blue. They seemed familiar. She looked past them to the town beyond, built up on a rocky hill above the harbor.

The castle was nobly proportioned, its many small glass windows glittering yellow in the dawn. There were bright dots of color along the walls, either banners or uniformed guards, Sibyl could not be certain at that distance. But even at a distance, she recognized the town. "Liniris," she said, "do you realize where we are?" Liniris shook her head. "I guess we *were* a little off course," said Sibyl. "We are in Tredana!"

DANSEN THE LEARNED
The History of the Kings of Tredana: Mathon Breadgiver
an extract

It is with deep and continuing sadness I must now relate the last events in the reign of Mathon, which occurred in the 40th year of his rule and the 62nd year of his life. Although he had never fully recovered from the treachery and maltreatment of the false king, Ddiskeard, the years he spent in exile were, as I have shown, not without their work, and their rewards. It happened in this most eventful year that Leron the Prince was called away to Sundrat, the first he ever had left the city of Rym Treglad since it was built; and for the first few weeks thereafter, Mathon did not much remark upon his son's long absence, thinking him gone but a few days. At length, however, he began to call upon his name more frequently, and being turned aside with soft answers, flew into a rage. Calling a stableboy to saddle his horse, in anger he rode away by a western road, doubtless supposing himself to be in Tredana and the road the one that led to the King's lodge. The stableboy knew not better than to obey the King, and much was he made to fear when Sentell, the King's groom, told him that horses had been forbidden to the King these eight years past, by direct word from the Prince himself.

Sentell and Gannoc both rode after the King, and not far from the city found him lying in the dirt, his horse nearby, for it was a young half-broken animal newly brought from Sundrat. They took him up with tenderness and care and brought him back to the Palace, but nothing could be done for him except to ease his pain and give him water, for something was broken in his back or neck. Gannoc has told me that as he stood by the King's bedside, Mathon of a sudden opened his eyes and spoke commandingly, demanding the mirror from the wall. And when the Steward held the mirror up, he looked a long time deeply into it, then closed his eyes and fell back on his pillow, saying, "I have seen death. It is not terrible." A little later he said, "I have been too many years a-dying. You must forgive me." And a little later yet, "Salute my son for me." And it was many minutes before the Steward knew that he was dead. Then Gannoc called us all to come and kiss our dear Lord's hand, who had been our own good King in happier days and a fairer master no man could wish for. We buried him in sorrow not long after, thinking it was a heavy thing for Leron to come home and find his father gone, himself for several weeks a King and all unknowing. Of course, we did not then know that he would not be returning to Rym Treglad.

Chapter Three

It was storming when Leron arrived in Tredana, a storm swept in from the ocean with heavy rain. Despite Ginas's protests of danger, he was traveling with her disguised as a singer, carrying a harp as he had eight years past and itchy under ten days' growth of beard. When the Players arrived at the gates, they were hurriedly penned together in a small alleyway for the night, high stone buildings on either side. Guarding the alley's mouth two kingsmen leaned sullenly on their spears, cold, their leather and chain-mail armor sodden. Inside Ginas's wagon, Leron watched her silently tell the cards, oblivious to the furious rattle of rain on the curved wooden roof. The wind shook the carts despite the protection of the alleyway.

She sensed his impatience, for not looking up from her reading she spoke aloud, answering the questions in her mind. "Tomorrow it will be possible to learn if the *Damar* has arrived in port and discharged her cargo. We can learn nothing tonight. Be easy, Prince." But Leron fidgeted where he sat. Home at last in Tredana and penned like a sheep on the fringes of the town. Perhaps the *Damar* had already arrived, given up her goods and sold her slaves and gone. On the road to Tredana, the simple fact of travel had helped keep him from brooding. That and the excitement of being in disguise, in possible danger. But now he was safe in Tredana and there was no way of guessing Sibby's fate.

For twenty minutes he sat passively, his head in his hands, then jumped to his feet. The rain had died down a little, but it was as windy as ever. He reached for his cloak, and Ginas looked up in surprise. "Where to, my lord? We are not allowed out until morning."

Leron pushed his right arm through the narrow slit and adjusted the folds on his shoulder. "From Castle Hill I can see the harbor. Enough to tell whether a large ship like the *Damar* lies at anchor. And if I see no ship, there are places I can go where there might be news of a sale of slaves." He adjusted the feathers carefully under his brooch.

Ginas rose from her seat. "No, you must not! You will never leave here safely, and you must not expose yourself this way."

"Think only that, rather than sit dumbly and be surrounded by the enemy, I have chosen to cast for a fate. Who knows, it may take me into the castle itself. I wonder if they have posted guards above." He pointed over his head in answer to her questioning look. "Above, on the roofs of the town. It will not be the first time I have gone out into Tredana secretly, by night." She put up her hand as though to stop him, and he nodded insolently at her table. "Lay out the cards for me, Ginas. You will be the first to know if I am to return safely."

He laughed at her scandalized look and slipped out through the door. On the top step he stood quietly, listening for the soldiers in the dark, but there came no sound from the alley's entrance. He swung down noiselessly onto the cobblestones, inches deep in water, and as quietly went to the corner of the wagon yard. The shed at the back had a steep slate roof that came to within twelve feet of the ground; the building against which it was built was much taller. Using the corner as a brace for back and feet, Leron wormed up to the edge of the roof, then pushed with his feet against the higher building so he slithered backwards onto the sloping tiles. They were slick with rain, oily to the touch, but at length he straddled the ridgepole, still undiscovered. Now he could see that the taller building was a warehouse. Once on its great roof he would have a clear run up to the corner of the main street, for the warehouses all were built in blocks of five or six. And here he was repaid for casting a fate: a rope was hanging from a beam above, which protruded from the stone sill of a large window where cargoes were unloaded. He stretched perilously upwards, slipping on the treacherous roof. He risked a bad fall and threw his weight upwards one last time, catching the rope in one hand then the other before the jerk of his weight on his wrist could break his hold. The rope was slimy and wet and it seemed an eternity before he could get a firmer hold, and walk his way up under it to the beam. From there to roof edge was a matter of a few feet; and still no alarm had been given. The warehouses were very wide, their roofs almost flat, and Leron skidded along rapidly, stumbling a little in the dark and rain, but safe from falling or detection from the street below. The familiar shapes of Tredanan stone chimneys, leaded gutters, and fanciful bronze weathervanes lightened his worries considerably. He was back home and as free as he had been at sixteen, secretly away from the castle at night.

At the end of the row he threw himself flat on the tiles and peered down cautiously. Now he knew exactly where he was; the street below, which he had to cross, went through a roofed and enclosed market space a little farther on towards the castle. It would be a useful bridge across to the other side. He turned to the right, and following the road, scrambled from building to building. They were of differing heights but so close together he had no difficulty. The market square was still as he remembered, built right across the road tight against the buildings on either side. In the day when it was open, any traveler on the street was forced to pass through; at night there was no choice but to take another route—or go over, as he intended.

The timbered roof at the market was uneven and irregularly gapped with ventilation holes; what mud and plaster roofing he could see was cracked and slippery. He let himself down cautiously then flattened himself as he heard horse hoofs in the street below. When they died away down a side street, he rose to his hands and knees and began a rapid scuttle across to the solid roofs of the other side. As he passed one of the many small air holes he suddenly froze at the flash of a small light below. He moved his face slowly over and placed one eye to the opening. Directly below he could see the light clearly, the top of a round dark lantern muffled on all sides. It threw a little light upwards, and none at all on the men who stood around it.

He heard first a familiar voice, the stranger from the woods outside Sundrat. It could be no one else. "Hey, c'mon. You can see I'm here alone. I came in good faith. Which one of you's the leader?"

He was answered by another familiar voice.

"Why have you come?"

"Don't play games. You don't like the kingsrules better'n anyone else. I got an offer for you from the captain of the guards. Now, who's the boss here?"

"The brigsmen do not keep us from our nabs and stickling."

"Well, y'better watch your step or you'll all end up in one of those slave ships. Now which one of you's this Huffing Dick?"

An edge of the lantern cover was turned back, and in the narrow shaft of light Leron could see a familiar embroidered cloak covering massive shoulders. Huffing Dick swept a wide bow to the leather-clad stranger, his rags and tatters fluttering. "I am he. A chainster tried the napping line once, on one of mine: he went back to the waters all done up in nicest canvas, stones to his feet."

There was a rasp of metal, and a short narrow blade gleamed in Huffing Dick's hand. "Now give me your message before I slit your pipe." A little jump of light on moving metal, and the dagger went spinning out into the dark. As Leron had seen once before, there was a lethal length of heavy chain hanging from the stranger's hand. Huffing Dick did not move. "Were you trained for the wars or the pit? No matter." His men on either side took the stranger by the arms, and one returned Huffing Dick's dagger to him. "Why so dumb?" he asked. "You want to pipe it privately?" The other nodded, and Huffing Dick gestured with his hands.

Obediently his men moved away into the darkness, and he was alone with the other in the middle of the room, the lantern at their feet lighting their faces for Leron, crouched overhead. "Now, what do you want with the footsmen? I will drop the fancy speech. Look!" He raised his arms high, and the rags made fantastic shadows. "There is no velvet under this. Tatters only. You can speak free with me."

"You could have velvet there, or anything else you want, if you work with the captain and his men."

Huffing Dick threw his head back with a deep barking laugh. "So, the dogs and cats should hunt together? Tell your master that footsmen like their own ways best."

"He could make it worth your while."

"And how should we make it worth his?"

"Listen, look, and point out certain people as he might require. Nothing more."

"I am an outlaw by King's writ: this would buy my freedom?"

"Yes."

"Easily said, young man. Your captain will need better proof
than the word of a nameless messenger. I could bring the true
prince in chains to the false king, and still be sent to the gallows
for my pains. You'll want a better lure for this old fox."

"In a week I can bring you a promise signed by the king.
My captain has an audience tomorrow."

"In less than a week, then, one of my men will tell you
where to come. He will know you by these berries in your
hat." Huffing Dick handed something to the other, chuckling.
"But I tell you now, I've been a wild stickler and skimbler-
skambler all my days, and do not look to end them in the
service of a king who dislikes poetry." He laughed again and
gestured in the dim light, and his men were around him again.
"Do not leave until we are gone, or you'll not live to regret it.
Canny now, come."

There was very little noise below, but the hall emptied
rapidly of men. The messenger from the king's guards waited
patiently below with his shuttered lantern several minutes, then
walked to the door and disappeared. Leron waited as patiently
himself, then carefully wormed the rest of the way across and
pulled himself up onto the farther set of roofs. He smiled with
satisfaction, knowing now that he had friends of a sort in
Tredana. It was still several hours to dawn, but lighter out and
less windy; the rain had died down to a chilly drizzle. He hurried
off towards the castle, more surefooted now in the semi-dark.

From the high roof of the old counting house, which abutted
the castle walls, Leron stood looking out into the dark. In
another hour or less he was sure he would be able to see the
entire harbor clearly, and still have enough darkness left to
cover his return to the Players. It was very still, except for a
few wakeful roosters fitfully discussing the dawn. The sea smell
was piercingly familiar: a breeze that had come in at his bed-
room window the first twenty years of his life. He closed his
eyes, trying to imagine himself off on a youthful excursion,
and found he was smiling with anticipation.

The gates to the old orchard were less than twenty feet from
the edge of the building on which he sat. He looked around
and lightly swung from roof to buttress to wall to road and
stepped around the corner.

The orchard was empty and unguarded as he had hoped, the shaggy old trees pruned back into ugly, misshapen spiked cudgels and between them the ground cleared in neat paths, trimmed and gravelled. Leron stepped carefully onto the crushed stone, to leave no mark on the turf. It seemed impossible that the tunnel entrance could have remained undiscovered so long.

His hand brushed aside the leaves of a small apricot that was fastened flat across the opening: underneath the niche was still unclosed. The opening was partially filled with rubble, broken pots and bits of stone. He scrambled over the small mound and found inside why it had not been explored by the gardeners. A wall of brick along one side had given away with dampness, almost filling in the narrow angle where the tunnel began its long climb up through the thick castle walls.

Leron wormed his way through gingerly, feet first. There was fresh air on the far side, but no light. He went along with one hand tracing the damp walls for guidance, silently counting the levels as he climbed. At the fifth turn he paused, then crept past the corner in utter silence. Here the tunnel was speckled with light, coming through the carved stone bench in the King's chamber, which concealed the tunnel's end. And not just light, there were voices also. Leron carefully put his eye to a small opening and looked in.

In the uneven light of flaring torches set in brackets on the far wall, Dastra moved across the room, impatiently sweeping her full skirts to one side with a clenched hand. "For God's sake hold your tongue," she snapped, and a whining voice from somewhere to Leron's left stammered and stopped. "Faugh! It makes me sick to see you. Be glad I visit with you at all." She whirled and nervously struck her hands together. "This emissary from Vahn will demand an audience with you, that I know. But by God, you'll hold your tongue, sir, or I'll see to it you'll wish you had. You'll never receive a guest again." The wordless voice whimpered and made what was obviously meant as a placating sound. Dastra's eyes narrowed, and she pointed at the unseen speaker. "No tricks, now! I will bring the nobleman Gizmir in, you will nod when he speaks, and I will talk for you. It is a formality, nothing more. His master Bodrum of Vahn does not care about the state of your health. Only the state of your realm. Is that understood?" Again the eager, pathetic response. "Very well, then." Dastra moved back towards the door, the torchlight gleaming in her silvery hair and sculpting her proud figure with sensuous shadows.

Then Leron's cramped view was blocked by a scuttling figure that rose from where it had been huddled on the floor, a slight figure dressed in black. Its hands were gloved in black silk, its head hooded, and its face masked. Crawling towards the queen it raised a gloved and twisted hand in supplication. Dastra stepped back towards the door. "Be easy, my lord," she said with a twist of her mouth. "I will send your majesty's attendants in to you." She twitched her skirt away from his fumbling grasp and slipped out through the door, closing it firmly behind her. The black-dressed figure rocked back on its knees, crying and clutching at its head. Leron recognized his cousin's ring flashing in the light.

As Ddiskeard struggled to rise, the door opened again and two young men came in. They lifted the shrunken king under his arms and carried him to a padded chair, with straps ready to restrain him. Ddiskeard's lips were white and bleeding, his eyes pale in the darkness of his masked face. The masking seemed stuck to his flesh in places. He was buckled in and left alone and soon his whimpers and sobs subsided. His head rolled back to one side, and he was asleep, breathing loudly through his open mouth.

Sickened, Leron made his way back through the corridor in the walls. Outside it was almost full light. He hurried around the corner and scrambled up onto the roof, where he saw no ships at all in the outer harbor. Past the fishing fleet he could see some figures on the breakwater: sailors no doubt whose boat had broken up. They would be able to walk to land, however. He put their troubles aside and hurried back across the drying tiles. Perhaps the *Damar* would come into port today.

The sun rose fully as Leron scrambled back, and the Players were already on their way to the main square. He heard their music before he could see them, looked out from the shelter of an ivy-covered chimney, timed his jump carefully and landed in their midst just as a turning in the road blocked the kingsmen's view. He pushed his way along through the group and caught up with Ginas, winking at her. At the first crossing, they met kingsmen on horseback, who commanded them all to back against the walls and clear the streets. On fat shiny horses that steamed in the crisp autumn air, the kingsmen cir-

cled and pushed, gathering all the passers by into a compact
crowd, to make room for a procession.

Leron pulled himself in close to the wall and craned his
neck to see over the heads. He could just see the approaching
riders' conical felt hats and gold earrings: soldiers of Vahn.
Twenty men preceded the emissary and twenty more followed
after, their horses decorated with ribbons and glittering trappings. The nobleman Gizmir—for the emissary must be he—
was a heavy man, as massively built as Bodrum. Leron could
not see his face clearly, but the long rippling beard was chestnut, the color of Bodrum's own. Some close relative of the
master's, no doubt. Four sumpters followed the procession,
carrying rich gifts. Leron's eyes followed the figure of Gizmir,
and he wondered if a shrewd, cruel Vahnian trader would think
the alliance worth its purchase once he was presented to the
black-shrouded King. A longing to oversee their meeting grew
strongly within him. He had thus far behaved with the utmost
irresponsibility, and thus far his skin was whole. So when the
chamberlain from the palace came to the Players that afternoon,
to hire musicians for the banquet that night, Leron unques-
tionably accepted his good fortune. He would cast for a fate
again, and hope once more for an advance.

There was still only the one ship at quayside when Leron,
carrying his harp, accompanied two other Players to the palace.
It was an ornate vessel, doubtless the ship of the Emissary
Gizmir. At the gates the chamberlain met them, leading them
not to the Great Hall but down familiar stone passageways to
a small supper-room in the north tower. Leron lightly touched
a stone-carved dog on the head, as he had a hundred times
before, and was startled into caution by the chamberlain's rep-
rimand. "Now, none of that, sir! Behave yourself, or it's down
to the scullery with you."

As he showed them into the supper-room, he explained they
would eat later, in the kitchens, and be given a bed there by
the fire. They settled themselves into a corner and began playing
softly. By the small fire Dastra was sitting at supper, opposite
the nobleman Gizmir. Apart from the servants, they were alone
together, with not even the customary empty chair to signal
the absence of the king. Dastra did not look up as they came
in: she was leaning close to her guest, smiling and gazing

intently into his face with her large and brilliant eyes. In return Gizmir smiled back from time to time, but inattentively. His chief interest seemed the heaped-up plate before him. One hand was constantly caressing the goblet from which he drank deeply between mouthfuls of food, waving it under the wine steward's nose whenever the level had dropped a little. With his other hand, he scooped up liberal portions of meat and bread, from time to time stroking the crumbs from his glossy beard with the side of his hand. There were little pouches of fat beneath his eyes, but for all that he was a handsome man, strongly built and massive as a bull. At length he sighed deeply and reluctantly put down his cup, pushing back a little from the table to ease his belly. Leron strummed the harp more softly, straining to overhear, his eyes politely downcast.

"A tolerable meal, your majesty. You do better by your table here in the east than we'd heard. Pity I bothered to bring so much food with me. Ah well, anything would taste good after that filthy voyage. Had to eat one of the horses—died in the slings." Leron stiffened with surprise, and not for the rudeness alone. Gizmir's voice was well known to him. He raised his eyes slowly, unbelievingly, while Dastra spoke in answer.

She had lowered her eyes with an old familiar trick and moved herself slightly closer to her quest. "We shall do our best to satisfy all your wants, my lord, and make your visit here both profitable and entertaining."

In return Gizmir looked her up and down, openly examining her bared arms and shoulders. Dastra flushed, but not unhappily. Gizmir drank again, deeply, then belched and leaned forward towards the queen, speaking softly in her ear. "On future shipments from Vahn might I suggest you hire some of our artisans and inlay-workers? This chamber could easily be improved. The ceiling's high enough, it could be quite elegant in a simple way—a better setting for yourself." Dastra flushed again, and her shoulders moved slightly. "A pity," he went on, "that I had not foresight enough to bring with me a few musicians for your entertainment. Then you might have heard some real singing, and fine playing too. Better suited to you than this—admittedly charming—rude entertainment."

Leron looked back to his harp, feeling the blood warm in his face. This made his own adventure tame by comparison. Odric! Odric of Treclere in masquerade as his father's emissary, calmly insulting those who would delight to have his head off, had they known whose head it was. Before he had made any conscious decision his fingers chose for him. Memories of their first meeting brought a melody from the strings that the other Players amplified with the ease of much improvisation. "Seasons pass and the seed is sown . . ."

Startled himself, Leon turned the tune aside into other variations, but Odric had not failed to recognize his own melody. He shifted his bulk slightly and looked around in seeming unconcern, and Leron could feel his heavy-lidded gaze upon him. "These are some of your famous Players, are they not? They don't get so far westward as Vahanavat. They are not unskilled, that I can see, despite the oddness of their dress. Good lad, very good!" He gestured approvingly, and Leron, furious at being singled out, bent his head farther over his harp as he played on. From the corner of his eye he could see that Odric was beaming with delight at his presence there, and also at his discomfiture.

Dastra was clearly unsuspecting. She only glanced at the Players and then back at the emissary. "So, something in our realm finds favor with you?" she asked coyly, and Odric nodded and touched her arm.

"Yes, that tune for example. Very clean, very elegant." She murmured something softly in return, and Leron saw he would have no chance of talking to Odric that night. It was the queen's clear intent to make a close companion of her guest, and if Odric could extricate himself, he would prove a diplomat indeed.

As Leron thought these words, Odric took another swallow of wine and drew back slightly. "Will the king join us tonight or wait until tomorrow? There are of course certain matters of state and business that must, ah, regrettably intrude."

Dastra stiffened a little. "He is indisposed, sir, as I told you." She smiled. "There will be time enough tomorrow for diplomacy." She leaned forward again, but Odric stayed pushed back in his chair.

"Then, madam, if you will excuse me. . . ."

Dastra met his eyes coolly and placed a delicately strong hand upon his wrist. "Tomorrow morning, my lord, is soon enough. You will have time a-plenty to order your thoughts in the morning, before you meet the king in the afternoon. But tonight I cannot be so inhospitable as to turn you out of doors."

Odric shrugged philosophically and looking past the queen

to Leron, smiled and shrugged again. "Tomorrow morning, then. We are agreed." Leron nodded imperceptible assent as the chamberlain came in through the door to usher the Players out, in response to some secret summons from the queen. Dastra as before did not look up, but Odric waved impudently with his free hand and thanked them for their service. His other hand was firmly held by Dastra.

So Leron slept under his own roof at last; and it was warmer in the kitchens than ever it had been in the king's great chamber. At dawn they were allowed to return to their carts in the city, and midway through the morning Leron slipped away into the crowd and hurried towards the quay, clutching his harp so that Odric could vouch for him should he be stopped.

The Vahnian ship was hung with colored bunting and shining with paint and gold leaf. The guard who showed him in was a youth of eighteen or so, vaguely familiar in his features, but Leron quickly forgot him as the polished wooden door with its great brass handles swung noiselessly to behind him, leaving him alone with Odric.

Odric moved around the table and quite simply held out his arms. Leron fell into them and almost had the breath squeezed from his body. It was a relief when Odric took him by the shoulders and pushed him back to look at him, shaking his head in disbelief. "You crazy young fool! What are you doing in Tredana? Is your neck nothing that you should so risk it?" At this Leron threw back his head in laughter, and Odric joined him. "I know! You were about to say the same to me." He drew Leron down onto a bench with a hand on his shoulder. "This is a happy meeting, friend. And a fortunate one if we escape with our skins."

"If I keep my head I'll not quibble about skins. But what of yourself? After last night I'll wager that you've lost at least your virtue."

"Now there you would be wrong. There is something about that lady chills the blood. She found the nobleman Gizmir a disappointment, I fear, and a nasty drunk moreover. Now, my next step will be to work some deadly insult in amongst my excuses."

"I collect your mission is not to secure favor with Tredana?"

Odric laughed again. "No, I shall insult them within an inch

of my life. It seemed the easiest way to break this foul alliance
between Vahn and Tredana; one put into my hand by a kind
fate when the true Gizmir's vessel fell prey to ours. The break
should be bloodless and complete."

"Excepting your blood, of course."

"Better that than sit and wait in Treclere. Perhaps you have
noticed, dear friend, that the life of a prince is in no way more
interesting than that of a minstrel, unless he make it so."

Leron smiled ruefully. "I cannot argue that just now, at least
not with this harp on my back. But do you think a few insults
will do the trick?"

"A few? No. But I have forged in Bodrum's name a list of
demands no state could ever stomach. I expect to be successful.
Now tell me, what of yourself?"

Odric listened attentively to Leron's story, interrupting from
time to time. "On one thing I can be of help, in a way. I have
a list from the Master of the Harbor. The ship of Captain Delgar
is long overdue from Sundrat. No one has reported seeing it
since leaving there twelve days ago."

Leron paled a little. "The storm, do you think?"

Odric squeezed his shoulder reassuringly. "No, no. I rode
that blow quite comfortably in this little boat, and the *Damar*
is a great and famous ship. Perhaps there has been some fortunate intervention. From what I have heard of Delgar, anything
that hints at his delaying is a hopeful sign. He is usually as
prompt as he is pitiless. Now, if he arrives, I can confound his
plans a little."

"I hardly dare to hope."

"You must. There is no more we can do for now. But I
have a great respect for your young cousin's abilities."

"So very young no longer, Odric. Old enough to fear at
Delgar's hands. And from what I hear, she is more lovely than
Simirimia."

Odric looked grave, then shrugged fatalistically. "Perhaps
she inherited more than appearance: perhaps some power also."
He got to his feet and looked out of the window, up towards
Castle Hill. "What may I expect this afternoon in audience?"

As Leron tried to describe the scene he had overheard between the king and queen, Odric's shoulders twitched in distaste. "There is a sickness in the palace worse than whatever
foul rot infects the king. There is a cruelty there would frighten

me, were I easily made afraid. Last night was more difficult than you might think. I have never had so little taste for sport. I do not think the next man in her power will escape so easily."

"Do you think you will face trouble tonight?"

"Possibly. Not the same trouble, that's for certain. She has no fondness for the nobleman Gizmir now. But she might decide to have me trussed and handed over for the celebrations on the Sacred Hill." He was obviously joking, but saw the bewilderment on Leron's face and paused to explain. "Of course, I had forgotten that you are not aware of the practice in Vahn, now most unhappily brought to Tredana. Vazdz, you see, is best worshiped in blood and fire, and the more dearly bought that blood, the better. I have already heard rumors that this year's festivities will go beyond a few sheep and a white horse or two. But I doubt she'll slit my throat, at least not in public. Easier to break the alliance and send me home in my shirt or some such gesture."

Leron was uneasy, however. "I have to return to the Players this afternoon, but tonight I am going to come again to the palace. It's safe enough over the roofs. Then if you are in any trouble, I may have warning of it. In any case, I'll meet you here tomorrow, if you will."

"It is unnecessary. You saw Kerys outside, did you not? He insisted on accompanying me here. I can send him to the Players on some pretext to fetch you. Do not risk yourself for me."

"I enjoy the journey along the heights looking down, never fear." Leron sighed. "It gives a momentary illusion of power."

The first of the fall festivities took place on Sacred Hill that afternoon. Leron had finally mastered all sixteen stanzas of the latest Clerowan ballad, but there were too few in the crowd to make it worthwhile singing. Without a proper audience, the Players lost heart in their performance. They concluded the little drama and subsided into acrobatics, fortune telling, casual songs and harmless games of guess-the-shell. Two or three even strolled out towards Sacred Hill to watch the rituals, but Leron did not accompany them. Ginas had explained to him more fully about the Great Sacrifices, and he did not think it would amuse him to watch white roosters being beheaded, or the disemboweling of a steer or horse. The eagerness of the crowds he found disquieting.

He sat on the step of Ginas's cart, his harp held loosely on his knees, and plucked the strings up and down the scale until Ginas asked him sharply to stop. He looked up surprised into her sombre eyes.

"You return to the palace tonight?"

"That is my plan."

"Better, lord, if you do not go."

"Odric is as a brother to me."

"It is not Odric concerns me. Come within."

She held aside the heavy velvet curtain for Leron to pass, then pulled the folding wooden doors together and dropped their pin in place. "Sit."

Leron obeyed, and Ginas went to stand next to her table, turning the lamp up slightly so the room smelled of oil. She placed her hands on the table and dropped her head. "Lord, you never should have come. Rather, I should not have sent for you. The fault is mine, and other faults—You have been brought into known danger here, and my Liniris and your cousin into unknown danger elsewhere. I have interfered where I should have been content to observe."

"You were told—"

"Nothing! I learned, I studied, I read, but the decision to act was mine. I thought to influence fate favorably."

"You brought Sibby here."

Ginas gestured with despair and sat down. "Yes, and to what purpose? And who is to say she might not have come otherwise? Perhaps her destiny like her lineage is more than mortal."

"Ginas, speak with me frankly. Why do you despair now? Have you read something in the future I should know?"

"I despair because I can see nothing. The cards do not work for me. The great Book of Ornat is silent under my hands."

Leron looked from her hollow eyes to the glassy ring on her hand. "Can you see nothing in that?"

She turned the ring on her finger, angling it into the light, and nodded. "Too much, too many pictures, and too few answers. There are fires on sea and land, danger in the hills and woods and under the water. I have seen you both king and in chains, and blood runs everywhere."

"So long as I am not yet king, why let chains concern us?"

Ginas shook her head. "I did not mean to tell you without proof. I dreamed of Rym Treglad this morning, and a voice spoke, saying, 'The rains have come and the old king is no more.'"

Leron carefully placed the harp on the floor and pressed his hands against his knees. "A dream?"

"A dream, but I swear"—and her fingers touched her throat—"that the voice spoke truly."

"Then he can never come home." Leron jumped to his feet and turned his face away, tight with tearless grief. "If I have lost my father as well as Sibby, be assured I will not abandon Odric. If there is danger I had best go now. I will rejoin you when I can."

Leron unbuckled his dagger and slipped it into his boot, took down his cloak and left. He managed to enter the orchard unseen without resorting to the roofs. A little way along into the tunnel's private depths he finally fell forward on his knees and cried for the death of his father.

There was dirt on his face when he picked himself up off the floor. He stood for a moment with his hot forehead against the cold damp wall, then wiped his face with his sleeve, shook his head and began the slow climb upwards. The curtains must have been drawn in the king's chamber for there was no light coming through the secret panel, and it was hard to see even as far as the bed. His father's bed. Leron pushed the panels silently apart and pulled himself into the room; behind him they closed as silently.

The room was not empty. The masked and withered little king lay in a heap of black on the curtainless, bare bed, the backs of his gloved hands pressed against his silk-covered face as though to ward off blows. Eight years ago Mathon had lain there suffering from the effects of Ddiskeard's plots and poisons; but this was worse. He listened to the light, rapid breathing, wondering if Dastra would bother to wake him for the audience or carry out her revenge on Gizmir herself. He considered setting out in search of Odric, but the loud click of a key-turned lock surprised him. It was too far to the bench and secret panel: no hangings shrouded the bed. He sprang at the shallow storage closet let into the panelling by the head of the bed and prayed that it was not full. Apparently no linen had been wasted on the king for some time. It was empty and thick with dust. As he carefully drew the door shut, he could hear the great door to the passageway pushed open. The sound of Dastra's voice came vaguely to him; he opened the door a

cautious inch and he could hear more clearly. There was a
deeper voice answering hers, not Odric's.

"And here is our sovereign lord, a lovely portrait of grace
and power, think you not? Do you still fear to do it?" Her voice
rose shrilly on the last words, then subsided into a pleased and
throaty murmur. "Ah, my sweet, you are my king already.
And will be more—" She laughed again, and Leron could not
help the risk of another inch of space, to which he put his eye.

Dastra stood by the bed looking down, her hair undone in
a silver froth down her back. She wore a very thin silk un-
derdress and hung on the muscular arm of the tall young man
standing beside her. Bare armed and legged, with a tunic open
to the low-belted waist he stood with legs apart and his free
hand on his hip, arrogant, tanned and wide-shouldered. The
stranger of the woods, the messenger to the footsmen, leather-
clad no longer.

Dastra released his arm and bent over her husband so that
her hair fell across his face. Ddiskeard twitched and muttered
something, then awoke and seeing her reached up eagerly. She
pushed him back contemptuously, but he struggled up again
and took her wrist in both his hands, trying to kiss it. She
gasped, and her companion pulled her free, then dealt Ddiskeard a heavy backhand blow. The king cried out thinly, like
a bird, and fell back on his pillows weeping. But the young
man did not let him go. He pinned him down with a hand on
his narrow shoulder and hit him several times more across the
face. Under the masking the flesh must have been very tender,
for the king choked and cried and clawed helplessly with his
hands until he fell back in a faint. Leron's knuckles whitened
on the door jamb.

Dastra laughed and clapped her hands. "Oh, Michael! You
are splendid. You will do it, then?" She pressed against his
arm once more. "For me?"

Michael picked her up and carried her across to the bench
by the window, kissing her face and throat while she sighed
ecstatically. "For both of us," he said and set her down.

Now they were more clearly in Leron's line of vision, sitting
over his only means of escape. Dastra had pulled a little away
from Michael and was preening, arranging her hair around her
shoulders and swaying her slender body back and forth. "Tonight at midnight, then, we will be free. I will ride the white
mare up the Sacred Hill and there will be flowers in my hair.

You can help me dress if you like. They will burn my lord's murderer before my eyes, and the mare's blood will mix with the ashes to cleanse the altar." She put back her head laughing again, and Michael pulled her to him and kissed her mouth.

"I guess it's a good thing I came along to that audience yesterday," he said, and she added, "It is a better thing that you returned today."

Michael ran his hands up and down her back and looked over her shoulder at the bed. "Who will they find with him?"

She looked at him coyly. "The murderer? He's here already, waiting for an audience. A foreigner. The guards will show him in and turn the key . . . and I will find him here with his victim." She put her head to one side, considering. "Should I faint?"

"Just call for help. I'll come with the guards." She made some joke, and they laughed, pressed closely together, then Dastra pushed him away.

"We really should hurry. Can I watch? I've never seen anything like it before."

"Nothing to see," said Michael with a shrug. He got up, walked over to the bed, and then more quickly and more coolly than Leron could have believed possible, pulled the helpless figure up against his chest, put an arm around his head and a knee to his back and snapped his neck. "Just like a chicken," he said and grinned at Dastra.

She looked at him with enormous eyes, her color high, shivering. "It's done?" she cried, and he nodded, amused at her excitement. She pushed at Ddiskeard with her hand, and the body rolled a little on the bed; she laughed, kissed Michael in passionate gratitude and took his hand. "I must dress. Come to my room with me. We will have the emissary from Vahn sent up, and I must arrive not long after." She pulled Michael out after her, and they locked the door behind them.

Leron wiped the sweat from his face. Revenge had never been less appetizing. He considered dashing to the tunnel, to wait there for Odric's entrance, but the risk seemed too great. So he waited the next long minutes out, his eyes avoiding the barely rumpled bed. Soon he could hear the steps without, then the door clicked open and Odric entered, blinking a little in the curtained dimness. The steward behind him spoke a few words and nodded respectfully, then closed the door and left him there alone. This time the lock turned more softly than before, and Leron doubted that Odric had heard it. Odric approached the bed then stepped back in alarm as the closet door swung open and Leron stepped out, a finger to his lips for silence.

Leron took him by the shoulder. "No time to explain. They have killed Ddiskeard and intend to find you with him, to destroy you. Here." He jerked him over towards the window and pressed the spring. He pushed Odric towards the opening. "Go in first. I am following." Odric swung himself through the narrow passage with astonishing lightness, stumbled on the unseen steps and righted himself. Before Odric was all the way down into the tunnel himself Leron heard the key turning in the door once more. He looked around desperately. The outer door was already beginning to open. He shoved Odric all the way through and pushed the spring to close the panels after him, then sprang across the room to hide behind the opening door.

It stopped inches short of crushing him against the wall, and there was silence from the other side of the heavy wooden panels. Leron could imagine Dastra standing there, looking for her victim. She moved a few steps farther into the room, one hand slightly raised in apprehension. As soon as she was clear of the door Leron shoved it shut with his shoulder and leapt on her as she turned. He grabbed her by the throat and she clawed at his face, but he forced her back against the foot of the bed, looking for something with which to tie and gag her. There was nothing but a dawning look of recognition in her eyes. He reached into his boot for his dagger, to hit her with its hilt and make an escape, but as he drew it something cracked his hand open and the weapon went flying across the room. He tried to turn, his right hand hanging useless and another great crack seemed to explode behind his eyes. He sank to his knees and then fell forward as the chain in Michael's hand fell a third time, across the back of his neck.

SONG
by Huffing Dick (banned in Tredana)

Tell me, where's that goodly king
who wore so well the golden crown

and made the birds of fortune sing
ennobling the Tredanan throne
with a peculiar babioun
all dressed in black, a diamond ring
and crown to call his very own?
Where is the king who did this thing?

Tell me, where's this babioun
who thought prosperity to bring
looked in the glass and saw a man
where others can see no such thing?
He's gone from carefree capering
with retinue about the town
to dancing on a shaky string
nor string nor steps to call his own.

But king or prince or babioun
slave or free or wandering
we dance but never call the tune
and plan nor start nor finishing.
So brother footsmen, wake and sing
shake your metals, knowing soon
Ddiskeard will be shivering
black as ever was his gown. ————

Princes everyone are doomed to death.
Of course, that's true of any who draws breath.
Angry or annoyed? Curse, cry, or crawl
In any case the wind will take us all.

Chapter Four

When Sibyl and Liniris reached the beach, they were blue-lipped and shivering. Their heavy, dripping cloaks were a slight protection against the wind but drenchingly cold, and they had no feeling in their feet at all. Sibyl rubbed the gritty salt from her eyes and mouth and put out an arm to support Liniris, who could hardly walk. There were a few men farther down the beach, seeing to their boats and readying their gear for the day's fishing. One raised his hand in greeting and came hurrying over, a dark-faced man of middle age with close-curled, grey-streaked hair. His voice was rich and gravelly.

"You lost your boat on the seawall, did you not?" Sibyl nodded, nervously. They were in no condition to make a break for freedom. "Bad fortune, that. You'll not be from around here?"

"No, up the coast."

"Ah, one of the villages, of course. Poor lads. Will your master beat you for breaking up his vessel?"

Sibyl looked at him dumbly, then felt a sudden surge of relief. Liniris's long hair was hidden under her hood; Sibyl's cloak was thrown back but her curls were only inches long, and both were dressed as men. In answer to his question she dropped her eyes and nodded, squeezing Liniris's arm for silence.

"These autumn winds are treacherous things. He had no business sending out two youngsters like yourselves, in tricky weather. Next time I warrant you'll remember where the mouth of the harbor lies. Many of us learn the hard way. Here, come along with me, you'll catch your deaths if you stand here in the wind. We have some breakfast cooking. Something warm."

The fishermen, busy with their own concerns, did not press the strangers to talk. Their host had them sit near the fire to dry out and generously served them sausage and fried bread and hot spiced ale. Only when they had finished eating did he question them again. "And how far's the walk you'll be having now to home?" Sibyl looked at him blankly, her mind racing. She had no idea where the fishing villages might be.

Besides her Liniris spoke for the first time. "We come from Crommerton. Ten miles or so." Sibyl thanked Liniris in her head, and buried her face in her mug.

"Ah, Crommerton. This'll not be the first bit of bad luck yon village's had. You lost two men some months ago, if I remember."

"Ay," said Liniris, her voice suddenly much huskier and her accent slurred a little. "Father and son together, washed up on the beach like so much driftwood." She shook her head as though at the memory, and Sibyl tardily recalled that Liniris was by trade an actress. The Players must have passed through Crommerton on their way to Sundrat.

"Happen then he'll not beat you, but be glad to see you alive."

Liniris shrugged doubtfully and held her cold hands to the fire. They were very small and fine-boned and she hastily tucked them under the folds of her cloak once more. Someone hallooed to their host, and he scrambled hastily to his feet. "That's us loaded then and ready to go. Take care now, lads. Just kick the sand over the embers when you leave. And if ever you need a hand again, ask any man here for Nicca, that's myself. Good luck." He turned their thanks aside and ran down to his boat, being held on shore by two of his fellow fishers.

When the boats were all safely out through the surf, Liniris began to giggle. Sibyl joined her, and they laughed for what seemed minutes. Sibyl sobered first. She looked at Liniris. "Where do we go from here?"

"My people are probably in Sundrat still, or on their way to Rym Treglad. It will take us nearly two weeks walking just to reach Sundrat, and by then they will be that much the farther north."

"How long on horseback?"

"Seven, eight days." Liniris rearranged her tangled hair beneath her hood. "But we have no horses."

Sibyl stood up and began brushing the sand off her fire-warmed clothing. "Liniris, here in Tredana we're in danger, right? We have to sneak around like criminals. Okay, let's be criminals, then. Or, to be more exact, horse thieves."

Liniris looked up at her. "But what if we're caught?"

"We wouldn't be any worse off than now. I know where the king's household has its stables. At least, where it used to. My horse was kept there once. I think we should aim at the top."

Liniris looked at her blankly. "The top?"

"The better our horses, the quicker our journey and the sooner we all arrive safe in Rym Treglad. Look, they left some sausages." Liniris's cloak had a deep patch pocket inside, which Sibyl stuffed with leftovers. Then they covered the fire as Nicca had asked. Sibyl squinted out to sea, at the now tiny boats. "I hope," she said, "that someday we can repay him."

It was Sibyl's idea to go boldly ahead to their objective and try for a job at the stables. Liniris was doubtful, but Sibyl became more positive as she considered the idea. "I can't believe things are so very different in this world. At home there's never enough people to groom and clean out stalls and feed. If we act like runaways who will do anything to be near horses, I bet they'll take us on, at least for a few days. It will give the regular grooms time to slack off. You do know something about horses, don't you? You must." Liniris nodded. "Of course. At least, I've never done it myself—I only hope they're not too big."

At any other time Sibyl's plan might not have worked, but the head groom was ill and the stableboys and undergrooms already inattentive to their charges' needs. When the two arrived at the stables, there was an argument in progress, two grooms complaining that they had to miss the celebrations on Sacred Hill. The much harassed second groom welcomed the strangers with tearful relief. He sent the restive ones away and immediately set about showing the newcomers their duties. They could sleep in the straw storage area, wash under the pump, and eat in the servants' kitchen three doors away. Here was the chopped straw, here the oats, the barley; the stalky hay for this horse and the fine green dust-free hay for that one; the hoof oil, the body rub, the bandages for leg and tail, the brushes, picks, combs, shears, scrapers, and thin silk rubdown cloths. Sibyl delighted in it all, but Liniris was clearly staggered by the amount of work involved. She paled a little when she saw the mountain of manure produced by thirty horses in only a week, and hefted one of the square bottomed shovels doubtfully. Their first job, of course, was mucking out.

Sibyl waited until the second groom was out of earshot, then took Liniris into the room where grooming implements were kept. "Put back your hood," she said. "You're about to lose your hair." Liniris did not protest, for she recognized the sense in Sibyl's decision, but tears welled out from between her fingers as she crouched on the rough brick floor, and blue-black glossy waves of hair fell around her. Sibyl snipped a little more around the ears, then ruffled the pitiful remainder with her fingers. "That'll do," she said, "but I wish there were some way we could grow beards." Liniris tried to laugh but it was difficult. Sibyl picked up the longest strands and wound them into a tail. "Put it in your pocket. It will be something to show your children—if we survive to have any." Liniris wiped her eyes and nodded, then they tackled the first of the stalls working together.

By nightfall Liniris and Sibyl both had blistered hands. As they cleaned each stall, Sibyl had Liniris trot the horse in question around the yard, ostensibly to check for lameness or sore feet, but actually to choose the best-moving horses. Many were clearly unsuitable, but there were eight or so Sibyl thought had possibility. Unfortunately none were in hard condition, and she feared that they'd have trouble lasting the course. As they settled down that night into the sweet yellow straw, Liniris suggested leaving the city and stealing horses from pasture. Sibyl shook her head. "In the first place, there'd probably be no harness, and I don't know about you, but I don't like the idea of riding bareback for a couple of weeks." Liniris looked aghast at the thought. "And in the second place, this way we know something about the horses we steal. It gives us a better chance of getting away. Do you want to go climb on the back of some nice-looking animal and find out no one's ever ridden him before?" Hastily Liniris agreed that Sibyl's first plan had been best.

They curled up together for warmth, the two cloaks over

them, and Sibyl was glad not to be alone the first night away
from the ship.

Morning came very early. The horses began to call for breakfast
shortly after dawn, and Sibyl and Liniris stumbled around carrying water and loads of hay at the direction of other stable-
hands. Liniris almost cried when she saw the thirty immaculate
stalls all soiled again. "How could they do it?" she asked in
anguish, and Sibyl laughed. Their meticulous cleaning pleased
the head groom when he paid a short visit to the stables, and
he instructed the second groom to show them how to exercise
certain of the horses. This included four of Sibyl's private
choices, she saw with satisfaction. But by afternoon she felt
less pleased. There was no easy way that she could see to take
any of the horses outside the complex. It might be weeks before
they were trusted any farther than the riding ring. She was
about to confess as much to Liniris when a wonderful chance
came their way.

There were two white horses in the stable, a broodmare of
about twelve and an elderly stallion, morosely aloof in a special
strong box at one end of the yard. The mare was muscular and
well built, not very tall, with a round white belly and enormous
dark eyes. She was handed to them that afternoon with instructions that she be washed spotless; they tied her between the
training pillars and spent several hours soaping and scrubbing.

Sibyl began to feel quite fond of her as the afternoon wore
on. She had a pleasant trick of resting her head against her
groom's shoulder and blowing out gently against the human's
neck. She responded to petting by caressing in her own turn
with eager thrusts of her heavy head and fell into a reverie with
eyelids closed as they combed and untangled her silky long
mane and tail. Clearly she had once been a darker grey, for
there were small dark spots on her nose and around the base
of her tail, her skin was dark and her hoofs black. Sibyl oiled
the hoofs after cleaning them and carefully clipped a little
excess fur from around the fetlocks.

She looked up to see the second groom smiling. He held a
lump of white chalk in his hand. "When she's dry, see you
cover those speckles with this. There's not to be a spot on her,
orders from the queen herself. She's going to use her, tonight
y'see, at the ceremonies. Poor old girl." He placed his hand

on the mare's forehead as he spoke—for a moment Sibyl had thought he meant the queen.

Liniris looked up from braiding the luxuriant tail, horrified. "She's going to be used for the offering?"

"Not in the common lot, no, no. The Queen will ride her up the hill, y'see, and then they use her blood to make the paste. Cleanse the land, y'see."

Sibyl was sure that he did not mean the queen this time, but she wished he did. She placed one hand protectively on the little mare's neck. "She's to be killed then? Tonight?"

The groom nodded and handed over the chalk. "Now if it had been that one, I could see it." He jerked with his thumb at the stallion's box. "Like to see her ladyship on that one. He'd need killing then, oh yes. But it has to be a mare, y'see. Pity too, with her gone four months in foal."

Sibyl thought quickly. "Should we help the queen tonight, I mean, accompany her? How well does she ride?"

The groom laughed. "It's not for the likes of us, tonight. All the high uppity-ups tonight. Pledge allegiance to the throne, tonight, they do. The queen'll do all right on this old girl. Tell you what though, with the noise in the streets and all, perhaps you should go along as far as the hill. Take another horse with you, and you can ride back double." Sibyl looked at Liniris with satisfaction.

As they bandaged and blanketed the mare so she would stay clean, Liniris put her arms around the shining white neck and hugged her. "Sibyl, if I have to ride a horse for weeks it is going to be this one. I have made up my mind."

Sibyl tucked under the last braid on her mane and sewed it tight. "Yes," she said, "I really think it should be. Let's put her in and clean up that old fellow."

Liniris followed her gaze to the stallion box. "Him? We can't take him! He's mean, and besides he's too old."

Sibyl shook her head. "He still has plenty of spirit. Somehow I feel it may be useful to have two white horses there in the dark tonight."

When they led the old horse out, Sibyl almost changed her mind again. He was thin, his withers sharp and bladed, his bones a little too angularly marked, his neck stuck out before at an uncompromising angle. But his eyes were large and lustrous, his ears proudly pricked, and he lifted and set down his feet with an easy grace, despite the swelling in his joints from too long standing in a stall. As he snuffed in the smell of other horses, his head lifted a little, and by the time they had him cross-tied at the pillars, his heavy neck was arched up beautifully, his large square nostrils red with excitement.

He submitted to their grooming with a lordly indifference, holding each hoof up in turn to be picked without their asking for it. The yellow stains and crusted dirt washed away and his hair began to sparkle in the sun. He had far finer blood in him than the mare, but had been far worse neglected. There were ridges from past lameness deforming his front feet and the marks of accidents or blows crisscrossing his chest and flanks. One of the stableboys came out to watch as they finished with their grooming. "Now he's nice and clean, are you going to ride him?"

Sibyl looked up from scrubbing his tucked-up belly. "I would if I had permission."

The stableboy laughed and poked his companion. The other said, "Pay no attention to him. That horse is not for riding. He was a state gift to the king eight years ago at the coronation. The finest from the desert. They used him for stud awhile, before the king's illness. The queen is not interested in horse breeding, so now he stands idle."

Sibyl looked at the horse carefully, trying to imagine him with fat and muscle covering his bones, and perhaps a different color. "Was he darker then?"

"Handsome indeed, the darkest grey. Only his mane and tail had turned, and a little about the eyes. It is a pity how they fade."

"A gift from the desert—from Dzildzil?"

"Yes, the chief horse captured from the old Karif's stud, when they killed him. Dzildzil meant to ride him, so I hear, in a procession through the desert capital. When he recovered a little from that, he gave him to our king. Be advised by me and stay content with washing him."

Sibyl waited until they had wandered off, then turned to Liniris triumphantly. "This is his horse, Ajjibawr's! I had one of his colts once. Well, that settles it. You shall have your mare, and I shall have this one."

Liniris shook her head. "But you can't ride him."

"They can't ride him. But I know something they don't. Mubassa, Ajjibawr's horsemaster, taught me to ride my colt. All the horses he trained had a special signal with the knee, to make them rear. Let's get a saddle and see if I am right."

The old horse stood patiently while Sibyl adjusted the thick sheepskin to protect his bony back. Most of the saddles were very cumbersome. She chose the lightest one and he stiffened a little as she dropped it into place and fastened the girths. "I know, old boy, it's been a long time." She sorted out the bridle and presented it for his inspection: he sniffed, then put his head down calmly, opening nicely for the bit and keeping his head comfortably low while she fastened the straps. Then he champed the bit in an exploratory way before standing still again. He seemed ominously relaxed. Liniris nervously held the bridle as Sibyl prepared to swing up.

Sibyl's stomach thumped as she put her toe in the stirrup, then pulled herself on as lightly as possible, careful not to touch except as necessary. She sat down nervously erect, legs loose and hands quiet, and the old horse stood as quietly. "If I remember correctly," she said to Liniris, "a certain pressure with the left knee signaled the horse to rear, and then it would buck if the legs were tightened or the heels used. That way, Ajjibawr felt his horses were safe from stealing. He said whoever could figure it out deserved his prize." Sibyl lightly flexed her calf muscles against the horse's sides. That merest whisper of movement was enough to set him into a steady trot, head flexed and tail lifted.

At first he creaked a little as they circled the stableyard, then he began to warm with the work and his breathing quieted. He stopped when Sibyl sat back, the reins almost untouched. She sat there happily patting his neck, then stiffened as the stableboys reappeared. She thought that she had hardly moved, but the change was enough to make the old horse sidestep and fret. She quickly slipped her left knee forward and gently pressed his shoulder. He reared high in eager obedience, whinnying enthusiastically, and she threw herself forward on his neck and swung to the ground, trying to make it look like a fall. "You crazy fool," she shouted, secretly caressing his neck with her hand. "Why did you do that?" The stableboys, who had been staring in stupefaction, laughed and moved on. "He'll do," she said to Liniris, as she slowly removed the saddle, caressing the horse and making much of him. "And my riding will have to improve or I'll break my neck."

They completed their chores in good time, shamelessly secreting in the straw those items that would prove useful on the trip north. Although it was awkwardly heavy, Sibyl set aside a clay pot of oil to rub on the horses once they were on their way. With the oil and a good roll in the dirt the horses would be white no longer. For weapons they chose two heavy hoof rasps, sharply hooked at one end. Then they hurried off to eat an early supper.

On the walk back to the stableyard, Sibyl tried a shortcut across one of the back alleys. The outbuildings surrounding the palace made a maze of streets and courtyards and dead ends. The path they followed took a subtle turn, not leading to the stable but twisting off between high walls. Liniris wanted to retrace their steps but Sibyl hurried stubbornly on, sure that it would come out where she thought. Suddenly the road widened out onto a major avenue, bordered by tall trees. Sibyl looked around with amazement. "I've been here before. We're on the other side of the castle. There's an orchard here somewhere, that's where Leron. . . . Liniris, go on back to the stable. You were right, we have to go back the way we came. I'll catch up with you. I just want to check on something. Please!"

"Sibyl, we have to prepare for tonight."

"I know, I know. I'll be right along, I promise." She darted out into the deserted street and ran along in the shadow of the buildings, then disappeared into a dark gateway, while Liniris turned back with a sinking heart.

In the orchard, Sibyl paused. She was not sure where the opening was. It might take longer to find it and see if it were still open than she should risk. There was a movement among the trees; she pressed herself back into the shadows and stood still. Then a slight sound behind her and powerful hands on her throat. She threw her weight backwards and stamped on her attacker's feet; but as she twisted and struggled, the other let go so suddenly she almost fell. "You have escaped! By all that's wonderful! But how? I saw you beaten and bound!"

Now it was her turn for surprise. She put her hands to her bruised throat and tried to speak. The other put his arm around her and drew her back in among the shadows. "My friend, my friend, forgive me! But I was so sure you were truly caught I never suspected—I took you for a kingsman." His voice was familiar.

Castledown

Sibyl choked and managed a throaty whisper. "Odric?"

"Gizmir no longer, that's for certain. What shall we do now?"

"Odric, don't you know me?"

"Prince, what are you saying?" His hand swept her smooth cheek, and Odric suddenly stepped back, taking her shoulder in a hard grip. "You are not Leron. Who are you? How do you know me?"

"Odric, let me go." The pain had brought tears to her eyes and she was shaking. "It's me, Sibby. What are you doing here? Aren't you glad to see me? Where's Leron?"

THE GLORIOUS HISTORY OF THE BENEVOLENT REIGN OF DDIS-KEARD, KING OF TREDANA, GOVERNOR OF VILLAVAC, LORD OF THE EASTERN SEAS AND PROTECTOR OF THE TRUE FAITH... an extract

Now it happened in those days before Ddiskeard generously assumed the heavy duties of protector and guide to his people that the city of Tredana knew not the worship of Vazdz, mindlessly allowing the seasons to pass and the years to turn without making any of the propitiations and sacrifices necessary to the continued fertility of the land and to the benefits of rain and harvest, thereby causing the chance of grievous harm and hungry failure, were it not that Vazdz in his mercy stayed His hand and allowed the grain to ripen, doubtless seeing in His all-wisdom that the day would come (as we have lived to see it) when autumn would bring to Tredana a full and proper measure of ritual, the high and holy days of the Great Sacrifice, performed on Sacred Hill with a full measure of grave and pious panoply.

There is not a man in Tredana today has not lived to see the truth of Vazdz's great teaching, which is that there is no gift better pleases the earth and ensures its harvest than the blood of a pure and innocent beast, mixed with that from an unbeliever's heart.

Chapter Five

When Leron painfully opened his eyes, the first thing he saw
was Dastra's face. He closed his eyes and opened them again,
but it did not go away. She was there, smiling a little; and the
leaden feeling in his arms and legs was as much the weight of
the chains and manacles as it was the after-effects of the blow.

"My prince has returned to my side. Impetuously. So murderous in his ardor. I could be quite content, if only I knew
just how this trick was worked. Where is Gizmir?"

"A thousand miles away," said Leron truthfully. There was
an impatient movement to his left, but he did not dare move
his head for fear of blacking out again.

Dastra made a quieting movement with her hand. She sat
down opposite Leron in a rustle of lace and put her hand on
his aching knee. "There is little advantage in lying," she said.
"You burn tonight, whatever you say. But I can speak with the
priest. He will grant a quick end before the flames are high,
if you speak now."

Leron looked at her coldly. "I have nothing to say except
that I would go through any peril on earth to return you to the
island prison whence I so foolishly rescued you. But I will give
you a little information more—the nobleman Gizmir was never
here. It is all a matter of disguise, and you were fooled by the
masking."

"It is impossible! He had a neck like a bull and a great
beard! Besides, there was no time."

Michael came wavering out from the blind field on Leron's

123

left and placed his hand on Dastra's shoulder. "It makes no difference. Look, from what you've told me he makes a better murderer than that other guy. When this is all over we can seal up the room and forget about its secrets."

"Perhaps we should explain to him that the king is dead."

Leron looked up wryly. "Yes, I know. Just like a chicken." He was sure his wrist was broken. It only surprised him that his neck was not. He tried to move his head a little more, broke out in a sweat, and stopped. Dastra was looking at Michael in dismay.

Michael shrugged. "Won't be telling anybody anything after tonight." He leaned forward and took Leron's chin in one hand, snapping his head up. "Why don't you look us in the eye, huh?" Leron's chain-weighted hands raised a little from off his knees but he bit the exclamation back.

Dastra watched them with satisfaction in her eyes. "There will be a great crowd there tonight. Nobles and landowners and people of the court, bidden by oath to come and swear fealty to the crown and to Vazdz. What better time for all to see with their own eyes the perfidy of the false prince, slinking into the palace for a murderous revenge? Why, had it not been for my guard, my loyal guard, that dagger would have been in my breast!" Leron closed his eyes wearily, then snapped them open as Michael jogged his chin again.

"You are very courageous tonight," said Leron softly. He looked insultingly at Dastra. "But you have proved that already." This time it was Dastra who hit him, and she must have slapped him several times for he promptly fainted and did not recover consciousness until much later in the evening.

The second time he revived it was to find his head being soaked in icy water and cold cloths applied to his neck. Before he could take advantage of the chains' removal from his wrists and ankles they were snapped back in place, and he realized he was newly dressed in a white tunic and black hose. The silent servants shaved him and trimmed his hair roughly, handling him with surprising gentleness. The one who held the razor finished by sprinkling on lilac water, and Leron almost laughed. He did not think the delicate scent would last long in the smoke of the sacrificial pyre.

Next Leron was brusquely bundled to his feet and half carried out into the corridor. The chains were so massive, with such short play between the legs, he would have had a hard time walking even with a clear head. Below in the courtyard an ox sledge waited, decked with wreaths of pine and sheaves of wheat, oats, barley. The oxen were snowy white and glimmered in the torchlight. Their long horns had been painted red and garlands looped their gentle stolid faces. Leron was bundled up onto the platform and a kingsman clipped his wrists to the short post behind him. There was a horse guard all about, fretting and stamping at the slow pace of the oxen. They jerked their imperceptible way across the cobbles out into the streets, brightly torchlit. The crowds were thinner than Leron would have expected. It was clear that they had been told who he was. He looked down into their faces openly, it being too late for fear or even distress, but saw bewilderment and pity more than hate. There were some cruel words said, some missiles thrown, but nothing that caught the temper of the crowd. One small stone thudded against his shoulder, and he saw the thrower's arms suddenly pinned behind him by a dark and tattered form. There were many footsmen out tonight, and not just for the picking of pockets. Wherever an angry taunt was heard, it silenced quickly; and Leron could see the dark rags of the footsmen threaded through the multi-colored crowd. It was a slight favor, but he was grateful for it.

An hour at least they crawled through the winding streets, three times more slowly than a man would walk. At last they passed the gate and began the approach to Sacred Hill, which in Leron's father's time had been a pleasant garden with roses and olive trees. Here, outside the city, there were armed men in evidence everywhere, but not kingsmen. They were the household groups of retainers and bodyguards, the ordinary retinue of traveling noblemen and landowners, who had journeyed to pledge fealty that night. Most of these men-at-arms did not even look up as the sledge rumbled past, absorbed in gaming and gossip.

It was full dark of the moon. Whatever little sliver of light had been in the sky earlier was gone. Now there was only a clear black sweep of distance overhead, with tiny points of light marking the long way down into its recesses. There was a light, cool breeze and the half-stripped trees rustled. Leron looked up giddily and felt that he was falling into the sky. Then a wisp of torch smoke swept across the path of the lum-

bering sledge and he shook off his torpor. For the first time
he tested his manacles, his arms knotted with strain under his
loose-sleeved shirt, but it was useless.

Implacably the oxen set down one slow foot after the other,
too slow to count their rhythm, but too certain for any hope of
stopping. Up, up, up, around the turn, and finally a true halt
imperceptible at first. They were on the flattened summit of
the hill, above a dark anticipatory crowd, and the stake of green
pine bundled round with wood stood close at hand. A low
marble slab stood nearer, at the edge of the hill, dark-blotched.
The oxen were uncoupled and led away into the dark; Leron
stood up as straight as possible in his bonds and looked im-
passively out across the crowds. Clearly there was nothing left
but to die, and it might as well be accomplished with dignity.

A noise of horns and pipes broke incongruously upon the
crowd. The guards stepped back, leaving Leron alone on his
platform, and the first of the new procession appeared partway
up the hill. A dark-robed, hooded priest stepped out of the dark
to welcome them. He raised his hands and all the little murmurs
of the crowd hushed into silence. The pipes shrilled and wailed,
drums beat, and the parade appeared over the crest of the hill,
men and women garlanded with ivy. In their midst a white
horse stepped daintily along, her mane and tail braided in dark
ribbons that showed green in the torchlight. Dastra was seated
sideways on her back, dressed in a long white clinging gown,
her hair bound up in flowers. The small silver bells on her
wrists and ankles chimed faintly with each step.

A cloaked and hooded groom stood at the white mare's head
and held her motionless in the middle of the clearing, while
Dastra looked out over the heads of the crowd, remote and
marvelously beautiful. The priest stepped past her and raised
his hands again and began to talk. Leron's mind was wandering
now. He had trouble concentrating on the invocations to Vazdz,
the pleas for rain and sun and harvest. If I am to be killed for
rain, he thought with a touch of annoyance, it might as well
have been done in Rym Treglad where we need it. Now Dastra
lifted one slim arm and began to talk. Tonight they would have
to pledge to her alone, for the king had given his life for his
people. There was a murmur at this, and she raised her hand a
second time for silence; the small bells sang. But, she explained, the blood of his murderer offered to Vazdz tonight
would buy assured prosperity for the realm. It was not common

blood they offered to Vazdz, but the blood of the false prince, Leron son of Mathon, last of the godless kings. The power was with Vazdz.

Two kingsmen unfastened Leron from his post and pushed him forwards, well into the view of the crowd below. Whatever their beliefs in Vazdz, he thought, my powerlessness now is enough to discredit me forever. Dastra pointed at him and at the pyre. "He will light a great flame to heaven," she cried. "Vazdz will be pleased."

She sat back in her cushioned saddle and looked into Leron's eyes for a long triumphant moment. Her expression changed ludicrously however as the quiet mare suddenly threw up her head, snorting. The groom did something with his hands and the mare shook her head as though to avoid some irritation, then unexpectedly half-reared, once more tossing her head. Dastra clutched at her neck, then lost her balance and tumbled to the ground. Leron threw back his head and laughed. Fate had been at least a little kind.

Dastra had hardly left the saddle when there was a thunder of hoofs in the distance and another white horse appeared out of the darkness. It had the thick, cresty neck of a stallion and carried its long tail proudly flagged up over its back. It pivoted sharply around the group and skidded to a halt on Leron's right hand, rearing almost vertically with a great stallion scream, then subsiding quietly and standing motionless.

Leron looked at the rider in disbelief, which was certainly echoed by the crowd below. His mirror image sat there, dressed as he in black and white, dark eyes wide with anger. The other looked out over the crowd and then contemptuously down at Dastra, who from surprise had not yet regained her feet. "If the power of Vazdz relies on such strumpets," cried the other, "then I say down with the powers of Vazdz." The rider pointed at the waiting pyre and in moments there was a crackling sound, a column of smoke and a sudden leaping tongue of flame. "Nothing but wood shall burn tonight: if Vazdz has any complaints let him come to us." The horse reared up again then stood facing the crowd as his rider stood in the stirrups. "I speak for the True King, Leron. You have come to pledge your fealty tonight. Will you bow to false usurpation and bloody ritual? The King is before you: the time to decide has come."

The crowd was moving and murmuring now, and torchlight glinted on nervously unsheathed swords and daggers. "Put by your weapons! We are not murderers here! Who wishes to go, depart now in safety; but after tomorrow your lives and estates are forfeit for your treachery." There was a palpable hesitation below, and Leron, cursing his bonds, wished fervently for some band of men however small to show the way to those who would be his followers. There was a light touch behind him, and a loud click; the manacles fell to the ground, and the leg shackles followed after. He looked down to see Huffing Dick on one knee, lock pick in hand. The footsman bowed his head, and Leron touched it in acceptance of his pledge. Then the older man grinned. "I have no sword to offer you at present, but this little picklet proved a needier weapon. I suspected you from the start," he added with a smile. "Tonight we'll drink your success." He turned to the crowd and cried out in a louder voice, "Stand forth, me beauties, and show yourselves to'r king."

A rustling of movement in the crowd below, and then hands and voices were raised from every quarter of the throng. The rider on the white horse slipped to the ground and held the stirrup for Leron. "The horse is Ajjibawr's," cried the rider. "Use no leg, or you'll be thrown worse than Dastra." On foot it was evident the horseman lacked several inches of Leron's height and breadth of shoulder. Leron leaned his good hand on the other's arm and swung up carefully, then looked down incredulously into the other's widely smiling face. There was a great shout from the crowd below, and Leron raised his hands above his head. By now the pyre was roaring with flame, and the light danced harshly over them all. Below the shout turned to cheers, and swords being lifted in salute.

"My people," he cried, "I shall take your pledges one by one. It is as my cousin has said. You may leave now if it likes you; but if you stay and swear to me, it will please me better. My return will not be marked by bloody revenge. We shall see the false kings humbled across the continent and bury deep the bitter past." A burly figure elbowed through the crowd of footsmen, which had gathered protectively round, and Leron leaned down and took him by the shoulder. "I present to you all my friend and ally, Odric, true heir to Vahn and sovereign of Treclere. He and the Karif Ajjibawr, not dead as all supposed, support us; do you doubt then our success?" As he stood up in his stirrups for their cheers, he did not doubt it himself. He looked round for Sibby to present her also, but there was no sign of her; nor any sign of Dastra.

MISSIVE
from *ADABA TAYYIB*, Mekrif of the Karabdu to *BODRUM VIII*, Master of Vahn

Thou who illuminist the heavens with thy sunlike presence, permit this the least and lowliest of petitioners to interrupt thy august meditations. I send this letter by the hand of one who is well known to you, one who has by a grievous mischance lost all his caravan in the desert (such is the awesome power of Vazdz). We have provided him with horse and food, (seeking in return no recompense) that he might bear this message to thee in all safety and comfort.

O Mighty One, this thy humble slave urges in all sincerity that thou seekest not to ally thyself with the Holy Reader Dzildzil in his desert capital, for there is many a long day's ride of sand between the farthest reaches of his land and thine, and all therein as well as all along the ocean shore may not, alas, be friendly to thy most auspicious purposes. Indeed, the sudden growth of gross impiety among the Karabdu is a thing to marvel at, nor strive to contain. For the Karabdu are without form and cloudlike when thou seekest to attack, yet like that cloud they may conceal within themselves a bolt of lightning with which to strike thee down.

May Vazdz open thy eyes and may these words be read as they were written.

III: WIDEGAME

Chapter One

As the two ships approached Rym Treglad, Ajjibawr went up onto the deck so that a familiar face might greet the harbor master and reassure him of their intentions. Even at a distance he could clearly see how parched the land had become over the last summer; the recent rains had created a shiny surface, everywhere split and cratered like the crackled glaze of an old plate. He had never seen the little settlement look so desolate.

Within a few hundred feet of shore they came upon the shallows, where they dropped anchor and prepared boats to go ashore. As they did so, a boat put out from the dock to meet them. Meladin the Navigator, standing there with them on deck, shouted as he recognized a friend.

"Alwyn, Alwyn," he called, hands to his mouth. "How do you here in Rym Treglad? Shadow me all and row mimpsy, there be high winnories aboard this windcar."

The boat drew alongside, and the one called Alwyn looked up delightedly. "Meladin, me hearty. I see you dragged off in metals many months past, and here you come steering home a great windcar, as brigsome as you please."

Meladin cut him short and gestured towards Ajjibawr. "Not only before the wind, but side of Clerowan the White. Better me that!"

Alwyn's eyes opened wide and his jaw dropped as he looked

up into Ajjibawr's face. "Clerowan the White! And just this
morn as ever was, a friend of yours came calling through the
town for news of you."

Ajjibawr looked at Osmin in surprise, then drew in his
brows. "A friend? What friend is this?"

"He called himself the Tayyib and demanded to see you."

"Adaba?" Ajjibawr carefully released the railing and relaxed
his hand. "Can it be?"

Osmin shrugged. "Anything is possible with a Tayyib." He
smiled, and Ajjibawr could not help but smile in return.

They swung the first boat over, and Ajjibawr went ashore
with Osmin and two sailors, while Hakma stayed behind arranging departures and the off-loading of the cargo. Alwyn had
preceded them onto shore, and a knot of curious onlookers was
gathered by the time their own boat had beached. As Alwyn
helped them pull the boat ashore and hold it steady, he explained that he had already sent a messenger for the Tayyib
with the news of Clerowan's arrival.

Ajjibawr waited for Shirkah's boat to land, and then together
they approached the town. In the first small square, they stopped
as a voice boomed in the air about them, rattling the poles of
the houses and raising a flock of sunning birds.

"Ajjibawr likKarif! Adaba Tayyib wannamat!" A great figure strode across the square towards them, followed by several
others, dressed in the brilliant silks of the desert, red and blue
and green and white. As always the Tayyib wore his grizzled
hair long and unkempt to his shoulders: he was dark for a
Karabdin Mekrif, no doubt the result of his ancestors' many
raids on villages outside the desert. He fell heavily to his knees
before Ajjibawr, looking up slyly under heavy grey brows, and
seized his hand to kiss it. Ajjibawr pulled away frowning, and
spoke, but pointedly not in the Karabdin tongue.

"Karif no longer, Adaba. And some say by your own choosing. No man kneels to Clerowan the White. Your journey is
in vain if the news you bring is for the Karif and not for
Clerowan. Get up."

Adaba climbed slowly to his feet, assisted by two of his
sons. His face was set in heavy, humorous lines, and he shook
his head. "For a plain man, this Clerowan sounds as proud as
our Karif once did."

Ajjibawr smiled reluctantly. "True, O serpent. But I spoke

the truth. Tell me your news, but do not expect my help."

Adaba looked around the samll group, and recognizing Osmin, nodded in greeting before returning to Ajjibawr. "I speak here because my news is urgent and I speak quickly because the need for an answer is also urgent. It was four months ago, and I among the northernmost of my tents, when there came to me news of a great caravan from Vahn, carrying messages and goods from Bodrum, on whom be the plague, to Dzildzil." (Here he spat.) "So I availed myself of this convenient messenger, lightening his load, and sending him back unaccompanied to Vahn well-horsed and victualed with my message in his pouch. And because of this letter I welcomed shortly thereafter a messenger from Dzildzil (he spat again) with these words for me."

Ajjibawr interrupted him. "Another time we will have the full tale, O Tayyib. For now, the bare bones only."

Adaba shrugged, and carelessly flicked his hand. "It shall be as you say, O Karif. The word that came to me from the Valley of Kings was simple enough: a summons to come and show myself and explain my manifold trespasses against the Holy Reader and his men. So I left the tribe of my brother's sons to watch at the northern edge of the Land, and sent the tribe of Killalla to maintain the western shore; then gathering the ten old clans of the grassland I rode upon the valley. But alas, news travels in the Land even more swiftly than my brown mare, and the valley entrance was shut upon us, the back door also. So I spoke with one I had long been friendly with, and from him learned that in answer to a plea from the Tredanan King (on whom be manifold plagues and diseases), a force had left already to join with the Tredanan army and be at their command. So I disposed the clans of my kinsmen about the doors of the Valley and came here as you see, with ten men only, passing the forces of Dzildzil (he spat) with such stealth and swiftness as you may imagine. They loiter on the edge of the Tredanan realm, awaiting the forces of Ddiskeard. But I had it in mind that much might be accomplished should the Karif return now, while the forces of the Holy Reader are few and scattered, to encourage the small flame I have set into a mighty blaze that will burn the sands clean again." He paused and smiled. "And, having heard that one Clerowan might lead me to Karif, I came as you have seen."

Osmin stepped forward eagerly as Adaba finished speaking, to take him by the hand. He turned to Ajjibawr with a glad look on his face, faltering as he read the unmoved expression there. Ajjibawr spoke softly. "So, the Land would like a Karif once more? To rescue his denouncers and the murderers of his swordbrother? Let them deal with Dzildzil as they please. He is of their own choosing."

Adaba shook his head. "They were ignorant, they have repented; some have already paid for their mistakes in blood. The Mekrif Gandana died outside the valley at the hands of Dzildzil's men, and he died with your name on his lips, your true man once again. And there are others. It is time for you to return." Adaba spoke so urgently he forgot to spit at the mention of Dzildzil's name. As Ajjibawr remained silent, Adaba went on shrewdly, "There is more at stake here than politics alone. The widow Halila has been forced to leave her encampment, by order of the Holy Reader. She dwells perforce within the valley, and it is said he importunes her day and night to marry him, and thereby give his reign support amongst those who seem not wholly convinced; notably her own tribe, the Shibayi, whom he fears."

Ajjibawr looked at him incredulously. "This is impossible." Adaba dropped his eyes but shook his head firmly. "No, my lord, it is the truth. Do you not think the time must now be ripe for a return? Surely the young prince, your friend, would welcome a desert alliance."

Ajjibawr gestured with his hand, and Osmin stepped up obediently. "I must go with Shirkah to talk with the Steward Gannoc, and see what best can be done to untangle the events of the past few weeks. Stay with the Tayyib; and if he can put a lock on his tongue, you may tell him a little of our recent adventures. I shall rejoin you later." He looked at Adaba sternly. "You may go. We will speak of this again." Adaba bowed his head respectfully, concealing his sly look of triumph with scant success, then drew Osmin in among his own men and silently retired.

Before Shirkah and Ajjibawr had taken many more steps towards the palace, the central great door opened and Gannoc hurried out, followed by Dansen whose skull cap had been knocked askew in his haste. They embraced there in the street, and Dansen was overjoyed to meet Shirkah, muttering under his breath, "It is just as Herrard said."

Ajjibawr looked at him keenly, his hand still on Gannoc's shoulder. "Herrard? My brother Rassam is here? He moves quickly for an old man."

Herrard appeared in the doorway and greeted Ajjibawr familiarly in the Karabdin tongue, then looked at him severely. "No older than yourself, O brother by blood. Truly, the weight of forty summers is heaviest at this season when summer fades." Then he politely switched to the common tongue, greeted Shirkah with respect, and the five of them withdrew into the palace.

Briefly, Ajjibawr related the story of his voyage aboard the slave ship, and how his plans had been forced into immediate action. That Sibby had arrived yet not met with Leron perturbed Gannoc greatly; that she and Liniris had disappeared seemed equally grave an omen. Ajjibawr narrated all with carefully schooled emotion, aware nevertheless that he was communicating more than he intended. For the other details of the voyage he turned to Shirkah, who spoke briefly of Ruave and her release, to Dansen's especial delight. Pleased as the Rym Tregladans were by the rain, the temporary disabling of the Moraganas pleased them more. In their turn they described their plans and the decisions of their council. Gannoc turned to Dansen. "Do you wish to speak of your weapon?"

Dansen did not answer directly, but spoke to Ajjibawr. "There is a man in town who calls himself the Tayyib. Has he spoken with you?"

"Yes."

"If the Karif wishes to return to the desert and forge an army there, there is something he can do for us that will change the whole course of the coming struggle."

Ajjibawr smiled dryly. "Dansen, you have studied the ways of the Karabdu too well. Come, speak plainly."

Dansen looked at the afternoon sunlight lying on the window ledge and rose to his feet. "First, I shall demonstrate." He took a piece of paper in one hand and a small lens in the other, and standing by the window held the two in the sun. In moments the paper had smoldered into flame, and he dropped it with an exclamation and put his singed fingers in his mouth. "The result is so swift I am never prepared," he explained with an apologetic look at Gannoc.

Ajjibawr raised an eyebrow. "As children in the desert, we

often played such games, with bits of broken glass."

"That is it, you have the glass in quantity. We do not. And in small size it is a toy, a toy for children and dreaming students. But I have made calculations for a great lens"—he gestured widely with his hands—"that can throw the power of the sun many hundreds of feet, across great distances. And only in the desert are there furnaces, material and knowledge sufficient for its fabrication."

Ajjibawr nodded slowly. "Who would show my artisans what to do?"

Herrard raised his hand a little way from the table. "Dansen has explained the whole thing thoroughly, and I have copied all his notes and figures. If it can be done, I can do it. Not for nothing were we students once together."

"Then it seems best on many a count that Ajjibawr return from the dead." He sighed wearily. "Yet I do not like to leave these other matters unresolved."

"There are men of yours here in the city, Clerowan's men. Are there any you especially trust? They could go south as quickly as any and look for Leron in Sundrat, to assist him. Furthermore, they would stand as good a chance as any to examine matters in Tredana."

Ajjibawr looked at Dansen affectionately. "Dansen, I bow to your wisdom. I have had with me for companion Osmin, whom I trust as my own eyes. He will know what to do; and if a rescue is needed he is as skillful as any." He looked at Gannoc for confirmation and the steward nodded, a slight relief in his face.

"It is a good thought. I cannot lie easy at night thinking of our king's peril."

"King?"

"Mathon is dead these several weeks."

Ajjibawr bowed his head in brief respect. "It was a merciful release for him, but the news will weigh heavily upon our young friend." The others nodded gloomily. Then Dansen turned to Shirkah, who sat by, silently listening.

"How came you into the clutches of Vahn?" he asked. Shirkah smiled slowly as he told the story of his brother's treachery. "Now I live only to return to the north and settle matters with my brother there; once that is done, my men and whatever ships we can capture will lie at your disposal." He held out his

hand to Dansen and then to Gannoc; as Gannoc took it, he
smiled and spoke. "You have lost your brother by birth, but
here you see those who would be your brothers by blood."
Shirkah smiled widely in return.

THE BALLAD OF CLEROWAN THE WHITE AND THE
KINGSMAN OF SUNDRAT
(as sung in the northern provinces of Tredana)

It fell all in the early spring,
When new fields they were plowin',
The King has sent one hundred men
To capture Brave Clerowan.

Bold Gwillam was their Captain cruel,
And thus the Kingsman said,
"Before a month has come and gone,
I'll have Clerowan's head."

"Before a month has come and gone
For mercy he'll be beggin'."
Away into the fields went they
To capture brave Clerowan.

Clerowan he rose in the prime
And taking two or three,
He caught a lamb of ten month's growth
And feasted heartily.

And as they sat there at their meat,
A messenger came runnin':
"Fly, oh, fly, my master dear,
The Kingsmen they are comin'."

And when Cruel Gwillam he rode up,
A black look lookéd he,
To see these three poor men at meat
And drinking heartily.

"O mercy, mercy," cried Clerowan,
"Have mercy on us three—"
"No mercy," cried Cruel Gwillam then,
"Such thieves should hangéd be."

Clerowan smiled a little smile
And motioned with his hand
And all about Cruel Gwillam then
The outlaws they did stand.

Away into the hills they went
And cursing with dismay,
The Captain thought on ninety men
Not twenty miles away.

And when they stood all in the hills,
Clerowan called his men:
"Come tell to me, my brave men all,
How shall we serve these ten?"

"O mercy, mercy," Gwillam cried,
Clerowan smiled again.
"I sang that tune but two hours since—
What mercy had you then?"

"You came here for my head," said he
"Among the springing flowers—
Answer me, O Brave Gwillam,
Why should you leave with yours?"

"O mercy," Gwillam cried again,
"O spare to me my life."
Then Brave Clerowan laughed aloud
And he took out his knife.

"We do not want you life, Gwillam,
Nor yet your head," said he.
"But you must dance a little yet
To cheer my men and me."

So in his mail and helmet there
For full three hours or four

He danced for Brave Clerowan's men:
They laughed till they were sore.

Back to the King he rides again,
Through green fields they were sowin',
And safe with his hundred men he bides
Cursing our Clerowan.

Chapter Two

Matters were arranged promptly as they had planned; and although Osmin was loath to let Ajjibawr depart without him, he submitted with good grace. Adaba nodded approvingly as he watched Osmin ride away with six men at his back. "The Bakra are all honorable. That one has no heart except to live and die for you. It will be no worse than if you went yourself. Some years I saved the head of his brother's murderer, thinking to please you with it; but it is no great trophy now."

Ajjibawr looked up in surprise. "You have avenged Ab'Bakr?"

"His murderer did not live a week. I would have left the deed for you to do, but you had left the desert."

Ajjibawr nodded slowly. "And now I shall return." He held out his hand to clasp Dansen's. "When Leron returns, he will of course receive my official messages. But I promise you that you shall have your great lens before spring. It was a fortunate flood washed you upon my shores, nine years ago."

Dansen smiled up into his face, then looked at Adaba and his impatient sons. "You are going so soon? You will not even spend the night?"

"I have stayed away eight years, and now am anxious to be home again." Ajjibawr flushed. "You will honor me if you can relay another message for me," he said, and Dansen nodded courteously. "You may tell your companion of nine years past that when we meet again she may have a stronger talisman than a ring of glass; and a home in the desert if so she wishes."

Dansen nodded without comment, and Ajjibawr turned to Adaba with a lifted eyebrow. "I assume we ride?"

Adaba smiled slowly. "Yes, we still have horses in the desert: and some of them are swift."

His sons ran into an alley between two buildings and reappeared leading several restless horses, fully accoutered for travel. One was a little taller than the others, pale dun with tall black stockings; Ajjibawr recognized him and laughed. "And what fool rides The Thunderer?"

Adaba made a deprecating gesture with one hand. "Not I, O Karif. But he has learned manners since last you sat him; and you yourself have said he is the swiftest of the Tayyib bloodstock."

Ajjibawr matched Adaba's gesture with his own hand. "And if we have no need to stop, then all is well?"

Adaba silently handed him a headcloth, and as Ajjibawr wound its familiar folds about his head, Adaba's sons swung up and Adaba took hold of The Thunderer's bridle. Ajjibawr shrugged, then swung up himself as easily. The horse screamed and tried to stand on its hind legs, then bit the Tayyib's arm as he relinquished the reins. Ajjibawr sat quietly and allowed himself a small smile. "Manners indeed. Pray to all the gods that your other words have more truth to them than this tale of The Thunderer's manners." He turned a little in his saddle and raised his hand in salute to Dansen; and then the dust of their departure was thick between them.

The Tayyib's horses were bred chiefly for endurance, not speed; a necessary quality for brigands who must always be ready to outlast an irate pursuit. Familiar as he was with the Tayyib's boasts, Ajjibawr could not help marveling at the distance they covered. More than seven hundred miles of difficult terrain lay between the Tayyib's northern tents and the city of Rym Treglad; they covered it in less than two weeks, riding no longer than ten hours in each day. By journey's end Ajjibawr offered to buy The Thunderer, still in good flesh and condition and fresh for each morning's start, but Adaba laughed and shook his head. "I will make a present of him, if you wish, O Karif. But he is of value only over distance. Let him rest but a little, and even I would hesitate to put my saddle on him."

"So the tale of new manners was a false one?"

"No, my lord, no, no. Recollect, he had just traveled nearly two weeks to reach Rym Treglad. The Thunderer always im-

proves his manners on a journey." Ajjibawr sat back in his
saddle and laughed, relaxing his reins a little, and The Thunderer, scenting home a few miles ahead, made a great leap out
from under his rider's control and set the pace for a fine arrival
into camp.

The eldest of Adaba's sons had ridden ahead from the pre-
vious night's encampment, and the entire village was standing
there in welcome. For the first time in eight years, Ajjibawr
saw the flutter of strong red and blue, green, yellow, and orange
silk against the soft-shaded contours of the desert; the sparkle
of sun on upraised swords and gold-embroidered clothing; the
warm black mass of low and welcoming tents. Where they
halted, a company of men sprang up to take their horses; old
warriors knelt in tears and young ones who had never before
seen the Karif fell face down on the sand, their hands outstretched before them. Ajjibawr looked at their numbers proudly,
then brought them to their feet with a gesture. One in particular
he noticed, a slender, arrogant boy who gladly rose from kneel-
ing and offered his sword to the Karif with scant humility.
Ajjibawr looked at Adaba. "He is one of yours?"

Adaba summoned the boy over, and Ajjibawr gravely took
the proferred sword and returned it with a nod of acceptance.
"The most fanatical of my bodyguard, O Karif. An eater of
fire, a devourer of my enemies. His name is Shadith." The
boy looked pleased at the description but said nothing, waiting
for Adaba's sign to step back, and as he did so Ajjibawr nodded
approvingly.

"You are fortunate."

They had eaten sparingly on the journey, and Adaba had
determined to make amends for this the very first night. While
his bodyguard brought scented water and towels and finely
worked embroidered clothing, Adaba, with surprising delicacy,
left Ajjibawr alone to wash, shave, and dress. It was more
common for a Karif to be attended at all times, but Adaba
knew Ajjibawr and his peculiarities well: he gave over his own
tent and went to supervise the preparation of the feast.

Outside the tent in the harshly bright afternoon, the cooking
fires crackled palely orange and tall. Adaba was engaged in a
wrangle with the cook, but he saw Ajjibawr immediately, and
made a little motion with his hand. The young bodyguard
materialized at Ajjibawr's side, the great sword magically
changed for a round brass salver set with cups and a steaming

pot of thick sweet coffee. He would have knelt to offer it, but Adaba lumbered up and preemptorily poured a cup himself, which he knelt to offer to the Karif, looking around as he did so to make sure his gesture was noted by all. Before he took the cup, Ajjibawr leaned over and put his hand on the older man's shoulder. "So, the Mekrif of the Tayyib kneels in his own camp?"

Adaba gestured vaguely over his shoulder. "I kneel for their sake more than for yours or mine. It is well known I have never knelt for Dzildzil."

Ajjibawr helped him to his feet, and they drank their coffee standing. Then Adaba led Ajjibawr on a brief tour of the encampment. Of the more than three hundred men under Adaba's direct control, nearly forty were his own sons, the fruit of twenty-eight marriages spanning more than thirty-five years. He had fourteen wives still living and was known to have sworn never to take another unless it be his last. "It has made me more particular," he explained. In this camp he had gathered nearly half his fighting force; he had deployed the others across key points to observe the movement of Dzildzil's men.

Well separated from the rest of the camp, he had an orderly complex of dug-out stables and sand paddocks. It was the cleanest part of the camp, and Ajjibawr commented approvingly as they watched the weanling foals at play, bucking, nuzzling and nipping, then calling pitifully for their missing mothers. Adaba nodded proudly. "Past winters have been hard and many a good broodmare failed before her term, sick with the infections that sweep the camp. This winter we will take care that no one visits here but the grooms." He smiled and put a hand on the Karif's arm. "Tell me," he said, "do you have races for these young ones in your camp?"

"Weanlings? No. How is it managed?"

Adaba held up his hand and smiled. "You shall see tonight. It is a good sport and shows us early which ones merit attention."

When they returned, it was nearly dusk, and the food was ready. Adaba placed Ajjibawr on a low cushioned seat while the rest sat on the ground. He had ordered that a sheep be stuffed with chickens and the chickens stuffed with vegetables and lumps of butter; he enthusiastically whacked the carcass open with a two-handed sword, and the stuffing exploded out onto the platter. Then he handed his sword to Shadith and gestured towards the head. Despite his seeming lack of muscle, the young boy severed the sheep's neck with one easy swing, and Adaba carefully located the eyes and brains to give to Ajjibawr on the point of his dagger. With this same weapon he gestured to Shadith. "You see? He is an expert, dangerous, as I told you." Ajjibawr nodded, and they ate on, absorbedly.

It was full dark by the time the remnants on the platters had been taken to the gazelle hounds where they waited impatiently on their leashes. Ajjibawr settled back against his cushions, and coffee was once more put into his hand. He took a pinch of snuff and sneezed contentedly. Adaba slurped his small cup dry and held it out to his servants, rattling it on its saucer for a refill. "What is the Karif's pleasure? A race or a story?"

"A story. Now that I have eaten I can think more clearly. The way in which you force your foals to race is obvious. Your stories, however, are not always so, and their ends never so clearly in sight as the mare to whom the weanling runs. So it shall be a story."

Adaba chuckled. "Very well. I have a good story to tell, which you will not have heard, having been so long from the desert." He settled back himself more comfortably and cleared his throat.

"It happened that spring was late last year; the rains came after the snows and did not cease; by the edge of the true sands all lay muddy and desolate; and the hearts of men longed for that which would reassure them summer is coming. This was true of the Vahnian soldiers as well as among the Karabdu, perhaps more so for the Vahnians since they are soldiers away from home and in a strange land. So one of their bold captains, named Howanis, famous years past at sea and now upon the land, a strong man with a sword and heavy with taxes and the impressing of Bodrum's law upon his allies in the desert, desired to marry. This is not strange, for many desired likewise. I myself was tempted to take another wife last spring. But this Howanis desired for wife a maid from among the Karabdu, and there were not any families willing to receive his suit. Until, however, a man among my tents proposed his youngest daughter to Howanis, who accepted and even met the high price he had been set. Perhaps in Vahn a scrawny child is considered beautiful; who can guess the logic of an alien heart?

Or perhaps it was her yellow hair. In any case the match was made, and Howanis eagerly welcomed to his tent the fair-haired daughter of the Karabdu. But before the dawn—" A rustle in the audience distracted Adaba, and a voice murmured something about a scream; the Tayyib thanked him for the correction and picked up the story once more. "As I said, he welcomed her to his tent; and when there came a scream some little time later, those accustomed to Howanis and his ways remarked it not. But a little before the dawn his servants visited him, to tell of a horse stolen in the night, and they found his body lying there, curious in its headlessness; there was no weapon near and no sign of the woman. And it was not long thereafter that the head of Howanis returned to his camp, flung at night by a horse-borne warrior who called for the armies of Vahn to beware the might of the desert, little though they might think it now. And throughout the summer it went on, that soldiers from Vahn would meet a single warrior who would rob them at sword point and steal their horses and weapons and send them home on foot with the same message. Adaba's voice had slowed and now he stopped. "This story is unfinished. I think however, that we shall live to hear those words made truth."

Ajjibawr took another pinch of snuff and having sneezed he rubbed his nostril gently with one finger. "And the soldiers of Vahn made no inquiry into this matter, and no one came to you, the Mekrif of the tribe, to demand redress?"

Adaba spread his hands reassuringly. "No, no, I did not say that, O Karif. Of a surety they came straightway, loudly demanding that I surrender the murderer of Howanis. I explained that she roamed the desert as free of my control as—"

"As once you were of mine?"

"It is as you say, Karif." Adaba smiled. "In any case, she was not mine to surrender. But I told them that which did not please them greatly. They asked how I intended to deal with this brigand, and I said..." he paused to laugh, his hand at his throat. "And I said that if I caught her I would put her in my tents where she belonged. If a man cannot have the youngest daughter of his own follower, who then may he take?"

Ajjibawr raised an eyebrow. "Who indeed?"

He looked around and saw the Mekrif's young bodyguard sitting cross-legged and straight-backed upon the ground, a bared sword once more across the knees, blue eyes proud in a

thin white face framed with a ragged fringe of pale gold hair.
"You are indeed fortunate to have for bodyguard one so skilled
with a sword."

Adaba nodded proudly, then whispered to Ajjibawr behind
his hand. "She is happier as a boy, and I am an old man. I
pretend I do not know, and it saves me much trouble. Besides,
it amuses me."

Ajjibawr put his hand on Adaba's arm. "So, the old wolf
waits, for once?"

Adaba stretched and yawned, signaling time to retire. He
leaned over and again spoke close to Ajjibawr's ear as the
others all took respectful leave. "Karif, you know how little
the love is that I bear for the way you live your life; if men
were meant to live alone they would not be born with—"
Ajjibawr raised a hand in humorous protest, and Adaba shrugged.
"However, I am at an age where it seems wiser to consider
carefully each action. So, today you see me carefully considering. Tomorrow is in the hands of fate."

THE TEACHINGS AND DEATH OF MARAJ
as seen and narrated by Mumar the Pious (trans. Rassam)

*Word reached the valley during the first year of reconstruction
there that a man was wandering from tribe to tribe in the desert,
teaching the word of Vazdz and encouraging the people in
submission to the Holy Reader, and Dzildzil was pleased to
hear of this man, who was called Maraj, and to hear of the
holy example which he set to all men. He invited Maraj to
teach in the Valley and for the first four years of the Holy
Reader's reign Maraj came and went with respect, and many
men gathered to hear him when he spoke.*

*But as the days passed Maraj grew thin and unkempt, his
hair grew down upon his shoulders and his clothing grew thin
and patched; the dust of the road was on his face and his eyes
turned ever inward. And he spoke to the people in riddles,
confusing their minds, often crying out to Vazdz with loud
reproaches in public places. And when some wise men went
to him and asked for an explanation, he laughed in their faces,
and then cried, "I have true knowledge of God and it will make
me an outlaw in your eyes."*

*Not long thereafter he was indeed proclaimed an outlaw
and put in prison, where, his jailers report, he spent the nights
in prayer and tears and the days in fasting and meditation.
And the night before his trial he was heard to repeat one word
over many times, which was, "Illusion." Yet in the morning
the word he was heard to repeat was, "Truth." And at his trial
he said, "Salvation will come to the Karabdu only if they remain
on horseback and forget the walls that close them in; but they
must also forget their fool's honor which will be a harder thing
for them." He was asked, "What is this fool's honor?" and he
answered, "It is this, that to forgive an enemy is wrong." And
he did not repent him of his many heresies and misguided
teachings until nearly half the sentence had been carried out,
which was a thousand blows; but the executioner had expected
this repentence and stayed not his hand, afterwards removing
the head as Dzildzil had commanded.*

*And it disturbed many people who watched that he had not
repented of his sins, and that even on the way to be killed he
had been observed to dance in his chains and to sing. Thus it
was that many tales began to be passed about, that another
had been killed in his stead, or that he had returned from
death, and other stories too foolish to be worth recounting.*

Chapter Three

A messenger disturbed their breakfast the next morning, riding furiously into camp and throwing himself at Adaba's feet. He was another young man Ajjibawr did not recognize, one who would have been a child eight years ago; but the hard-ridden sweat-streaked horse was clearly of his own Ziliman blood-stock, and the young man suddenly recognized him. He threw himself onto the sand a second time, and Adaba leaned over. "The fourth son of your horsemaster, Mubassa. Mubassa was killed for laughing when Dzildzil was thrown by your grey horse, whom he had followed into captivity; his four sons live to follow you and see their blood avenged."

Ajjibawr had the young man rise and looked at him critically. "Mubassa's fourth son—you must be Masala, then." The boy nodded. "No son of Mubassa would have ridden a three-year-old colt so hard, except for some great tiding. What is your message?"

The boy broke into a wide smile. "Great tidings indeed, my lord. The greatest we have had these eight years past. The Tredanan king is dead, his wife has fled with some few followers, and Leron has been acclaimed king in a great ceremony, receiving the fealty of many powerful lords."

Ajjibawr rose to his feet, and Adaba looked at him triumphantly. "It has begun, then, O Karif."

150

Ajjibawr laughed proudly. "Where there were four false kings there now stand only three. How long, do you think, before we make it two?"

Adaba pushed away his plate and stood also, wiping a greasy hand against his coarse grey beard. "No longer than a short ride to the valley, and perhaps a day or two for argument within. Masala, do you rest or ride?"

The tired messenger had been slumped against his horse's side, but he straightened up proudly, a hurt look on his face. "You shall have a fresh mount from my stable and ride with the bodyguard. Shadith, you may show him. Go and make ready: we ride within the hour."

As the two hurried off, followed by the tired horse, Adaba grinned at Ajjibawr. "No wonder you are so anxious for The Thunderer. Clearly, the Ziliman stud can use fresh blood. Why he has not come half the distance we traveled." Ajjibawr smiled but made no answer, tapping his fingers against the hilt of his dagger. Adaba looked at him more keenly. "You do not wish to ride, then? For what would you wait? Osmin will soon reach Sundrat, if he had not already, and hear the news. Doubtless he will speak with the new king, who will therefore expect an alliance with us. We must strike before Dzildzil can gather his forces again!" He spat loudly.

Ajjibawr shook his head. "There is a greater need for subtlety than for strength. I do not wish to slaughter half the Karabdu in order to preserve the other half."

"But they are traitors, Karif! And of untrustworthy tribes!"

"The Karif cannot hold any tribe in special love or hatred, except it be his own. No, I have a plan and it is your Shadith has given me the idea. I think I can enter the valley unsuspected, if you will help." He put an arm around Adaba's shoulders. "Surely, Mekrif, with your extensive family you have some extra clothes that I can wear. Women's clothes?" He explained his scheme to Adaba, and the old warrior laughed aloud in delight, sending his servants scurrying to comply with the Karif's wishes.

They rode within the hour as Adaba had said, and Karif and Mekrif rode stirrup to stirrup in front, just behnd the men who bore the banners of Tayyib and Ziliman. By good fortune they did not encounter any men along the way, either soldiers of Vahn or tribesmen of the Karabdu, and on the evening of the third day they made camp in a narrow defile, near to the desert capital but reasonably secure from discovery.

As they sat by the fire that night over a game of Castledown, young Masala came over awkwardly and bowed his head. "There was some other news, Karif, which I forgot before because I did not understand. Also, I told you that the false king is dead, but not that it is rumored that his murderer was the queen."

Ajjibawr raised his eyebrow at Adaba. "I have told you, have I not, of that lady's sojourn in the desert? You see, I did not exaggerate." He turned back to Masala. "What was your other news?"

"Perhaps the meaning will be clear to you. The one who gave me these messages said, 'The daughter of Simirimia has returned in alliance with Leron.' Yet it is well known that Simirimia of Treclere was a bitter enemy to Tredana."

Ajjibawr laughed aloud with relief, and Adaba looked at him curiously. He explained, "She is the one for news of whom I sent Osmin to Sundrat and Tredana. She was also my guest nine years ago, in company with Dansen and Dastra." He turned to Masala. "Your father helped her with the horse I gave her. She is no enemy to Tredana. And if she came safely ashore there, then I will worry no longer. Clearly her power is even greater than I suspected." He laughed again after Masala had left and idly looked down at the board feeling many years younger and lighter at heart.

Adaba looked at him shrewdly. "So, you have not been a complete hermit these past few years?" He did not wait for an answer but turned seriously to the board, surveying his stone army as though they were riding into real battle. Tentatively he toyed with an admiral, then drew back his hand with a muttered apology and pushed instead one knight in front of the others.

Ajjibawr shook his head warningly. "The Tayyib is careless tonight." He calmly blockaded the knight's retreat and smiled. "I have a siege."

Adaba sprang up and circled round to look at the board from over the Karif's shoulder. Desperately he examined each route to escape or counterattack and saw each avenue blocked. "Siege? You have a Castledown, O Karif." He shrugged and sat down again. "It is good that you have returned, if only to keep me from too constant winning."

He motioned to a servant who silently removed the board

and began to pack the pieces carefully into their fitted traveling case. "You leave us tomorrow then, as planned?"

"As planned I leave, and also as planned you will stay here and not ride out as foolishly as that knight you just sacrificed."

Adaba nodded. "I will stay safely here, but three days only. If you have not returned by then, look for a rescue."

Next morning Ajiibawr dressed himself with humorous assistance from Adaba, who knew far more about the arrangement of women's clothing than Ajjibawr. With powder he helped put a little more grey into Ajjibawr's fair hair than was there already, frowning at the way it had receded from the temples. "The hair of women rarely decreases with age, Karif. Nor would I guess that any could have so rough a cheek, no matter how ill-favored."

Ajjibawr ran a hand across his chin and grimaced. "I trust no man has the chance to caress it," he said dryly. "And I shall not forget to shave."

Adaba threw a heavy woolen cloth over Ajjibawr's head, carefully tucked back the longer ends of hair and modestly crossed the shawl over his chest. "Do not forget, Karif, to keep your sleeves from pushing too far back. There are not many old women carry sword scars on their forearms."

Ajjibawr laughed, then frowned at the golden hair on the backs of his hands. Adaba offered to shave it off, but here Ajjibawr drew the line. "I will not be attracting the attention of others. Is the basket ready?"

Adaba nodded and opened a large woven pedlar's pack full of lengths of lace and embroidery, whalebone combs and carved mirror backs from Vahn, vials of fish oil useful in the making of essences, and other items pillaged from Adaba's various households. He briefly discussed the current price of each, and Ajjibawr committed them all to memory. Then he hefted the entire pack onto his shoulder and stooped under its weight, drawing the cloth across his face. Adaba shook his head. "Perhaps I should wait for two days only."

Ajjibawr straightened up and shook his head. "Three days, you rogue. I am sure the disguise will be sufficient for those who do not suspect."

By the time Ajjibawr had reached the gates, he was genuinely stooped under his load, bent over in the uncomfortable pack saddle of the ungainly white mule Adaba had chosen for him to ride. "If the Karif must ride into his capital dressed as a pedlar, then he should ride a mule. But at least let it be a white one," Adaba had said. The guards at the outer entrance did not look up, waving him through impatiently, and soon his hoof-beats echoed all around, resounding from the tall rock walls that nearly met overhead, protecting the cleft that led into the valley. Here, nothing had changed; the hard-packed trail, the slight smell of damp on the stony cliffsides, the perpetually dim light; Ajjibawr straightened a little and breathed in deeply the familiar smells. Then the small circle of light before him grew into a tall triangle as he approached, becoming at last a small view of the immense valley's floor.

No amount of description in Adaba's camp had prepared him for the rebuilding in the valley. The broad plain, lying slightly below, was covered with thickly clustered sandbrick buildings, squat and poorly designed for the most part and irregularly daubed in pale shades of blue and green. Even at a distance the fetid smell of the town made Ajjibawr draw back and raise his cloth across his face.

The mule, standing half-asleep, was finally urged on, and they picked their way down the stony path towards the nearest buildings. On the farther wall of the valley, where the enormous carving of Vazdz and the tombs of the Nine First Kings adorned the cliff face, there was a sparkle of color; apparently the rock was hung with flags. A market had been set up against the crude walls that encircled Dzildzil's palace in the center of the town; a narrow channel of water ran through the small square and disappeared under the palace walls. The water stank, and dust covered everything with a fine white powder like flour. Ajjibawr set up the goods from his pack in the shade of a sick and dusty tree, head bent but ears and eyes alert. At noon several sellers of meat and bread set up small braziers and began roasting mutton on skewers, for lunch; this and a little thick coffee he purchased with a fine show of aged reluctance, counting out the coins with trembling fingers.

He was disturbed at his meal, however, for there came a screech of brass horns and the gates were thrown open in the palace wall. Hurriedly goods were gathered up and the merchants pulled back out of the way, as three pale golden horses, their heads checked absurdly high, came trotting out into the square, drawing a light chariot behind them. A mounted guard rode on either side and behind, and the entourage cut a wide swath through the small area.

A man who had been selling pottery bowls next to Ajjibawr grabbed him by the sleeve and pulled him back out of the way as the procession wheeled around and disappeared down one of the side streets. "Careful, old mother, or you'll be run down." Ajjibawr thanked him with a quavering voice and downcast eyes.

Another merchant laughed. "That or be carried off to the palace. I wager there's not an old woman in the city safe if the Widow Halila refuses his suit."

The pottery merchant began carefully setting out his bowls once more, carefully wiping the dust from their blue-glazed sides with his sleeve. "Now, now, friend, speak cautiously. We are in the shadow of the palace. It is not, after all, as though the Holy Reader's interest in the widow is a personal one." The other made some ironic reply, and the afternoon began to settle down quietly upon them, in a thick haze of dust and heat.

For a while Ajjibawr sat there quietly, sweating under his heavy robes. He sold an ivory mirror back to a young woman with three or four children hanging onto her skirts, giving her a very cheap price because she looked so tired. He was slowly realizing that Adaba's trade goods were all much finer than the average run of things sold on open market. Much more the type of thing sold door to door in the better sections of town. Of course. He slowly stooped over and packed up his things with exaggerated care, huffing a little as he maneuvered the pack onto the white mule's strong round back. His neighbor lifted a hand in farewell, then hurried over to take advantage of the shade where the mule had been tied.

It was not hard to find the better part of town. Enclosed gardens separated the houses, and plantings showed green above high walls; the house fronts were massive with finely carved shuttered windows, and wheel tracks in the dust turned in at each bolted gate. "Fine things, rare oils, sea shell carvings"—he coughed and tried again in a higher voice. "Rare oils, essences, sea—" A shutter opened out in the wall above his head.

A pretty girl with a long tail of very fair hair hanging over one shoulder leaned out. "I am trying to make rose essence," she said. "Do you have any oil that will hold the scent?" He fumbled in his pack and drew out one of Adaba's precious vials, calculating a cost that would make up for the loss on the mirror back.

"Ah, my dear," he said, a wicked amusement rising in his breast, "I have it right enough, distilled in Vahn and as pure as your lovely young cheek. But it will cost you dear. Three golden krahs it cost me, and ill could I afford the expense. But you may have it for only a half-krah more."

The girl made an impatient gesture, then nodded. "Very well, old woman. Let me see it." She reached down her hand, and Ajjibawr made a play of trying to reach up, stooped over as he was.

"It's too far for an old woman, my pretty. You'll have to come down, my dear."

The girl pulled the shutters closed and a moment later appeared at the door, clutching a silk purse in her hand. She snatched up the vial and unstoppered it, sniffing carefully. "Yes, that is the oil." She undid her purse. "Here are three krahs and a quarter, quite enough and you know it well."

Ajjibawr bit his lip to keep from laughing. "Then, my dear, you'll not grudge an old woman a favor? It does my heart good to see one as fresh and pretty as yourself. Give me a kiss now on my cheek and maybe I'll not feel so cold in my bones when I go to sleep tonight."

The girl looked startled, then leaned forwards ungraciously and brushed her lips against his face. She smelled delightful. "There, now." She put the vial carefully into her purse and jumped at the sudden sound of trumpets. "Go to the Widow Halila's house, if you have any more oils to sell," she said more kindly than before. "Her servants distill many essences from her garden and are often buying different oils."

"But which is her house, my dear?"

"There, where the Holy Reader's chariot is just leaving."

He thanked her and with difficulty turned the mule around towards the end of the street. At the far end gates had been drawn back and the three pale horses reappeared, picking up their legs and waving their silky white tails. Their heads were strapped so high they could turn only with difficulty, and the driver swore as he swung them around in Ajjibawr's direction. A wheel of the chariot went off the edge of the road, into the shallow sewer, and the Holy Reader, standing behind his driver,

was thrown against the side of the chariot. He was in a furious
temper, and he took up his gold-tipped ivory wand and began
beating the driver on the neck and shoulders. They wheeled
towards Ajjibawr in a thick cloud of dust, and he had a short
close look at Dzildzil high above him in the chariot. The ruler
was a young man, no more than thirty, with fair hair almost
white and protuberant bright blue eyes; his lips were large and
fleshy. He was dressed all in cloth of gold, with gold and white
sandals and a heavy gold bracelet on his right wrist; the driver
he was still belaboring wore a cotton tunic, striped white and
gold. They rushed past, and Ajjibawr pressed himself and the
mule against the wall, his sleeve across his face to keep out
the dust, fascinated by the Holy Reader's unbridled rage. Apparently the Widow Halila had yet to give a favorable reply.
He took up the mule's halter and began to walk toward her
house.

THE ANNALS OF DZILDZIL
Chronicle of Year Seven . . . an excerpt

   *It happened that following the execution of the madman
Maraj for heresy in Year Four, those who had been deluded
by his teachings into heresy did not entirely forsake their ways,
although there was no public sign of their presence. But in the
Year Seven the hand of Vazdz caused the truth to be brought
to light, for a young man of the Shibayi tribe tried to kill the
Holy Reader as he knelt in public prayer at the time of the
Autumn Sacrifices, and was surprised and taken by the Holy
Reader's guards with a dagger in his hand not twenty feet from
the spot where the Holy Reader knelt. And when he was questioned, the young Shibayi did not at first admit to any reason
for his action, but upon being urged further he confessed that
there were within the city a group of men who still believed
that Maraj had spoken truly concerning Vazdz, and that these
impious wretches had together decided that Dzildzil must be
removed from his high office through death, and that they had
converted this young man, swearing him to secrecy and convincing him by cunning arts to work their will. Shortly after*

*this confession the youth expired but not before he had freely
given his interlocutors the names of these "Marajites," who
shortly thereafter were taken and destroyed in public show by
the order of the Holy Reader. And great was the gladness of
the people to see their city purged of this foul corruption and
to know that the heresies of Maraj were gone as they had never
been.*

Chapter Four

For many minutes Ajjibawr hesitated outside Halila's house, unable to nerve himself to action. When he finally called out his wares, it was in a husky voice, and he had no difficulty with the aged quaver. He need not have distressed himself, however, since when the shutters opened a servant only came to the window, who questioned him about his wares and then asked quite politely if he would return on the following day. He nodded humbly and moved on.

That night, as he sat with his back against the recumbant mule, huddled in his shawl against the chilly night air, he once more went over in his mind the unanswerable questions Halila would ask. Ah well, if she did not want to see him, it would be easy enough to go away, and when he was Karif once more he would see that her privacy was respected. He slept fitfully and awoke at dawn.

The mule breakfasted comfortably on the weeds, brambles and patches of grass that covered the public grazing area; but Ajjibawr went hungry. He tightened his sash against his empty belly and set out towards the market square, hoping for some coffee. He did not feel like eating. In the market all was in an uproar, and a crowd of people filled it to the walls, awaiting word from the palace to confirm news of some great battle just outside the Valley entrance. Ajjibawr listened with apprehension. Adaba had promised to lie hidden for three days. Yet who else would be battling with Dzildzil's forces just outside the capital? At last the gates were opened and one of Dzildzil's

captains appeared, distinctive in his golden livery. He had one
gloved hand on the shoulder of a dirt-streaked warrior who
bore a narrow sword cut across his face, and the other hand
held up for silence.

"Good People, loyal followers of the Holy Reader, in this
the eighth year of peaceful submission to the will of Vazdz.
There is glorious news for you today." Ajjibawr stepped back
into the crowd and grasped the mule's halter more firmly. "We
have had a skirmish at our very gates, and although the impious
brigands made good their escape, we have killed three and
taken one prisoner. And the prisoner we have taken is a man
infamous in the annals of the desert, loyal to no chief in his
half-century of misspent life. Here is the man whose sword
brought down the horse of the foul brigand: Talal, step forth!"
The warrior stepped forward to cheers from the crowd. "And
here is his prisoner, the infamous Tayyib!"

Ajjibawr bit back a groan of despair and reached instinctively for a sword that was not there. Helpless in his muffling
disguise, he saw his old friend dragged forth, his arms pinned
behind him, by contemptuous armed guards. Adaba's face was
swollen and black with bruises, one eye shut, blood from his
nose and mouth caked in his beard. As they watched, Talal
swaggered up and hit him across the face once more. The first
time Adaba remained impassive; after the second blow he twisted
in the guard's grip and kicked the young man on the knee,
almost knocking him over. Talal and the guard both turned on
him for that, until he hung almost unconscious in his bonds.

Behind them the palace gates were once more filled with
men as several guards appeared, roughly pushing a large group
of old men out into the street. Most were clutching at unfastened
clothing and several had dark bruises on their arms and bewildered faces. Once more the captain held up his hand for
silence. "There is word," he said, "that a dangerous traitor in
league with this same Tayyib has entered the city already, in
disguise. Good people, beware of everyone you meet. Examine
each one carefully: who unmasks this disguised warrior earns
a golden reward from the gracious hand of the Holy Reader
himself."

Ajjibawr gritted his teeth angrily, wracking his brains for a
weapon or a way to help the Tayyib. If they were searching
old men now, it would not be long before they considered old
women. He pulled on the balky mule's halter and tried to worm

his way out through the press of people. Perhaps he could get
help from Halila's household. He was almost at the edge of
the throng when the crowd surged back, and he was once more
pinned in place. Horsemen were trotting into the market square,
a small company of six with the banner of Vahn overhead.
They were dressed in the heavy leather armor of their country,
sewn all over with shiny metal discs and were wearing tall felt
hats and gold earrings. The leader spurred his horse forward
and held up his hand, coughing in the dust and speaking hoarsely.

"We have had news of your victory," he said. "We are come
to take the prisoner to Vahn. Long has Bodrum desired the
pleasure of seeing the Tayyib's head on a spike above his gate."

The Captain of the Karabdin Guard looked sullenly up at
him. "Wait, and you can have his head to take back and not
bother with the care of a prisoner on your journey."

"Bodrum desires to remove it with his own hands. We have
had our orders these many months."

"Too bad, then, that you did not capture him yourself."

"By treaty you are under us, and therefore what your men
accomplish they do in the name of Bodrum."

The Vahnian captain pulled his horse in a tight, impatient
circle, drawing his long sword as he turned. "Bring us our
prisoner," he said and the Karabdin captain angrily made to
obey. For a moment Ajjibawr could see directly up into the
Vahnian captain's face and with a shock he recognized young
Shadith beneath the darkened skin and hair. Hope leapt up and
he looked at the others, but hope died as he saw them to be
just as they appeared, mercenaries from Vahn. Adaba was
pushed forward, still bound, and Shadith placed the point of
her long sword against his shoulder, and poked him back against
the guards.

"So, the old dog is leashed at last." She flicked the sharp
point across his face, lifting one bloodmatted lock of hair and
letting it drop again. "If it were not for my master's orders, I
could take his head now, or perhaps one of his eyes." She
touched the point against his swollen cheek, moved it delicately
up against his lid, then dropped it again against his heaving
chest. "We have many an old score to settle, he and I. This
journey to Vahanavat will be a pleasant one, I think. Who is
the brave man brought him in?" Talal stepped forward proudly.
"You may ride with us, if you like. My master will reward
you with a full heart." Talal looked at his captain, and the

other nodded. Shadith nodded curtly to one of her men, and they brought up a packhorse and roughly bundled Adaba aboard, tying his feet uncomfortably tight beneath its belly. She smiled at his discomfort, and when he looked her straight in the eyes, she laughed, showing very white teeth. Once more she poked him with her sword. "You will learn what it is to snap at the heels of Vahn. Come."

Talal scrambled onto the horse they brought him, and the small troop wheeled about and slowly cantered away, Adaba being thrown forward and back helplessly to the motion of his horse. The captain looked after them in baffled anger, robbed of his triumph and his prisoner, then went inside and closed the gates behind him. Slowly the crowd dispersed, and the market square returned to sleepy quiet.

Ajjibawr did not know what shook him more, his old friend's danger or the unimaginable treachery he had witnessed. Or perhaps not treachery. Had the tale of Captain Howanis been a story only, a way of tricking Adaba's confidence? Doubtless she had betrayed him into last night's battle and also revealed Ajjibawr's own presence in the city. The old wolf of the Tayyib, betrayed and taken by a girl of sixteen years. What a reckoning they would have when he gathered the Tayyib's men and rode for a rescue. More than ever he shrank from meeting Halila again, but for the Tayyib's sake there was no time to waste: he would need a weapon at least before he left the city. And whatever she might say, it would not be like Shadith. There could be no question of any betrayal. He turned down her street and forced himself to walk up to her window, where he rapped on the shutter lightly. He rapped again, and it opened.

The same servant looked out as yesterday, a kindly-faced woman he did not recognize. She smiled. "We were hoping you would return. Oils are in short supply this year, and many of our distillations are ready. There are so many brigands beset the trains from Vahn. Wait, I will come down." A moment later she was at the garden gate. "Bring in your beast and tie it to that ring. There is hay and water there. Come, follow me." The garden was cool, untouched by the sun until noon or later, with graceful tall bushes, late drooping roses tied up along the walls and neat paths of white stone winding between the flower beds. He tied up the mule by a stone trough full of water, where it began tearing hungrily at the hay. He undid

the pack and followed the servant across the garden, up wide
shallow stairs and through the tall folding wooden doors into
the high-ceilinged porch that ran along the garden side of the
house.

There was a large round pool in the middle of the room,
raised a few feet from the floor with a broad stone lip. Some
flowers floated on its surface, and there was a flash of fish
within. On a low table by the outer door stood many bottles
and jars; above on strings hung bunches of drying flowers and
herbs awaiting distillation. The room was cool and sweet smelling, and Ajjibawr remembered with a sudden pang the curious
mixture of pungent herbs Halila had always worn as her own
scent. As he set out his little flasks, his hand trembled. There
was a light step behind him, and he turned unwillingly.

Halila crossed the room slowly and sat down on the edge
of the pool, drawing her deep blue skirt around her. A thin
silk scarf of the same blue fell from her head to her waist; the
hair that showed around her face was perfectly white. She
folded her hands in her lap and looked at him with unchanged
dark blue eyes; an old woman, but never lovelier.

"You have brought us goods from Vahn?" she said and
Ajjibawr nodded dumbly, feeling a sudden warmth in his face.
"No need to look so stricken," she said. "We do not ask their
provenance. Enough that they reach their destination at last,
despite the perils of the journey. What have you here?" Ajjibawr
took up the various vials and described their contents, and
Halila nodded quietly. She looked at her drying flowers and
made some calculations in her mind, then selected and nodded
to her servant. "Take these flasks to the storage room and see
they are put away carefully. Then bring me my strongbox."
The woman nodded and left, leaving them alone; Ajjibawr
turned away.

"Show me your other things," said Halila. "What have you
in shell?" Ajjibawr took out a cleverly carved comb, with ships
and sea serpents beautifully detailed, and held it for her inspection without coming too close. She took it gravely and
examined it against the light.

"Strange," she said, "how things return from our past to
disturb our present. I could have sworn this comb belonged to
Shalimi Mekrive, third wife to the Tayyib, dead these past five
years. Have you anything else? What about that ring?"

Ajibbawr touched the double thread of silver he wore on the last finger of his left hand. "It is not for sale. It was a gift to me."

"Surely a pedlar will sell anything?"

"Anything that is for sale. But this was given me twenty-two years ago on the eve of my wedding, and loyalty is not for sale."

Halila looked down at her hands and twisted her own silver ring around her finger. "Perhaps because there is no market for it?"

He spread his hands. "Perhaps it is as you say."

Before Halila could answer, a young servant girl came hurrying in. She stopped when she saw Ajjibawr and looked at her mistress with wide eyes. Halila smiled. "It is all right, child, you may speak freely to me."

"My lady, there is more news of the Tayyib." Ajjibawr looked up sharply. "He was yielded up to Vahn as we heard, but it was a trick! The man who captured him, Talal, has just been returned to the city, tied to a horse, and they say his right hand has been cut off, and a message was pinned to his clothing. It said that his hand was taken because with it he had struck the Tayyib. And that the debt would not be called clear until they had taken his head, fairly, in battle."

Halila smiled dryly. "Fairly. I suppose that means when he has learned to use a sword left-handed." She shook her head, then lifted her hand in dismissal. "Go, child, and do not chatter too loudly of these things."

The servant left, and Halila looked back into Ajjibawr's face. "So, there is some loyalty yet." She lifted the comb and held it out to him. "Take this back to the Tayyib. If he lives much longer, he will need another bridegift."

Ajjibawr dropped to his knees before her and buried his face in his arms against the edge of the pool. Halila broke the brief silence. "Did you really think I would not know you? I knew you when I looked from my window yesterday to watch my visitor depart, and saw an old woman steal a kiss from a foolish girl." She laughed. "Such a risk, my love, and for so small a reward."

"I came to your window yesterday."

"I did not feel strong enough to see you yesterday."

Ajjibawr looked up. "Were you frightened?"

"Yes."

"I also."

"Clearly." She tenderly touched his cheek with her hand. "So rough for an old woman."

He kissed her hand and held it in between his own. "You and the Tayyib are agreed on that point. How has it been with you, these past eight years?"

Halila placed her free hand over his. "Not bad, at first. It was always pleasant in my encampment, good water and grass and much to keep me busy. And messages from the outlaw Clerowan to cheer me from time to time. But once I was made to move here, life became less pleasant. I do not care for the city; there is only a small garden to keep me occupied, and of course, there were no messages."

"I sent them still, and wondered that they were not answered. I did not know why until three weeks ago, when Adaba met me in Rym Treglad."

"You made the trip in three weeks? It has been eight years. Why such haste to return, now?" She gently touched the back of his neck. "You are learning to bend a little, after all these years?"

He straightened up and looked at her, then took her face gently between his hands and kissed her. "My neck is as stiff as ever. But there were too many signs to be ignored, even for one so foolish as I. Can it be of any help now to say that I never should have left?"

She stooped forward and pressed his head against her. "No, it cannot help now. Have you forgotten what I asked when you left? I asked you not to widow me again, who had been widowed once by you before."

When the servant returned with the strongbox, Halila and her visiter were sitting apart on the edge of the pool. She counted out the coins carefully and handed them over, then directed the servant to leave them alone until dinnertime. "This pedlar has traveled far. You will spread a rug for her in the garden where she may rest before setting out again." The servant nodded and left, and Ajjibawr looked at Halila curiously.

"You do not trust your own servants?"

"All of them, no. Many were supplied me from the royal household."

"How often does this Dzildzil importune you?"

"He visits nearly every day, or has for the past few weeks. But he does not importune me. He talks, I listen, and finally he goes, vowing to change my mind the following day. It is only a small disturbance in my calm."

"He has not threatened?"

"Nothing that could make me fear. You may hear for yourself when he comes today."

"I have a better idea." Ajjibawr stood up and stooped over to take her hand. "Send out those servants you do not trust. Then let me take your place today. I have heard interesting rumors in the camp of the Tayyib. I think I can make an agreement with the Holy Reader that will bring him to his defeat."

Halila smiled but shook her head. "I should love to see this, but it is impossible."

"It is possible." He drew one fold of her veil across her face. "The Widow Halila will be modestly attired, with downcast eyes and for once a decorous tongue. At least she will seem that way at first." He kissed her forehead. "Hurry and call the servants. We may not have much time. And perhaps you can teach me how to sit. Adaba was not able to explain what I should do with my arms. They always seem too long."

The Widow Halila received the Holy Reader that afternoon on her long, low porch, dark-shuttered against the sun. The only light lay in narrow stripes across the polished stone floor, and the lady sat in a carved chair inlaid with ivory, set near the pool. As was his custom Dzildzil strode in and stood opposite, arms folded behind his back and legs spread out a little. He was silent until the young serving girl had poured out the coffee and set the cups on their small brass tray, and bowed and left. He took up the cup impatiently. "Have you considered since yesterday?"

The widow gazed serenely into the water's depths, her cup untouched on the fountain's lip beside her. "There is no freedom from the chains of mind, except one were a bird upon the wind," she quoted in a low voice and crumbled a bit of bread into the water.

Dzildzil sat down in his chair. "I do not need poetry quoted at me. There are scholars enough in my own palace."

She looked up. "But was it not your own namesake Dzildzil who wrote, 'The desert has bred up warriors numberless as the sands: it is time to nurture wise men now as numberless as the stars?' How many wise men have you my lord?"

Dzildzil set down his cup. "I did not come here in the dust and heat of noon to talk philosophy. I have come for an answer."

"There are no answers short of the final answer. I am an old woman, my lord. Soon I may die. Was it not the first Dzildzil who also wrote, 'Let woman take one older than herself?'"

"Did you follow those teachings when you married the last Karif?"

"He had killed my husband, and I was not then accustomed to being a widow. Yet I paid for my own folly, for did not the first Dzildzil also say, 'Who plants the seed must be prepared for the fruit?' I should want someone steadier now, if I married again."

"I am not as the old Karifs."

"This is true." The Widow Halila crumbled a little more bread onto the water. "Yet the old Karifs had one virtue at least. Neither took another wife while he lived, and I was always held in honor."

"If they never took others in name, you and I both know well that they took others in fact. But they would not have insulted your family any more than I. Even the Holy Reader may respect the Shibayi." He paused. "But greatly as I respect them, do not think I will meekly allow you to live on comfortably in this place, flaunting my wishes. You have said yourself you are an old woman. Do you wish to spend you last years comfortably or not?"

The Widow Halila's hands tightened in her lap. "What is my comfort compared to yours, my lord? There are younger women in my tribe who would welcome the Holy Reader's suit."

"But they are not former Karives, and that twice over. Alliance with me will return you to power."

"It would not be without benefit to you also, my lord."

"I have not denied that. I am prepared to be generous, however. I shall honor your wishes so far as is possible, once we are married and your family has at last pledged loyalty to me."

"My family and my family's family. The Great Shibayi. They have never been invited to the capital, my lord. How then may they pledge their loyalty?"

"If you will give me your promise, they shall be allowed to come and witness it."

"Very well, my lord, you will have it, upon that and one other condition."

Dzildzil was silent a moment. "You have finally consented?"

"Call for my family to come, and we will stand up before them and before all the people and I will accept publicly the one who is ruler of all the Karabdu, giving him the seal of acceptance that has always been my family's to give. My other condition is a simple one. That the more may witness our union, I wish for the ceremony to take place not in town but at the foot of the great image of Vazdz."

Dzildzil stood up. "I am glad that you have seen reason. It did not please me to think of having to punish one of your venerable years. How soon can you be ready?"

"As soon as the Shibayi may be gathered in the city."

"Very well. I will send you word when it is to be." He nodded and strode out of the room.

No sooner had the doors swung to behind the Holy Reader than the Widow Halila tore off her veil and flung it to the floor with a savage sounding expression. The tray of coffee cups might have followed it, but for the arrival of the true Halila who laid a hand on his arm. "Softly, my dear. He was quite amiable today."

"How has he threatened you before?"

"In a most ridiculous manner. I, who can neither cook nor clean, he threatens with being a servant in his palace."

"If he lives, I will have him for a stable boy, and you may give him orders."

"Then your horses will suffer as much as he."

He laughed and put his arm around her. "You have spoiled my fury." He drew her closer and pressed his face against the top of her head, in the soft fragrant coil of hair. "We shall win out, you and I. If Dzildzil orders things before I have returned from making arrangements with the Tayyib, you will know how to spin matters out until I can return. It should not be more than a few days, however. I doubt he can muster all the tribes of the Shibayi so soon."

She nodded, then gasped as he tightened his arms. He released her hurriedly, and she smiled. "It is nothing—a small pain that comes under my heart. I will not have it much longer." She pushed him back. "You must dress and go before the servants return."

Hastily Ajjibawr resumed his original disguise and left the cool house and garden for the shimmering heat of the streets. He raised a hand in brief farewell to Halila, watching from the latticed window, then turned towards the valley entrance. There was a large armed guard now at the outer end of the pass, but he was allowed to go on through without any trouble. By evening he was well away, and before full night he had reached the edge of the narrow defile.

A sentry stopped him with harsh words, and he answered harshly. "Where were you when your master was taken?"

The other jumped off his horse and took the mule's bridle in his hand. "Is it you, Karif? Truly, the fault was not ours. He heard of a small train passing and he vowed to pick it clean. It was chance brought an army upon him and his bodyguard. But he has returned safely. Have you not heard? He is here, and he awaits you!"

"I have heard." He pulled off his uncomfortable robes and bundled them onto the mule. "Bring this beast down. I will borrow your horse." Dressed only in his long tunic he swung aboard and delighted to feel the free evening air on his bare arms as he slowly cantered down the sandy slope. He entered the encampment and two boys, seeing him, ran to take the news to Adaba's tent. When he dismounted, the Tayyib was standing there in his open doorway, arms spread wide in welcome.

"You are come in good time, Karif." His voice boomed through the quiet encampment. "Tonight we celebrate my wedding."

Ajjibawr threw back his head and laughed, then turned to the sentry trotting towards them on the mule. He thrust his hand into the pack and rummaged around, finally drawing out the comb of shell. "Halila bid me return this to you. She said that if you lived you would soon need a bridegift again."

Adaba took it, and as he turned back towards the tent Ajjibawr could see that he limped from his beating, and his face was swollen and discolored. But his laugh rang as heartily as ever. "It is a fine comb, I remember it well. But the bride has no more hair than a boy. Ah well, she can use it for her horse's tail." He took Ajjibawr inside and summoned a servant to bring the Karif proper robes. He helped him draw them on, then pulled him through to the farther division of the tent, where a feast was spread along a long narrow rug. Shadith stood there near the charcoal brazier, still dressed as a boy but handsomely so in a long embroidered shirt of soft blue cotton belted with gold-embroidered leather. She smiled broadly for the first time since Ajjibawr had seen her, and when he took her hands and kissed her forehead to give his blessing to her, she blushed and dropped her eyes.

Adaba looked at her proudly. "You should have seen her play her part this morning. She has a brain to match her courage!"

"I did see." Adaba and Shadith both looked up, surprised. "I was in the crowd and cursed the seeming treachery."

Adaba raised an eyebrow, then grimaced at the pain, touching his bruises tenderly with one hand. "I will confess, I lost faith for a moment. The company she led was not of ours."

"So I could see."

"She captured them just after I was taken and held their captain hostage here for proof of their behavior. Until we were safely distant from the capital, she kept up the pretense, and when she drew her sword, I thought, now my head also will roll in the sands as I have caused so many others to do. But no, she severed my bonds, and then, as Talal started to draw his own blade, she cut off his hand as neat as might be, saying it was because he struck me with it." He looked at her proudly and shook his head delightedly. "Tomorrow we will campaign again, but tonight all is in honor of the Tayyib's truest body-guard and final wife."

So they sat and ate, and Adaba caused there to be singing and dancing, apologizing to Shadith for the poorness of the entertainment and promising a finer celebration when they returned to his encampment. She said little in return, looking from time to time into his face with such a fierce devotion that Ajjibawr was taken aback.

At the end, when coffee had been brought and the fires had died down, Ajjibawr touched the Tayyib lightly on the sleeve. "I will not disturb you tonight with talk of politics. But some things you must know, that we might discuss them tomorrow." Briefly he described the situation in the desert capital, and his plan for tricking Dzildzil. "We must send word to Halila's kinsmen before they are summoned by Dzildzil. I would also talk with some of these Marajites of whom I have heard, for I feel that the religious schism between them and the Holy Reader can be turned to our advantage. With them and the

Shibayi we can open the doors to the valley, front and back, and bring in your faithful men before Dzildzil is aware."

Adaba nodded. "I am not overly fond of these Marajites with their talk of forgiveness, fasting and penitence. But they may prove a useful tool. It is good that the Shibayi are to be summoned. The Holy Reader tried once to break their power. Now they will help break him. Dzildzil will wish he had left the Karive in peace, and not sought for greatness beyond his station." He smiled at Shadith. "And I may suffer for my foolhardiness also."

He took up the marriage goblet that waited alone in the center of the feast and drank from it, then held it to her lips. She covered his hands with her own and tilted it back to finish it. He nodded approvingly. "You already know how it is to cut off a man's head. Tonight I will show you how to cut out one's heart." He drew her to her feet, nodded courteously to Ajjibawr, and ignoring the others drew Shadith with him beyond the curtains into the inner chamber.

THE ODE OF ADABA TAYYIB

Here in these hills of sand where we made our camp
I draw rein and stop, calling the years to mind:
the places where our tents once stood and the cooking fires
     burned
are bare and swept by the wind, nothing but circles of black
     ash left.
It was loud here once with the sound of our sheep and our
     goats,
with horses calling for grass in the hungry morning and chil-
     dren crying
but the sand does not remember us, we are gone as we never
     were.
Over the land we pass as lightly as the wind
and we leave windlike no memory of our ever having been.
So too my life will blow away, an empty tent abandoned.

There is no comfort in these hills for an old man:
the young girls with their hair like the sun shine otherwhere.

Mirar with her red lips and three sons is no more
and her sons have their own sons, their own tents and their
      horses.
Shalimi whom I stole at night, riding her father down
and wounding her brothers carelessly—how I laughed to pay
      their price
sending them stolen gold while we drank from the same cup—
she is gone also. And Yashir the slave from Vahn, who danced
and left her master to travel on alone, and taught me to sing—
but my voice is cracked now and harsh like the wind, and she
      is dead.

Numberless as the stars they shine on our passing
while we like restless comets wander, no part of the sky
to call our house: what need have they of an old man,
with tents and flocks and children to call about them?
Here in these hills of sand where we made our camp
I draw rein, and wonder who will mourn my going.
The sword that fits my hand? The stirrup that knows well
the weight of my foot? Perhaps the speckled horse
who will drink at the pool and wander away unnoticed
when Death has taken his bridle out of my hand.

Chapter Five

The day of the Holy Reader's wedding dawned clear and blue.
By the time it had begun to get hot, vast crowds were already
assembled, carrying baskets of bread and skins of wine in
pleasant anticipation of a festival day. They settled at the foot
of the enormous statue of Vazdz, which stood in a niche carved
out of the rock of the valley wall, more than two hundred feet
in height. The wings that spread out on either side of the head
glistened with fresh gilding, as did the flame he held balanced
in one great hand and the round crown held in the other. The
face that had been blank years past was covered now with a
mask of pure gold, enameled in black with the chief teachings
of Vazdz as set down by the first Holy Reader. As the crowd
waited, the slight breeze changed direction, and the heavy smell
of the town began to drift over. Heavily armed, the Royal
Guard sat motionless horses along one side of the gathering,
watching with suspicion the numbers of proud Shibayi tribesmen who had come at Dzildzil's invitation.

At length the Holy Reader appeared, drawn in his chariot;
he was helped to alight and stood in the bright sun proudly,
clutching his short rod of office in one hand. From the recesses
in the cliff behind him, where stairs and tunnels led up through
the cliff to a passage, which gave on the desert outside, the
Widow Halila appeared, attended only by an old woman dressed
in black and heavily veiled. She herself was dressed in cloth
of gold as the Holy Reader had instructed her: she seemed to

falter as she went to stand beside him, and her attendant steadied her with a hand under her arm.

Now Dzildzil could be heard, an impassioned speech full of the workings of Vazdz and the inevitable success of those who did his will. At long last he touched upon the purpose that had drawn them all together. Halila of the Shibayi, wisest and noblest of women, twice Karive of all the Karabdu, had accepted him and now added her acclamation to theirs. He closed his fingers on Halila's wrist and drew her forward, to make her obeisance first to Vazdz and then to Vazdz's chief servant, the Holy Reader Dzildzil. He pointed graciously to the cushion on which she might kneel and Halila looked down at it for a long moment while the crowd waited. The fitful breeze lifted her veil and spread it out on the air behind her, and there was a faint odor of smoke, passing over the crowd almost unnoticed. She looked a little longer, than spat contemptuously on the cushion and turned to face the people. Deep amid the crowd there was a rasp of metal as the Shibayi drew their swords. Those who were unarmed began to hastily move away, pushing and shoving in their anxiety. Dzildzil did not move at first, then raised his staff to strike the old woman down. The staff was struck from his hands, and he turned to face Halila's attendant, now dressed in white, the black overcloak in a heap around his feet. He screamed for his bodyguard, but the panicked crowd was between him and his protection. Ajjibawr reached forward deliberately and took him by the ear, twisting it until he was bent half over, and dragged him up to stand before Halila, facing the crowd also. Halila raised both hands, and this time there was perfect silence as her voice carried to the farthest listeners.

"You have come to see me acclaim the leader of the Karabdu. I will not disappoint you. The Karif Ajjibawr, Mekrif of the Ziliman, has returned from exile. The story of his death was false. Now smell the stink of the city behind you and decide. Will you live as this creature would have it"—and she pointed at Dzildzil, still writhing in Ajjibawr's stern, ignominious grip—"or clean and free as our ancestors have done?"

Ajjibawr threw Dzildzil roughly to the ground and bent his head to receive Halila's kiss on his forehead. The Shibayi cheered and held their swords up: light flashed on their blades, and two or three of the Royal Bodyguard nervously shed their weapons and dismounted. The others grouped more closely together, however, anxiously looking about for other members of Dzildzil's troops. They saw a movement from within the city and cheered themselves, for a small group was riding towards them from the town, under the gold and white banner of Dzildzil; over the town itself the air was curiously dark.

At that moment, however, there was a roar and rush of hoofbeats echoing on rock behind them, and one by one an army began to pour out of the cliff, like a spring of water leaping out into the light, horseman after horseman, Tayyib, Killala, Ziliman, men of all the great tribes with swords held up, shouting the name of the Karif. The back entrance to the valley had been opened to an army of conquest, while the bulk of Dzildzil's own forces were far away, awaiting alliance with Tredana.

The army of invasion spread out in two long wings on either side of the Karif, their clothing bright and their horses dancing. At this, the Royal Bodyguard began to back up in close formation, looking in desperation towards their faraway reinforcements still approaching from the city. As they did so, another army appeared, spilling into the valley from the far side, partly forcing a way among the buildings, partly spreading out to surround Dzildzil's small mounted force. One of the bodyguard, bold with desperation, jumped his spotted horse over the tumble of men at his feet and charged the Karif, his sword held high. Ajjibawr stood quietly to meet his attack, then ducked the blow and seizing the man's leg, tossed him onto the ground. In a moment he had the sword from the man's hand and had pulled himself onto the horse. It fretted in a tight circle, almost trampling the wretched Dzildzil, who had covered his head with his arms and lay there motionless. Ajjibawr raised his sword, and his people cheered. He forced the horse mincingly sideways over to where Halila stood and leaning over swung her up as though she were a girl. When they were both secure in the saddle, he turned to address the crowd. Already a black round column of smoke was rising from one portion of the city.

"Look behind you," he cried. "The palace burns already, and the rest of the city follows before nightfall. We are Karabdu and need no roofs between ourselves and the sky; nor any protection from the will of Vazdz. And look before you, up into the hillside." He swept widely with his hand, and all could see that the many caves and crevices of the fissured cliff were filled with dark-clothed figures. "These are your brethren too, whom Dzildzil would have murdered one by one, the followers of Maraj to whom I have given the valley. They have no need of the city which cast them out, however. Take what you must from your homes, but quickly: the valley shall be clear by night, and no wall nor roof nor doorway shall stand to see tomorrow's sun. You all had tribes once; return to them now. The Karabdu will live like men and not like cattle."

Anxiety seized the crowd, and there was a sudden uproar and a rush back towards the city, where Adaba's men were posted to supervise an orderly retreat, firing each section as the homes were emptied of people and livestock. The last of Dzildzil's men were bound, and the Holy Reader himself, shaking and weeping, was hauled to his feet by young Masala to stand before the mounted Karif.

Ajjibawr looked down at him coldly. "I have promised you already to my wife, as a stableboy. Masala, see he is securely chained, and show him his duties when we return to camp. He shall learn to work, and doubtless Vazdz will lighten his sufferings with many wise sayings, spoken directly into his ear as has been his wont these past eight years."

To Halila he spoke more softly. "Do you desire to save anything from your house?"

"I need nothing. My servants will be brought to camp?"

"Of course."

"Then I am ready to leave."

Slowly they cantered across the gritty plain, and as they drew level with the outer buildings of the settlement, the horsemen standing guard lifted spears and swords in salute. On the far side they found Adaba, moodily overseeing the city's destruction, Shadith at his right hand carrying a sword.

Leaving his lieutenants to continue their work, Adaba brought his horse up next to Ajjibawr's. "In a week's time, O Karif, we will be able to gallop an army one hundred horses wide across this plain in both directions."

"That is well. But we will not bring our forces here again. I have given the valley over as I said. The followers of Maraj will not allow cities to grow nor armies to pass; so long as they live and study here, we may be certain that the valley is free of corruption. Who guards the outer gate?"

"Your own people, Karif, the Ziliman. They are few in number, but they have cause to be fiercer than any others. They have set up camp for you already, and for the lady Halila."

"Will you join us there tomorrow? There is still much to discuss."

"Tomorrow then."

As they reached the entrance in the cliffside, Adaba saluted and wheeled about back towards the burning city, and Ajjibawr set his horse at an easy pace along the stony incline. In the dark of the tunnel he drew Halila a little closer against him, and she suddenly sighed, half turning to rest her face against his shoulder. "I have dreamed of this often," she said, "but never thought to live to see it. Is the city gone in truth?"

"By nightfall, entirely. Let a few seasons wash it clean, and it will once more be a pleasant place."

"I will be glad to die as I was born, free, with no walls around me."

"And so shall I when the time is come, but surely it will not be soon for either of us."

Halila turned a little in his arm. "In the ordinary run of things, it should be sooner for me by twenty years; but I fear it will be sooner still than that." His left arm encircling her held the reins behind her back. She took his right hand and laid it flat against her left side. "I am turning to stone while I live. It started here"—she touched her breast—"and grew in a few months from a small spot to a space as wide as my hand. That was a year ago. Now my whole side is corrupted, and there are small places on the right as well. I do not know how long before it reaches the heart. I cannot move my left arm easily; I awake in pain every morning and lie down in pain every night. Trapped in the city, I would have made an easy death for myself, except that I lived to speak with you again and see you take your proper place once more. And my wishes have been fulfilled."

Ajjibawr harshly jerked on the reins and the horse stopped, throwing up its head in protest. Under his hand her side was stone-hard as she had said, filled with an unnatural warmth. Even his gentle touch made her wince, and he hastily took away his hand, bringing it up in a caress against her neck. For many minutes they sat there, she with her face buried against his shoulder, and he with his against her hair. Finally he raised her face and kissed her, setting the horse forward with a light

pressure of the knees. "Whatever can be done, shall be," he
said, and they rode out into the sunlight on the farther side.

There the Ziliman warriors waited, and when they saw their
Mekrif they raised their spears and shouted. As Ajjibawr cantered up, they fell into formation around him, and a young man
drew alongside, bowing deeply from the waist as he rode, a
wide grin splitting his face. "We have made camp not far from
here. All awaits the pleasure of the Karif."

Ajjibawr nodded and following the young man's lead they
crossed a narrow plain of soft sand and climbed a short hill
protecting a deep valley with water and trees at the bottom. A
great tent had been pitched a little apart from the others, with
rugs spread all around it on the ground; already food was
cooking. In the center Ajjibawr brought his horse to a quiet
stop and gently handed Halila down. "See that you find me a
better horse than this spotted one for tomorrow, and an ambling
mare for the lady Halila. If we do not have an ambler here in
camp, you have my permission to steal one from the Tayyib."
The young man grinned again and bowed obediently, taking
the reins of Ajjibawr's horse. At the tent, Halila's youngest
servant waited, still breathless from her journey slung over a
warrior's galloping horse. She needed no urging to take care
of her mistress, and Ajjibawr left them alone together.

When he stepped out of the tent, a familiar face greeted him,
Emr, once of his bodyguard. Emr bowed as though there had
been no lapse of years since he had last served the Karif and
took him around to show how the camp was fixed, for men
and supplies. Ajjibawr nodded in approval as each arrangement
was described to him. "It is well. We will stay here some few
days, until we have made all necessary plans with the Tayyib;
then we must ride for the southern shore and see to the repairing
of the great glass furnaces there. Our friend Rassam the Traveler will be joining us before then; he will direct matters at the
furnaces." Emr nodded unquestioningly.

"The Lady Halila and I do not wish for a public meal tonight.
Let the feast go on as planned, but see we are brought our food
privately, in the tent. How many hounds are here?"

Emr counted rapidly on his fingers. "Ten bitches trained for
chase, two dogs and seventeen puppies."

"Choose me the largest and gentlest of the bitches, one with straight hind legs and simple markings. She will be for the Lady Halila, so choose accordingly and bring her to my tent tonight." Emr nodded again and silently accompanied him back to the tent signaling a young man to stand guard with drawn sword by the entrance, as he went to carry out the Karif's wishes.

Within the tent Ajjibawr spoke to the young servant, who sat silently in the outer room. "You may go. I can attend to the Karive's wishes."

The girl spoke up timidly. "She sleeps, Karif."

"It is well. I will not disturb her. Have you powders for her? For sleeping?" The girl shook her head. "Then speak with Emr and have him bring me some, when the food is brought. Now go." She hurried out, and he paused a moment before lifting the inner curtain. Halila was sleeping heavily, turned on her right side. Her white hair spread out on the pillow was not much lighter than the palest gold it had once been; her face was smooth except for small lines near the eyes. The thin wool blanket had slipped down in her turning; Ajjibawr carefully pulled it up over her shoulder then turned his head hastily aside so his tears would not fall on her face and awaken her.

Later that evening Emr appeared and supervised the servants, who set up a simple supper in the outer room, silently, while Halila slept on. Pressed closely to his legs was a wonderfully tall and graceful hound, with a luxuriant white coat irregularly blotched dark grey and black. Her narrow noble head was on a level with Emr's waist and within the tent she moved delicately, her tail tucked decorously under her high arched back. Ajjibawr raised his hand for her to lie down, and she flipped one small ear forward in a comical expression of attention, then obediently collapsed in a graceful curve on the floor. He nodded. "You have chosen well." Emr bowed and followed the servants out. Later Halila awoke, and although she would not eat, he forced her to drink a little wine and take the powders Emr had provided. The bitch was called in for her approval, and it came up to her immediately, to sniff her outstretched fingers. The hound slid a sideways look at Ajjibawr, then trotted around to Halila's other side and fell to the ground with a sigh of relaxation, thrusting its slender head under her hand. Soon it was asleep, and Halila stroked the soft fur and smiled, saying little. Ajjibawr sat back against the pillows so

she could lean against him and carefully breaking a wide round
of bread into small pieces, he soaked them in the goblet one
by one and had her eat them. She laughed at his solicitude but
submitted, and in this way between them they ate most of one
flat loaf; but Halila suddenly choked and turned her face away,
covering it with her hands and sobbing bitterly.

Ajjibawr set the goblet aside in consternation so it spilled
unheeded onto the carpet. "What is wrong? I did not mean to
force you."

Halila shook her head. "I was remembering," she said in a
muffled voice, bending her head down against the hound's soft
side.

He turned her round to face him. "And I have never forgotten. At our wedding feast you fed me with you own fingers,
and I thought in my innocence that life could hold no greater
excitement. I learned I was wrong very soon, as I recall." She
smiled, and he used the edge of his sleeve to wipe her eyes.
"You taught me how to live when I was young. Perhaps it is
time now for me to learn the rest of my lesson. I know now
nothing lasts forever. You shall be my teacher again, and show
me how a good end may be reached." His voice broke on the
last words and he settled down farther against the pillows so
she could rest more comfortably. The powders had their effect
and she soon slept again, but he was left awake through most
of the long night.

Next morning Ajjibawr went out early, leaving Halila still
heavily asleep, to walk around his encampment in the first light
of day. The bitch trotted delicately at his heels. Thus he was
first even before the sentries to see a distant figure on horseback
come galloping through the oddly layered light of morning,
distorting as it approached until finally both man and horse
were close enough to hold both shape and color clearly. It was
Rassam the Traveler on a rangy black; and as his old friend
drew nearer and saw the Karif waiting for him, he stood in his
stirrups foolishly at full gallop, waving his arms above his head
and shouting aloud like a young warrior. He threw himself off
the horse before it had fully stopped and threw his arms around
Ajjibawr, almost lifting him from the ground. The hound drew
back in amazement.

"It is done! Ah, my brother, to see you as Karif again makes
my heart lighter by half its burden."

"How did you learn the news? When did you return to the Land?"

"I came ashore but yesterday, and bought this miserable beast from a village on the coast. As I rode nearby the valley, one of the Tayyib's sons cut across my path, all black with smoke and filled with the glorious news of your achievement. It was he directed my path towards your encampment. He also said to me that Dzildzil lives."

"If he has not been kicked to death yet. Come, I will show you." They walked over to the stable area where Masala, long awake, was supervising the feeding and grooming of his stock. Ajjibawr handed him the reins of Rassam's awkward, sweating horse. "Have the would-be-king see to this animal. It must be walked for an hour and thoroughly groomed. When it sleeps, you might give him a fan to keep the flies away."

Masala grinned and then bowed soberly. "It shall be as you say, O Karif." He took the bridle with great respect and summoned Dzildzil with a curt toss of his head. They watched for a moment, and then Ajjibawr put his arm around Rassam's shoulders.

"Come break your fast. There is coffee ready, better than any you have had these past few months. I know you bring much news, and I am eager for it."

They ate in silence and then settled back with their coffee. Rassam breathed deeply with delight and shifted his weight against the cushioned saddle that formed his support, looking out over the awakening camp. "I dreamed of such a return," he said, "but often it seemed that it would never come. Now, if only I could convince you to breed dogs as cleverly as you do horses . . ." Ajjibawr dropped his hand on the bitch's head, and she changed her already graceful sprawl for one even more beautiful, pushing her nose against his leg.

"Our hounds suit us well."

"But they are full of foolishness. Do you not remember my Sweetmouth? That was a dog. Intelligent!"

Ajjibawr smiled. "Our hounds are long of leg and large of eye, they are loyal, soulful and filled with the joy of the chase and the song of speed. It is for lesser dogs to be witty."

"Very well. I know I shall never convince you. You have had, of course, the great news from Tredana?"

"Only in brief, that our young friend Leron has ascended his father's throne."

"That is brief indeed. The story is better than that."

Rassam sketched the events in Tredana as he had heard them there, and Ajjibawr threw back his head and laughed with delight as he heard described the scene at Sacred Hill. "Would that I could have seen that!"

"You are not entirely uninvolved, Karif. The horse that Sibby took from the royal stable is your old grey, a gift from Dzildzil to Ddiskeard years ago."

"My horsemaster Mubassa was killed by Dzildzil because of that horse. It was one of the finest I ever had. It must be noble yet despite its age. I am glad she has it for her use. She is well, you say?"

Rassam nodded. "She is well and glad indeed to hear that your ship sailed on to Rym Treglad."

Ajjibawr mused a moment. "Our next step must be a council of kings, for winter will soon be come and gone, and spring will bring campaigning against Vahn. Where is Odric now?"

"He tarries in Tredana, awaiting the news from the desert."

"I will send a rider today with messages for all."

"If the Karabdu can hold the center, a sea-borne force could try and take Vahanavat, Tredanans and the Zanidai allied."

"The Zanidai? How does it then with Shirkah?"

"Well. He caught his brother cleverly, and put down the rebellion. It is a good story, which you must hear some time. One of the smaller ships from Vahn he intends to use to take certain families farther north, men he feels he still cannot trust: there he plans to leave them, well supplied, but without boats or timber, to build a fishing village to which he will send ships twice a year. The other small ship he placed at my disposal, retaining the *Damar* to lure still other ships from Vahn unsuspectingly into his harbors, should more be sent. At Tredana I went ashore more cautiously, and after meeting our friends there left the ship with Leron, for dearly he desired to have one noble ship at least; he sent me on my way in a swift small yacht, which put me ashore on the southern coast, and here I am."

"What news of Osmin and my men?"

Rassam sighed. "None, as yet. That Captain Gwillam, the same Clerowan knew well, is yet to surrender—he and his company of one hundred men roam free a little north of Tredana, and Osmin may have had to turn aside to avoid them."

"Osmin is wise to the ways of Gwillam. I am sure he will win through safely."

He cocked his head to one side slightly, listening, and behind him the hound lifted her head from her paws and raised her small grey ears. "There are many men riding this way. Either we are under attack, my friend, or the Tayyib comes as requested. He is away from camp early for a new-married man."

Rassam looked up in amazement. "Again?"

"This time is a little different." By the time he had told Rassam the story of Shadith, Adaba had arrived with a good company of fifty men.

Shadith was not in her usual place with the bodyguard, and Ajjibawr asked after her. Adaba waved his hand in the direction from which they had come. "She follows, a little more slowly, bringing you special prisoners, O Karif." He greeted Rassam warmly, threw himself heavily down onto the ground between them and accepted a cup of coffee. He shook his head and sighed. "Only now," he said, "do I realize what it is to be old." He did not elaborate, but Rassam raised his eyebrows at Ajjibawr and they both smiled.

Behind them the curtains parted, and Halila stepped out into the light. Before Ajjibawr could get to his feet, Adaba had turned and seen her; he smiled broadly and swiftly moved to kneel at her feet and take the hand she gave him. "Karive!" he said and kissed it. "Welcome to the Land again. Every year that I see you, you are grown more lovely."

She bent over and touched his head affectionately. "And every year I see you, you are married again. It is well I rejected your suit and married the old Karif, blackguard though he proved."

"If it were not for my vow, my suit would be open still."

"What vow is this?"

"In Shadith I have married my last wife. You will understand when you meet her. Now had I married you forty-five years ago, there might have been no other women in my tents."

"Perhaps." Halila laughed and turned to sit on a low chair brought by a servant for her. "But you would miss that army of sons."

Before she could sit, the hound had also to greet her, trying to stand and drop its long legs across her shoulders. She smiled but raised her hand, and the dog dropped down obediently,

heaving a sigh of disappointment. Then Halila gave her hand
to Rassam, welcoming him graciously, and lastly put her hand
over Ajjibawr's for a brief moment before accepting food from
her servants. She was dressed in her favorite blue, and except
for the darkness under her eyes, there was no sign of weakness
or pain in her serene face.

Adaba listened closely to Rassam's news, and shook his
head disapprovingly when he heard of Dzildzil working in the
stables. "Cut off his head and be done with it, Karif. You
cannot afford to let him fester in you like a wound." He turned
to Rassam. "Mark my words. We will live to regret it, if
Dzildzil is allowed to live on."

Ajjibawr gestured impatiently. "I cannot kill him now, in
cold blood. He will grovel and weep."

"Yes, and he will slit your throat too, if he has the chance.
You did not hesitate to kill the old Karif."

"That was in a fair fight. He opened a wound in my body
from shoulder to hip, before I cut off his head."

"Give Dzildzil a sword then, if it makes you happier."

"And hope he falls on it without my help? I doubt he knows
which end to hold." Adaba snorted contemptuously and Halila
broke the following silence.

"The old wolf is right, my lord. If you do not wish to do
it yourself, there are others to whom he owes the blood-price.
He killed Masala's father: let Masala then take his revenge."

"If he must die then I must do it, for I represent all the
Karabdu and thus all blood-prices will be paid. We will discuss
this later."

Adaba grunted an agreement then suddenly smiled as he
heard the sound of arriving horses. "Shadith must be here. Now
you will see my surprise. The king in Tredana will soon face
a far worse problem than you have here." He chuckled crypt-
ically, then rose to his feet as Shadith approached, followed
by two others of the bodyguard. She made a proud gesture
with her hand, and the young men behind gently pushed forward
their disheveled prisoner, who angrily twitched herself free of
their clasp and put up her hands to smooth the hair back from
her face.

Ajjibawr rose slowly and nodded his head. "So fate has
brought you back under the tents of the Karabdu."

"Fate! My escort and I were captured by brigands! I demand

to be taken before the Holy Reader! He will see that we are treated with due courtesy."

Ajjibawr controlled his twitching mouth and turned to Adaba, fumbling in his sleeve for his snuffbox. "Would it be wise, do you think, to grant her an audience with the Holy One so early in the morning? He is so busy with his duties." He found the box, flicked it open, took a pinch and sneezed.

Dastra's eyes suddenly opened wide as she recognized him, and she looked from one face to another in sudden shock. "But the Karif—is dead."

Ajjibawr gave her a little mocking bow. "You must not believe these rumors. Stories fly across the desert more swiftly than wind across sand. I have even heard that the usurper of the Tredanan throne was murdered by his own queen."

Dastra did not move but her large blue eyes widened as though in shock, and tears began running down her face. Adaba looked at her with bleak disfavor. "You will save the king much trouble if you cut off her head also," he said at last, and Dastra stepped back in real terror.

Ajjibawr shook his head. "He would not thank me for it, though it were in his best interests. He is not desert bred." He turned to Shadith. "See she is secured against escape. One of my wife's servants will see to her needs while she is our prisoner." He looked to Halila for confirmation and she nodded. "Where is this escort she mentioned?"

Shadith pointed back towards her horses. "He is still asleep from a blow to the head. We have him tied across a horse."

"Very well. Then see that he is also secured, and I will have him returned to Tredana also."

"It shall be as you say, Karif." She hurried her prisoner away, and Adaba watched her go with a fond expression.

He turned to Halila. "You see?" he said, and she smiled.

That morning the messages to be sent to Tredana were written; and tentative plans for a council were made, to include representatives from Tredana and the desert and Treclere. It was agreed also to keep the news of Shirkah's restoration in Zanida a close secret, so that Vahn might continue to send ships north. Rassam had Dansen's plans with him and he made ready to depart the following day for the southern coast, to oversee the restoration of the glass furnaces. That afternoon they saw the messenger off, and Ajjibawr returned to his tent alone to wrestle with the problem of Dzildzil. Halila joined him there and put her cool hands against his face.

"Eight years ago you never would have hesitated."

"Eight years ago I had never left the desert. My neck has not bent, but my heart seems somehow changed."

"You are learning your lessons with no further help from me."

He put his arms around her and they stood leaning together quietly. "No pain?" he asked, and she shook her head.

"None," she answered and although he knew that she lied he did not argue further.

At dinner that night he spoke with Adaba, and told him Dzildzil would die the following dawn. They debated giving him warning, and Adaba was against it. "Let the miserable wretch spend his last night in peace."

Ajjibawr laughed bitterly. "He will spend it more easily than I." After dinner they sat back and listened to one of Adaba's interminable stories, made more palatable for not having been heard for nearly a decade, and around them the noises of the camp settled into peaceful quiet. It was almost time to retire when a shout was raised from near the stables and a sound of running came through the dark.

One of Adaba's bodyguards threw himself prostrate before them. "The prisoners! They have escaped!" They sprang to their feet, and Adaba grabbed the man by the shoulders.

"Which prisoners? What of Shadith?"

"She is hurt, Mekrif. They have escaped all three." Adaba threw the man from him with a curse and followed by Ajjibawr and Rassam ran down towards the stables.

There, all was in an uproar, a confusion of torches and swinging lamp. Masala lay spread out on the ground, dying, a dagger in his back; Ajjibawr took his head on his knee but the young man could not speak and was coughing blood. Nearby Adaba stood with Shadith hanging limply in his arms; her pale hair was soaked with blood from a welt across her forehead. Dastra was gone and Dzildzil also; from what they could piece together her escort had freed himself and rescued them all. Adaba clutched Shadith to him with a desperate intensity, rocking back and forth. "I will cut off their heads myself," he roared, "and leave them for the rats and birds to devour."

In Ajjibawr's arms, Masala rallied a little. "Do not worry, Karif," he managed to whisper. "They stole the Traveler's black, and that poor piebald of yours. The two worst horses here. I know you will overtake them..." He laughed. "They did not need to use a knife. I would have given those horses to them..." He laughed again and coughed a little more blood and fell silent.

Ajjibawr laid him gently down when he was certain he was dead. In Adaba's arms Shadith had not stirred, and Ajjibawr had them bring wet cloths to lay across her head. He also summoned four of the bodyguard and told them to take horse immediately. "Try to bring the woman back if you can," he said, "but you may deal with the others as you see fit." They saluted and galloped off. He turned to Emr. "Bury the boy properly. We will tend to Shadith at my tents."

They walked slowly up the hill and carried Shadith into the tent. There they could see that she had been stabbed also, but high in the shoulder: Rassam helped Halila bandage the wound while Ajjibawr tried to comfort the Tayyib, but the old man's eyes were running freely and he kept making futile clutches at the hilt of his sword. "You see now," he said at last, "what good comes of sparing these dogs. Kill the enemy and be done with them!"

Ajjibawr watched Halila change the blood-soaked cloth across Shadith's head for a fresh one. "Yes," he said at last, "I see. And do not worry—we will not be over merciful again."

CONCERNING DEATH
from the teachings of Maraj (Rassam's translation)

By all the stars of nightime,
by penitent tears of sorrow,
by all the cares of living,
surely you have known our weakness;
surely you have seen our sickness;

Eager to begin the race
we set our faces to the wind;

there is no time to cross the space
between our hasty start
and wished-for end.

No advantage at the start
can change the end: no craft nor art
can alter what is written:
spur on your horse to speed, as fast
as he may run comes up the last
short race no riders win.

IV: SIEGE

Chapter One

Leron was crowned king in the Great Hall of the castle of Tredana, one week after the events on Sacred Hill. It was a week of endless attention to detail and a thousand and one decisions. First there was the question of loyalty. Then the morass of civil business to be entered into. The tax rolls were in abysmal order, and census records were in poor shape, rife with omissions and forgeries. In each of these matters Odric proved a valuable counsellor, and it made Leron sorry to hear him talk of returning soon to Treclere.

Word had been sent to Rym Treglad, but it would be weeks at least before Gannoc could be expected in Tredana. Not only would he have many matters to settle there: there was also the danger of the journey itself, since several large forces still loyal to Dastra roamed in the countryside north of Tredana, notably Gwillam and his one hundred men.

Perhaps Leron would not have felt so lonely and troubled had it been easier to understand Sibby—Sibyl, she called herself now. When she had returned that first night from looking for Dastra, he had swung her around, and they had embraced each other laughing on the hilltop. She was almost as tall as he, and he would never forget how good it had felt to have her in his arms. Alone in his chamber Leron sighed, looking sourly at the circlet of gold so recently placed on his head. It did not seem likely he would have the chance to feel her there again. She was as distant now as though she had never returned.

But the damage was done. He was at last understanding the truth in a song he had often carelessly sung.

> *I have seen a woman's arms white in the moonlight*
> *and never again shall I lie easy at night.*

Leron threw the circlet onto his empty narrow bed and went out into the corridor.

Below in the chilly antechamber to the Great Hall several men were respectfully waiting to bring their various affairs to the attention of the king. Leron nodded pleasantly but went past them into the open courtyard, with so determinedly abstract an expression on his face none dared break his silence. The Players were camped now within the palace walls, but Leron did not stop to speak with them either, although he returned the smile of Ginas's granddaughter. A pretty child, but short hair did not suit her as it did Sibby—Sibyl. It was not that Sibyl avoided him or was in any way aloof. She had been helpful and a wise voice in council—an excellent friend in every way. Leron realized he was scowling and hastily rearranged his expression. He had set out aimlessly on this walk, but seeing the captain of the Castle Guards hurry past he stopped him just inside the gates.

The captain saluted. "My men are holding some prisoners below, fishermen accused of smuggling and of secret agreements with the traders from Vahn. I was on my way to question them."

Leron fell into step beside him. "Very well. I will come and listen."

Below on the harbor's narrow strand a group of men stood near a tangle of nets between two long boats newly beached. The three fishermen were close together, sullen and defiant, reproaching the impassive young guardsmen who watched over them. Their leader, a stocky dark-faced man, turned bitterly on the captain as they approached. "Just tell us where you heard these stories, that's all I want to know. Me and the lads have fished these waters for thirty years and never a word was ever breathed about our doing anything but fish. Just tell me who accuses us." He turned to his companions. "I'll lay you odds it was Dikrat or his father. Ever since we ran afoul his nets he's had it in for us."

He suddenly noticed Leron and his face lit up. "Now where'd

you scare him up? There's one of the lads I was telling you
about. One of those spies I helped from off the Vahnian vessel.
Ask him, he'll tell you how I gave him breakfast. Speak up,
lad, tell the captain what really happened."

The captain looked at Leron in bewilderment, and Leron,
feeling very slow-witted, asked, "What is the story here?"

"These men have been accused of helping to land two spies
from off a Vahnian vessel. I am not sure what he means by
these last words . . ."

The fisherman shook his head and ran a hand over his thick,
greying curls. "Tell him, explain to the captain how it was."

"Friend, I do not understand what you are saying."

"Did the crash addle your wits so you've forgotten being
dried by my fire and fed with my breakfast?"

The captain stepped forward angrily. "You may not speak
like this!"

"I'll speak as I please, if this boy calls me a liar to my
face."

Leron put his hand on the captain's shoulder. "Softly, now."
He turned to the fisherman. "I do not know who you are nor
have I ever seen you before. Perhaps you can find another way
to answer the captain's questions."

"The truth's always been good enough for me. Happen
you'll be a stranger to it yourself."

The captain interrupted again. "You may not speak to the
king like this!"

"King is it? King, now? A funny sort of king this is, who
calls himself a fisherlad from Crommerton."

Leron suddenly laughed aloud, and they both looked at him
in surprise. "When was it you fed and dried out these two
lads?" he asked. "Was it the morning after the great storm, ten
days past?"

"Aye."

Leron turned to the captain. "Then this will be a fisherman
of whose kindness I have heard already. He helped a kinsman
of mine whom I greatly resemble. Your name is Nicca?" The
fisherman nodded, bewildered, partially appeased. Leron spoke
to the captain again. "Who brought this complaint against
Nicca?"

"Another fisherman, a certain Dikrat, who swore it was the
truth."

Leron nodded, then held out his hand to Nicca. "I am Leron,

and I am now the king. I thank you for your kindness to my cousin. Whatever you catch in the future, do not bother with at market but bring directly to my kitchens. I promise it will be bought, and always at a fair price. And tell Dikrat to bring any future complaints directly to me."

Nicca bowed awkwardly over his hand, then he and his friends clapped each other on the back and repeating their thanks made a hasty retreat. As Leron and the captain turned to go, Nicca's warm rough voice could be heard distinctly. "Now that was a queer business there, all right. But he's a proper lad, that one. Fair as fair."

Leron put his hand on the captain's shoulder. "It is a hard task, I know, but be suspicious of neighbors bringing complaints against neighbors. If those in power are too eager to believe in tales, then too many tales will be brought. I can condemn no man out of hand, however strong-seeming the evidence." The captain was clearly puzzled but he bowed his head submissively, and Leron checked an impatient sigh. He complimented the man for his loyalty and went back to the castle.

That night in the small dining room, after a meal shared with Odric, Kerys and Sibyl, Leron described the afternoon's incident. He shook his head gloomily. "Will they all be trying to even old scores by carrying tales to my men?"

Odric shrugged. "If it is as it was in Treclere, yes, for a while. After a few months matters will smooth out, your power will not seem so new, and life will go on as before."

Leron rested his chin on his hands. "We will have to work something out, by law. We cannot let the power of the throne be invoked for such trivial ends. There should be some way of settling disputes routinely and fairly."

Sibyl smiled at him. She was curled up in the big chair nearest the fire, with a brown cat lured from the kitchens asleep in her lap. "That was nice, what you told Nicca about the fish. I was hoping he would be rewarded somehow. I should have remembered him sooner."

Odric chuckled. "I would object that he must be a fool to have confused you, had I not been guilty of the same mistake myself. Yet to look at you now here together, the resemblence is strong but far from bewildering."

Leron tilted his head and looked at Sibyl critically. "They said the same of my mother and Sibyl's father. Brother and sister, alike when seen apart, yet different when seen together."

Sibyl looked at him as carefully. "When I look at you, it's like looking in a mirror: but the person behind the face is so different."

As she continued to look at him, Leron flushed and turned to Odric. "When do you plan to return to Treclere?"

"I already feel guilty to have been away so long. Perhaps within the next few days. I can leave Kerys here to wait for the news from the desert, and the results of your council with the Karabdu. Then he can follow after in that ship that Herrard brought. The navigator, Meladin, seems to have learned a little since he erred so badly when Sibyl was aboard. I can return the *Damar* to you in the springtime, filled with men."

Kerys, who had been moodily silent all evening, nodded ungraciously, and Odric looked at him in exasperation. "Whether you return in ten days or twenty, Kalla will doubtless be waiting eagerly for you. What difference can ten days make?"

Kerys jumped angrily to his feet. "You don't understand!" he finally managed in a thick voice, heading for the door.

It shut very loudly behind him, and Odric heaved a great sigh. "No, I do not understand. He conceives a sudden passion for this girl just as we leave and can talk of nothing else throughout the journey. If she is going to be untrue, I hardly think ten days can make a difference."

Leron said nothing, secretly commiserating with Kerys. Then Sibyl spoke up casually, bent over the cat and stroking its upturned stomach. "What do you think the news from the desert will be?" Her face was pink from the heat of the fire.

"I am sure it will be good," Leron answered. "Adaba Tayyib is a great warrior and would not have come for our Clerowan had the time in the desert not been right for a return. I am sure that when we next hear from Clerowan he will be once more Karif, and Ajjibawr again. The might of the desert will be a comfort in the coming campaign against Vahn." Odric nodded and Sibyl shifted her position, cradling the cat to keep it from awaking.

Suddenly the door clicked open and Kerys stood there, pale and silent. "There is . . . there is a messenger here . . ." he stammered and stood aside as two guardsmen entered holding the arms of a powerfully built man in chain mail and leather leggings. A large and heavy bag of stained green cloth swung from his belt.

Leron stood up slowly, and behind him Odric also rose to his feet. The warrior pulled himself free and stepped forward with an insolent twist to his mouth. "I came under the white flag from Gwillam. If you be after killing messengers, then I'll die with it unspoken."

Leron raised his hand. "You are free to speak and go."

The other laughed, showing all his teeth. "Well said, that. I have a present from my captain, taken but a few miles north of here from the last owner, and that fairly." He fumbled with the string that drew the bag shut. "He bid me give you this and say many will follow it." The bag was free of his belt and he held it up, prolonging the moment and chuckling deep in his throat. "Here, then, is the head of Clerowan the White: as fall the champions so too the armies will perish."

He spoke the last in a singsong voice, shaking the horrible burden clear of its cloth covering to fall with a dull thud onto the floor, rocking a little before it came to rest. There was a sudden smell of decay and a quick glimpse of bloody tissue, fair hair and one wide open blue eye before Leron could pull the heavy cloth off of the table and throw it over it.

In her chair Sibyl was bent over gasping into her hands: the cat leapt to the floor in consternation, then sat back and licked its shoulder, quickly regaining composure as Leron walked up to the messenger. He hit him so hard across the face he fell back against the guards and blood spurted from his lip. "You can take that answer back to Gwillam and tell him he knows where to come if he desires the full message. Now be off before someone cuts out your tongue." One guard seized him by the arms and pulled him out of the room while the other at a gesture from Leron gathered up the cloth and the thing it covered from the floor, following his companion out.

Leron turned and saw that Odric was bent over his chair and holding onto its back for support. The cat had come over to smell where the head had been, sniffing with its mouth half-open and its eyes wide. The hair along its back stood up, and it rapidly turned and trotted out after the others. Sibyl had not moved. He went up to her chair hesitantly and dropped to his knees. At first she stayed bent over, rocking back and forth but silently; then she looked up and seeing Leron's tears began

to cry also. He put his arms around her, and she clung to him
with her face buried against his neck, her tears running down
his skin, her body shaking. Soon he could no longer tell if he
were crying for the death of a friend or in sympathy with her.
It was hard to be sure of anything except that she was in his
arms and he did not mean to let go so easily again.

Odric stayed for Leron's wedding, delaying his departure from
Tredana by another ten days. The ceremony was to be the
simplest, an exchange of vows in private at the castle. There
would be a public ceremony later but Leron set no date in
deference to Sibyl's wishes.

A few days before the wedding, Odric found a baraka among
the Player's collection of instruments and with his foolishness
and singing began to make Sibyl laugh. Leron could not understand her continuing soberness, and her reaction to Odric's
clowning lifted a great weight from his heart. The Player maid
Liniris also seemed to enjoy his fooling. Leron often saw her
with Sibyl and with Odric; and sometimes Kerys was with them
too, still scowling. Tonight Odric was trying to make up a song
about the footsmen but had trouble getting past the first verse.

> A rimbler-rambler skimbler-skambler,
> purse-nab stickler went out riding,
> saw a taxman on his tall horse,
> saw the monies he was hiding.

He was sprawled in a low chair with the baraka small in
his large hands; Sibyl and Liniris sat nearby curled on the floor,
watching his fingering closely and from time to time borrowing
the instrument to try it themselves. Leron stood at the door
watching a long while until Odric looked up, and Sibyl turned
with a smile.

"You should find a harp," she said, and Leron shook his
head ruefully.

"No time for that yet."

"Well, find one for me, then." He laughed and went on to
meet those who waited to speak with him; but the next afternoon
he had an instrument maker sent for and ordered a fine harp
to be especially inlaid and strung in time for the wedding
supper.

* * *

Next evening, the day before the wedding, Odric's story had advanced only a little.

> *"Woe is me," then says the stickler,*
> *"I've been taken of all I prized."*
> *Sharp the taxman looks him over,*
> *"Where was this you were surprised?"*
>
> *"Past those trees there, in the valley,*
> *be surprises by the many.*
> *Hold your horse and hide your ring,*
> *conceal your money if you've any."*

Liniris had gone to walk with Kerys at his request, and tonight Sibyl sat alone by Odric's feet. Leron sat down opposite, and she leaned back against his legs and he dropped his hand on her curly hair. "I can see how this is going to work out," he said. "But even a very cowardly taxman would think twice before hiding his money in plain sight of a footsman."

Odric plonked the strings and bit his mustache reflectively. Sibyl laughed and brought Leron's hand down against her warm soft neck. "Perhaps the footsman was in disguise as an old woman."

"That," said Odric, "happens only in ballads. This will be exactly like life, and he will be disguised as another taxman." They all laughed at this, and Odric put the baraka into Leron's hands.

He awkwardly coaxed a few tunes from it, unfamiliar with its fingering. Then Sibyl took it, and as she played and sang, he lightly rested his fingertips against her throat and shoulders, feeling the song gently vibrate in her bones.

> *"Once I had a truelove, and now I have none—*
> *Once I had a truelove, and now I have none—"*

She had chosen an oddly melancholy song to sing, and the tune had a plaintive twist that made his eyes sting. When it was over, she laid the baraka down, and Leron leaned over to wrap his arms around her and to lean his head on her shoulder. From the click of the door he realized that Odric had discreetly left them alone.

After a while she turned her head a little, and he kissed her;

they kissed until Leron thought he would faint if he leaned any farther over and gently slipped down next to her on the floor. This was better, with the chair to lean against. He settled her in his arms more firmly, and as they kissed again she moved her hand timidly from his arm to his shoulder to his face. After a while he could bear it no longer and pulled his mouth free, hugging her against him and burying his face against her neck. It was several dazed minutes before he remembered the ring in his pocket: his fingers were still trembling as he fumbled for it.

Sibyl, lying quietly against him, did not notice at first when he slipped it into her hand, but at his urging she opened her eyes and held it up. In the half-lit room, the seven large crude diamonds filled with a marvelous light. They were arranged to make a six-petaled flower, the desert rose: the ring had been his mother's and Leron had been delighted to find it in the palace strongroom. It was too small for Sibyl's ring finger, but she slipped it on the last finger of her hand and then hugged him without speaking.

Later when he led her down the hall to her door, he opened it for her and pushed her gently inside. "You had better lock it," he said, and she began laughing, hanging onto the door frame with her hair ruffled. He wanted to kiss her again, but instead he backed away. "Tomorrow we can lock it together." She looked at him more soberly, then pushed the door to, and he heard the bar slip home. Alone in the dark hall he raised his arms above his head in silent exultation, then stretched and walked off quietly to bed.

Well-wishers who could not be excluded from even the simplest of ceremonies were invited to the palace in the afternoon, in hopes that by suppertime they might be gone. Washed and brushed and dressed with the greatest care, Leron received them courteously in the Great Hall, impatient for Sibyl's arrival and the guests' ultimate departure.

Mistress Gemarta, who had been head cook for Mathon, had returned to serve Leron, noticeably older but kindly still and as deft with pastries and clever with baked meats as ever. She had far exceeded the simple foods he had asked for, and the long table was covered with a fantasy of foods shaped into birds and animals. There was a roast pig in the center of the table, sliced and reformed under his crackly skin, ready to fall apart at the touch of a knife; at either end were deep silver basins filled with spiced wine. A group of Players, more gaily dressed than ever, were playing and singing at one end of the hall. Ginas, standing near them, saw Leron and taking a covered goblet from her granddaughter's hands approached him.

"This is a great and fortunate day, O King. In its honor I have prepared a special gift for you."

Leron smiled at her, looking over her shoulder in a vague search for Sibyl. "You have brought my cousin back to us. What greater gift could you possibly bring?"

"Nothing greater, O King. But I have prepared a special potion according to an acient herbal receipt, that is said to insure a long and happy life." She held out the drink, and Leron could not graciously refuse. He took it, and and as he touched its sweetness to his lips, he finally saw Sibyl approaching through the crowd and he drank it off hurriedly. He returned the cup with murmured thanks and held his hand out to her.

Sibyl was dressed in a long narrow dress of ash grey silk; her dresser had tried to fasten sprays of tiny white dried flowers in her short hair, but they were slipping down onto her neck and she looked even younger than eighteen. She smiled and took his hand then saw the cup in Ginas's hand and her black eyes grew enormous. "What is this?" she cried. "Another one of your special potions? How dare you meddle in our affairs again?"

Ginas drew herself up proudly, but Sibyl was the taller; she stood there magnificently with one hand pressed over her heart and her nostrils flaring, no longer young at all. "This is the end!" she said at last. "The end! Do you understand? No more interference. We will do as we please, and you can go play with your cards as much as you like, but not with us! No more interference! You are not welcome here."

She yielded to Leron's pressure on her arm and turned, giving him her other hand as well. "Please," she said in a much softer voice, "I will explain to you tonight. But don't listen to her now; we can be free, we don't have to do as she says."

Ginas looked at Sibyl coldly, replacing the cover on the empty goblet. "So you will explain everything tonight?" It was said in an oddly challenging voice, and Sibyl looked at her proudly.

"Of course. But I would not expect one so skilled in manipulations as yourself to know anything about honor."

Ginas drew back, and Liniris took her by the arm. Before

Leron could ask for an explanation, he was undone by the look in Sibyl's eyes, and he drew her closer to him mindless of the crowd. "What is it, sweetheart? You cannot be in tears tonight."

She answered obliquely, gesturing at the crowd. "How much longer will these people be here?"

"An hour or two, no more—" he put his arm around her shoulders and led her away in the general direction of Odric. To those who congratulated them, she was gracious and poised, and if Leron had not had his arm around her he would not even have guessed that she was shaking. He was beginning to feel shaky himself.

Odric raised a goblet to them in greeting, and Kerys, less moody than usual, clasped Leron's hand warmly and nerved himself to kiss Sibyl's cheek. His face changed to a scowl as Odric pinched her chin and kissed her lips heartily. On the table the pig had already been taken apart, and as the food disappeared so too did the guests. Sibyl suddenly noticed that the polite servants were graciously assisting the guests to leave and she gasped, then looked at Leron who grinned back shamelessly. She squeezed his hands and leaned up against him.

"I do love you," she said, and he lifted his eyebrows.

"It is just as well," he answered and drew her arm in under his. He nodded to Odric and Kerys. "We will see you again. Tomorrow." Then he deftly swept her out through a side door and closed the noise in behind them.

She was silent as he led her up the stairs and into the small round tower room, yellow with the friendly light of candles. It smelled of smoke and bunches of dried herbs and oranges, these last imported from Vahn and making a magnificently exotic centerpiece on the small table. He drew out her chair and began to serve her supper, and she looked at him in surprise. He smiled. "Until tomorrow morning, no more servants. I am yours to command."

She put her hand over his. "Then please, no food. Maybe later. I can't eat now."

He nodded. "I am not very hungry either." He touched the goblet. "There is this to be drunk, though, and words to be said."

Again she restrained him. "Let me speak my words first. Then you can decide about the goblet." She went over to the low couch by the fire and sat, holding out her hand, and he came to sit next to her. She looked into the flames silently for a moment, then leaned her head against his shoulder. "I'm going to begin at the beginning," she said, and started with a more complete story of how she came to Sundrat than he had heard.

As the story of the voyage unfolded Leron heaved a sigh of relief and tightened his arms around her. He only interrupted once. "Liniris thought she was helping me?"

"Yes. Oh, I don't know if it made any difference. Probably not. I—I wanted to make my own decisions."

She was silent, then hesitantly picked up the story and carried it through to the end. Leron pressed his lips against her forehead. "Thank you," he said at last. "I thought it must have been that way but did not know how to ask. He was a good man, and a hero. It is not remarkable that you should have loved him. As a friend I also loved him."

She looked up in surprise as he suddenly chuckled. "I think that potion must be taking effect." He removed the drooping flowers from her hair and kissed her ear and then the side of her neck. "I am as helpless in its grip—as you shall be in mine!" She took a moment to adjust to his swift change of mood, straining back against the pressure of his arms and then suddenly yielding. His lips had made their slow way across her face to her mouth when she broke free to say one last thing.

"The marriage cup—"

He did not follow her gaze to the table, intent on the tiny buttons that fastened her dress at the nape. "It will keep until morning," he said at last, and she took his face between her hands and put her mouth on his.

At dawn he remembered his words and ventured out from under the covers for a quick dash through the chilly morning air. Safely in bed again with the cup he gently woke Sibyl, smiling down at her with fond delight. Warm under the covers, she snuggled against him without opening her eyes, until he pressed the cool silver side of the cup against her bared shoulder. She sat up protesting, and he uncovered the goblet with a flourish. "I think it is time," he said, "that we make this official."

She stretched and looked at him under heavy lids. "I thought we had."

"No. The order of the ceremony was somehow reversed."

He drank from the cup and held it for her to do likewise. She drank deeply, and he leaned over to put the cup on the floor. She put her hands on his shoulders. "Is it official now?"

He nodded and she smiled. "Perhaps we should really make sure."

"Very well. As I said, I am yours to command. But don't expect me to always give in so easily." She threw back her head at this, and he began to kiss the spot where laughter bubbled in her throat. They were late for breakfast.

POEM IN OCTOBER
by Sibyl
Written in Tredana

*Blood warm the earth beneath my feet
is black and clotted. Every spring
some green has come, unfolding to the sun.*

*But I will choose to disregard the spring
I have no leaves waiting to open out
no need to flower or sprout.*

*Better to sit and watch the busy sun
wind through the sky, inciting trees to leaf,
to join in that old circle dance
under each grinning mask
silly with grief.*

Chapter Two

It had been chilly when Leron married Sibyl, but a few days
after came the warm week of weather known as Karabdin
summer. The sky brightened from grey to blue, cloudless as
June; the orchard was thick in fallen apples and their sweet
spoiling odor filled the palace grounds; the trees along the
garden walls were varied in shades of red, gold and brown.
From the higher rooms of the castle it was possible to look out
beyond the town into the fields; on the east the water glittering
as blue as the sky and to north, south and west a wonderful
embroidery of golds and brown, oats, wheat, barley and rye,
broken with curly patches of still-green trees and bare-clipped
pastures.

For Leron time passed in a daze of delighted distraction.
He had never been so happy in his life. Never before had he
enjoyed the undivided affection of one person: he welcomed
tasks and council meetings because each separation led to a
reunion.

Karabdin summer had been in for several days when Odric
finally took his departure, leaving Kerys as they had planned
to follow with further news, once messengers had arrived from
Rym Treglad and the desert. The evening after Odric sailed,
Sibyl managed to draw Kerys out a little from his moody
silence, and as they still sat together at table he suddenly began
telling them his misfortunes, turning to Sibyl for sympathetic
support whenever the tale faltered. It did not seem possible

that they were nearly the same age.

Kerys told them how he and his younger brother Varys had fallen in with Odric by chance, while on their way to Vahn at Bodrum's unbrookable command. "We were so bored," he explained, gesturing vaguely with his knife as he put away what seemed to Leron vast quantities of food for one so slender. "It was so wonderful to see him again. Even when he was just our tutor in Mindo'ila he was always good to us and took us on long walks and taught us how to play the baraka and how to fish and how to make fires even if it was raining. And when we found out he was also our half-brother we neither of us wanted to leave him. That is why it is so hard to understand his treachery."

"Treachery? That is a strong word."

"It is the truth!" Kerys pushed his long dark hair back from his forehead and looked up from under it defiantly. "What else can it be called? She was mine, and he took her away."

Sibyl raised her eyebrows a little. "Odric? Are you sure?"

"Of course I'm sure. It happened this way. I met Kalla one day at the market. I carried her basket for her, and one thing led to another—" Leron chuckled, and Kerys scowled. "It wasn't like that. That's what I tried to tell her father. We were only talking in the garden. He said that was fine, but he'd have the dogs after me if I came again. So next night I had to meet her secretly. We didn't want her father to get angry. You understand, don't you?"

Sibyl and Leron both nodded gravely, and Leron asked, "And the night after?"

"Well, in secret again, of course." He brooded. "Then Varys ruined everything. Odric asked where I was once, after supper, and Varys just told him. You would think he is a halfwit. He could have made something up, if he'd only thought about it. Of course I gave him a good hiding when I found out, but the damage was done."

Sibyl looked at him in amazement. "You beat up your brother? Don't you like him?"

"Like him? I love him more than anyone in the world, except maybe Kalla and Odric. But he should have known better. And so should have Odric. You won't believe this, but he went right to Kalla's father and apologized for my behavior! Apologized! As though I were a child! And said that he would see to it I behaved more honorably in the future! And said he would

see we were chaperoned if Kalla's father consented for us to
visit again in the future!"

"And he did?"

"Yes, later. But when Kalla comes, Odric is always there,
and she spends more time with him than with me! He plays
and he sings and she laughs and acts as though I weren't there.
I found her first. It isn't fair."

Sibyl had been drinking from her goblet, and when she heard
this last she choked a little and set it down. "You found her
first? What was she, missing?" Kerys looked puzzled and turned
to Leron for support, but he was laughing at Sibyl's response.

"Tell me," he said at last, "how old is this Kalla?"

"Almost sixteen."

"Does it not seem reasonable that a chi—a girl of sixteen
would find someone like Odric attractive? He is the ruler in
Treclere, after all, older, more exciting. Perhaps she saw you
in a more, a more sisterly light."

"She didn't act sisterly in the garden."

"Ah yes, when you were—talking."

Kerys did not rise to this comment. "Besides," he said, "it's
the same thing all over again now."

Sibyl looked at him kindly. "You mean with Liniris?"

Kerys cut ferociously at his meat, scowling once more.
"Why can't he ever let me alone?"

Leron smiled at him. "Truly," he said, "I do not think Odric
is trying to steal anyone from you. But you cannot be forever
blaming the other party should her interests quite naturally shift.
Each has the right to make his own decisions."

"But if I found her first—"

"She was not territory to be claimed! She had a life before
you, and will have one after." Kerys lapsed into sulky silence,
shaken but unwilling to make any concessions.

After he had retired, Sibyl got up and came to stand behind
Leron with her arms around his shoulders. "You have a generous mind," she said, half-mockingly, but the pressure of her
arms was warm and approving.

He reached around and pinched her on the leg. "As a point
of fact, I am at the moment full of the most selfish thoughts."

"Why don't we go somewhere so you can share them?"

In the darkest part of the night Leron awoke. There was a
clear sound of horses on the roadway, and then there came a
knocking at the gates. Silence afterwards: nothing then of any

urgency. He pulled the coverlet up over their heads and settled back into the warm universe of their bed. For a while he lingered in the warm and blissful weightlessness of half sleep then drew himself in even more closely to Sibyl and slept again.

It had become Sibyl's habit to arise early and go for a ride before breakfast; when Leron awoke later, she was gone, and there was no warmth left in the hollowed pillow next to his. He hung out the window a moment, looking for a glimpse of a white horse in the fields below. Perhaps she had returned already. He dressed and hurried down to breakfast.

Neither Kerys nor Sibyl were sitting there by the small fire, but a familiar figure in brown velvet rose from the table smiling. Leron had forgotten the disturbance in the night. "Dansen!" He crossed the room in a few strides and put his hands on the other's shoulders. "Was it you rode in so late last night?"

Dansen swallowed his last morsel of bread and nodded. "I beg your pardon for not delaying my breakfast, but the events of last night built up an intolerable hunger."

Leron smiled reminiscently. "For me also. I will join you while you tell me what has been happening." He carved himself some meat and bread and nodded for Dansen to begin.

"First, my lord, I will say that we are all well in Rym Treglad. As you may imagine, the news of your accession here was the cause of greatest rejoicing, and it will doubtless interest you that many settlers have decided to stay on in Rym Treglad, forming there a colony loyal to your majesty. It is the formation of the colony and the drawing up of a charter that delays Gannoc; when these matters are settled, he will return to be your steward here and counsel you in the choice of a governor for Rym Treglad."

"He has no wish to be governor himself? There could be no one better."

"He anticipated that you might offer him this honor, and has already instructed me to refuse it, saying, he would prefer to be at your majesty's side."

"As I should prefer to have him. Very well, I must wait and listen to his counsel. The rains have come, I hear?"

"Yes, and Mariti has fish once again in the garden pool. She has sent you a message . . ." he rummaged in a fold of his gown and produced a tattered scrap of parchment, covered with wavy lines and blots of ink. "I held her hand but she held the pen, and as she wrote she explained that she was telling you she loved you and would be glad to see you soon."

"And I her." Leron folded the parchment carefully and tucked it in his belt. "Now what of yourself?"

Dansen shrugged. "When Ajjibawr landed in Rym Treglad, I spoke to him about the glass furnaces, and when our paths most fortunately crossed last night he told me that even now Herrard is in the south overseeing matters. I intend to join him there and take the first lens made across the sea this winter, as I said before—"

Leron dropped his knife, suddenly cold in his heart. "Last night. This is impossible. The Karif is dead."

Dansen looked at him perplexedly. "Dead? On the contrary, he has returned to his people and is surer in his power than ever before. Dzildzil is dead. Where did you hear this other report?"

"Report? I saw his severed head with my own eyes."

"Last night I also saw his head most assuredly secure upon his shoulders. Wait—I think I understand. Let me tell you what happened."

Leron drank his ale and breathed deeply, trying to slow his pulse. "Tell me," he said at last.

"I came by boat as far as Sundrat, and there I and my escort of ten men took horses from your majesty's stud farm to come the last way by road." He blushed. "I am not yet comfortable on the water. In Sundrat we were warned of this Captain Gwillam and his men, and told to stay to the High Road and only ride by day. We did so, until we were near to Tredana, and then I felt a foolish impatience to see my home again and those who were with me felt this also. Ten miles or so to the north, we were set upon, in that valley where the road drops between cliffs and is so dark even by day."

Leron hit the table with his hand. "This is intolerable. Were any injured?"

"Young Alric, Gannoc's nephew, took a spear through his shoulder. But there was more noise than harm in our encounter, and the noise brought our rescue upon us, for by great fortune the Karif and his escort were not far away, coming to Tredana also in answer to your messenger, and the outlaws fled before the Karabdin forces. This Gwillam, you will recall, was an old enemy of Clerowan's, and after we had talked, Ajjibawr sent a small force to escort us to the city gates and took the rest of his men off after the outlaws, telling me to say he would call on you tomorrow at the latest."

"You have not explained how I saw his head here, on the floor."

Dansen frowned. "I fear this must explain poor Osmin's fate. He was sent south from Rym Treglad with six men, to aid you if possible and to discover the fate of Sibby. I fear he and his men all fell to Gwillam's hand. Did you examine the head closely?"

Leron scowled at his plate. "Of course not. I had it removed and buried. It was fair haired, and the eyes were blue." He hid his face in his hands. "You are right. It must have been poor Osmin's."

Dansen leaned over and touched his arm gently. "You do not seem pleased at the resurrection of a friend. Is Sibby here?"

"Yes, she is here," said Leron harshly. "We are wed and this morning she is out riding. When she returns, you may tell her the glad news."

Dansen sighed in sympathy. "I see. But my lord—"

"Dansen, please! I do not need philosophy with my breakfast."

Leron got up and went to the window, tapping on the stone sill with one fist, his stomach in knots. There was silence, then Dansen suddenly spoke up. "Out riding? Outside the city? Surely this is not safe. Gwillam may yet be near. It was so dark last night I doubt the Karif had much luck in his hunting."

Leron whirled around. "You are right. I must send the guard—no, I must ride out myself." He rang the bell for service and questioned the chamberlain as soon as he appeared. "How early did the queen ride out? Was she alone?"

The man thought. "Three hours it would be now, sire. And the young nobleman from Treclere, Kerys, he rode out with her. They said they were going to have a run on the beach, sire, north of the city where it's nice and flat."

"At least she is not alone. But the northern beach. That is not so very far from where you had your trouble." He turned to the chamberlain again. "I will want my horse in ten minutes, also the household cavalry and six guardsmen."

Dansen left the table. "Surely it is not so serious, my lord. I spoke without thinking. Now it is plain light—"

"But the beach is deserted, and the road is lonely. And what greater prize for any hostage-taker than the Tredanan queen?

Besides, she had never been away for so long, going out so early. An hour and a half, no more . . ." Dansen followed him as he hurried down to the courtyard, and there they found the cavalry mounting and the guardsmen waiting. Two men held the little bay stallion that was Leron's new favorite, for it was very fresh and angry for having been taken away from its grain. It bugled noisily and tried to unseat him as he leaned over and touched Dansen's shoulder. "We will hope this is unnecessary. 'Til later—"

He whirled the horse around on its hind legs, and they went clattering out over the paving stones, the guardsmen in close formation about him and the captain riding level with his stirrup. As they went out through the streets he explained the reason for their expedition, and the captain snicked his sword in its sheath. "We have many a score to settle with Gwillam. The boys will be happy to meet him."

"Hope, rather, this is all unneeded." The captain nodded deferentially but there was a keen look in his eyes and he kept touching his sword hilt as he rode.

It was still early and quiet in the streets. The road north of the city was empty, and it was hard to tell much from tracks on its hard dusty surface. They cut through the woods towards the beach, as Leron knew Sibyl would have ridden, and came out on the sands. Here the marks of her horse and that of Kerys were plain. They had trotted past the high tide mark and then begun a gentle canter along the hard-packed sand. Here one had splashed through the water and the tracks were gone. Here they had begun a gallop. Leron gave his own horse its head and down the beach they galloped together, towards the curving shoulder beyond which would lie several miles of sand all in plain view. They rounded the corner and Leron drew rein sharply. There were figures on the beach far ahead: a large mounted force. The sun winked from their weapons, and great silk flags snapped in the seabreeze. The Karabdu. This was almost worse than outlaws. He began to blush, imagining what Sibyl would think to see him galloping out like this. But it was too late to return now. They had been seen. He picked up a gentle canter and tried to compose in his mind a plausible speech of welcome.

No one rode to greet them as they approached, however, except a sentry who recognized them and raised a reassuring hand to the lookout posted nearer the main force, and as they drew nearer he saw that the Karif was dismounted from his

golden horse and that there was a figure lying on the sand
before him. There were many greys among the horses there,
but not a single white. He drove his horse on again, sick with
apprehension. He could now see that the figure on the ground
was Kerys, being restrained from rising by one of the Karabdu;
there was a white bandage around his head and his boot had
been slit to relieve a swelling ankle.

. Ajjibawr looked up at Leron with harsh lines deeply etched
from nose to mouth. "So, Leron of Tredana," he said with a
contemptuous lift to his lips. "You arrive a little too late as
usual. I hope you are tending your realm better than your wife."

Leron drew his horse backwards and sideways and clenched
his hand in anger. "What has happened here?"

"Nothing of great moment. Your queen is a prisoner and
her escort left for dead on the beach; no need for you to leave
your breakfast so early."

Leron tried to take his sword from his scabbard with some
vague idea of striking down the Karif as he stood, but his
fingers fumbled and he was blinded and had to cover his eyes
for a moment with his hand. Ajjibawr suddenly came up to
him and put his hand on his arm. "My friend," he said in an
altered voice, "my friend, forgive me. I have been up all night
chasing that blackguard. I did not mean to speak so. We will
find him together, and Sibyl will be safe. He would not dare
to harm her."

Leron nodded and rested his hand on Ajjibawr's shoulder,
still bent in his saddle. "Does Kerys know anything can help
us?"

"We will see. He has just awakened." Leron swung down
from his horse and they went to kneel by the young man's side.

He was very white but eager to get up and put out his hand
anxiously to take Leron's. "You are here! Oh, my lord!" And
he burst into tears.

Kerys was not very helpful. The attack had been so sudden
and unexpected, and he had been struck senseless almost immediately. It had happened soon after they arrived on the beach,
so the trail was cold by now, and since the men who surprised
them had been mostly on foot, there would be no easy trail to
follow. Ajjibawr looked out at the nearest strand of trees to the
west. "There are sixty thousand acres of deep woods there:
Clerowan found them useful in his time. It will not be easy to
follow them."

Leron knelt, put his arm around Kerys's shoulders and helped him to his feet. The cloth fell from his head, revealing a deep and ragged wound. Ajjibawr touched his face gently and turned his head to see the damage more clearly. "I have seen a wound like this before," he said. "How were you struck down?"

Kerys was still confused, and he leaned against Leron, trying to pull his thoughts together. "It was a chain," he said at last. "There was a tall man with a chain, and he flipped it in my face before I could move."

"Ah," said Ajjibawr and turned to Leron with a bitter expression. "I have to apologize to you, my friend. That this man still is free I must lay to my own carelessness. I had three prisoners in my grasp, Dzildzil, Dastra and this man who accompanies her, the fighter with the chain. They escaped, and my men brought back only Dzildzil. It seems the false queen and her champion have joined with Gwillam."

Kerys interrupted. "But she knew him. Sibyl—I mean, the queen. She spoke his name and tried to strike him."

Leron soothed him and held him as one of the Karabdu deftly wound a bandage in place around his head. "I know, Kerys," he said at last. "I have felt the weight of that chain also. One of his names is Arleon, and he is as dangerous a man as the first Arleon was."

"She called him Michael."

"Yes, that is his other name."

At a gesture from Ajjibawr, one of the men took Kerys up before him on his horse. The Karif then turned to Leron. "We had best return to Tredana and hold council there. If we blunder in among the trees, we will only give more hostages to their hand. We can make our plans while we await their demands."

Leron hesitated, his hand on the bridle. "We should send some men—"

Ajjibawr dropped his heavy lids and shook his head. "It would be activity to no purpose. They know who their prisoner is and will try to turn it to their own advantage. They know they harm themselves if they harm her." Knowing that the Karif spoke the truth, Leron sadly remounted. As they cantered back along the beach he could not help looking back over his shoulder, but the marked-up sands were empty of any sign, and the spaces between the trees were dark and quiet.

As they rode back in force through the streets of the town, the people stood and gaped at the barbaric magnificence of the

Karabdu, their brightly fluttering robes and savage-headed horses
hung with tassels and ornaments, their large silk banners gau-
dily colored in scarlet and turquoise. Leron barely noticed. He
and Ajjibawr disposed of their men in the courtyard and went
inside. There Dansen joined them and Ajiibawr greeted him
warmly, but the scholar could see from their faces what had
happened. Kerys was taken protestingly away to have his ankle
set and strapped, and the three men went into the small room
where food still lay out on the table.

"You were quite correct," said Leron with a twist to his
mouth. "I did leave my breakfast. Will you join me now?"
Ajjibawr threw himself down on the bench and passed his hand
across his heavy eyes. He accepted some wine and bread, and
as he ate, Leron told Dansen what they knew.

"I do not understand entirely," said Dansen at last. "Who
is this Arleon? How came he by that name?"

Leron shrugged. "I do not know exactly. But he is from
Sibyl's world, though descended from ours as is she. It was
in a house belonging to his family that Sibyl first found her
way here; I think his family must trace back to those survivors
of Old Treglad's destruction who disappeared at the time the
first Arleon set out on his wanderings. There were those in his
family, according to the chroniclers, who joined with the break-
ers of the Temple. Was it not said that Simirimia was in touch
with the Otherworld? Perhaps she spoke with sympathetic voices
there, the family or followers of these new Arleons."

"Sibyl does not know?"

"Nothing for certain. Nor do I think this Michaël was aware
of his heritage."

"A heritage of infamy. How came he here?"

"He followed her."

Leron did not elaborate but Ajjibawr sighed. "So even a
child of eighteen can have a past to haunt her." He sat back
and slowly drew out his snuff box. "I think," he said, "this
Arleon is a more dangerous man than Gwillam. Gwillam had
a certain cunning, but I cannot imagine him insinuating himself
into a queen's company, effecting her escape before a crowd
of thousands, fleeing safely into the desert, effecting there an
escape from under armed guard and thence joining forces with
a hidden group of outlaws and all in a matter of weeks. If he
replaces Gwillam, the outlaws will become a major power."

Dansen nodded. "And he will place a high value on the

queen's return. Let us hope Gwillam can keep him in control."

Ajjibawr took his pinch, sneezed and rubbed the back of his hand slowly against his nose. "First, I will see that no force is allowed to cross the desert." He looked at Leron. "You have men to hold Villavac? Good. We will draw up lines south and north. I am sure the outlaws will hope to make their way west, to join with the forces of Vahn. They have no friends left here, not in the east nor in the south. I will see that Odric is alerted also and has his scouts active south of Treclere. I will send him messengers overland, and you can double our efforts when you return Kerys by ship."

Dansen interrupted. "My lord..."

Ajjibawr tapped his snuffbox on the table impatiently. "I have not forgotten my promise to you. I will not remove those men who now assist Rassam. You will have your lens, and quickly. It will be well if you test it soon, for we may be drawn into open war with Vahn before the spring, and while I do not fear for the desert, I do fear for the coast if you face Vahn with neither ships nor any weapon of defense."

Dansen nodded. "Those were my sentiments exactly. With your permission," he turned to Leron, "I will take the first one made by ship to Melismala, and see how we do there. I can be back well before spring."

Leron looked at him bitterly. "Is that all you can think of?"

Dansen shook his head, his kind face worried. "Leron, my dear lord, no, no, no. But it is the only way I can help. Do you want me to ride after the outlaws? I will, if you ask it. But what would I do if I found them?"

Leron laughed despite himself and reached across the table to take Dansen's hand. "I am sure you would think of something. You are right, of course. To strengthen our defenses against Vahn is the greatest help you can give. Forgive me."

"There is nothing to forgive. Her safety is precious to me also. And besides, I know how I would feel it if were..."

Ajjibawr looked up, an arrested expression on his face. "If it were?..."

Dansen blushed and dropped his eyes. "A lady you do not know."

Ajjibawr nodded slowly, and once more his heavy lids dropped to conceal his eyes. "Yes, it happens to us all." Then he startled Leron with his next words. "I must return to the

desert immediately. My wife is ill, and I do not care to be
away any longer than is necessary."

While Leron tried to assimilate this, there was a small commotion in the courtyard below. Before they could go to the
window, the door had opened and the chamberlain was there,
making a discreet noise in his throat. "A messenger, sire—"
Leron looked up eagerly and saw beyond in the hall his captain
of the guards, hands triumphantly tight on a prisoner's arms.
It was the man who had brought them the head, pale now with
terror; he gulped nervously when he saw Leron standing before
him, and then gasped and tried to step back as Ajjibawr also
arose from the table.

The captain jerked him forward. "Speak your piece," he
said, and the outlaw bowed trembling before them.

"I've been sent—"

Ajjibawr smiled slowly and put his hand on Leron's shoulder. "Sent? I think the word you want is sacrificed."

The outlaw looked to Leron for protection, and his eyes fell
nervously when he saw none there. "I've been sent with a
message."

Leron unclenched his hands. "From Gwillam?"

"Gwillam would never have sent me back. No, not Gwillam.
He's dead, and there's a new chief now."

Leron sighed. "So what message does Arleon have for us?"

The other started and hissed between his teeth. "So you
know Arleon then? You'll know he means as he says. 'Hands
off,' says he, 'I want no trouble or there's a lady dead for it.'"

Leron's fists clenched again, and the outlaw suddenly tore
himself free and threw himself onto the floor at their feet. "He
made me come. He'll kill me if I go back. I didn't have anything
to do with it. Let me stay."

Ajjibawr pushed him with his foot. "Why is your new captain so eager to be rid of you?"

There was a silence, and he finally mumbled, "I made a
mistake."

Leron laughed bitterly. "And so you ask us for mercy." He
turned to Ajjibawr. "The mistake he made was to bring us
Osmin's head for yours. Until this morning, we all supposed
you dead."

Ajjibawr's calm for once was broken. He looked at Leron
and then leaned over and pulled the outlaw to his feet, shaking

him by the shoulder. "What of the men who rode with Osmin? Do any live?" The other shook his head and whimpered as Ajjibawr threw him back against the captain who took him once more by the arms.

"Did Arleon have anything more enlightening to tell us?" asked Leron, and the outlaw looked up nervously.

"Only to warn you that there'd always be a knife ready and not to try anything. But I can tell you his plans! They're heading west, towards Vahn—"

"By what road?" The outlaw shook his head, and Leron turned to Ajjibawr. "We learn nothing we did not already know."

"Nothing of immediate help, it is true. But I have the murderer of my sword-brother here. Will you yield him to me?"

"Of course, but—"

"There will be no mistake this time. Dzildzil caused much grief before he was retaken and killed. I do not make the same mistake twice." He spoke to the captain. "Take the prisoner below and bind his arms. I will meet you in the yard." The other bowed and pulled the unhappy man out.

Ajjibawr raised an eyebrow as he saw the surprise in Leron's face. "Do you think it is kinder to wait? Or safer?" Leron shook his head. "It is quick, the sword. Quicker than he deserves. It is hardly the first time I have taken a man's head." Dansen made a little gesture of protest, and Ajjibawr turned on him angrily. "Perhaps you both should attend me below. In days to come it may be a skill you will wish for."

FOOTSMEN BALLAD
by Odric
written in Tredana

A rimbler-rambler, skimbler-skambler,
purse-nab stickler went out riding,
saw a taxman on his ambler,
saw the monies he was hiding.

"Woe is me," then says the stickler,
"I've been taken of all I prized."

Sharp the taxman looks him over,
"Where was this you were surprised?"

"Past those trees there, in the valley,
be surprises by the many.
Hold your horse and hide your ring,
conceal your money if you've any."

"I've no fear," then says the taxman,
"In my boots I've hid my money.
Many a trick I've learned collecting
thirty summers tight and canny."

"Thirty summers tight and canny?
Well then," says the rimbler-rambler,
"Now's the time for change—I'll have
your ring, your money and your ambler.

My clothes are new," the rambler says,
"I'll change them for your bits and tatters.
Your old boots have a weighty look
and that is all that really matters.

"Learn and listen," says the rambler
"Secrets should be shared with none.
Love a brother if you must
but never trust your life to one."

Chapter Three

Sibyl enjoyed her gallops along the beach, but this morning the old horse took it hard, and she pulled him up in concern. He was eager to continue running but his breathing was heavy and the sweat shone on his neck. With a word to Kerys she swung off and loosened the girths. Silver rubbed his bony head against her gratefully, leaving a streak of foam across her shirt and stood there quietly blowing while she patted his neck and felt of his legs.

"I'll just walk him out a little," she said to Kerys and turned the old horse towards the water. She had not reached the first line of foam when she heard a sudden noise and turned to see Kerys being pulled from his saddle by two men dressed in leather. She reached up to remount and the loosened saddle slipped. She righted it and quickly jerked on the straps, but before she could fasten them in place they had taken her by the arms. She jerked her crop from under the stirrup leather as she pulled herself free. As she swung at the man nearest her she saw his face and gasped.

"Michael?" she cried, and he grabbed her wrist and forced her fingers open so the crop fell to the ground.

He was grinning at her surprise, and he held her arms so another man could tie them with a cord. "You were expecting maybe Paul Newman?" He laughed and then suddenly noticed Kerys struggling free. He took a few quick steps across the beach and whipping out a chain from his belt, flicked it hard across the boy's face so he fell motionless to the ground. He

then took Sibyl by the arm and had another man bring the two
horses as they slipped silently into the forest. Sibyl let herself
be jerked stumbling along for a few yards, then pulled herself
free and tried to run back towards the beach. Michael caught
her easily and hit her across the face. It was an unwise move,
and he realized it immediately, for she planted her feet and
bared her teeth at him.

"I don't know what the hell this is all about," she said, "but
if you want me you're gonna have to carry me." Michael cursed
impatiently then lifted her with some little effort and threw her
across the back of Kerys's horse, helpless, on her stomach. As
they continued on, her ankles were bound also.

Sibyl had some vague idea of marking where they went,
but slung face down as she was, it was all she could do to
avoid the whipping branches, let alone notice the trail. When
they arrived in the clearing her face was bleeding with scratches,
and she was dizzy and sick to her stomach. She was also filled
with fury, and as soon as she was allowed to slip to her feet
she whirled around and would have fallen, forgetting her ankles
were bound, if Michael had not caught her arm once more in
his hard grasp. There was a stocky older man in the center of
the clearing, and he grinned with delight as he saw her and
nodded to Michael. "So you've brought me the queen as you
boasted. Very pretty, very neat. I did not think you could do
it."

Michael shrugged. "It was nothing."

The chief's eyes narrowed. "But you will be rewarded as
if it were something, never fear. What are those horses?"

Another outlaw spoke up. "Karabdin horses, sir. That white
one was the queen's. We thought you would want them, too."
He faltered as Gwillam looked at him contemptuously.

"What would an outlaw want with a white horse? A pretty
target he'd make. Still . . ." he went and put a hand on Silver's
neck and the old stallion drew himself up proudly, snuffing in
the unfamiliar scents. "We will give him a try. Give me a leg
up: the old wound's sore today."

A young man helped his chief into the saddle, and because
of his assistance the loosened saddle did not slip. Gwillam
settled himself in easily and gave the horse some leg. The old
horse was tired but he obediently rose up vertically on his hind
legs, trembling a little with the strain. Gwillam began to shout
out in anger, but the saddle twisted and suddenly came off in

a rush, dropping him between the horse's hind legs. As he fell Silver staggered and kicked himself clear of the straps, then stood quietly. One foot had hit Gwillam on the side of the head, however, and the outlaw chief lay silently on the ground. There was a superstitious hush in the clearing as Silver shook himself and began nosing the ground for grass, snorting at the pine needles. Sibyl laughed.

Michael ran across to where Gwillam lay, checked his breathing and pulse, then stood up. "He is dead," he said. "If any of you would choose another than myself speak quickly."

A few of the men looked sideways at Sibyl, then at Michael. "What about her?" one asked and Michael laughed.

"You fool," he said, "she's our safe conduct. Tredana won't harm us while she is ours."

"And the other lady?"

Michael laughed again. "She'll make a great guard."

Michael knew Sibyl too well to underestimate her now. He did not trust to ropes but had one of his men bring heavy chains to fasten her wrists and ankles. There had been a small fire already lit, and with bellows an outlaw brought up the flame and hammered the closing links together. They gave her less than three feet of play between her legs and less than two for her arms.

The smith shook his head as he did his work, but Michael cowed him into silence. "Question me and I'll send your questions into Tredana, and you with them. That reminds me . . ." he searched the group and brought forth a man Sibyl recognized with disgust. "You're the one who made that little mistake?" The man nodded nervously. "I'm going to give you a new message to take to Tredana, and four of the boys will go along to see that you enter the city as told. I wouldn't advise you to come back."

"But sir, Clerowan—"

"Exactly. You idiot, can't you tell one man from another? You don't deny that was Clerowan set upon us last night? Or perhaps he has a twin." Some other men shook their heads. "That was Clerowan, sure enough, Karif or whatever he calls himself now."

Sibyl looked up from testing the heavy chains. They were crudely made and already hurt her wrists, their rough joins chafing with every move she made. She looked at the outlaw and narrowed her eyes. "If you have made a mistake and Clerowan still lives, be assured he will have your head, if not for his own sake then for mine. You can take him that message from me, if you like."

The outlaw, already pale, raised his hands protestingly, but Michael gave him curt instructions and left him to the mercy of his escort. Then he walked over to Sibyl and lifted the length of chain between her wrists, approving its weight. "So you got this Karif on your side, too. I have to hand it to you. You work pretty fast. And Queen of Tredana!"

"She is not!" Dastra pushed her way through the men and stood dramatically with both hands clasped on her heaving breast. The rough leather clothing became her and she was as lovely as ever. She looked on contemptuously as Sibyl raised her bound arms to wipe the drying blood from her face, then stepped up more closely. "She is a dirty little stranger who tried from the first to usurp my position. Now we shall see justice done."

Sibyl stretched painfully, drawing herself up to her full height, and looked down at Dastra. She curled her lip. "I know I'm not as clean as usual, but little seems hardly appropriate."

"Indeed, you're as tall as a horse. Leron's taste seems to have deteriorated sadly."

Sibyl began laughing and looked from Dastra to Michael and back again. "So has Michael's," she said at last, and left him to explain the cryptic remark.

She was not left long in peace. The outlaws never stayed long in one place, and the chief difficulty was to get her on horseback without removing her chains. Michael finally threw her up sidesaddle and she hooked her right knee awkwardly around the pommel. Soon, she thought, she would take an opportunity to wind her chained hands around somebody's throat. Preferably Michael's. But she could wait a little: clearly there was no immediate danger. She concentrated on trying to absorb the rhythm of the horse's gaits in her oddly twisted spine and legs. It was difficult and amazingly uncomfortable and she wondered that anyone would ride in such a manner by choice. On the first stop she had an inspiration when Michael lifted her down to stretch, and rubbed her left hand in the dirt to cover the sparkle of her ring. Leron's ring.

They made their way along twisting paths into the woods. At first she was confused, then her sense of direction began to return and she could begin to guess where they were in relation to the city. She was riding on Silver, a little to the rear of the company, with only two men riding near her, one of whom held her reins. The horses cleared a broken branch in the path and she was thrown far forward on Silver's neck. This gave her an idea and when she saw another obstacle ahead she prepared herself well in advance. Silver jumped, she threw herself forward and pushed the heavy embossed bridle over his ears. He threw up his head as the top straps fell in his eyes, then shook the bit clear and leaped sideways. She kicked him with her one available heel and tried to guide him with her hands on his neck. Excitedly he snorted and wheeled, then made a sudden dash between the two nearest horses and lengthened out into a gallop. It was all she could do to stay in the saddle. She ducked low on his neck to avoid the overhanging branches and called to him for more speed. Suddenly he slid to a stop, his hind legs folding up under him so quickly she would have fallen off had he not thrown up his head. Her sense of direction had led her well: the highway was before them. Or to be more exact, below them. There was a rocky drop of nearly thirty feet to the road's surface. She clung to Silver's mane weeping with anger and frustration as her pursuit encircled her.

Michael did not say anything, but he grabbed her by the hair and shook her so hard she thought her neck would snap. "You try anything like this again," he said at last, "and if you ever get back to Tredana no one'll recognize you." She bit back her answer and looked away proudly. A rope was tied around Silver's neck and once more she fell into line behind the others.

The next few days of captivity were overshadowed by an impatience to escape, but she was watched closely and constantly and no further chances came close to presenting themselves. The nearest she came to being alone was when Dastra amused herself with taunting her. At first she tried to force her to wait on her, but Sibyl sat calmly unhearing or simply lifting her hands to let the chains clink meaningfully. Dastra was desperately curious for details of Sibyl's relationship with the Karif and her marriage to Leron, and it amused Sibyl to answer so laconically that Dastra was wracked with jealous curiosity. Once Dastra so forgot herself that she hurled a plate of soup in Sibyl's direction. Unable to move swiftly because of the chains, she took most of the rapidly vanishing heat and pain on her shoulder. Michael slapped Dastra, and to Sibyl's disgust she saw that Dastra simpered under this manly show of force. Michael seemed less impressed with her tactics also, and not long after began to look more often and more appraisingly in Sibyl's direction. For the first time a deep sense of unease was added to her continuing anger and frustration.

Securely chained, closely watched, Sibyl counted the passing days with increasing helplessness. Outwardly she remained placid, infuriating Dastra, but inside her head she was actively searching out every means of escape. They were going steadily westwards, of that she was certain, skirting Tredana and slowly approaching the mountains, beyond which lay Villavac. Once, in Villavac, she had helped to rescue Leron. She would not think about Leron now—it made her feel sad and helpless, and she needed all her energy. The first few evenings she had tried to reassure herself by playing with the powers discovered on shipboard, but the chains had somehow numbed her spirit, and the ability to make a campfire blaze more brightly seemed ridiculous. The problem, she told herself, will be in getting Michael to stand in the fire while I concentrate, and she laughed our loud, startling the others. She slumped forward, her head on her knees, and tried to picture the Karabdu tracking the outlaws down. They would ride up and cut the men to pieces with their swords. She pulled her bound arms apart and snapped the chain taut, a habit that irritated the thick scabs on her wrists. Many evenings they bled, and she went to sleep with the taste of blood in her mouth.

One night as she slept huddled against a tree, as far from the others as possible, she heard a familiar name that roused her from her lethergy. "We'll go more carefully," Michael was saying. "They say this old loyalist Glisser is about, who was an outlaw under Ddiskeard. He knows this area well. He may have had word from Tredana and be looking for us. We'll have to stay close together and be ready to use our hostage if it is necessary. Those ships from Vahn cannot be so many miles ahead of us now."

Another outlaw shook his head. "It's another week or more to that inlet."

"A week then. That's not forever. If we go carefully we'll make it. We've gone this far." That evening he had more sentries posted than usual, however.

Glisser. Sibyl leaned her head back and closed her eyes. Odd to think of that beefy, blustering farmer as an outlaw. How glad he must be to have his land back again. He had bought Herrard's wonderful dog. She had forgotten to ask about the dog when Leron told her about Herrard. Leron. Her eyes filled with tears and she turned her face against her shoulder, weakly sobbing. And miraculously a dog was there, cautious at first and then licking her wet face and whining. She raised her hands and it jumped at the clink of the chain, then pressed against her again and snuggled its nose against her neck. She hugged it and it did not flinch. "Who are you?" she asked and the dog pressed closer. "Don't you have a home?"

It sat back and looked at her, head slightly to one side, and the dim firelight gleamed yellow on its short fur. "Sweet-mouth?" she said hesitantly and the dog thumped its tail on the ground, raising its lips in an encouraging grin. "Sweetmouth! Oh, my god!" She wracked her brains for a way to send a message and suddenly felt the glass ring against her throat. Fumbling in her haste she undid the leather thong and beckoned to Sweetmouth. He lay down and looked up at her expectantly, turning his head aside so she could fasten the token to his collar. This done she buried her face against his head and he licked her again, still gently whining.

Then sparked with a sudden mischief, he dashed into the center of the camp, grabbed a piece of bread from the ground near the fire, and dashed out into the dark again as the men threw angry stones after him. She laughed at his excellent imitation of a wandering tramp dog, then sobered as she wondered how well the ring would be understood. At least they would know it had come from someone related to the Karabdu, a friend, and helpless. Or perhaps Sweetmouth had his own way of transmitting messages. No wonder Herrard had had such faith in him. That night she slept much better than usual, imagining help to be on the way.

LETTER
from GLISSER, Provisional Governor of Villavac
to THE KING

SIRE:

We have posted men all along the roads as you commanded
and furthermore sent our most trusted scouts into the woods
and mountains, accompanied by those dogs most skilled in
tracking. If the outlaws of whom your messenger spoke are
within fifty miles of the town, be assured they shall be found,
surprised and taken.

And as it is Your Majesty's avowed intention to avoid any
chance of violence or bloodshed the while the outlaws hold a
hostage, I would counsel against the sending down of any
Karabdu to assist in the search, but it of course will be as
Your Majesty commands.

Confident therefore of your imminent success, I conclude
this letter in hopes of soon sending word of such a triumph.

Chapter Four

If help was on the way, it was taking its own time in coming. A week passed after the appearance of Sweetmouth in the camp, and Sibyl went from hope to depression to hope again. They had left Villavac behind and were skirting the lower edge of the mountains: soon they would reach the edge of the fens and be able to follow the river valley southwest, to the inlet where Michael hoped the forces of Vahn still maintained a naval outpost. Sibyl wore her chains a little more easily now, but there was a continuous ache in her shoulders and lower back and the dull rage bottled up within her made it hard to think clearly. By now she was uncomfortably filthy and this added to her anger. Her scalp itched and her clothes stank. She had refused Dastra's earlier cold offers of assistance, but by the time they reached the river she was able more easily to stifle her pride, and accepted calmly.

The evening was chilly and the water cold, but no washing had ever been more delightful. Sibyl staggered as she tried to keep her balance on the slippery rocks of the river bottom, and it made her skin crawl to fasten the dirty clothing back in place over her wet, clean body. Dastra roughly helped her belt the long shirt of coarse linen back in place and Sibyl slipped again, a link of the chains twisted among the rocks where she stood in about a foot of water. "Please help me keep my feet," she said, "I want to wet my hair."

Dastra held her hand as she half knelt awkwardly, trying to dip her head in the water. Then Dastra gave her a sudden spiteful push so she fell forward heavily on her hands, bruising her face on the rocks below the surface. "Wash your clothes while you're at it," said Dastra and pushed her back with her foot as she tried to rise. "We wouldn't want the Queen of Tredana to be dirty." Three or four times Sibyl half rose to her feet, but each time Dastra was able to catch her off-balance and push her back in, and the chains were now all twisted around her feet.

Finally she had to give up for a moment and catch her breath, stretched out in the cold water with her head just above its surface. Dastra daintily picked her way out over the stones and pushed once more with her foot, this time at Sibyl's head. It was too dark to see well but Sibyl sensed it coming and twisted around to ward off the blow with her hands. The short slack of her chains clipped across Dastra's ankle, and Sibyl made a half turn with her hands, tightening the chain and jerking Dastra off her feet. She fell with a splash, but her cry was stifled by Sibyl's hands. Then Sibyl had the other by the hair and was pounding her head against the river bottom before she could control herself. Fortunately the water softened the force of her blows, and Dastra did not seem to be dead. But she was certainly unconscious. Awkwardly Sibyl struggled ashore and pulled Dastra onto the bank after her. Then she leaned forward to pull up the chain between her legs and clumsily went back into the water, hurrying along the slippery rocks, stumbling upstream and leaving no trail behind her.

She was desperate to put as much distance behind her as possible, but soon her teeth were chattering uncontrollably and her feet were so numb she could no longer feel the rocks, and she stumbled more often. The last time she caught herself her hands were numbed also, and she cut her palm without feeling anything. The taste of blood as she tried to warm her hands with her breath was her first clue, and then she could feel the edges of the wound with her tongue. She looked around desperately and saw in the faint moonlight a glitter of rocks in the center of the river where it narrowed ahead. Twice she stumbled in deep swift channels but the rocks were everywhere about, and she finally hauled herself to the center and from the center across to the other side. Large trees hung out over the water at crazy angles, their roots undermined by the widening river, and on to one of these she managed to pull herself up. There was a crotch in the branches big enough to curl up in, insecurely poised out over the water: with a bitter laugh Sibyl passed her chained wrists around a short branch and fell back with her full weight on her manacles, secured from falling in her sleep. For a long time she shivered, aching in the cold night air, but finally she fell into a doze.

The faint predawn awoke her. The trees were full of noise, birds and small animals muttering as they began a new day, but she could hear no sound of man. Her clothes were still damp and her hair also: her throat was aching and she was weak and dizzy. She leaned down towards the water, trying not to breathe, listening. There was no voice, no step, no sound of approach. As far as she could see downstream the river banks were empty. Stiffly she unwound her numbed hands from their support and scrambled to the ground. The chains on her feet caught in some roots and threw her to her knees, and she suddenly went crazy with frustration, crying and screaming curses heedless of the noise, tearing at the metal with her hands and straining her legs apart. Now she could understand the fox who chewed off his paw in order to go free: she would have used a knife on her own flesh given the chance. Bent over she tried to gnaw at the clumsy joined links and the pain of biting down on metal finally brought her to her senses. She wiped her face against her sleeve and set out again, stooped over to hold the chain up off the ground.

The woods thinned out and rapidly gave way to flat bottomland, rich and spongy underfoot. There were sheep in the fields ahead, browsing between the harvested stalks of grain and moving in slow, purposeless formations across the wide flat land. Incredible that civilization should be so close. A distant small white figure she had taken to be a sheep stood up on thin legs, lifting a stick. It was a boy in a heavy wool cape, and the large woolly shape next to him was his dog. She stumbled thankfully towards him, across the endless, spongy, difficult pasture.

As she fell to her knees for the fourth time the dog suddenly bounded forward, running directly towards her. It planted itself in her path with head lowered and hackles raised. She lifted her hand reassuringly and the dog growled, squinting its narrow yellow eyes. It had an enormous neck and was half again as large as a sheep. Its eyes never left her and she stood patiently

still, awaiting the arrival of the boy, who was running towards
them barefoot at great speed, brandishing his stick. The sun
was finally up and she could feel her clothing beginning to
steam.

"Go away, go away," she heard him call as he drew nearer.
He could not have been more than nine or ten years old. "Go
away or I'll set Wolf on you." Wolf growled softly in anticipation. The boy stopped a few feet behind his dog, almost in
tears, waving his stick above his head. "Go away and leave
my sheep alone."

"I don't mean any harm," she said softly. "I'm cold and
hungry. I wouldn't hurt your sheep—I can't hurt them." She
spread her chained hands helplessly, and as she did so realized
her mistake.

His black eyes grew enormous with apprehension, and he
looked at her more closely, taking in the chains on her legs as
well. "You're someone bad," he said at last. "Where did you
escape from? I'm going to go get my uncle. He'll take care of
you. He's strong. You're a bad man."

Sibyl shook her head. "I'm not bad. I'm not a man. I'm a
woman and I've escaped from some bad men, really." The boy
looked at her rough riding trousers and long shirt, her short
hair and thin scratched face.

"You're a bad man and a liar," he said at last, "and my
uncle will make you tell the truth." He turned to the dog.
"Watch him!" The dog lay down obediently, softly growling
in his throat. The boy looked at Sibyl again. "You'd better not
move until I get back. If you do you'll be sorry!" He turned
and sped off, squelching through the rich, wet, flooded pasture.

Sibyl straightened herself a little and the dog sat up, showing
his magnificent teeth. "Come on," she said, "I'm just trying
to get comfortable. You try standing here without moving."
The dog took one step forward, then flopped down heavily
again. His eyes had never left her face, and there was an
undercurrent of growling in his heavy breathing. Minutes passed,
and Sibyl's dizziness returned. There was no part of her body
that did not ache intolerably. If she tried to shift her weight
onto one leg the other would tremble violently, and the dog,
alert to each small change, would growl his warning to her.
Now the morning mists were burned away and at last her clothes
were dry, but inside them she was cold and shaking. She stag-

gered as she stood there and the dog rose to his feet. "Wolf," she said, and he looked at her intently. "Wolf, if I had a gun in my hand I would take the greatest pleasure in blowing apart your head with a slug. I only wish you could understand what I am saying." She was speaking very levelly and softly and the dog squinted at her in concentration. It occured to her that if she could blast the captain of the *Damar* she ought to be able to stop a dog, but there was no spark of power inside her, nothing but a terrible weariness. "You know, Wolf," she said at length, "we have this all wrong. Dogs wear chains. People don't. Want to switch?" Wolf's attention flickered and at last Sibyl could see two small figures approaching in the distance.

When the boy and his uncle were about fifty feet away, Sibyl sank at last to the ground and, as she had hoped, the man called off his dog before it could spring. Then he clapped his nephew on the shoulder. "By all that's amazing. So you spoke the truth. An escaped man in our own pasture." He looked around the field shaking his head, as though the whole aspect of the land had suddenly changed. "Well, now we know to believe what the lads said this morning, about a big fight down along the river. My lord should reward us well for the returning of this one."

The child clutched his staff with both hands, leaning on it in imitation of his uncle. "But what will we do with him? They're all away at the farm today."

"Take him straight to my lord's house. You've never been there? It's nothing so special but you might as well see it before you're much older. You, now. Get up. And don't think I don't know how to use this." Incongruously he drew a rusty knife from his sash and brandished it at Sibyl.

"Where are you taking me?"

"Back to them as you escaped from. My lord Glisser and his men."

Sibyl scrambled to her feet. "Glisser? You know him? He's nearby?"

"Ay, and you'll not escape him this time. One of the lads said as how there were hundreds of you fellows taken prisoner in the night. And hundreds killed, too, from what he says." He held up his hand. "Not that Glisser'll kill you, I shouldn't think. They do say as most of the killing was done by those Karabdu. Swords. But Glisser's in charge and he'll deal with you fairly. Now come along."

Sibyl held out her hands. "Do you think I got those scars in a single night? I've worn these chains for weeks. I was a prisoner of the outlaws. I escaped. I will welcome the chance to see Glisser."

The older man narrowed his eyes suspiciously. "That's as may be. We will see when we get there. But don't try any tricks. I know your kind." He curtly ordered the dog to return to the sheep, then took the boy by the shoulder and gestured for Sibyl to precede them, following the general direction of the river upstream. The going was still difficult, but she exulted silently as she scrambled along. Sweetmouth had carried her message as she had hoped. Of all nights to run away from camp. What had Glisser thought? Did Michael tell him she had escaped, or deny ever having her? Knowing Michael, it was likely he had said she was being held in another spot and had continued to bargain with her life even though it was no longer in his hands. And the Karabdu had been there, too. There were many tribes. Not necessarily Ajjibawr's. For the first time in weeks she wondered what she looked like. Must be pretty bad to scare a child so. She continued on with new energy and at last they came out on a narrow track. Here the shepherd let her rest a few moments and she sank down gratefully.

He looked at her a little more kindly and must have seen how exhausted she was, for he handed his knife to the boy and held his small wineskin to her lips so she could drink. She thanked him and slowly got to her feet again. "Glisser will reward you well," she said and did not elaborate. They walked on a little way farther and there came a sound of hoofbeats in the distance, a fast canter. Then, coming over the edge of the hill they could see a horse approaching, dark brown and fluttering with the trappings of the desert.

The shepherd shook his head and muttered. "I'll be glad when these foreigners go back home." The horse drew nearer and the sun shone on the rider's fair hair. A dip in the road hid him and then he was almost on top of them. He drew rein sharply and the horse stopped so suddenly the rider was thrown forward on its neck. It was Michael, and he was grinning.

He drew his sword and saluted the shepherd gravely, but he could not keep from covertly savoring Sibyl's expression. "So you have our prisoner safe," he said. "You have done the crown good service today. Now I will relieve you of your burden."

The shepherd shook his head, thanking him. "I'm taking him to my lord," he said. "I'll feel better handing him to Glisser myself."

Michael smiled easily. "This one is the Karif's. I was sent to find him and bring him back if possible." He pulled down his shirt a little at the neck to reveal a gaping bloody slash. "He looks mild enough now, but he gave me this cut with his sword when he broke free. A devil, or we never would have chained him so."

The shepherd nodded. "That would explain it, still..."

Michael drew a small purse from his belt and leaned down courteously from the saddle. "There is a reward, of course." The shepherd gawped delightedly at the coins within.

Sibyl raised her hands pleadingly. "Glisser will reward you better for my return. This man is lying. He is not even one of the Karabdu."

The shepherd shrugged. "He's pale enough."

Sibyl stamped with fury. "Whoever heard of one that can't even ride? He flops on that horse like a sack of flour. He's lying. Believe me, Glisser will be generous."

Michael sat back smiling. "He is a dangerous warrior for one so young. He knows it is a long hard tramp to Glisser's, and he hopes for some chance to escape along the way. You will not regret handing him over." He swung off awkwardly and put out his hand towards Sibyl. "Come along now."

She backed away. "Don't you dare put your hands on me again."

"A little too proudly said for one in your condition. You know, I don't think you want to try and identify yourself any further. Somehow you don't look the part." He smiled at the shepherd and shrugged. "A terrible liar, also."

Sibyl turned and tried to run but Michael caught her easily and pressed her chained hands back against her throat until she slumped in his arms. The shepherd helped him throw her over the horse's shoulders and Michael pulled himself up behind her.

"If you see the Lord Glisser," he said in parting, "be sure and tell him that you helped return the prisoner in chains. He will know whom you mean and give you further reward." He chuckled as he said this and continued chuckling as they cantered off down the road.

* * *

Before they reached the sea inlet, Sibyl had fallen ill, and
Michael carried her aboard the ship from Vahn. She did not
hear what arguments he used to convince the captain, but the
ship sailed soon after; and later as she lay sick and coughing
in her tiny room she learned that Michael's luck had apparently
returned, for the small fleet had been planning to leave even
earlier, for fear of being trapped in a bottleneck by Odric's
forces. Now they were safely aboard, Michael could easily
have ordered her chains struck off, but he did not; and if it
were possible for Sibyl to hate him even more she did at this.
But at first she was too ill to concentrate on anything, even
hate. She coughed until there was blood in her mouth and the
simple act of breathing seemed more trouble than it was worth.
In the stuffy cabin she burned with heat but the water that stood
in the jug by her bed seemed too far away to fetch and too
heavy to lift; she looked at it, thirsted, and fell asleep without
drinking.

A week or more passed in this way, until one morning she
awoke and tried unthinkingly to get out of bed. She was almost
too weak to sit up, but otherwise she felt so normal she laughed
with relief. Apparently they desired her health, for as her appetite returned good food was sent in to her, as well as hot
water and soft soap for bathing. Moved by some obscure feeling
of guilt or compassion Michael brought her a clean shirt, slit
along the sleeves, and helped her bathe and change and then
sew up the seams again, crudely with linen thread. Although
she shrank from any suggestion of their former intimacy, the
need for clean clothes was stronger, and Michael was silent,
leaving as soon as she was dressed. When she awkwardly went
to comb out her damp and curly hair she frowned at her appearance and turned the mirror to face the wall.

There was a small porthole above the bed and with difficulty
Sibyl hammered it open, for it had apparently been shut many
years. The room filled with cold autumn sea air, and she fell
back gratefully onto the newly clean bed with a wool blanket
up to her chin and dozed. It was as grey as November on the
water, sea and sky perfectly matched to each other for color.
She drifted a little and began counting days and weeks in her
mind. There were some gaps of which she was unsure, but
even so it must be mid-November by her reckoning. It was late
September when she arrived in Sundrat and partway through
October when she was married. How long had she been in

chains—three weeks, four? Then it was late November. The happy days of October seemed months past. If only there were some way to send a message to Leron—surely a political hostage could send a letter. So many weeks—at least he must know she was alive and would return. She pressed his ring against her face and slept comfortably for several hours, breathing the clean salt air.

In her sleep she was in a shadowy dream forest, dark and overgrown. A cloak hung heavily from her shoulders and one end was lapped about a sleeping child, heavy in her arms. The woods were familiar but she was lost, and the panic rising in her throat made the trees seem deeper and darker. Then the bushes before her parted and a man on a white horse stepped in front of her: a pre-Raphaelite knight in red velvet with yellow hair and a long curling plume to his hat. "Are you lost?" he asked and she nodded, unable to speak. He removed his hat with a flourish, drawing from it a folded parchment. "A map to the forest," he said gravely. "With it you may find your way out." She took it eagerly from his pale hand and then stopped, struck with concern. "Won't you need it yourself?" she asked and he shook his head as he settled his hat back in place. "No," he said, "I always know where I am going." Turning the horse aside he disappeared into the trees again. The image was so vivid Sibyl looked at her clenched hand as she awoke and was surprised to find it empty.

She sighed impatiently. "At least I'm not carrying that damned child," she said as she swung her legs over, then paused, pressing one hand involuntarily against her belly. Again she counted the weeks, and this time fell forward with her arms around her knees, weeping silently and despairingly. What other explanation could there be? It wasn't just a question of being a few days off—this was seven or eight weeks. At length however she pulled herself together and washed her face. "If you are in there," she said, addressing her belly, "you sure must love life to hang on through all this. We'll do what we can at this end to see you're taken of." She went to her porthole again and looked out over the empty sea and found she did not feel nearly so alone.

As usual she ate in peace, alone in her cabin, but later that evening there was a knock at the door and it opened immediately to admit Michael. She looked up from where she sat propped against pillows under the open porthole. "Why bother to knock? Or does that serve in place of a trumpet fanfare? It's so hard to get a good fanfare nowadays."

Michael looked less self-confident than was usual, and he held up his hand. "C'mon, Sib—"

"To where? A dance maybe? Black tie and chains? I've got a better idea. You can play Alexander ruling the world, and I'll be Diogenes. That gives me the chance to say, get the hell out of my doorway."

"Sib, I'm trying—"

"What's the matter? It must sound better in Greek. Alexander was impressed."

Michael frowned, then gestured deprecatingly with his hands. "If you'd just be a little more reasonable none of this would be necessary."

"You mean I wouldn't have had to've been kidnapped? Someone should have explained this to me before." He cursed softly and clenched his fists, but he sat down opposite her making no threats, until she was quiet again. "Okay, Michael, talk. You see here the original captive audience."

"Sib, don't you see what a great chance we could have if we worked together? We know so much. They're still fighting like the Middle Ages here. Swords and arrows and stuff like that."

"A sword was pretty effective on your neck."

Michael touched the thick scab. "That was your friend the Karif. If I hadn't stumbled it'd been my head."

"Maybe next time."

Mike scowled. "C'mon, Sib. Don't you understand? We could make gunpowder—"

"And cotton gins and steam engines and B-52 bombers? Too bad one of us didn't take physics, so we could go the whole way and split an atom and be done with it. And just how do you intend to make gunpowder? There's an awful lot of caves to be scraped for saltpeter before you fill one cartridge case. And I didn't do that well in shop. The rifling in my gun barrels might be a little crooked."

"We'd just make a cannon, first, to scare them. Even a grenade or a simple bomb. I bet there's a petroleum deposit somewhere—"

"If there is, some farmer's probably using the stuff to keep his cattle's feet from cracking, and I say hooray, I hope he never thinks of another use. Look, I can understand your missing your bike, but what the hell do you want with bombs?"

"It would be so easy, no one would be expecting it. Think of the power—"

"I had plenty of power in Tredana and bombs weren't exactly at the top of my list of interests. Nor were motorcycles. And speaking of bikes, how did you follow me here?"

Michael shook his head. "I have no idea. I got drunk and decided to drive over Weeks Bridge. I think I fell off. I came to in the water, but it wasn't the Charles. It was salt, and I came ashore near Sundrat. How did you do it?"

"The first time I broke into your uncle's house, on the hill. It was locked up after those people disappeared from it. I didn't know that then. And when I came back I forgot about having been. Do you know that your name is a name from this world?"

"Arleon?"

"Yes. It was an Arleon who founded Tredana, thousands of years ago. He fled from old Treglad, and he stopped in Vahn on his way. Some of his family disappeared. They might have come into our world. He was an unscrupulous bastard."

Michael laughed. "And a successful one. This is real interesting. I guess I'll have to drop the Michael and just call myself Arleon from now on. That should impress this Bodrum."

He stretched and stood up. "We've got a coupla days before we arrive in Vahanavat. Think about my offer."

"You haven't made one, yet."

"Oh, come on. You know what I'm saying. We gotta stick together here. I'm willing to forget about this Leron nonsense— of course, you'll have to play the Tredanan Queen as long as Bodrum's around, but we can probably get rid of him eventually."

Sibyl threw the blanket back and set her feet on the floor. The chains clanked noisily on the boards. "You're willing to forget? Leron's my husband."

"Okay, so he's your husband. Marriage is pretty informal here, I've noticed."

"It's for life."

"Even if the Karif comes around?" Sibyl blushed and dropped her eyes. "You forget I had a chance to talk with him a little before he lost his temper." Michael touched his neck lightly.

"He must be a real good friend of Leron's to be all that anxious to rescue Leron's wife."

"He is."

"Okay, okay, we'll leave it at that. But if you're smart you'll think a little further."

Sibyl clanked her chains restlessly. "Don't forget to lock the door on your way out."

The day they sailed into harbor, Sibyl turned her mirror around. The reflection was not wildly encouraging, but there was a definite improvement. She brushed her hair vigorously into shiny black curls and pinched her cheeks for color: The circles were nearly gone from under her eyes. With the ring sparkling on her finger she drew herself up proudly and then laughed with helpless bitterness at the chains, plain even in the dim, distorting mirror.

She was ready when Michael came to the door and she pulled free of his clasp on her arm. "Let's not rub it in," she said. "I think the chains make it clear enough." A boat had already been sent ashore, and on the quay the seneschal waited, strange and magnificent in his tall felt hat and gold earrings, the embroidery on his robes marvelously rich. Behind him the low white roofs of Vahanavat stretched out, broken here and there by the green tops of trees. The air was chilly and dry, the ground brown underfoot.

Sibyl shivered and raised her chin a little higher. The seneschal looked at her narrowly, and she curled her lip in disdain as she looked back. He turned to Michael. "You are expected. You will follow me." He spoke curtly, and a guard or escort of six men fell in around them as they followed him to the palace. As they passed in under the high arched gateway, Michael began to smile with satisfaction. Sibyl shivered again. She was not so sure.

LETTER
from LERON, King of Tredana and Lord of Rym Treglad to
BODRUM VIII, Master of Vahn

I write firstly to inform you that my usurping cousin and your late ally Ddiskeard is no more. I have assumed the throne of my father and I have joined in alliance with Odric of Treclere and the Karif of all the Karabdu, of whose return you have doubtless already had word. We do not seek any quarrel with Vahn but neither do we hold any friendship for her.

I write therefore to further inform you that the Queen of Tredana, my cousin and my wife, has been foully taken prisoner by an outlaw whose published intention is to bring her to Vahn as hostage. If he should accomplish his purpose I charge you to see to her safety, comfort and swift return. For any aid you can give we will not prove ungrateful, but any harm she is caused will be repaid a thousandfold.

Chapter Five

Bodrum the Eighth, Master of Vahn, received them in his office, a pleasant lofty room set high above the palace's central courtyard. The ceiling was painted with scenes of ships at sea, in muted tones of red and cobalt blue; the walls were narrow strips of inlay between tall rectangular windows through which the cold air whistled. Sunlight lay across the polished stone floor in broad yellow bars.

Bodrum had charts spread out on his massively carved table, and was measuring distances with a pair of brass calipers when they were shown in. He waved the guards away impatiently and stepped forward, ignoring Michael, one hand graciously extended towards Sibyl. Surprised, she held out hers without thinking, and the master's small eyes widened with apparent shock. He snapped his fingers to the seneschal. "Send for the armorer at once, and bid him bring his anvil."

The seneschal left them alone and Bodrum, still without acknowledging Michael's presence, led Sibyl to a low, pillowed chair and had her sit. There was a heavy velvet robe hanging over its arm and she spread it gratefully over her knees. "There is a fire in your chamber, of course," he said, "but first we must remove these fetters. We did not know until today of your presence within our realm. A message from Tredana but now arrived, and we have not had the time to answer it. This man is the outlaw of whom the message spoke?"

Sibyl nodded. Bodrum turned and looked at Michael. Like Odric, he was under six feet, but massive through the shoulders and far heavier than his son; there was more chestnut in his hair and beard and his mouth was smaller and more prominent. The furs and velvet he so casually wore made him seem even larger, and Michael drew himself up to face him although he was the taller.

"I am the one who has brought you the Tredanan Queen for hostage. My name is Arleon."

"So is mine," said Bodrum. "But we do not boast of that connection here."

The seneschal reappeared, with the armorer and two servants carrying a small anvil. The armorer was a small man with enormously muscled arms. He considered the problem at hand seriously, without any show of surprise, then quickly and skillfully severed first the major lengths of chain and then, working more delicately, the manacles and ankle clasps themselves. Sparks flew from his chisel as the mallet thudded rhythmically against it. The job completed, he silently gathered up his tools and the broken chains, bowed and departed still without a word.

Now Bodrum took Sibyl's hand and bowed courteously over it. "We will send a reply to Tredana in the morning," he said, "and enclose in it any message you may wish to send. Doubtless the trip has been tiring for you. We will conclude our business with this man and do ourselves the pleasure of dining with you this evening. I think you will find all your needs attended to."

Sibyl had been rubbing her chafed wrists; now she slowly drew her arms more widely apart and pain leaped through her shoulders as she passed the limit that her chain had allowed. She nodded, and Bodrum drew her to her feet, summoning the seneschal with a nod. "The Tredanan Queen is our guest. See that her needs and wishes are met." Still half-dazed, Sibyl followed him out, nor did she look at Michael as she left.

The room to which she was brought was warm and comfortable, with a fine view over the harbor. The fire burned warmly and bright, the bed was deep in pillows and warm coverings; on a table near the fire stood food and fruit and jugs of wine and water. A board of Castledown was set up on a separate table, and a baraka hung with silk ribbons lay propped against it. A girl sitting on the ground by the door was handed to her as her servant, and at the instuctions of the seneschal she took a pot of salve from the table and began to tenderly soothe Sibyl's wrists and ankles as soon as they were alone. When Sibyl expressed no desire to sleep, the girl was delighted and began showing her dresses so she might choose her wardrobe for that night; she did not understand Sibyl's wild laughter.

The contrast with recent weeks was so ridiculous even laughter could not serve for long. Sibyl fell silent and quietly selected a sober-colored gown. The girl's face fell, and Sibyl suddenly snapped awake. There was no need to be modest; this capitivity was none of her own choosing. She selected again, a dress of clear red with green and gold embroidery, and sat back calmly for her hair to be dressed. The girl worked with utter absorption, and Sibyl drowsed, soothed by the light attentive touch. She allowed the girl to paint her eyelids with kohl, and selected a slightly acid extract of chrysanthemums from the scents offered her. When the round brass mirror was held up for her attention, she opened her eyes wide with satisfaction. It was not the face of a weak prisoner but the proud face of a queen.

By now the early dark had descended, and the girl helped her to dress. She was terribly stiff, yet felt enormously light on her feet, free now of the dragging weight of metal. Although it was painful, she raised her hands above her head and stretched as the dress was pulled into place. Now she felt equal to the task of dealing with Bodrum and learning his terms. The supper chamber was empty when she was shown to her chair, but Bodrum entered soon after. He waved the servant back and poured her wine with his own hands, then sat down closely opposite with his own cup in his hands, leaning intensely forward.

"Now," he said, "you appear as you should always look, the Queen of Tredana in form as well as spirit." Sibyl blushed to have her secret thoughts so exposed and would have sat back a little, but that he spoke so softly she was compelled to stay quite close. His eyes were a light reddish-brown, and they were looking deeply into her own, so much so she found herself looking helplessly away. "Do not be afraid of us," Bodrum said gently. "We are not like this rogue Arleon. We know the honor that is due your position."

Sibyl looked up into his eyes. "I am not afraid," she said half-truthfully. "But I would like to understand my position here."

Bodrum narrowed his eyes in concern and leaned still closer. "The part of a hostage in time of war is a trying one, troublous to the proud of spirit. We will see that the way is made easy as possible until the terms of your return have been properly arranged. You need fear no harm nor indignity at our hands.

All it requires is your word of honor."

"My word?"

"That you will not seek to escape."

Sibyl, used to the weight of the chains, lifted her hands higher than she intended. "I cannot give my word," she said. "I was not captured in war. I was kidnapped by force, and I have no greater wish than to return home."

Bodrum drank from his goblet and once more settled his weight forward. "That is most understandable," he said gently. "But you must believe us when we say you will return more surely and more swiftly by letting these matters take a politic course. Your city has petitioned for your release, we will set our terms; they will be met, and you will go free. We have reigned here forty-seven years and these matters are well-known to us. You need have no fear of giving your word."

Sibyl drank thirstily from her goblet, wondering what to say. Bodrum smiled at her. "We will not press you for your word tonight. Tomorrow we can speak on this further. Let us eat now, and afterwards we will show you our communication from Tredana."

They ate silently, Bodrum speaking only to press more food on her, or beg her to try another Vahnian delicacy. "You must not be so thin when you return to Tredana," he said, "or they will think ill of us in Vahn." The food was good, and Sibyl had no difficulty eating. How could this be the monster of Vahn? He reminded her more and more of Odric, with his ready smile and gentle voice. Only his eyes were more serious.

When the table was clear, Bodrum offered Sibyl a plate of dried fruit and nuts and had her goblet refilled. He drew a folded parchment from the breast of his gown. "When we received this message we were most surprised. But recently we learned of the revolutionary events in Tredana and the desert: we were not aware of the existance of a new Tredanan Queen, far less her presence within our realm, a hostage."

Sibyl unfolded Leron's angry message, and her hands trembled as she held it to the light. It was brief and to the point, and she let her fingers rest on his written name in a secret caress as she looked once more at Bodrum. "I can add nothing to what the king has said. Surely there are settlements which may be made, short of war."

"That is our desire also. We have asked that a representative be sent, so we may negotiate these matters personally. In the meanwhile, if you will add your personal message to our assurances of your well-being, we will see that the letter is safely delivered." A quiet servant stepped forward from out of the dark recesses of the room, bringing a pen and parchment.

Sibyl hesitated a moment, under no delusions concerning the privacy of what she was to write. Certainly there was no advantage in length: tell all the story or none. She chose the simpler course.

> Dearest,
>   The journey was trying, but in Vahn I am safe and well, although I can never be happy until I return to Tredana and your arms.
>
> Sibyl.

Bodrum nodded approvingly at the briefness of her writing, and smiled as she sealed it with wax. "That is well," he said. "Now there need be no question in Tredana's mind of the truth of our claims." He stood up. "Tomorrow we will talk further. If there is anything lacking necessary to your comfort, pray do not hesitate to inform our servants." He smiled in dismissal, once more an expression that did not reach his somber eyes, and Sibyl left. He had not asked for Leron's message back, and that night she slept with it under her pillow, tightly clasped in her hand.

Next day Sibyl considered giving her word as Bodrum had asked, but she could not. Bodrum took her refusal courteously, explaining that it made necessary her removal to Almond Island. He assured her however that despite the greater security, there would be no lack of comfort. Almond Island was a rocky outcropping less than five hundred feet from shore, with a small jetty and beach. Most of the island was covered with an impressive stone fortress, towered at each corner. It enclosed an open garden several acres in extent. She was taken there by open boat and installed by the seneschal in a large high chamber. The whole of the western tower was given over to her use, and a staff of servants was at her command. In addition, Bodrum had arranged for three fine Karabdin mares to be taken across and stabled there for her amusement; there was a large ring for riding in the garden's center, with goalposts for the mounted game of Zir-i-bala. There were musicians as well, and a baraka and a harp should she wish to play herself.

For a long while Sibyl tried to convince herself that it was still the fall of the year; but one night there was a light fall of snow and she could not fool herself any longer. The snow depressed her, and for several days she found herself drawn to the top of the tower more frequently, fascinated by the cold grey curling waves that slapped and broke on the stones far below. One day as she leaned far over, looking down, the sun suddenly caught on the diamonds in her ring and almost blinded her in a burst of color. She stood up and drew away from the edge, angry with her weakness. Soon there would be a message.

Winter had been in for several weeks when Bodrum came to spend some time on the island. It was his favorite retreat from the city, he explained, a summer palace originally, but also a welcome lodging in the winter. He stood on the top of the tower and looked eastward with her.

"There is snow in the mountain passes," he said. "No traveler can pass through Karseni until the weather breaks. Doubtless the messenger we both await will be here when the roads clear." He sighed. "Whatever the news from Tredana, there will of a certainty be war for us with Treclere this spring. There is one there who claims himself our son, attacks our ships and waylays our merchants. He is known to Tredana, it is said."

"Yes," said Sibyl. "We know Odric."

Bodrum sighed again heavily and gestured for her to precede him inside. Below in her sitting room he waited for her to settle by the fire, then sat down at her right, leaning forward with his head in his hands. "What is not well known," he said at last, "is that this same Odric has with his own hands murdered the two young princes of Vahn, the most dearly beloved sons of our body."

There was a suspicion of tears glittering in his eyes and Sibyl reached forward to put her hand on his. "No, no, you are mistaken. I saw Kerys with my own eyes in Tredana. He is well, and he spoke of Varys also."

Bodrum squeezed her hand and then drew his away to cover his eyes. "That was not Kerys, but an imposter," he said at last. "Irrefutable proof of their death has been received in Vahn."

Sibyl looked at him in concern and horror. True, she had seen Kerys only once before, years past, but surely Odric would

have no reason for such an elaborate charade. He was their
friend—and what of his mother, cruelly murdered by Bodrum
when Odric was a baby? She had heard that story more than
once. She rubbed her scarred wrists uneasily. "Why would
Odric have anyone impersonate Kerys?"

As so often happened, Bodrum answered her thoughts rather
than her words, speaking even more softly than usual. "His
hatred of us goes back over many years," he said. "Once he
was well received in Vahn, beloved for his talent with voice
and baraka. But he was of low birth, his mother a strumpet
found murdered with her latest lover, and this preyed on his
mind until he made up stories of a secret, higher birth. Nothing
less would do than that his father was the Master of Vahn. I
do not doubt but that he believes these tales himself, now."
Bodrum laughed bitterly. "And now to ensure his claims, he
has had murdered those who had the true claim to the throne."
Again he buried his face in his hands, and his shoulder shook
under Sibyl's gentle touch. There was a short silence, then he
shook his head and stood up. "We regret the intrusion of our
grief upon your own melancholy," he said. "If you will excuse
us tonight—" he turned hastily and went out.

Next day was clear and sunny and cold, and Sibyl took
advantage of the weather to ride in the ring after breakfast.
Bodrum appeared by the rail as she put the bay mare through
a simple routine of circles and turns and changes of lead. He
smiled approvingly. "Your skill becomes you well. As does
your new appearance. The Tredanan King will not be too dis-
pleased with us when you return. He will see that you have
been cared for tenderly." He spoke with deep sincerity, his
face not many inches from her own, and Sibyl blushed, her
embarrassment causing the mare to fret and sidle. Bodrum made
to leave, but first he touched her cloak gently. "I shall see you
are sent one in red. It becomes you better than this drab green."

After Bodrum returned to the city, Sibyl was seized with
restlessness. The other towers of the fortress were used pri-
marily for storage, although Bodrum maintained apartments in
the eastern tower opposite. But in the walls themselves, there
were many small rooms she had only partially explored. Pulling
the cloak warmly around her she went to walk on the battlements, following the little stairways down into the inner passages and rooms, then up again onto the broad stone wall. Most
of the rooms were thick with dust, silent and empty; some had

birds' nests in their corners. But in the northeastern stretch of
wall there were oddments of furniture that interested her and
good views across the narrow straits to land. In one room there
was a table and chairs most beautifully carved with dragons
and monsters, and Sibyl spent pleasant minutes running her
hands over the wood and admiring all the subtle twists and
turns of the design. In the farther wall there was a heavy wooden
door instead of an open archway. Supposing that stairs up to
the battlements lay beyond, she walked over casually and turned
the brass handle. The opulence of the room beyond stunned
her, and as she stood there she was greeted by a deep and
sinister laugh.

Sibyl had clearly wandered further than intended, all the
way to Bodrum's rooms in the far tower. The chamber could
be no one else's. Again the evil laugh rang out, and she looked
up to find herself face to face with an enormous green parrot.
He was hanging nonchalantly upside down from his polished
stand, on a level with her face, and his scarlet beak barely
moved as he laughed a third time and righted himself.

There was no one else in the room. Sibyl hastily made to
go, and the bird lifted its head surprisingly high from its hunched
shoulders. "You cannot go," it said quietly and watched her
closely with one bright eye. It polished the edge of its beak
against the stand and spoke even more softly. "You cannot,
cannot, cannot go. Never again, no, no, no. Aha!" And it leapt
a little in the air, rearranging the feathers in its wings. "You
must do better than that, my friend," it said confidentially, then
screamed heart-breakingly, loudly, ending in a fit of sobbing.
It flipped upside down once more and spread its wings. "Do
not make me do that again," it said with a leer and it chuckled
deep within its iridescent throat. It was still chuckling as Sibyl
shut the door and hurried back the way she had come.

Next day a red cloak appeared as Bodrum had promised,
trimmed with fur. Boredom had drawn Sibyl to the mirror, and
she could not resist trying its effect, turning and twisting to
piece together a comprehensive view in its small dull surface.

As she turned sideways she could not help but notice how
prominent her belly had become. She pressed her hands against
it awkwardly and counted in her mind. Four months—no, five.
As though in answer, there came a funny flutter under her
hand, and she pressed the spot with her fingers. It fluttered
again and she began laughing with delight; it was real, it was

there, and moving with complete independence.

The week that followed was the briefest and happiest of her captivity. She put all thought of the parrot out of her mind and did not go exploring along the walls again. When Bodrum returned to Almond Island he looked tired and careworn, but he immediately noticed and commented warmly on Sibyl's appearance. They ate supper together, and only when they had finished did he set a document case upon the table and slowly open it.

"We did not wish to speak of this before dining," he said. "Nor did we wish to spoil your content. But a messenger has arrived and his message must be delivered."

The child moved feebly, and Sibyl pressed her hand below her breast in apprehension. Bodrum's quick eyes noticed. "You are well?"

"Yes. I—I am carrying a child."

Bodrum sighed, then he smiled briefly. "We shall write of this to Tredana. Perhaps the news will move the King's hard heart."

"How do you mean?"

Bodrum gestured at the papers with his hand. "There is no message here for you directly. I have received a Declaration of War, and the appointment of an intermediary to negotiate terms. Tredana offers nothing for your safe return, but the King writes, in appointing the Karif he feels he has provided adequately for you; and that the Karif may pay for you whatever price he sees fit." Sibyl rose to her feet, shaking. Bodrum stood aside to let her pass, his face twisted with sympathy, and Sibyl nodded blindly as she hurried out.

For several days thereafter Sibyl had difficulty sleeping. She did not eat at all; the smallest swallow of water or bit of bread triggered a nervous nausea and she paced her room restlessly or sat dry-eyed by the window doing nothing. The ring that had been Leron's mother's she angrily threw in the fire that first night, and now she nervously pressed her bare finger against her lips, missing its shape but too proud to rake through the embers for its remains. Not long after, Bodrum sent word that the Karseni pass was clear and that the Karif would arrive with his men to parlay within the following month. A few days later, he came to Almond Island for a short stay and spoke with her most kindly. He insisted that she eat and instructed his servants accordingly; then had her dress warmly and took her to walk on the tower as before.

It was cold but not unpleasantly so: the sky was calm and the sea grey and absolutely flat. "We have passed the longest night," he said at last. "Soon you will notice more light in the afternoon, and the dawn will not be so late in coming." She nodded, not trusting her voice. "It is possible," he said after a brief silence, "that the Karif will not be concerned with your ransom. This matter is not of importance to the Karabdu." She nodded again.

"If Vahn cannot claim you as a hostage, perhaps it may persuade you to stay in a more honored position?" He clasped both her hands and stood looking closely into her eyes, only an inch or so the taller. She looked away.

"I do not understand," she said, and he released her hand to take her chin and raise her lips to his. For a moment she was too surprised to move, then she gently pulled away, shaking her head. "Please," she said, "it isn't possible."

His beard was very soft and warm, and her heart was beating wildly. Bodrum looked sad. "Have you been unhappy here?"

She shook her head. "No, it isn't that. But I can't break my word. I can't be an enemy to Tredana, or to Leron."

"Tredana is not so loyal to you." He touched the tears running from her eyes with one hand, and it was all she could do to keep from falling into his warm, strong arms. "If you cry up here, you will freeze in the wind," he said. "Very well, we will not press you. But do not forget our offer." She shook her head and let herself be led inside.

That night she cried for what seemed hours, clutching her pillow until it was so wet she threw it onto the floor. She wanted to tear Leron's throat out with her bare hands, but she also wanted him to love her again, and the conflict exhausted her. Leron could have come himself in the time it took the messenger to arrive. It could have been his kiss on her mouth. She could have been ransomed and tonight they could have been warm under the covers together. Instead she was alone and crying herself sick. What a joy it would be to make him suffer also: she would have her revenge if it took a lifetime.

In her uneasy sleep she imagined that she was trying to leave the castle. She went as far as the door and pushed against it, but it was locked and as she pushed with her whole weight against the panels, she felt again the soft fullness of Bodrum's body pressing back against her own, and she awoke in terror.

It was a moment before she could be sure she was alone in the room. There was a faint light from the snapping embers in the fireplace, and a small streak of light at the window. She sat up and pulled the covers around her chin. What was wrong with her? Bodrum was her only friend. She hadn't been afraid this afternoon. Yet now with the aura of the dream around her, the thought of his arms made her shudder. The feeling would not go away, and finally she got up and wrapped the quilt around her. The privacy of her bed had somehow been invaded.

Sibyl went to the window, and there was just enough moonlight to glitter on the water below and make each small wave a stark triangle of shadow. It touched the edge of the board of Castledown as well. Weeks past she and Bodrum had played several games one afternoon, here at her window. She had almost forgotten they were captive and captor. That was the time Bodrum had spoken to her about the history of Vahn and had been so pleased the one time she won the game.

One thing that he had said stayed with her still, relaxed and unthinking though she had been at the time. She had lost a game foolishly to his siege, and they had been laughing as she set up the board once more. Then Bodrum suddenly looked at her sharply and spoke soberly. "It is good that you now know we are not your enemy. In years to come you will learn that there is no such thing as enemy, as there is no such thing as friend." He cut short her protest. "We would not expect you to understand yet. When you are older, it will be unavoidable, unless you close your eyes. When you learn not to look for enemies, you will not lack for friends: when you learn not to look for friends, you will not mourn their inevitable loss."

Directly below, a shape broke up through the water and fell back again, disturbing her reverie. Something large—whale, shark, dolphin? As she watched, another twisting leap and a faint splash. It was not far from the little balcony that jutted out over the water from the bottommost room in the tower. It was impossible to sleep, and she did not feel like thinking about Bodrum. She pulled her red cloak on over her nightdress and laced on a warm pair of fur slippers. She was silent on the stone floor, and the maid did not awake as she went out through the antechamber.

The dream had been wrong: the outer door was not locked. She went down the winding stone stairs quietly, one hand on the wall for guidance. The bottommost room was not used in wintertime, being too cold and damp, but its door was also unlocked. Tall windows on either side of the low fireplace of carved stone gave onto the balcony. Despite the cloak, she shivered a little as she stepped out onto it, a few feet above the water. It was darker here under the shadow of the tower, difficult to see clearly. Then she heard the splash again, and for a moment the shape of a dolphin showed against the darker water. There was a thump and another dolphin broke through, making an anxious, high-pitched, chattering sound.

Apparently they were battering themselves against part of the tower. She leaned out farther but could not see what they were doing. Suddenly there was a tiny gleam of light on the water, and she had a momentary glimpse of a grating in the rock, through which seawater washed. The light came from behind the grating, and it was against those bars the dolphins had been throwing themselves. The light seemed to startle them for they drew back from the tower wall.

There was only one stair, Sibyl knew, that led down below the level where she was standing. Its entrance was near the kitchen, and it led to a small storage cellar. Perhaps the kitchen threw out its scraps at night and this had attracted the dolphins. She turned to go upstairs when another sound startled her, as high pitched as their chattering but long drawn out and musical, filled with suffering. It came from the grating in the stones. She held her breath and leaned out over the water again. The sound came again, higher and more intensely pain filled. It was followed horribly by a man's laughter.

She stood still with shock. What was the parrot doing in the cellar? The laugh was unmistakeable. And weren't birds supposed to be quiet at night? Silently she recrossed the room and went out into the courtyard. Well under the shadow of the building she slipped along until she reached the entrance to the kitchens. From under one door there shone a red light from the constant cooking fire, but the steps down into the cellar were dark. She went down noiselessly, shivering now from the intense night air. Below in the small cellar she stood still and listened. There was a scutter of mice among the flour sacks and dimly on her left a sound of seawaves. Her fingers trailed along the wall and found an opening in the dark. It was a passageway, pitch black, but wide and high roofed. As she stepped in, she could smell the sea and hear the slapping water far ahead. She stepped along cautiously, and the wall gave way

under her fingers, in good time, for there was a flicker of light
ahead and she stepped back into the small cell just as two
muffled figures passed, carrying a small lantern. Her heart beat
violently, and she stood absolutely still for several minutes.
Then she went out into the dark again and followed the tunnel
to its end.

There was a little light there, shining in from outside through
a double grating. The inner bars were set across the end of the
passage, bolted and chained and locked. The outer grating was
smaller and only barred together in the middle; the sea washed
in and covered the bottom of the small cell with several feet
of cold black water. A pale figure floated on its surface, surrounded by a web of hair. Sibyl stepped up to the bars and
touched them with her hand: they were achingly cold. As she
stood there, the outer bars shivered from a desperate blow. The
dolphins had returned.

The floating figure raised its face from the water and fell
back again weakly at the sight of Sibyl standing there cloaked
and hooded. Then it spoke, with the voice of a woman. "Kill
me as you have the others. You will never learn anything of
help from me." The dark slits in her throat fluttered clearly.

Sibyl strained her face close to the bars. "Are you one of
the Dylalyr? Why are you here?"

The other opened her eyes and tried to struggle to her knees,
but her body was dark with brusies, and she was very weak.
She pulled herself through the water and pressed her face close
to Sibyl's. She seemed even more fragile than Leron had described and spoke with difficulty. "Who are you?"

"I am from Tredana," Sibyl answered. "There I heard about
the Dylalyr."

"Are you also a prisoner?"

"A hostage, yes. Why are you here? Does Bodrum know?"

At his name the sea woman threw back her head in despair.
"He has torn my people apart before my eyes. But crueler than
that, he will not let me follow them into peace."

"What has happened? Are you at war?"

The other did not answer, bent over in the water, nursing
a hurt wrist and rocking back and forth in agony. "They will
tear me apart bone from bone before I tell. This is some trick
of Bodrum's. Tell him the alliance will triumph, and Vahanavat
will burn over his head."

Her delicate wrist seemed broken, and she doubled over in

pain. Sibyl found she was almost crying herself in empathy. "Please," she said, "perhaps I can help. I am Sibyl, the wife of Leron. Trust me."

The other looked at her more closely. "If you are Sibyl, I have heard of you from Dansen. My name is Arrod."

"Arrod! Leron spoke of you. How do you come to be here?"

Arrod took hold of a bar with her good hand and tried to draw herself closer, but drew back as Sibyl reached to help her. "Do not touch me. I cannot bear your touches."

She huddled against the bars. "I came here a prisoner from Melismala, in the hold of a ship from Vahn. We have had a great battle. Is it not spoken of in Vahn?"

"I don't know. I am a prisoner in this castle."

"I see. It was your Dansen brought Melismala the power to withstand Paradon; we destroyed their ships as they gathered to despoil the island; many ships burned, and those who sailed in them we did not suffer to return from our undersea kingdom to the air above. There was great rejoicing in Melismala, and we below the water were as happy as the ones above it."

"How do you come to be here, if you won the battle? Is Dansen all right?"

Arrod began crying with a sad whistling sound, her long white arms wrapped loosely around her knees, her hair spread out in the water around her and her broken hand hanging limply. "A ship from Vahn bound for Paradon came upon us as we rejoiced unsuspecting. There was no time for the weapon to be used. They did not dare approach the shore, but they took many of my people prisoner, for they know we cannot fight them hand to hand. And they brought us here so we might tell the Master how it happened that Melismala destroyed the fleet from Paradon; and that he might amuse himself with our destruction."

Her voice dropped. "And worst is that Dansen had prepared to join us in the water, as some men may, who care not for risk or any danger of strangeness. When we were taken, he came back into the air again and tried to follow us. No man may risk a second journey undersea. We will never meet there now, even if I live."

Sibyl took hold of the bars and pulled angrily. "I don't understand this very well, but there isn't time now. If you were free, could you return home? Are those dolphins out there your friends?"

"The Mahiva wait for me outside, and they will see me home. But I cannot escape. I will die here as the others have done and only hope it will be soon."

Sibyl strained again, but the bars were set tightly and firmly locked. The farther sea gate was far flimsier, fastened with a simple bar, but out of reach. Helpless with fury Sibyl blasted the bar in her mind, and it seemed to shift a little, though it might have been the changing light on the water. She pressed her hands to her eyes, trying to remember the feeling of power from before, pushing the bar with all her strength of thought. This time she could hear the rasp as it moved. She strained the harder, until her shoulders trembled and there was sweat on her face.

Arrod gave a weak cry of amazement, and Sibyl looked up to see the bar slip sideways and the gates open a little. Arrod tried to pull them back but they were stiff and far beyond her power. She cried aloud strange sounds, and the dolphins reappeared. They threw themselves triumphantly against the opening and pushed the grating back until the narrow opening was wide enough for Arrod's body.

Tenderly they gathered around her, clucking and chirping. "I must go now," she said, "but the Dylalyr do not forget. Do not despair, Vahn will not successfully besiege Tredana much longer. Dansen's weapon will burn this empire down. You will be free soon, as I am now." As she spoke, she disappeared into the darkness and the little cell was empty. Sibyl shivered, slowly realizing that she was drenched with sweat. So much effort to move a little bar. But at least the powers were there when most needed.

Sibyl drew her cloak around her and hurried back down the passage, thence safely upstairs and back to the tower and her own room. She hung the cloak out by the dead fire's warmth and quickly sponged herself clean with cold water. Then she suddenly knelt on the brick hearth and searched the hot ashes with anxious fingers. The ring was black and so hot it burned her, but when she washed it clean she could see it was undamaged and the diamonds winked bravely bright in the slowly growing light of dawn. She kissed it and carefully drew it onto her finger again; she fell asleep with it pressed against her mouth, her other hand comfortably tucked under her sleeping child.

She did not see Bodrum that day, but he sent for her on the

next and received her graciously, holding her hand a moment
longer than was usual and looking her closely in the eyes.
There were signs of strain under his own. "We will meet the
Karif tomorrow," he said at last. "He does not seem to trust
the honor of Vahn, for he brings an army with him. But he
has promised to meet with us here, alone. Soon we shall know
if there are any further messages from Tredana."

Sibyl drew her hand away. "May I be permitted to speak
with him?"

"In the future, of course. Tomorrow would not be correct.
We shall assure him of your safety, never fear. Have you
thought further on our other words?"

Sibyl sat down and drew her skirts around her ankles, crossing her arms protectively in front of her belly. "I have thought,"
she said slowly. "And I realize you know very little about me."
Bodrum gestured impatiently, but she shook her head. "No, I
think it will interest you. Before the death of Simirimia of
Treclere, Vahn was not so powerful as it is now; it was, I
believe, a vassal state. I am the daughter of Simirimia."

For once Bodrum showed surprise, and the pink mouth
twitched in the depths of his beard. "We had heard you were
a cousin to the king."

"I am that also. My father Armon was twin to Leriel, the
mother of Leron. Through him I am descended from an ancient
priestly house of old Treglad." She stood up and walked over
towards the window. "Certain small powers I have from my
mother, and better ones yet from my father, for the house of
Leriel and Armon could dream the future truly. Last night I
dreamt I saw ships from Vahn besieging the Tredanan harbor,
and I also saw flames arising from Vahanavat. Do you think
I am misled in my visions?"

Bodrum paled slightly, but he smiled as he walked up to
her. "Often we dream in parables. How do you read your
dreams?" He placed one hand on her arm and shivered. He
turned her towards him, and for all his acuteness failed to read
the changed look in her eyes. "Perhaps the flames were for
passion," he said at last and wrapped his massive arms around
her. There was the horror of the nightmare in the soft full
heaviness of his body pressed against her. She did not struggle
for fear of tightening his grasp, but pulled free as soon as he
took his mouth away.

"No, my lord," she said quietly. "Whether the message from

Tredana is kind or cruel, I have no desire to be anything but loyal to my city and my king."

"They do not desire your return."

"But I desire it, in any case."

He shook his head and took hold of her arms again. "You will be happier with us." Once more he folded her in his arms, and this time she could not control herself and fought to be free. His massive arms easily contained her, and she could feel a laugh deep in his chest. He must have laughed so when he snapped Arrod's wrist between his fingers: it was the sound his parrot knew so well. But when he spoke, it was as gently as ever and she realized that he did not yet understand the depth of her revulsion.

"Do not fear for the child," he said. "I am a patient man and can wait a matter of months." When he took his lips away a second time, she gasped for breath. "Shall we inform the Karif of our happy intentions tomorrow? Tredana will believe the news better if it comes from him."

Sibyl pulled free, restraining with difficulty a desire to wipe her mouth clean with her hand. "I cannot make up my mind so quickly."

An impatient frown passed over his face, but he smiled again immediately. "Very well, we will talk with the Karif and learn what news he carries. But we shall prepare him for the news that is to come." He smiled gently and bowed his head, indicating that she might leave. As soon as the door had closed between them, she wiped her face with her hand and then her sleeve, and once out in the courtyard spat on the frozen ground as well. But as she went up the stairs to her room she was smiling. She could not yet see her way out of the forest, but at least the traps set within it had become a little more apparent.

She was up early the next morning to watch the fluttering approach of the Karabdin army. They drew up their lines beyond the town, out of sight; but nearly a hundred men accompanied the Karif to shore. They sat their horses quietly, and their banners hung still in the cold air. A tall figure in white dismounted from a golden dun and approached the waiting boat. The red-embroidered headcloth hid his face, but it was Ajjibawr. She leaned against the parapet of the tower, and her hands shook.

He entered the boat unaccompanied but for Bodrum's men, and she watched it disappear around the tower's edge with sharp anxiety. What if there were treachery? An hour passed, or more, and as she waited to see the Karif's safe return to shore, there was a step behind her, and she turned to see Bodrum, his eyes alight with triumph. "Our first talks have gone well," he said. "See, he returns to shore, his crest a little lowered." Sibyl followed his pointing hand and saw the boat making its way back, the Karif impassive in its midst.

"What was his message?" she asked, and Bodrum smiled reflectively and put his hand on her arm. As he did so, she read the words from his mind as easily as though they were printed on paper, and she drew back, flaring her nostrils with anger. She brought up her hand between them. "You dare bargain with my life? Is this your honor?"

Bodrum looked at her in amazement, his clever eyes wide for once. "Do you deny it?" she cried. Below them the boat reached shore, and the Karif wearily pulled himself onto his horse. Sibyl watched him mount and turned back to the still silent Bodrum. "You told him that the Tredanan Queen and unborn heir were in your power, and the price of our continued life was his swift departure. Do you deny this?" Bodrum did not answer. "Speak up, you reveal nothing new. I can hear the words in your mind."

She did not understand that this was true until she said it. She made an angry motion with her hand, and Bodrum stepped back; she tossed her head, and he stepped back one pace farther. "And then you dared to say that if we lived, the next child would be your own. Fool, you have lost your chance. You will have to rethink your future."

Bodrum's first dismay had given way to anger, and he took her by the wrist. "Come below," he said roughly, "and I will give you a taste of your future here."

She jerked her wrist free and laughed in his face. "I never gave you my word," she said, "and now I am going to escape." He reached for her again, but she stepped lightly up onto the low parapet. The water seemed very distant, but it could not be more than four or five stories down. Forty feet at most. And if she did not survive, at least there was no hostage left to Bodrum. His hand was at her ankle. She jerked free and stumbled forward, pushing far out to avoid the rocks below. Time stood still in the winter air; then the water rushed up and knocked her sprawling, and silently closed a dark door over her head.

LETTER
from BODRUM VIII
to ORLOS, Admiral of Vahn
aboard the *Sembat*, lying off Vahanavat

The one who bears this message also bears the name of Arleon, and by no mischance. He has been of use to us on land and it is our hope he will continue this same usefulness afloat.

Employ him as his talents merit, and do not be surprised if his rise is swift. It is our opinion that he will be of greater use in command than under it.

BODRUM VIII

Given under his hand and seal at Almond Island, on this the 12th day of the first month of the 47th year of his reign.

V: CASTLEDOWN

Chapter One

The swift fall through the air continued under the water, a rush of coldness around her as she sank. Finally the force of the fall diminished, and she began to struggle upwards again, already too cold to move her arms or legs strongly, too heavy with water to breathe. The air burned her face as she gasped and choked on the sea's surface, trying to fight the downward drag of her heavy clothes. With painful and increasing slowness she kicked off her flimsy shoes, but their weight was nothing compared to that of her full, heavy skirts, worse than chains around her legs. Her arms could barely move in their dragging sleeves, but she made a few weak strokes towards shore. It was too far, too cold, too heavy; she moved her arms once more on the water's surface, then closed her eyes as she sank again.

The water filling her mouth and nose made her open her eyes, and she struggled on another few feet. Then, incredibly, there was a horse's head rising out of the waves before her, a frothing yellow head with black-tipped ears and rolling eyes, most certainly no seahorse but a land animal forced into an alien element. The churning legs struck against her own and pulled her down; but as she sank, strong hands took hold of her dress and heaved her partway out of the water. She clutched at the ornate pommel, and the rider shifted his grip, so that when the horse's flailing legs finally bit sand and they plunged up out of the waves, he could swing her up over the saddle before him.

Commands were spoken and a heavy cloak flung over her, sheltering her from the sharp air; then the rider gathered her up more firmly and set the horse at a gallop back through the ranks of the Karabdu. In their camp she was handed briefly into another man's arms, then the Karif swung down and took her up again and carried her into his tent. There, still without speaking and working as rapidly and as impersonally as a groom in a stable, he cut off her freezing dress with the knife from his sash and began to rub her roughly with a blanket. She protested as the blood came back to her arms and legs and tried to pull free, but he held her sternly with one hand and continued until she was dry. Then he took up a heavier quilted covering and wrapped it around her. She huddled in it gratefully, still shaking and chattering as he stepped briefly outside.

In moments he returned with dry robes hastily pulled on and still unfastened at the neck, holding a small cup in his hands. He sat down with one arm behind her head to help her drink, and the sweetened coffee burned on her chilled lips. Finally he spoke, "Slowly," he said. "We have more coffee in camp should you require it."

At this she laughed, a little wildly, and dropped her head against his breast. He set down the cup and closed his arms reassuringly around her. His silk shirt was soft and clean smelling; but as feeling returned to her body, Sibyl sat back in embarrassment and pulled the quilt up around her neck. Ajjibawr smiled. "So," he remarked, "it seems you have survived."

"I was only thinking about getting away. I forgot how cold it would be."

"Yes. I do not ordinarily go in myself before midsummer."

He grinned, the tight skin crinkling on his temples, and Sibyl dropped her eyes. "Thank you."

"It was nothing. I only regret not seeing Bodrum's face when he learns."

"He knows already. He was with me on the tower. I got mad at him."

Ajjibawr nodded, taking a pinch of snuff from a large box on the floor. Sibyl settled back against her cushions, beginning to feel warm, and listened in comfort to the familiar sound of his sneeze. Ajjibawr ribbed the edge of his nostril reflectively. "What was it angered you so?"

He listened attentively, nodding from time to time, still

rubbing the back of his hand against his nose. As she told the story of the past few months, she took in every detail of the Karif's appearance with an eye sharpened by concern. He had never looked so weary that she could recall. The shadows under his eyes were startlingly dark against his pale skin; the fair hair receding from his high forehead was more streaked with white than she had realized. Nor did he sit as still as before; one strong-boned hand played nervously with the edge of the snuff-box, snapping the lid open and shut, open and shut. He listened carefully, however, and did not comment until she came to the part about Arrod.

"I cannot explain all she said," he remarked, "but I can tell you how Dansen embarked with his weapon. When I left Tredana, it was not known whether or not it would prove successful. We must send word to Leron at once."

Sibyl brought her arm up in front of her belly, feeling herself blush. "I must send a message also."

"Yes. You are well?"

The last question was said softly, and there was in it a challenge to meet his eyes but she looked away. "Yes. I'm fine."

"That is good." He spoke more formally, and when she did look up again there was no special intimacy in his eyes.

He rose to his feet and indicated the curtain with his hand. "You may have the inner room. This is a war party, and we boast few amenities. True, the Tayyib has brought his youngest wife, but he is a rule to himself. For now, borrow whatever of my clothing takes your fancy; for the future I will see if I can find some boy with narrower shoulders than mine to lend some clothes." One of Ajjibawr's saddles was set against the edge of the tent, and the ornate leather case fastened to it lay partially opened. He pulled out several documents and shook out one small letter sealed with red wax. He handed it to her. "I did not bring this with me because I thought it best to talk with Bodrum and learn his plans first. It is clear he would not have passed the message on, any more than he gave you the letter Leron sent earlier. I will leave you to read in private. There is a servant outside the tent, who will help you as you may require it."

He nodded and went outside, leaving Sibyl with the letter in her hand. She moved closer to the small brass lamp and pulled the quilt up more snugly around her. So there had been another message. How could she have believed Bodrum? The wax slipped off, and the single sheet unfolded stiffly. She read the brief and loving message several times through and pressed it against her face. As she sobbed in relief, the child within pushed back fretfully, and the seeming impatience made her laugh again. Soon they would both be home.

It made her feel strangely intimate to rummage through Ajjibawr's clothes. As she pulled on the shortest tunic she could find, the pleasant familiar smell enveloped her, and she felt comforted and relaxed. But how irritatingly masculine not to have a mirror anywhere. The one she finally found was small and suitable only for shaving. The razors fitted in the same case were frighteningly sharp, like weapons. It was impossible to imagine Ajjibawr with a beard. He was one of those men who seem naturally clean shaven. He had asked to be shaved as soon as he awoke from his illness on the *Damar*. A sudden warmth of tenderness swept over her, and she hastily closed the razor case and pulled on a woolen vest to go outside.

The sun was bright and yellow, but the air bitterly sharp; Sibyl marveled she could ever have thrown herself into the sea on such a day, for any reason. She felt so warm now, and so dry. Not far away Ajjibawr was standing in close conversation with a heavyset older man, dark for one of the Karabdu and with grizzled hair hanging onto his shoulders.

He saw her first and bowed gravely. "The Tredanan Queen is welcome amongst us. The Karabdu are ennobled by her presence among their tents."

Ajjibawr raised an ironic eyebrow and added, "You might also say, it is easier for us to deal with Bodrum now he has no hostage to hold over us. Sibby—I present to you the Mekrif of the Tayyib, Adaba, an old friend and sometime loyal subject."

Sibyl smiled. "I have heard many tales of the Tayyib. I had expected a much older man."

Adaba grinned delightedly and turned on Ajjibawr. "So this is how you speak behind my back. My Karif, to whom I owe all obedience."

"Do not speak too freely of all the obedience you owe, lest I ask for payment." He looked past Adaba and smiled. "Your bodyguard returns."

Adaba turned eagerly and hurried towards a group of young

men who had ridden in and were dismounting a little way away.
Their leader was of middle height and thin, with short, pale,
curly hair and intense blue eyes. He handed down his great
sword to one of the others and also his reins, but did not
dismount. Adaba went up to his horse and held up his arms,
and the youth slipped his own around the old man's neck and
let himself be lifted from off his horse; his left leg dragged as
the foot pulled limply from the stirrup. Sibyl watched curiously
as Adaba settled his burden more comfortably in his arms before
turning towards them; behind her Ajjibawr spoke softly.

"Now you will meet Shadith, wife to the Tayyib. He swears
this will be the last, and I think for once the old wolf does not
lie. Her story will be of interest to you."

Adaba set Shadith on her feet when they were near and
supported her with an arm about her shoulders. She limped
towards them and made a deep obeisance to the Karif. A scar
stood out red against her clear white forehead. Ajjibawr continued even more softly, "She is another one marked by Arleon.
Your young companion Kerys also. But Kerys was only stunned.
Shadith took a knife in the neck as well, and you may see the
result. It has affected her left arm also."

Sibyl smiled at Shadith, and the other met her eyes with
nervous boldness. She made a handsome boy, and it seemed
impossible that anyone so vivid and so young could already be
crippled for life. Sibyl put out her hand. "Please," she said,
"if you have the time, I would like to talk with you. There is
so much I must know, if I am to spend any time among your
people."

Shadith smiled suddenly, and her face changed completely:
she no longer looked like a boy at all. "I will be honored," she
said at last, then let Adaba lead her away, his arm about her
still.

Ajjibawr shook his head. "She will never learn to manage
on her own if he does not cease to hover over her."

"In the same case, wouldn't you show concern?"

"I would show it differently. I am not so sentimental."

Sibyl nodded, then shivered in the wind. "I think I would
like to rest a little. Has Bodrum sent a message?"

"One came while you were still inside. An invitation to
parley tomorrow, on shore, under the white flag. Today we
watch, but do not fight. You will do well to rest now—there
may be no chance tomorrow."

Sibyl went back slowly into the tent, filled with a strange discontent. It was a little warmer inside, and a small brazier had been lit in the inner room, the cushions arranged invitingly and covered with quilts and a rug of red fox fur. Most of Ajjibawr's personal effects had been removed to the small cold anteroom; all that remained was a carved wooden comb and a few pieces of clothing. The room now smelt of charcoal. Sibyl suddenly felt very alone and huddled under the covers against the cushions, presently falling into a deep exhausted slumber that lasted until dinnertime.

After eating, Sibyl sat back to listen with amazement to Adaba's story of the female brigand and how she had rescued him from the clutches of Dzildzil; the story ended with the Holy Reader's head being displayed on a pole. The simplicity with which Adaba described his revenge made Sibyl feel very much an alien. Of all those listening, only she could not follow the tale from beginning to end without question; only she wondered about the untold stories, the differing points of view, and all the conflicts possible in apparent justice. Ajjibawr's profile against the campfire was as straight and uncompromising as Adaba's story. If anyone should be tainted with the complications of life outside the desert, it should be he. Yet he was sterner than Adaba: Adaba was sentimental.

Next morning Sibyl woke to Ajjibawr's touch on her face. She smiled warmly and unguardedly up at him without thinking. He flushed and drew back, and Sibyl shrank under the covers. "What's the matter?" she asked. "Is it late?"

"No," said Ajjibawr, "but I thought you would want to know that Odric has arrived with an army. And before the day is over, I would not be surprised if we were at war with Vahn."

Odric swept her off her feet, swung her around, and patted her familiarly on the stomach. "So," he said, "we have Tredana's heir as well as Tredana's queen under our protection. I hear that Bodrum did not release you willingly."

Ajjibawr, who had been standing by with a strained tired look on his face, laughed at this. "She released herself, most dramatically."

Odric reached around and put his hand on a young boy's shoulder, pulling him forward. "I have to present to you my youngest brother, Varys. He rides with me as squire, though

I would have preferred him to stay safely home in Treclere."
Varys greatly resembled Kerys, and like him blushed and spoke
inaudibly when first presented to Sibyl.

She smiled at him warmly, then looked at Odric in concern.
"Where is Kerys? How badly was he injured? I thought he
would be recovered by now."

Odric tugged at his beard in irritation. "Well enough to have
run away, foolish puppy that he is. I hoped he might have
joined you here, but I see we must look further for him."

"Run off? What for?"

Odric shrugged his massive shoulders, raising his eyebrows.
"Varys knows better than I, and he knows little enough. I
suppose it was jealousy, ill-founded, I might add."

"The same thing still?"

Odric nodded.

Leaving Varys to take charge of his horse and supervise the
encampment of his men, Odric followed Ajjibawr and Sibyl
into their tent. Adaba was sent for also, and when he arrived,
Odric greeted him warmly. "I had hoped to see you here. There
is a little matter to be settled between us. Certain merchants
from my city seem to have mislaid a donkey train at the desert's
edge, and it occurred to me you might have seen it. There were
three loads of saffron and five of indigo."

"Those were your men?" Adaba raised his shaggy brows in
amazement, and his heavy-hooded eyes opened widely innocent. "They ran off at my approach so rapidly, I thought them
robbers. Three each of saffron and indigo?"

"Five of indigo and yes, one more, of henna. You have
seen it, then?"

"It is safe, untouched, my lord." He looked sideways at the
unsmiling Karif. "And it shall be restored to you in its entirety."

Odric's chest rumbled with discreet laughter. "I must thank
you for having guarded it so well. Now, when do we meet
with Bodrum?"

Ajjibawr clicked his snuffbox open and shut. "At noon he
will meet us alone, under the white flag, just ashore from his
island fortress." He briefly gave Odric the facts of the past few
days, and Sibyl's news from Arrod of the defeat of the Para-
donians.

Odric shook his head. "The Master has spread his forces
very thin. There are ships off Tredana and Sundrat, ships off

the southern villages that lie below the desert, and a full fleet here in the harbor. He seems to have left very little army ashore."

"I do not think he ever expected to have two forces attack. Your army he may have expected, but not so soon; the Karabdu until recently were his faithful vassals. Events have moved swiftly and found out his weaknesses."

"He knows of Dansen's glass?"

"He has heard of its power but has no clear knowledge of it, I am certain: this may have hurried him into an unprepared attack on Tredana."

"Then it seems we should hurry him further and besiege the city; he will not foolishly prolong it since he can always escape to his fleet. Once we are firmly entrenched here on land, Vahn will be a power without any base on shore."

"Has Leron made his intentions known on this?" asked Sibyl.

"He could not plan," said Odric, "not knowing Bodrum's conditions for your release. But he has agreed with us that Vahn should be destroyed."

"Very well. I will speak for him and agree with you all."

Ajjibawr got abruptly to his feet and threw back the flap of the tent, squinting at the sun. "I had best leave soon: the sun is nearly as high as it can reach this time of year." At his word two grooms brought up The Thunderer, as fresh and quick with his feet and teeth as ever. Ajjibawr looked at him critically. "It seems that none of us were harmed by our swim." He pulled himself quickly up, to avoid being bitten, and The Thunderer backed up several rapid steps. Ajjibawr suddenly looked at Odric. "Did the old one recover enough to come on with you? Good. Tell the queen." He nodded formally to them and cantered off to join his escort.

Sibyl looked at Odric expectantly, and he put his arm around her and gave her a squeeze. "When the Karif and Glisser fell upon the outlaws, they found your horse: the one that had been the Karif's years ago. It was too lame to come on then, so the Karif left it with me and asked that I bring it along for you if possible, since he was confident of your eventual release despite our disappointment."

Odric nodded to Varys and the boy hurried off, returning soon with the old horse sauntering along behind on the end of a lead shank, looking fat and pleased with himself. He rubbed

his head up and down against Sibyl, and she had to push him
away to keep from being knocked down. When she kissed him
on the nose, he shook his head and nipped at her gently. Odric
laughed. "I must go and see to the settling of my men."

"Odric—what about my ring? The one I put on Sweetmouth's collar. Did Glisser keep it?"

"Glisser? No. He returned it to the Karif. He must have
forgotten to give it back to you." He raised his hand in parting
and walked off with Varys. Sibyl put her arms around Silver's
neck and rested her face against his sweet-smelling side, warm
with the thick soft fur of winter.

At the sound of hoofbeats she turned and saw Shadith riding
up, alone. Not looking around for any assistance, Shadith braced
her bad leg in the stirrup and swung her good leg around in
front of her, then undid the stirrup from her foot using her hand
and slipped down as though from a sidesaddle position. On the
ground she hitched herself around to the horse's other side and
grasped the pommel, walking beside him to where Sibyl stood.
The horse, used to this routine, stopped quietly and stood unmoving. Shadith looked at her uncertainly, and Sibyl smiled
encouragingly. "You manage well, even without the Tayyib."

"It is not so difficult. I do not need help." She smiled briefly.
"But it gives him pleasure."

Sibyl sighed. "You are lucky."

Shadith answered, "Yes," so vehemently that Sibyl looked
up in surprise and saw the other's eyes drop in embarrassment.

Shadith spoke in a very low voice. "Do you mind that you
are carrying a child?"

Sibyl leaned against Silver and rubbed her cheek against his
soft shaggy shoulder. "No. I didn't plan for it or expect it. But
it isn't nearly as bad as I thought it would be. I feel fine. In
some ways better than ever. But in other ways it scares me so
I don't think about it as much as I should."

Shadith shivered a little. "I think about it, often. I have
never been afraid of anything before. But I never want to have
a child. Never. I want to stay the way I am and ride with the
bodyguard. I will kill myself before I become a mother."

Sibyl put up her hand in protest. "You can't mean that."

"I do. You are the first person I have ever told. I should
never have married." She met Sibyl's eyes and shook her head.
"It is not that I do not love him. Happily I would die for him.
But I will not become like the others and stay at home and

nurse babies in a tent and never ride with him again. Never. This is why I never wished to be like a woman."

Sibyl said hesitantly, "There are ways to help prevent having children. Counting days—"

Shadith laughed angrily. "Ask my mother, who has borne eighteen children. She told us how to count the days. The five of us who live today know what she knew, and also how little it helped her. I thought that you might know of something else."

Sibyl shook her head. "Nothing that would help us here."

Shadith looked at her curiously. "Will your husband take other wives?"

"No."

"Is he not angry that this child is not his?"

Sibyl felt her face flame red and choked on her answer. "What makes you say that?"

Shadith also blushed and dropped her eyes. "I am sorry. I thought it was spoken of. When the Karif's wife died, there was talk of his choosing another."

The sudden return of Ajjibawr and his escort spared Sibyl any further comments. Shadith smiled nervously and pulled herself onto her horse from the wrong side, leaning over to place her dangling left foot in the stirrup. She saluted in parting and trotted out of the way as the Karif approached and dismounted. Odric came cantering in close behind and swung down next to them. "You are back so soon!" he exclaimed. "Did Bodrum not meet with you?"

Ajjibawr jerked his head, and grooms took The Thunderer by the bridle, then went to take Silver's lead also at another look from the Karif. He stood back to let Odric and Sibyl enter the tent, then followed, unrolling the flap to fall behind them. There was a short roll of parchment in his hand which he threw down at Odric's feet. "There is nothing to be gained from repeating the bulk of his remarks, since they were as foul as they were meaningless. This message is more to the point."

Odric picked it up and scanned it briefly. He nodded a few times and puffed out his cheeks. "So, 'he who calls himself my son' may avoid the consequences of open conflict and hasten his 'inevitable defeat' by accepting this challenge? When has anyone in a position of strength ever suggested single combat? That this challenge has been made at all shows us his weakness."

"I told him I would deliver it, but that I did not think the lord of Treclere had any need to imperil his person in combat, when one considered the strength of our combined forces."

"What did he answer?"

"That we trusted to our men more than to ourselves. He did not, however, phrase it so politely."

Odric laughed briefly, reread the message and handed it to Sibyl. "His forces then are as weak as we supposed?"

Sibyl looked up from her reading. "Or so he wishes you to think."

Ajjibawr looked at her curiously. "You know a little of Bodrum's mind. You think this is a trick?"

"I don't know. But I wouldn't believe anything he says without trying to figure all the angles. He's very clever. You say he insulted you?"

Ajjibawr dropped his heavy lids and his lips quirked a little. "Actively."

"Then he probably wanted to make you angry, so you wouldn't consider the whole problem carefully enough. If we were to agree to single combat, when would it take place?"

"Within a week is usual."

"Perhaps he's trying to buy time, waiting for more troops."

Odric shook his head. "The rules of single combat prohibit further fighting."

Sibyl tossed her head. "Tell that to the army when it arrives and attacks you. I say, attack tomorrow, if you think you can win quickly."

Ajjibawr smiled. "You sound like the Tayyib. You must have been talking with Shadith."

Sibyl blushed. "However, I suspect there is truth in what you say. Unfortunately, strong as we are and weak though he may be, a siege is never short and often uncertain of outcome. Bodrum could gain time as well through a besiegement as through single combat."

Sibyl looked questioningly at Odric. "Why were you challenged, rather than the Karif?"

It was Odric's turn to blush. "My dear, I am a minstrel. I can fight passably well, but I have never met a man in combat. However thin Bodrum's forces may be, I do not doubt he has many a warrior able to best me. Whereas the Karif no longer even counts the heads he has taken."

"I offered to accept the challenge myself," said Ajjibawr,

"but was most adamantly refused. Either Odric meets his champion or we must attack. I suggest the latter, and also that we deploy our forces in such a way as to prevent being surprised from the rear, should he have more men coming."

"How soon is an answer required?"

"Tomorrow."

"Let us think on this further today, then. I suspect that the lady is right, and Bodrum seeks to force on us a choice favorable to his own private aims. Let us not be overhasty." And with this they left the matter until dinner.

There was an uneasy tension throughout the camp that afternoon. Some tents were struck and pitched in a different area; armor and arms were cleaned and burnished, horses were groomed. Food was used lavishly, and there was a smell of roasting meat heavy throughout the entire encampment, pleasant in the cold frosty air.

Odric, Ajjibawr and Sibyl ate together in the Karif's tent. After the meal, over coffee, Odric proposed a game of Castledown, and Ajjibawr accepted, clearly uneager to make any decision for the morrow. Sibyl arranged herself comfortably on the cushions, wrapped in a fur robe, and watched the progress.

Ajjibawr drew shell and spent much time pondering his opening move. It was an unconventional one, and Odric rose gamely to the challenge. They settled into a rapid group of skirmishes before making any important captures. As Sibyl had expected, the Karif went first into widegame, and for a while she lost sight of his strategy. Then Odric blocked him, and Ajjibawr rather recklessly cast for a fate, which set him back, although not hopelessly. He sat back and took a pinch of snuff while he considered the board, and Odric poured himself another small cup of coffee. "It is hard enough from up here to follow the plan of the game," he said at last. "Imagine how difficult it would be for the pieces were they sentient. The board would seem a vast and arbitrary place."

Sibyl accepted a cup of coffee from the Karif and watched him tentatively touch a figure. "I would like to see," she said, "a game of Castledown played where each piece could decide on its own moves."

Ajjibawr laughed. "One can imagine the chaos on such a board."

"Yes," said Sibyl, "it would be just like life."

Odric looked at her keenly. "You do not care to think of higher powers guiding our lives?"

"What higher powers? Vazdz? If he is like Simirimia, then he is not a higher power, but a more powerful power. If there are higher powers, I'd like to know what they offer us in return for taking our freedom. And if it's just a matter of strength, we can use our wits to turn our weakness into advantage and win out in the end."

Ajjibawr smiled. "There is an old tale in the desert, with that for a moral, concerning a baker and seven giants."

Sibyl laughed.

"We have some stories like that too."

Ajjibawr looked back at the board and shook his head. "I should have used my own wits before I cast that fate. I do not think I will easily escape our friend."

Odric sighed. "If only there were some way I could apply this moral to Bodrum's challenge. If this were a ballad or a campfire tale, I should certainly win because I am virtuous, however clumsy."

"I can assure you from my own experience," Ajjibawr said drily, "that virtue is unnecessary in the winning of combats." He smiled reminiscently, and Sibyl frowned into the sludgy depths of her cup. Soon after she excused herself and retired to the inner room.

There she had no difficulty in falling asleep, long before the game of Castledown was over. When she awoke later, it must have been to the sound of Odric's departure, for the oil lamp in the other room wavered and there was a gust of cold air that came in around the curtain. She pulled herself farther in under the covers, and looked out unseen through her tumbled hair. There were soft vague noises from the outer room, and once the Karif cursed softly under his breath. He raised the curtain between their rooms and stood there, dark and feature-less against the light. He fumbled with something at his neck and held it in his hand against his face for a moment, then stepped forward quietly and laid it on the cushions near Sibyl's head. Then he stepped back, and the curtain fell between them. In the semi-dark Sibyl reached out to gather up her ring on its leather thong, still warm. She touched it against her own lips and let the hot tears run out silently over her hand as she fell asleep again.

Karabdin Epigram:
THE WARRIOR
(Rassam's translation)

When the warrior mounts his horse, then his heart is glad.
His heart unfolds with the unsheathing of his sword,
and it sings to the echo of his galloping horse.
To hear the strike of metal on metal is pleasing to him,
and he cries, "Aha!" as his enemies fall before him.
Blood for blood is pleasing to his honor,
injuries he forgets not, nor friendship.
With sword and spear, a good horse and his honor
what more can any man desire of life?

Chapter Two

Just before she awoke, Sibyl had a brief and realistic vision of
Odric sitting in a chair, his face in his hands and tears falling
through his fingers. When he did not join them at breakfast,
the anxiety of the dream returned, although by now the vision
itself had grown very vague. It was with relief that she saw
him come cantering into camp, rocking heavily in the saddle.
Ajjibawr smiled, inviting him to sit and eat: in the pale morning
light the Karif looked more strained and tired than ever.

Odric waved away the offer of food but took some coffee
gladly; he sat next to the small fire and warmed each hand in
turn as he drank. "You were early abroad," said Ajjibawr at
last, and Odric nodded.

"So said the Master of Vahn when I woke him for a parley."

"You have spoken with Bodrum?"

"Briefly. I have seen his champion, and I have accepted his
challenge."

Ajjibawr set his little cup down in the precise center of its
saucer. "I fail to see the advantage to us in this."

Sibyl found she was clutching at the ring she had once more
hanging round her neck. Ajjibawr went on, "I trust there is an
advantage?"

"Possibly. I told him we would leave his lands if we lost,
nor trouble his city further; yet the borders of the desert and
Treclere would be closed against him, as would the ports of
the eastern shores. And if we win, he has undertaken to leave

quickly and in good order, opening the gates to us the same day that he leaves." He shrugged. "If I lose today, you may still fight in the spring, in all honor; if I win we may not have to fight at all."

"We do not fear to fight. And though I do not doubt your courage, I am dubious of your skill. Why have you taken this risk?"

"The champion does not appear formidable. He is very slight."

"Then he will have the larger target. Why did you accept?"

Odric shook his head. "There was no honorable way I could refuse. I did not mean to accept when I went to talk to him. I did insist that we meet today, though, lest Bodrum be planning some treachery as we discussed last night."

Ajjibawr said nothing, but his thin lips were pressed tight together. Sibyl could not control herself so well. "Odric, how could you? You know how much he wants to see you dead. And what makes you think he will keep his word if you win? Why did you risk our losing, anyway?"

Odric looked at them angrily. "To what do I owe my sovereignty in Treclere? To my birth? Bodrum was a vassal of Treclere, not its lord; and besides, he has two other sons, whose legitimacy he recognizes, unlike mine. I owe my place to a whim of Leron's, a suggestion accepted by a scared and leaderless people. Bodrum may be deceitful, but in this he spoke the truth: I have never proved my right to my position."

"Until today, you had proved it through your good judgment. Now I am not so sure." Ajjibawr got to his feet and adjusted the folds of his sash with great deliberation. "I am tempted to have you bound and kept in a camp while I arrange my own terms with Bodrum." He spoke very softly, and when Odric scrambled angrily up to face him he met the other's eyes calmly, one eyebrow slightly lifted.

"You would not dare!"

"You are in the Karabdin part of camp, and I am Karif." Odric lunged forward as though to shake him by the shoulders, and Ajjibawr turned easily, sending Odric to the ground through the force of his own attack. Then he leaned down and gave him a hand to pull him up. "Tell me," he said mildly, "do you think you can learn enough by noon to save you?"

Odric let himself be pulled to his feet and shook his head, ashamed. "No," he said at last, in a much lower voice, "but I cannot back out now. I have risen to the bait that Bodrum cast, and now the hook is firmly in my mouth."

"If we seem to fall out among ourselves and I imprison you, no one can fault your honor."

"No one? I would know. I cannot do it."

Ajjibawr sighed, and for the first time that morning looked Sibyl squarely in the eyes. "You were right," he said. "He is as clever as you said. It seems, alas, that a warning was not enough."

The few hours between breakfast and noon were spent in fruitless argument with Odric. Once set in his own mind, Odric could not be shaken loose from his decision. In grim resignation Ajjibawr sent word through camp, and the Karabdu, puzzled yet obedient, stood ready to attack or retreat as ordered. The Karif dealt with each contingency calmly, dealing with the safety of his men and of Sibyl as thoroughly as he did with Odric's arms and armor. Only as he ordered their mounts did Sibyl intervene. "Perhaps it would be well if he rode on Silver."

Odric, being fitted into a suit of mail, laughed bitterly. "So he can kill me as he did the robber chief? I assure you, the decision in this battle is likely to come soon enough. No need to hurry it."

"The horse didn't murder him. He reared on command, as he was taught. None of the younger horses here are as well trained. He jumps backwards and sideways and everything."

Ajjibawr nodded slowly. "If Odric can learn the signals and employ them properly, he might do well to ride on that old horse. It was a horse's leap helped me win over the old Karif. He avoided the sword on his own, then reared so I might have the full weight with my own stroke. And this horse too was well trained in his time, though it is many years since he helped me in battle."

"I started working him again in Tredana."

Ajjibawr smiled. "Were you planning on using him for combat?"

"I'd use him today if you'd let me." She laughed. "Though you might have trouble finding armor that's the right shape."

Odric looked down grimly at his own belly, straining the close-linked mail. "No more than I, my dear. Bring out your horse. I might as well perish grandly."

Ajjibawr spoke a few quiet orders, and soon a groom ap-

peared with Silver, saddled and bridled, his coat shining white
and his hoofs oiled black. The Karif nodded. "I like a grey
horse, but not when it fades to white. At least he is clean. Let
me see how well he remembers his lessons." He put his hand
on the stallion's neck, and Silver arched it tightly, flaring his
nostrils so wide the front edges almost touched. He swung
aboard, and Silver, moving in response to imperceptible signals, began the complicated figures of war. Sibyl forgot the
conflict facing them as horse and rider drifted past in a smooth
and effortless sideways canter. Then the pain of beauty lessened
as the more violent figures were practiced. Silver reared and
struck, kicked, jumped sideways and threw himself around in
the air. When the Karif was through, they stood quietly, Ajjibawr unmoved, the old horse breathing heavily and shiny with
sweat but proud as ever.

Odric broke the spell, shaking his head. "Perhaps a short
course on the uses of the sword would make more sense."

But Ajjibawr swung down and held the stirrup for him.
"The horse remembers well. I will tell you what to do, and
more important what things not to do. If he only leaps once at
your bidding, it may be enough. I doubt that Bodrum's champion will expect it, not from you."

The sun rose a little higher in the sky as Ajjibawr repeated
his lessons in a patient, even voice; and Odric listening carefully
began to master some of the broader signals. He had never
used a sword from horseback, and Sibyl's sense of foreboding
deepened as she watched his attempts at a smooth unsheathing.
When he swung, the blade narrowly avoided Silver's ears, and
Sibyl flinched. Finally Ajjibawr counselled him to carry the
blade in his hand and not attempt to draw it while astride.

Too soon the sun rose towards noon and it was time to meet
the Champion of Vahn, on the wide beach opposite Almond
Island. Leaving the Tayyib in charge of the camp, Ajjibawr
escorted Odric to the fight, with a bodyguard of only twenty.
Varys attended Odric, and Sibyl rode in front with the Karif,
despite his expressed wish that she stay in camp. At least he
did not insult her with the present of a quiet mount; her new
horse sidled and danced and tried to bite The Thunderer's neck
when Ajjibawr rode too close.

On the beach they drew rein, Varys following Odric as he
rode forward onto the flat ferry boat that awaited them. A single

polesman pushed them across the shallows, and Odric rode resolutely out onto the narrow beach of Almond Island. There the Champion of Vahn waited, Bodrum and his cavalry farther back.

Like Odric, the champion wore a metal helmet with a heavy nosepiece, shadowing his face. He seemed very young but sat his horse with confidence; when Odric raised his heavy saber in salute, the other unsheathed with a flourish the Karif might have envied. The light shone on their blades. The horses were backed away in fretful zigzagging lines, and then at a nod they galloped towards each other. The champion struck first, and Odric managed to catch the blow on his own sword, though it slipped off and struck against his shoulder in falling. He turned his horse, and Silver, remembering past conflicts, called out his own challenge and bit the other horse's neck. He did not release his hold right away, and the angle at which he stood blocked the champion's next blow. Odric struck the other on the shoulders, holding the sword so poorly it turned aside as it hit against the chain mail, but the strength of his massive arm bent the other over in his saddle. Then the horses pulled free and circled around each other once again.

Tears rose helplessly in Sibyl's eyes, and her stomach cramped with nervousness. She clutched the pommel of her saddle with one hand, leaning forward, and looked at the Karif. Somehow she had thought that Odric might win, as he had at Castledown. But there on the windy beach it was so open and cold and hopeless, the sun shining so bleakly. Ajjibawr did not meet her glance; he was leaning forward intensely, one hand clenched, breathing with each stroke and wincing with each fumble.

Sibyl looked back, and through her blurred eyes she could vaguely see the two contestants hacking away at each other, the heavy, deliberate blows of Odric in bitter contrast to the swift, clever strokes of his adversary. Only the quality of his chain mail and the rapid movements of Silver had kept Odric in the battle thus far. Momentarily the two pulled apart and Sibyl watched in horror as Odric took up his sword with his left hand, his right arm hanging limp and brightly bloody even at a distance. Now he was taking more blows across his broad shoulders; he bent in the saddle and jerked Silver away and Sibyl heard Ajjibawr sigh loudly.

Odric pushed in wearily once more and the Champion of
Vahn stood up in his stirrups, young and confident, with the
sword held high over his head in both hands. Again the blade
winked in the light, less bright now, marked with blood, and
the champion whistled it round in a deadly circle aimed at
Odric's neck. Odric did not appear to react, but Silver sprang
sideways, whirled and reared, independent of any signal from
his rider. Now Odric had his chance, and he brought his own
blade down in a clumsy blow, above the circle sliced through
the air by his adversary. With the weight of Silver's descent
behind it, the awkward left-handed blow just managed to bite
into the other's neck a little way: the champion jerked backwards out of the saddle and fell off over his horse's rump, his
sword spinning out over the pebbly sand. There was a roar of
approval from the Karabdin bodyguard, and Varys spurred his
horse forward to attend his brother. Similarly a rider trotted
out from the opposing ranks to look after the fallen champion.

They met in the middle, and Varys took Silver's reins and
helped Odric to dismount. Odric dropped heavily to his knees
and loosened his opponent's helmet. The helm came free in
his hands, he held it a moment motionless then threw it aside
and bent over his enemy, gathering the limp body up in his
arms despite the still bleeding wound in his right shoulder. He
staggered to his feet and the light caught on his helmet as he
moved his head from side to side in despair.

The rider from the other side handed something to Varys,
then turned and cantered back towards his troops, which were
already making an orderly retreat. Boats on the far side of the
island stood ready to receive them, and farther out, ships were
lying at anchor. In the center of the deserted beach, Varys had
dropped the horses' reins and was leaning against Odric. The
Karif cantered up to the water's edge, imperiously summoning
the ferryman with one hand and Sibyl clattered onto the wooden
deck close behind him. In the distance, a rider she was sure
was Bodrum looked back at them, and she felt that he laughed,
although it was much too far to see. Behind her, riders from
the Karabdu were already galloping back to camp with news
of the victory.

On the island Ajjibawr dismounted, and before him Odric
fell to his knees weeping loudly, the body of his opponent still

clutched to his breast. He put up one bloody hand to cover his face, and the tears ran out through his fingers, while the head of Kerys the young champion rolled back limply on its broken neck.

Ajjibawr stooped forward and gently loosened Odric's hold, taking the dead boy up in his arms. Sibyl swung down next to them and went to Odric. She bent over him and put her hand on his shoulder; he put his arms around her, burying his face against her cloak. There was nothing to be said, but she silently stroked his thick chestnut hair while he wept against her, and the tears ran from her own eyes.

Finally Odric pulled away shame-faced, muttering some apology, and Sibyl turned to Varys, who was standing by white-faced, his lips trembling. "Can you bandage his shoulder before we return to camp?" Varys nodded and turned blindly back towards his own horse, and reaching down his cloak from the saddle tore it in strips. Odric let himself be pulled to his feet and numbly let his arm be lifted and dressed.

The Karif turned to Sibyl and lifted her back into the saddle. "Let us return to camp," he said. "Varys will bring his brother."

Sibyl gestured to the paper he had taken from Vary's hand. "What was the message?"

"It is from Bodrum. He says that he considers your ransom well paid."

Sibyl followed the Karif silently at a slow pace back to camp. As she wiped the tears from her eyes, she realized that she was stained with Odric's blood, or Kerys's. "Why?" she finally said, and Ajjibawr answered without looking up.

"Why did Kerys fight his brother? You heard what Odric said before. There was jealousy between them. Doubtless Bodrum knew well how to inflame it."

"Odric would never have hurt him. He loved Kerys."

"And when Kerys was not mad with jealousy, doubtless he loved Odric."

"So love is jealousy and jealousy is death? Better to live your life alone, then."

"So it would seem." He spoke the last so bitterly, she looked up in surprise, but his face was closed as always.

In camp he left her and went to the Tayyib to discuss the entering of Vahanavat, rejoining her much later in the evening as she sat with Varys, near to Odric's tent where he lay alone.

"The city is open to us as Bodrum promised. He left, however, neither arms nor food. The grain in the warehouses has been fouled, all casks have been overturned and storage jars all broken. There will be famine within a week."

Varys looked up hesitantly. "There was a rich harvest in Treclere. Our storage bins are full. Perhaps we can supply the coast."

"You will have to. Is Odric awake?"

"He will see no one."

"He will see me." Varys watched wide-eyed as the Karif went into Odric's tent, his mouth grimly set. A little time passed, and then the Karif reappeared, and nodded to Varys. "Odric would speak to you."

The boy went in, and Ajjibawr sat down next to Sibyl, uncharacteristically dropping his head forward to run his hands through his hair. "It seems that Bodrum has accomplished at least one of his purposes. He was as clever as you said, and so much cleverer than we guessed."

"What purpose is this?"

"He knew that Odric would never consent to take a throne for which he had killed his brother."

"There was no way he could have known. Who would blame him?"

Ajjibawr rose wearily to his feet, then surprisingly reached for one of Sibyl's hands. "Who indeed? Who would blame any of us? But who among us waits to be blamed?" He kissed her wrist and returned her hand to her lap, turning to walk away, but she rose to her feet and called after him

"Ajjibawr—I want to go home." He looked at her patiently, spreading his hands a little in a gesture of concession. Then he opened his arms a little more, and knowing that she would be welcome in them, she forced herself to turn away.

LETTER
from BODRUM VIII, Master of Vahn
to ARBAB, DALLAL, MIMBASH, SAHLAR, PADESHI, ZEHAR and MULKE,
the Seven Warlords of Paradon

BROTHERS IN VAZDZ:

The time is at hand for us to join together in war as we have in commerce, to proclaim the truth of Vazdz and our sovereignty in the blood of the unbelieving nations. Reverses upon the continent have brought a legion of the unbelivers to our very door: and they are strong with the righteousness of corrupted faith.

Therefore I proclaim to you all a Holy War that we may once again be as secure upon the land as we now are upon the seas. In evidence thereto I enclose a representation of my sign of power.

Given Privately under his Seal and Hand by
Bodrum VIII, Master of Vahn

Chapter Three

That winter seemed the longest and coldest of Leron's life. The room he had shared with Sibyl he only used at night; the rest of the time that he was not at work he spent with Gannoc and Mara in their house built within the palace compound. The old king's chamber he caused to have bricked shut.

It was more than two months after Sibyl's capture and the departure of the Karif for the desert, the darkest part of the winter, that a messenger arrived with Sibyl's brief note. His ship, a slaver like the *Damar,* stood well out from harbor, and the boat that brought him in had a hard row through the choppy water; but he refused Leron's invitation to come farther in towards shelter. Sibyl's note was enclosed in a formal dispatch from Bodrum, which Leron and Gannoc considered carefully before answering.

The messenger revealed, as he left, that his ship was bound for Paradon before returning home, and Leron spoke without thinking. "Sail clear of Melismala if you would return to Vahn in safety."

The messenger looked at him shrewdly. "What is there to fear on Melismala?" Leron made a noncommittal gesture with his hand and the other laughed. "Our captain'll sail us safe through any dangers, I've no fear. The whole fleet envies us our Arleon."

Leron had already half turned away: now he turned again and walked up to the messenger. "Your captain is named Arleon?"

"Yes."

"You may tell him for me, then, that I would think more of his bravery had he delivered these messages in person."

The door closed behind the sailor, and Leron hit the table with his hand so hard that the candles jumped and one fell over. Gannoc carefully righted it and waited for the king to stop cursing. "I do not think it was wise to mention Melismala."

Leron stopped cursing and nodded in embarrassment. "No, it was foolish. But I do not think I was much believed. Arleon! How he returns to haunt us! I wish I could will the waters open and drop his vessel in."

"Mayhap Dansen will do that for us with his glass."

Leron sat down and dropped his head forward into his hands. "In that case, I would wish he were not carrying my messages."

He took out Sibyl's note and reread it and tucked it in the breast of his tunic again. "Gannoc, will this damned cold never end? I have never seen so dark a winter. It is hardly light by noon."

Gannoc dropped a friendly hand on his shoulder. "Come to our house, my lord. It is warmer there."

Leron half rose, then rubbed his eyes. "Gannoc, how can I stay here and send polite messages back and forth? I should be on my way to Vanhanavat right now."

"And give two hostages into their hands? No, my lord. You did well to send the Karif to parley."

Leron sighed. "Possibly." He touched the letter in his tunic. "At least she was safe when she wrote this. And that was not more than a month past." He shivered again. "Was the palace always so cold in winter?"

"Always, my lord."

"Strange that I never remarked on it before."

Now it was Gannoc's turn to sigh. "Our own hostage has not failed to notice it. If we burned fires as large as she demands, the chimneys would ignite, stone though they are. I would think eight years here would have accustomed her."

"She is uncomfortable?"

"She has sent the usual list of complaints. She does not care for Mistress Gemarta's cooking, nor for the furniture of her apartments; the servants are surly, the fires meager; the—"

Leron held up his hand. "Please, no more. I do not want to hear her any more than I wish to see her. Send her an extra load of wood with my compliments and some extra quilts. And another keg of the fortified wine, anything to keep her quiet. But tell her I am still too busy to see her."

"Very well, my lord. Now, if you will come with me, I think you will find our kitchen tolerably warm."

The courtyard, bright with winter sunlight, was not as cold as the dark passages of the castle. Leron and Gannoc stood a moment savoring the sun before turning down the alleyway that led towards the stables. A gate in the wall gave on Gannoc's small yard; there was a thick column of white smoke rising straight out of the massive chimney of his steeply gabled white-washed house.

It was two steps down into the kitchen, and Gannoc always had to remind Leron to duck his head under the massive beam that framed the top of the entryway. In the low-ceilinged kitchen it was warm with the roaring fire of the open cooking hearth; even the flagstone floor was not chilly underfoot. The walls were of white plaster with dark wooden uprights exposed; scoured pots hung from the oak mantel; and a large copper tub built into the side of the brick fireplace held boiling water that could be let out through a cunningly worked brass spigot with a wooden knob. This was an invention of Dansen's, modeled upon the water urns of the desert; Gannoc had the first example made and was quite proud of it.

As they stepped down, Leron bumped his forehead and cursed. Mariti had been playing on a blanket by the fire; she heard him curse and looked up with delight. Leron blushed as he recalled some of the phrases Mariti had picked up from him. Today she said nothing to embarrass him, however, but ran over and embraced his legs. He picked her up, and she first held out her arms to her father, kissing him several times, then turned her back on him and snuggled against Leron's neck. Her mother did not move from where she knelt by the hearth, combing out her newly washed hair in the warmth of the fire. It was as thick and long as ever, but the black was plentifully streaked with white, as was Gannoc's.

She smiled a welcome and winced as the rough comb caught in an obdurate tangle. "Sit down. There is spiced wine on the hob and a smoked ham in the oven. Have you eaten yet, my lord?" Leron shook his head and went to sit in a high-backed settle near the fire. Mariti sat in his lap and began pulling the short beard he had grown when mornings became too cold for comfortable shaving. She giggled when he winced but immediately sobered when her mother told her to stop.

Gannoc laughed and fingered his own beard reflectively. "If you wish a rude awakening," he said to Leron, "you should sleep here and wake to find the child not only in bed with you but trying to extract your beard hair by hair."

Mariti dropped her eyes and rubbed her face against Leron's. "I like your face better," she said, loudly enough for her father to hear. "It is softer."

Gannoc laughed at this and stepped nearer to the fire. Taking the comb from Mara's fingers he skillfully separated the tangle into three smooth falls that he rapidly plaited together. A towel hung warming by the fire; he wrapped it around her head, enclosing the thick plait and tucking the ends in securely. Mara laughed and let him pull her to her feet, and she hugged him before she turned to look after her ham in the oven below the boiling copper. Leron's eyes stung and he hid his face against Mariti for a moment. She lay still for a few seconds, then squirmed around and found her straw doll on the settle and carefully placed it on his other arm, opposite. It seemed that the doll had had a remarkably adventuresome and tiring day, and as Mariti related the intricately detailed story, Leron listened half attentively, watching Mara move quietly and comfortably around her warm kitchen. The ale was poured, the ham carved, a fresh loaf of bread broken open.

After they ate, he sat by the fire in perfect peace with Mariti asleep in his arms. Gannoc sat there awhile too, then rose and stretched. "I must see to your instructions concerning Dastra," he said. "Is there anything else I can attend to for your majesty?" Leron shook his head quietly so as not to disturb the sleeping child. Gannoc put his hand under Mara's chin and kissed her; then taking up his cloak from a peg by the door he stepped out into the bitter afternoon.

There was silence after he had gone, then Mara spoke quietly. "Have you spoken with Dastra yet?"

"Only to assure her of her safety under my roof. I had no wish to speak with her further."

"That I can understand. I have visited with her twice, and to me she has said little enough. But she has confided at some length in one of her maidservants, a girl whose mother used to work for me. She came to me this morning, in some confusion of mind, to tell me what she has learned from Dastra."

"Was there anything of importance?"

"Possibly. Of greatest importance is the fact that Dastra thinks herself to be carrying a child."

"So Ginas's prophecy is coming true."

"In more ways than one, my lord. She hinted that you of all people most wished her dead."

"For what reason?"

Mara laughed a little and dropped her eyes. "Because the child she carries is yours."

"No one would believe that!"

"No one who knew you, surely. But I have nevertheless recommended to Gannoc that her servants be changed frequently lest she make too close friends with any of them. It may save you much grief amongst those who do not know you well.

"Dastra also said that an attempt had been made upon her life already."

"Here? She is mad."

"Not here, but earlier, before she was taken by the nobleman Glisser. She said that when they were both prisoners, Sibby tried to kill her, and that those were the marks on her face."

"When they were both prisoners? She traveled with Arleon of her own free will. I would also say that he has more to do with this child, if child there is, than anyone in Tredana."

Mariti half awoke at his angry voice, and he soothed her back to sleep. Mara turned so the fire's warmth fell on the other side of her head. "What was the message from Bodrum?"

"It was strange in tone. As though the queen were his guest and not his prisoner. And vague in its implied demands. I have warned him that the Karif is on his way to negotiate in my name, and that the comfort and safety of his hostage is to be respected above all else. I wish I could trade him Dastra."

Mara laughed. "She would be happy to be traded. But do not fear. Her stories will not widely be believed. And I know that Sibby will return safely."

Leron closed his eyes. "And what about the rest of Ginas's prophecy?"

"What do you mean?"

"She called Sibyl here to prevent Dastra's child from being the firstborn of this generation." Mara did not answer, and Leron did not open his eyes to read her expression. So much had come true already, this would not surprise him. But he did wonder if Sibyl would understand why he had sent the Karif; and what her choice would be.

Six weeks past the winter solstice, the weather was no warmer, but the lengthening of the days raised Leron's spirits. There was enough sun now to make it worthwhile removing the heavy hangings that covered the windows, during the day at least. Gradually Leron's chamber began to lose its heavy smoky smell. He anticipated the spring by having all the hangings changed and washed, much to the discomfiture of the staff who had to wrestle with the sodden, freezing wool and velvet.

One morning after breakfast Leron took Gannoc for a tour of the battlements, to mark the stones loosened by winter. Gannoc began to make mental notes concerning the repairs. "Before we left Rym Treglad," he said, "Dansen was working on a new way of caulking tiles. I wonder if he left any notes on the mixture."

Leron stooped to peer through the outlook, clearing away the browned ivy with one hand. "Perhaps you can ask him this evening. Does that not look like his ship?"

Gannoc looked over his shoulder, eyes narrowed. "The prow is the same shape. But the sail is a different color."

"Perhaps it was replaced. Would a Vahnian vessel sail so boldly in?"

"I think not. Will you accompany me to the quay?" Leron nodded, and they went back in through the sitting room, careless of the gravel they tracked onto its newly scrubbed board floor.

A small guard joined them in the courtyard, already alert to the ship's arrival, and followed them to the quay. There the first boat was just putting in and a familiar figure leaped across the short span of water and scrambled nimbly up onto the dock. It was Meladin the Navigator, who had elected to sail with Dansen to Melismala.

He dropped on one knee before Leron, then rose, papers in hand. "I bring you messages from Talyas and the people of Melismala. They are released from fear of Paradon through the working of Dansen's weapon."

Leron took the papers and passed them to Gannoc, signaling Meladin to rise. "What of Dansen? Did he stay on Melismala?"

"No, lord, he lies ill on board. It was after the fight—"

Leron looked at Gannoc. "See that a chamber is readied. I will go help him ashore." He sprang down into the boat and Meladin followed him, the rowers turning the bow about back towards their anchored ship.

On their way Meladin briefly described the success of Dansen's glass and the complete rout of the pirates from Paradon. "We were on our way home then, leaving Dansen as he had asked and sailing nicely before the wind, when we met with a slaver from Vahn. We could see they had been fighting, though never a sign of any other ship did we see. They sent out boats to board us, but we fought our way clear, and as we went our ways, we heard him calling to us, Dansen. There he was in the water and never a word of explanation have we had from that day to this."

"Was he hurt?"

"Not so badly. But he took an awful chill and the fever was with him until a few days ago." .

At the ship, Meladin was up the ladder first and helped Leron to board. Everything was in good order, and there was a clean smell of salt and pitch. The largest cabin lay across the stern and opened onto the main deck. Meladin gestured to the door and then stood back; Leron stooped and entered through the low paneled door.

The cabin was cold and airy, its seven small windows opened wide. A small lantern swung from the low ceiling; there was a table and a chest and a built-in bed. Dansen lay under the covers, painfully thin and white with dark shadows under his closed and sunken eyes. Leron bent down and placed his own hand over one of Dansen's. "Dansen, my dear. You are home in Tredana." He repeated this, and there was no response, then the eyelids twitched and fluttered, and Dansen's brown eyes looked up into his, vaguely at first. He drew his hand from under Leron's and tried to smooth back his ruffled hair.

"My lord, forgive me. I did not know. If you will give me a moment . . ." He made as though to rise and Leron touched him lightly on the shoulders.

"Lie back and rest. There is no need for haste."

"But my lord, it is not right—"

"Lie back and tell me how you come to be here. Meladin tells me you were left on Melismala. How did you come to be aboard a ship from Vahn?"

Dansen closed his eyes and sighed wearily, turning his head

to one side. "I was never on it." Tears began silently running
out from under his lids and he put one hand over his face.
"Forgive me, my lord, I am still somewhat weak."

"Dansen, I never meant to distress you. Tell us later. Let
us bring you ashore now. Are you strong enough to come?"
Dansen nodded weakly and Leron went to the door to summon
help.

Although he protested he could dress and walk ashore on
his own feet, Dansen was bundled up and half carried ashore
by two sailors. In the palace, Gannoc had caused a small chamber near Leron's to be warmed with fires, and there Dansen
was firmly tucked into a featherbed while Gannoc sent a servant
for some of Mistress Gemarta's warm broth with barley. Unable
to resist, Dansen at last began weakly laughing, and Leron
nodded approvingly as he sat down at the foot of the bed. "Now
that is better. Make him drink all of that, Gannoc . . ." The
steward held Dansen firmly and forced the broth down. "It will
make you feel better. At least," said Leron, "that is what I was
always told when I was young. In fact, Dansen, I believe you
once told me those very words."

"So now your majesty is having his revenge?" Dansen sat
up against his cushions, pink-cheeked, looking ruffled and in-
dignant and more like himself.

"My dear Dansen, you see, you taught me too well the
virtues of tenacity. Twenty years has not been too long to wait
for revenge."

Dansen suddenly looked grave. "I trust I do not have to wait
so long, myself." Leron and Gannoc looked at him expectantly,
and Dansen settled back against his pillows.

"Let me begin by saying that my weapon is as successful as I
hoped, though more terrible than I had guessed. It is not easy
to control. Yet with it I would not hesitate to face the Moraganas
or the Great Naqra himself. Of the ten ships sent from Paradon,
only three can have returned, and they were burned. No man
from Paradon even set foot upon the island."

Leron indicated the papers Gannoc had tucked in his belt.
"So I understand from our friend Talyas. He swears eternal
friendship between Melismala and Tredana. You left the lens
with them?"

"Herrard is overseeing the fabrication of a second one. It
should reach us soon from the desert. By leaving the first one

with them I have insured their continued freedom." He spoke vehemently, and Leron held up his hand.

"Peace, Dansen, we do not question you. It is your invention to dispose of as you please. But this success over Paradon does not explain how you came to be rescued from the waters, nor menaced by a ship from Vahn."

"If you have read the message from Talyas, then you have also read the letter I sent by Meladin, when I thought I was staying behind."

"It does not explain much. You speak of an adventure."

"An unparalleled one. I embarked upon it, but was not allowed to complete it." He leaned back farther and closed his eyes. "There is a way for the heavy ones—that is what the Dylalyr call us—to live under the sea. A process by which our lungs may learn to accept water as easily as they accept the air. But the strain upon our bodies is great. A man may live under the water a time and then return to the air. But it has never been known for a man to then go undersea again, without it causes his death. I went undersea with the Dylalyr. It was foolish, I know. I could have returned to Tredana and waited and joined them later in the year, but I was so impatient. As impatient as I once was as a boy—and never again since. I remembered things I thought had gone forever.

"It is already warm in Melismala, did you know? There is a strange ocean current surrounds those islands, and the weather is never cold there. The beaches are very beautiful and there are trees covered with flowers, very sweet to smell. I forgot Tredana. I am sorry."

"Dansen, no one would constrain you. There is no need to apologize—"

Dansen smiled. "I know that. Still, I should have recalled my duties sooner than I did. But I was living in a beauty I had never seen before—the joy which I only glimpsed before, sometimes, when reading.

"At first being undersea is like living in a deep fog—one can see only a little way ahead, and the murk of the deeper water is frightening. But then one learns to read the motion of water across one's path, the delicate shifts of warm and cool. And the freedom is what a bird must feel, who never has to come to land." His face relaxed as he drifted with his memories.

"The fish we call dolphins they call Mahiva, and they are friends. They play with each other, and understand each other's language. It was the plight of one of the Mahiva drew us near the surface. He had been pierced with a spear and was drowning in the sea and in his blood. The others were trying to hold him above the surface—you will remember, my lord, that the dolphin like the whale breathes air and cannot therefore be truly classified as a fish?" Leron nodded submissively and Dansen smiled. "You do not remember, you were never a good pupil in matters concerning the sea. Ah well—we came to surface and that was our mischance, for the ship was still there, a slaver from Vahn, and it cast spears among us, killing and wounding some of the Dylalyr as well as the Mahiva."

He passed one hand before his eyes. "There was a boat out from the ship, and they drew in one of the wounded Dylalyr and killed him without pity. Arrod had warned me not to come above the surface, but I forgot all in my anger; a sailor had her by the wrist, and I tried to go to her but a spear struck me on the head and I fell back. The Mahiva protected me as they had tried to protect the Dylalyr, and shortly our own ship came among them and the Vahnian vessel pulled away. I was so weak from the shock of breathing air I could not call out or move my arms: surely I would have drowned had it not been for Meladin's sharp eyes and ears."

"Then you do not know what happened to your friends?"

"They went undersea, where I may never go again. But some were surely taken aboard the slaver. I hope they died quickly."

"And the Lady Arrod?"

"I do not know." He turned his head away on the pillow, one hand again covering his eyes; his mouth trembling.

Leron stood up quietly and turned to Gannoc. "We will leave you now. You must rest and eat. Perhaps you will receive welcome news from Melismala." Dansen nodded and they went silently from the room.

It was several weeks before Herrard arrived with the new glass, and during those weeks Dansen improved a little but seemed curiously listless in whatever he did, as though his surroundings no longer had any color for him. For a while the arrival of his old friend seemed to cheer him a little, but then he sank into lethargy again. This was soon interrupted by the slowly gathering menace of ships on the horizon; first one, then three, then seven, then finally twelve ships from Vahn, all well out to sea. Not long after their appearance, there came news from Sundrat of a raid in the darkness, houses set to the torch and men and women brutally killed. Leron sent his cavalry up the coast, to guard the towns between Tredana and Sundrat, but his forces were of a necessity stretched too thin and the raids grew more and more frequent. A few pirates were killed, but not in enough number to discourage them.

Dansen shook his head as he considered his burning glass. "They have had the news from Paradon and will not approach close enough to shore." Together he and Herrard discussed the problem, while Leron and Gannoc hopelessly reviewed the state of their small army. Finally they sent a messenger to the desert, for the purchase of weapons, intending to arm each village as best they could.

When the small troop of Karabdu arrived, bearing their load of bright steel swords and spears, double-curved bows and arrowheads, they also brought with them a messenger of Vahn who had arrived among them shortly before Leron's messenger. It was one of the Tayyib's many sons who led the group, and he smiled cheerily at Leron as he supervised the unbaling and the counting of the load. "I would have brought you the dog's head on a spear and his news in my saddlebag, but the Karif has commanded us to spare such vermin as these, rather than risk the anger of Vahn against its hostage."

Leron breathed deeply with relief and thanked him. The son of the Tayyib took the dispatches from their wary bearer and handed them over: Leron went into the palace to read in private. There was no letter from Sibyl, and his heart thumped in his throat. The letter from Bodrum was curious, and he had to read it through several times before he could make sense from it.

TREDANA:

We welcome the forthcoming meeting with the Karif and shortly shall you learn from him our news. We cannot ourselves communicate more fully as we would not be believed. Let it be said, however, that our prisoner does not find her confinement at our hands distasteful. Soon our ships will show our power to you: Admit the power of Vazdz and his servant the Master of Vahn and there need not be any further cause for war. Submit to our

*will as our hostage has done and you too will enjoy the
benefits of our loving guardianship.*

VAHN

Later when he showed the message to Gannoc, he could
not restrain himself but paced angrily back and forth before
the fire. "This is intolerable. What game does he play? What
good does he hope to gain from this?"

Gannoc shook his head. "It makes no sense to me. If he
meant to force himself in any way upon the queen, he would
not then invite the Karif to be a witness. He must know that
Ajjibawr would not bring you a false report. Why of all people,
the Karif—"

Gannoc halted himself in midsentence, suddenly red-faced,
and Leron looked up shrewdly. "Not very diplomatic, for once.
But correct as always. Of all people, the Karif will be least
likely to believe this nonsense—though Bodrum may not know
that yet." He sat down suddenly and dropped his head in his
hands. "Gannoc, will we ever see the end of this? Will it ever
be spring again?"

"The spring will be here soon enough, but I cannot answer
the other question, dearly though I should love to." He touched
Leron reassuringly on the shoulder, then left him to brood
alone.

It was not long thereafter that the first signs of spring did
begin to show themselves: wild bushes growing up against the
castle walls began to be covered with a feathery yellow blos-
som, the first flowers to open after the snow. Tredana continued
untroubled and the raids on the coast grew infrequent, leading
Leron to suspect that the ships were awaiting new orders from
Vahn.

He was also waiting for messages from the Karif or Odric,
for any news at all from the western shore. Then one morning
as he was working in his study Gannoc came hurrying in, a
broad grin breaking the blackness of his curly beard. He threw
his arms around him, trying to squeeze the breath from his
body. "Vahanavat has fallen! Bodrum has fled! The queen is
safe!"

Leron looked at him in amazement, then sat down with
suddenly shaking legs. "Where—how did you learn of this?"

"A messenger from the Karif. He killed two horses bringing us word. He is nearly dead himself, though he merely said, when I asked, that he was used to hard riding. But there, see for yourself." Leron spread out the messages with fingers that shook.

There was a laconic dispatch from the Karif, describing how Bodrum had fled the city and how it was being held in Odric's name by forces from Treclere. He warned that a greater naval force was on its way to harass Tredana, but Leron skipped over the details, to worry about them later. He read three times the part that said Sibyl was safe, then turned to her folded and sealed letter. Greatly though he wished to read it, he feared slipping the wax seal, feared reading of her safety among the Karabdu. He must have stared at it for several minutes before he broke it open, and when he read it, tears of relief came flooding out and he was thankful that Gannoc had left him alone. He reread his letter and slipped it in next to the other one in his tunic, wiped his face, composed his features and went to join Gannoc to plan the defense of the city against the new attacks of Vahn.

It was less than two weeks afterwards that he was alone in the garden overlooking the harbor, watching the emplacement of Dansen's lens on a small flat barge. He heard a step behind him and did not turn, supposing it to be one of the servants. Then he felt a hesitant touch on his arm, and looking down saw the light flash on his mother's ring on a thin but familiar hand.

LETTER
from ARBAB, DALLAL, MIMBASH, SAHLAR,
PADESHI, ZEHAR and MULKE,
the Seven Warlords of Paradon
to BODRUM VIII, Master of Vahn

BROTHER IN VAZDZ:

In sorrow we heard your message but in joy we match your sign to ours and welcome you to our company. We send to tell you, fear not, in our union there is strength and Vazdz will be our spear and our shield. We have spoken with the oracle at Inivin and it says, be patient, do not trouble your heart, there is help at hand greater than any force ever yet seen in the world of men and with this aid and that of the immortal Vazdz we cannot fail in this our undertaking.

In proof thereto we send to you our signs and seals.

Chapter Four

Birds were fussing outside the window long before it grew light. The cold soft air, half-winter and half-spring, gusted in at the uncovered window, and Sibyl could see her breath above her face. But under the covers she was warm and had no reason to leave the shelter of her bed. At rest and totally free, she drifted on the edge of awaking, unable to feel the pressure of the quilts or the weight of Leron's arm and shoulder. The window grew lighter, and some of the grey dawn filtered into the room, growing shadows behind the furniture. She awoke more fully, beginning to be aware of the warmth of Leron's breath on her neck and the fold of the pillow behind her head. Then Leron also began to awake, moving his lips sleepily against her throat, and she turned to answer him.

The second morning after Sibyl's return, Dansen joined them at breakfast. Mistress Gemarta had sent up a bewildering variety of sausages and breads and baked dishes and eggs cooked in a variety of ways. There was also Karabdin coffee as well as the more customary ale. Sibyl could never recall having eaten so much in the morning, and Leron, aware of her anxiety, pinched the small roll at her waist as he leaned past to help himself to more food. "Morning exercise will keep you lean and fit," he murmured meaningfully in her ear, and she blushed.

Opposite them Dansen was slowly taking apart a small sweet roll and eating it pinch by pinch. His somberness wrung Sibyl's heart. She had not spoken with him since embracing him on the first day of her return, when he and Gannoc and Mara all gathered to welcome her back. Leron had briefly told her of Dansen's return, and she had supposed, when she thought of it at all, that his grief was because of separation.

She blushed again, this time at guilt for her selfishness, and put her hand on Leron's arm. "I—I just realized something. You haven't spoken with the Karif, yet, have you—about our reports from Vahn."

Leron raised his eyebrows. "I think you have been aware of all my movements, this past day and a half."

Sibyl turned to Dansen. "Dansen, I'm so sorry, but I forgot there was no way you could have learned—it was so long ago . . . I spoke with Arrod in Vahanavat and helped her to go free; by now she must be safe in Melismala." Dansen dropped his roll on the tablecloth and looked at her in amazement. Impulsively she got up and went round to where he sat and squeezed his shoulders. "The dolphins were with her, and she said they would see her safely home. Bodrum had her in a seawater cell, below the tower where I was hostage; she told me how she was captured and how the worst part of it was having to leave you."

"She said that? And she is well? You are sure?"

"She was hurt a little—but I am sure she got home safely."

He was so delighted Sibyl could not bear to describe the whole scene truthfully. She could not avoid telling how the other Dylalyr had been killed, but Dansen was too dazed by his reprieve to take it all in at once. She squeezed him again, and he patted her arm vaguely. "I don't know what to say," he said at last, as Sibyl sat down by Leron once again. "I should not have let myself despair so easily." He suddenly smiled at them, and his tired face was transformed. "If you don't mind, I think I will try a little of that sausage," he remarked, and Leron silently filled a plate and passed it to him.

As soon as their meal was finished, Leron went to find Gannoc and attend to the business he had put off the past day and a half. Sibyl could see that the unnecessary grief they had caused Dansen pained him as much as it did her. She kissed him for their few hours' parting and went to walk in the garden alone.

That first week she visited the garden often, savoring the cold sunlight and the wild smell of spring in the air. It was beautiful there behind the old stone walls, peaceful and fresh, and Sibyl could not understand the reason for her deep discontent.

In Vahn she had been sure that a return to Leron, who loved her, would be enough. So here she was and still unsatisfied. She paced the garden restless and unhappy. How on earth could she be having a baby? She wasn't grown up herself yet. Another life would be on its own soon, a mind with a memory in which she would just be a parent. A parent! She wasn't ready to stop being a child yet. As seemed to happen so often now, she started crying. That was something else she couldn't understand. For the past few months everything was up and down and up and down. For almost eighteen years she had been self-assured and dry-eyed, and now she seemed to be in tears most of the time. It made her feel so helpless and so tired.

She leaned against the wall and made her tears go away, but the sick unhappiness in her stomach was still there, squeezing nervously. I don't want a baby; I don't want a husband; I don't even want to be loved, she thought. I just want to be on my own. A friend had told her that once, but she hadn't believed him, and now it was too late. She thought about Shadith and started crying again. Maybe I'll have lots of children, and then I'll never be free again. The thought was so terrible it dried up her tears, and she shuddered with her hands over her face, the words *too late, too late* repeating themselves in her head.

"What's the matter? Your lover leaving? I'm sure he'll come around if you ask him to." Sibyl looked up to face Dastra, silently come into the garden. Dastra gestured at her belly. "Of course, he might want to wait a few months."

Sibyl clenched her fist, and Dastra drew back a little. "What the hell are you talking about?"

"The Karif, of course. He's leaving to go back to the desert, as if you didn't know." She pointed at the lookout window. "His men are in the streets now. What will Leron say if your child has blue eyes?" Her quick eyes read the success of her last remark and her pale lips smiled.

Sibyl raised her fist again and the smile faded. "You watch your tongue or I'll twist it for you," she said. "I'm not as polite as Leron." She turned to look out through the narrow opening in the wall, and as Dastra had said, the street was filled with bright-clothed Karabdu. Ajjibawr rode among them on his shining gold horse, his headcloth knotted loosely around his neck and the sun bright on his pale hair.

She sighed and turned back towards Dastra. "At least there's no question in your case. There's no way your husband could have been the father."

Dastra's eyes opened very wide, a trick that made her look both innocent and beautiful, and then they closed a little and she twisted her mouth. "Perhaps not—but there are some who will think that yours could have been so." She laughed at Sibyl's stupefaction and swept back inside, leaving her alone in the garden.

Sibyl sat down on the bench below the window and leaned her head back. Mara had said something about rumors in the palace, but she had been so vague and tactful. Poor Leron. He had so many problems, and she was not the least of them. What if the child were blue-eyed? Perhaps she should have stayed with Ajjibawr. He had come so close to speaking, and she had turned him aside. What good would that do, anyway? She wanted to be like him more than she wanted to be with him. Strong and certain, independent. Her fate was already with her, its heart beating quietly under hers. She sighed and stood up. There was no choice, so probably it was best to give in graciously. Perhaps she could learn content.

At lunch she joined Leron with Gannoc and Ajjibawr. The Karif did not meet her eyes but murmured a polite formal greeting in a low voice. Leron carefully guided her to her chair and let his hands rest possessively on her shoulders a moment too long; she squirmed with impatience to pull free, yet hated herself for feeling so. The meal was tasteless and far too long, and she excused herself immediately afterwards, begging the need of a rest. At this Ajjibawr looked up unguardedly, and she blushed as she thought how vigorously she had ridden with the Karabdu on their return from Vahn.

She went to her private sitting room rather than to the chamber she shared with Leron, and tried to rest. She had just decided to give up and go riding when there was a soft knock on the door and a servant entered at her word. He had a message in his hand: the Karif of the Karabdu desired a private word with her before he returned to his army. She nodded acceptance and hastily tidied her dress, going to stand by the small fire. Perhaps she would absorb some strength with its heat. When she heard his step, she did not turn immediately, but her heart began its old wild leaping and she cursed herself in her mind. Then she turned and tried to smile coldly.

The attempt was not a success because Ajjibawr was looking directly into her eyes, not coldly at all. It was too late for subterfuge. She turned away and looked at the fire again. Ajjibawr moved a little closer and propped himself with one hand against the mantel. When he spoke, the depth of his voice shook her: she was always forgetting how deep and quiet his voice was. "Before I return to the Land, there are some things I would say to you." She nodded and did not look up. "You are no longer my guest or a responsibility upon my honor. Perhaps we can talk more freely here." She nodded again, swallowing. He moved his hand a little. "Can you not look up? I would have apologized before for what happened on the ship, had I thought you wished me to."

Sibyl turned away as the ready tears rose again, and she fought to keep from covering her face with her hands. She was afraid he would think it an invitation to be comforting, but he did not move; she sniffed loudly and finally faced him. "You don't understand." Her voice broke, and Ajjibawr looked at her very kindly, still not moving or trying to touch her.

"What do I not understand? Be generous and explain."

She shook her head. "I would rather be in chains to a Bodrum than hear that apology from you. Do you really regret it so much?" Ajjibawr's composure was upset; he turned away and fumbled for his snuffbox. Sibyl laughed weakly. "Are you going to sneeze or answer?"

He left the box closed in his hands and looked at her helplessly. "How can I answer?"

Sibyl leaned her forehead against the mantel, letting the fire grow painfully hot against her face. "I thought coming home was an answer . . ." She shook her head. "But I don't know now what I really want. I guess there aren't any answers."

Ajjibawr finally took his pinch of snuff; she looked up after he sneezed and saw him smiling sadly at her. "There will be some answers for you, as the years pass; but the questions will always change." He looked at her more soberly. "If there were no dissatisfaction, then you might as well be dead. Dear Heart, I am not young like Leron. Perhaps I never was as young as he. I cannot insult you with answers. You would not thank me for it if I tried, however well the arguments sounded today or tomorrow. We are all alone in our own hearts. Even that child you carry is alone and will have to find its own answers."

"There is one answer I will never be able to give truthfully."

Ajjibawr nodded. "I know. Fate is ever showing its strength and humbling our pride. But rest assured there will always be a home for your child in the desert, should such a refuge ever be required."

Sibyl's knees shook and she went to sit on the couch, covering her hot face with her hands. The Karif would never take advantage of her weakness. Soon he would politely leave, and she would never see him again; or for so long as would make no difference. Perhaps she would despise herself later; but later seemed very remote. She put out a hand to Ajjibawr, and he let himself be drawn down next to her. As he sat, he gently shook his head. "Dearest," he said, "let me leave. If you ask me to stay, you will hate me for accepting." She hid her face against him, as she had wanted to do for many weeks past.

He lifted her chin to kiss her and shook his head again. "If we must be foolish, there is no need to be mournful as well. Will it make you laugh if I tell you that I locked the door as I came in?" Sibyl looked up startled at the barred door. She began to laugh then despite her tears, and the taut skin crinkled around Ajjibawr's eyes. "That is better," he said and kissed her and she kissed him in return; then closed her eyes and waited for the tightening of his arms.

In the week that followed the Karif's return to his army, the ships of Vahn were joined by the rest of the fleet from Vahanavat. The ships soon numbered over twenty, and four were as large as the *Damar*. Only one fell prey to Dansen's glass, a small ship sent close to shore no doubt for observation. It approached the large flat barge on which Dansen had caused the lens to be mounted, and since it did not come within bowshot, it let its sails hang idly, oars shipped, clearly seeing no danger for it there. Some flashes of light came from the barge as the lens was adjusted, bright even to the eyes of Sibyl who watched from a distance, high on a parapeted walk of the castle. Leron stood nearby, but as distant as though a sword hung between them.

An orange slash of light cut across the dry, tarred hull of the ship from Vahn, and Leron involuntarily touched Sibyl's arm. There was no time for the men aboard to do anything but jump; their ship was outlined in fire, and the sails exploded with light before suddenly fading into a thin black skeleton of lines that toppled sideways into the water. The barge now rowed forward a little more quickly, covering its advance with a company of crossbowmen in the prow, and began picking up prisoners out of the water.

Leron sent Gannoc to attend to the disposal of these unwanted prisoners and turned to Sibyl. "If this Arleon is with the fleet, will he be able to understand how we struck down that ship?"

"He could figure it out." She watched the black fragments float and sink in the peaceful flat sea. "It might surprise him at first, but the idea wouldn't be that strange to him. I'm sure he won't let the ships in range again. How long can they stay at sea?"

Leron frowned, his arms crossed on the parapet before him. "The ships of Vahn are victualed for many months. And if they raid more along the northern coast, they may further provision themselves, at our expense. The Karif and his cavalry may protect the southern shore, but I fear for the north."

The following week brought them the news they had feared: a major attack on Sundrat with most of the city that lay outside the walls burned to the ground. It also brought a boat into harbor, sailing under the white flag, its parent ship standing well out to sea. Sibyl was in the council chamber when Leron met the messenger; Gannoc was there also, with Dansen. The Vahnian sailor stood with his arms folded across his chest while Leron read the brief message and handed it to Gannoc. "So, we are offered the chance of peaceful submission? That is most generous of the Master, and his First Lord. I fail to see, however, where he will petition for this power he says will add itself to his own. If he has sailed to Paradon for help, I can tell you now his journey is in vain. They fear our power and rightly so: they have lost more ships than one to the fire that we can throw."

The sailor drew in his brows angrily. "The Master has sailed to Paradon, but not for any mortal help. He will speak with the Lord of Inivin, and then you will see what it is to challenge us!"

Sibyl looked at Gannoc for enlightenment, and he spoke softly in her ear. "Vazdz is reputed to live in a land called Inivin, on the sourtheastern part of the isle of Paradon."

Leron looked at the sailor and laughed. "So, the mighty Vazdz must needs be summoned like a servant to the help of

Vahn? Where has he hidden himself these last few months, that he has not heard the news? Are his all-seeing eyes closed and his all-hearing ears stopped up? Your faith in Vazdz does more credit to your faith than to your sense. Wait, and I will give you an answer in writing to take back to your First Lord. Dansen?" Dansen sat down and carefully turned back his cuffs, smoothing the parchment with one hand.

Leron crossed his own arms and leaned back against the wall. He looked very tired and pale, but there was a lively glitter of anger in his eyes. "'Leron of Tredana sends greetings to the First Lord of Vahn and strongly urges him that he avail himself of the Master's absence and undoubted flight by surrendering the fleet to the mercies of Tredana, Treclere and the desert. Otherwise he may be assured there can be no peaceful landfall for him upon any shore in this continent.' Do you have the wax heated? Very well." Leron bent over and pushed his seal into the wax.

"Take this to your captain," he said, and the sailor took it arrogantly.

"When the Moraganas burn your houses and the Great Naqra sucks you into its belly, you will wish you had settled peacefully with us."

Leron shook his head. "The only burning will be of your ships, and as for bellies, your own will cry for food and water after another few months at sea." The sailor left, and Leron turned to them with lifted brows. "Well, Dansen, tell us, should we prepare for the attacks of Vazdz's servants?"

Sibyl shook her head dubiously. "Shirkah injured the Moraganas, but they are not destroyed. What is the Naqra? I thought it was just a decoration on the game board."

Dansen patiently explained, referring to Erlandus, and Gannoc paced about the room. "If these monsters are so powerful," he said at last, "why has Vazdz not sent them before to ravage us?"

Dansen shrugged. "Possibly the world is larger than we suspect. Perhaps there are lands beyond Paradon and Melismala. The Dylalyr believe so. Perhaps Vazdz has had need of his creatures elsewhere. Until very recently he had effective servants in his kings, Ddiskeard, Dzildzil, Gorga, Bodrum— what need in our lands of anything more monstrous?"

Leron came and sat down on the edge of Dansen's table.

He carefully moved his arm to avoid brushing against Sibyl, rubbing his eyes with his other hand. "There is then a danger of direct attack from Inivin?"

Dansen shuffled his papers. "It is a possibility, my lord. One which I would not disregard. Furthermore, there is something I once read—" he blushed and Gannoc came up to stand on his other side.

"We are waiting, Dansen. No blushing modesty. What strange new idea do you have to startle our slow wits?"

"No idea at all—nothing really—a poem that is quite ancient—I first read it years ago, and copied part into my collection of old sayings. When I came across it again last night, in its entirety, I was struck by certain parallels and copied it out to show you." He pulled out the sheet in question, scanned the text and looked up alertly. "As I say, this is very old, and the provenance is unclear. I will research it further if you think it merits it."

He cleared his throat, and read:

> *"Chains are worn instead of gold*
> *while hostages are bought and sold.*
> *Chains are struck and all go free*
> *to watch the land fight with the sea.*
> *Powers of air and Powers of water*
> *together challenge the Moon's daughter,*
> *Wing of Copper, Tooth of Bone,*
> *Eye of Fire, Heart of Stone,*
> *The oldest hunger earth has known:*
> *But which will bring the castledown?*

I fear my earlier reading was incomplete. Now that I have the whole verse clear, I cannot escape the similarities to recent events contained within it."

Sibyl leaned forward, and once more Leron moved away. "The first two verses I can understand," she said, "and also the third if Bodrum does get help from Vazdz to send against us. But what does that last part mean?"

"I believe," said Dansen, "that it is in part a description of the monsters Vazdz has at his command."

"And the hunger?" Leron asked the question so harshly they all were startled; Sibyl moved away in confusion. Dansen lifted

his eyebrows and did not answer as Sibyl went to the window,
to look out over the castle yard and wonder how to talk with
Leron.

There was no chance that day; he was busy through the
afternoon and immediately after an early supper went with
Gannoc to inspect the fortifications along the shore. Sibyl wandered restlessly from room to room and then went to intrude
herself on Mara, hoping to absorb some of her peace. Mara
had brought up apples from storage and was peeling and coring
to cook them down into thick preserves; the kitchen was warm
and fragrant. Sibyl sat down awkwardly and took over the
peeling. Each day she seemed to have less and less lap, and it
made it hard to handle things. For a while they worked in
silence, then Mara smiled as she took a new plateful of peeled
apples to quarter and core.

"Have you had a quarrel?"

Sibyl moved her shoulders irresolutely. "Not really. Nothing's been said."

"That is the worst kind of quarrel. Are you going to be
brave or wait for Leron to speak up? It may take him weeks."

"I don't know what to say."

"Confessions are never pleasant. But better to look back on
them than have a cloud over the future."

Sibyl dropped her eyes as the small sharp knife slipped and
slit the edge of her forefinger. "It wouldn't make him very
happy to hear what I have to say."

"I think he's unhappier waiting."

Sibyl put down the apple angrily and stuck the knife into
it. "Waiting for what? If everyone knows, why should I bother
to tell him? Tell him yourself." She began to get up and Mara
came over to her and put her arms around her. She was warm
and soft, and Sibyl leaned her face against her for a moment,
letting herself be soothed. Then she pulled away and wiped
her eyes. "I can't explain anything to him. I don't understand
it myself. And you wouldn't either."

Mara laughed softly and sat down by the fire again. "I don't
know why children always think they are the first people ever
to be alive. When you talk like that, you remind me of Mariti.
What would I not understand? I am fifty-five years old. I have
not been shut in a small room all that time. I have not even
lived with Gannoc all that time. For almost thirty years I lived

alone. Do you think I never wept into my pillow or despaired of the sun rising again? What would I not understand?"

Sibyl was forced to laugh and sat down again, but she couldn't speak. After a silence Mara began to talk, smiling in recollection. "A week before I was to marry Gannoc, I decided I could not. I sent him a message and left the court. I went to the estate of an old family friend, whose son had loved me once when we were little better than children. How free I felt. I went riding with him and wading in the streams and danced in the evening and laughed all day. Nor did I lock my door at night." She smiled at Sibyl's amazement. "You are very arrogant indeed if you think you invented love and pain and complications."

Sibyl blushed, and Mara continued her story. "Then I received a message from court. From Gannoc. He said he did not wish to see me again, but the queen was ill and if I would help attend her, he would make sure we did not meet. I returned and was with Leriel when she died. And then dear Mathon began to confide in me. How well he had loved the queen, and how poorly he had been able to express it. Her closeness with her twin, your father Armon, had locked him out so completely he hardly dared talk with her. And then there was poor little Leron, four years old and as good as orphaned, his father so remote in his own sorrows. Leron clung to me but he also wanted Gannoc, who was a better companion to him than his own father. So we arranged to meet for the sake of the prince. But for weeks we did not exchange a civil word. And in those weeks the image of my young lord grew dimmer, while I cried in my pillow for Gannoc to speak to me again. But because I would not say so, we spent many sad unnecessary weeks."

She smiled gently. "Gannoc at last proved the braver."

"And he was not jealous?"

"Of course he was jealous. But he was the one I married. And we have lived together now twenty-five years, so I suspect the jealousy has faded somewhat."

"At least you weren't married when you ran away."

"I don't think it matters so much when you run away. Surely it is of more importance that you have decided to come back? You were very young to promise your life away. Leron will understand in the end. You know he would rather die than lose you."

"I don't know that."

"You are all he has. Think about it."

Sibyl closed her eyes and leaned back against the settle. "Even this child isn't his."

"It will be, once it is born. A child is for the future: history need not concern you. Now, get up, go home." Sibyl's eyes flew open, and Mara laughed. "It is getting late, and if you let him go to bed and pretend to sleep, you will have to spend another night hating your pillow. Speak tonight and awake happy." Sibyl got up, and Mara wrapped her cloak around her, then hugged and kissed and hugged her again. "You are my first daughter, my lamb. Be happy." Sibyl kissed her back and stumbled out into the brisk night.

There was no sign of Leron in the palace. Sibyl had a fire built in their room and sat down next to it in her long night dress, a shawl around her shoulders. The logs glowed and fell apart, and she put on fresh wood. Finally she drowsed uncomfortably in her chair, and woke later in a cold dark room. A few bright sparks glittered in the barely warm fireplace. Leron touched her on the shoulder; he was fully dressed, and his hand was cold as though he had been outside.

"You should be in bed. I will not disturb you."

"In that case I will sit right here." She could not see his face, but his irritation was palpable.

"I do not understand. I cannot see the sense in not sleeping."

"I was sleeping, right here. And I will not get into any bed in this whole castle unless you are in it too."

"What new policy is this? I did not think you noticed whether I was in bed or not, these past few days."

"Really? I think someone who can lie without moving or turning for eight hours straight is very noticeable."

"You will not have to notice me tonight. I can sleep in the next room."

Sibyl pulled herself to her feet and groped her way to the chest by the bed's foot. "Then we'd better say good-by now." She pulled up the chest's lid and rummaged around blindly in the dark. "Can I live in Villavac? The palace there belonged to my father's family."

"You are not going anywhere in the middle of the night."

"Well, I'm sure not staying here."

She began crying angrily as she pulled out her clothes. "And you can have your damned ring." She tried to pull it off, but her fingers were swollen and it would not loosen. "I'll send it to you. What about Villavac?"

"Wouldn't it be easier to go to the desert?" Leron choked on the question, but he got it out and then stood breathing loudly.

"I don't want to live in the desert. If I wanted to live in the desert, I would never have come home."

"I thought you had changed your mind."

"So did I. But I was wrong. I'm sorry. I was stupid. But you never understood how scared I was. You still don't."

Leron began laughing bitterly. "Scared? You should find a more likely story. I have never seen you scared of anything, not even when you were a child."

"Then I guess you don't see very well. Or you might have noticed that I'm scared of being married, and I'm scared to belong to anyone, and I'm very scared about having this baby, and I'm scared of not ever being able to be free again."

Leron's voice faltered, and he stepped a little closer. "Why would you be scared of these things? It doesn't make sense."

"You called Kerys a child once when we were talking together. You forgot we were both the same age." She sighed and pushed at her clothes half-heartedly. "You still haven't answered about Villavac."

"Villavac is not much of a castle. I think you could be happier in Tredana." He touched her tentatively on the arm, and she raised her hand to take his. He held it hard, then put his arms around her shoulders. "Don't leave me again," he said softly, and she nodded, her face against his neck. Then she gasped as he stooped and picked her up, one arm under her knees and the other round her shoulders, staggering a little. Leron laughed. "A whole family is much weightier than a wife."

Next morning they lay talking in each other's arms as the dawn grew bright and full day finally filled the room. But slowly a strange smell mingled with the clean salt scent of the sea breeze; at first merely strange, then disquieting, then almost sickening despite its faintness. Leron reluctantly pulled himself out from under the covers and went to look out. He stood quite still, then turned and stretched a hand back towards the bed. "Come here," he said, in an odd voice, and Sibyl gathered up the quilt to wrap around them both as they stood in the chilly air. The sea was flat, with little wrinkles of waves, and the fleet of Vahn rode well out from the harbor, though closer than the day before. Beyond, to the north, growing against the horizon, a dark shape was rising, already much greater than the ships, though much, much farther away. The growing sickening stench came in on the wind from the water. Leron drew Sibyl against him, and the circle of his arm was painfully hard. "I fear that Bodrum has made the alliance he sought."

SONG
by ODRIC

My fingers, clumsy with a sword
were nimble on a string,
My tongue that stumbles on the law
knew well once how to sing.
Twenty-five years I sang for bread
and ate it without pain:
Eight years later with baraka
I take the road again.
Walking until I have put the hills
between me and my sorrow,
I am chilly now in the open air:
but the sun will rise tomorrow.

Chapter Five

The first day the Naqra appeared on the horizon, the sky did not grow much lighter than it had been at dawn. There was a grey haze over the water and over the sky, behind which the sun was a watery diffuse patch of light. Within the dimness, the shape of the monster slowly grew as a larger darkness; waves flooded in upon the beach and the sky was filled with the screaming of carrion-eating seabirds. The stench of the monster hung over the city.

The beacon fires by the harbor mouth were kept roaring that night; and several times Leron arose to look out the window and be sure there was no trouble abroad yet. He also kept the fire burning in their room, to try to ease the heavy rotting smell that increased with every passing hour. The following morning the sky was dimmer than the day before, brownish rather than grey; the smell and the noise of the birds was greater than ever.

At breakfast only Sibyl appeared to have slept; Gannoc and Dansen both showed signs of having been up all night. Dansen was leafing through records as he ate, shaking his head with frustration. "There is nothing here, my lord, nothing at all. The Naqra is mentioned, yes, but there are not even any myths to describe how it might be overcome. These chronicles from Vahn, which Odric sent me from Treclere, mention the smell as being most characteristic. So I do not think we can doubt that it is the Naqra."

Leron smiled at Sibyl as she poured out the ale, and she squeezed his hand before she passed him the goblet. "I do not doubt it at all," he said. "Do you not think your glass might startle or pain the creature?"

"It might, though all the chroniclers remark upon its armored hide. Perhaps I might aim at an eye or open mouth."

Gannoc interrupted him. "We have archers posted on shore and ready to go to sea also. Each company has arrows dipped in pitch. Even without Dansen's glass we might harry it away from our shore."

"How does it attack?" asked Sibyl. "What will it do to us?"

Dansen looked at her kindly. "No one knows. No one who has observed it closely has lived to record it. Even among the Dylalyr it is a mystery, one of the terrors of the deep sea where the sea people do not venture."

"Shirkah frightened off the Moraganas. We may be successful with this monster also."

Leron carefully broke apart a piece of bread and tried to speak casually. "I think it might be well if we reopened the palace in Villavac. I spoke with Gannoc, and he is willing for Mara to accompany you there, with Mariti, of course. There is a great deal would need to be done, of course, but—"

Sibyl looked at him so fiercely he was unable to continue. "How can you think for one minute I would run away! And what safety would there be in Villavac, if Tredana fell?"

Gannoc spoke softly. "I would like to have my family accompany you there."

"Have you asked Mara yet?" He shook his head. "I think you'll find she's just about as eager to go as I am." Her set face softened. "You should make up your mind, Leron. One moment you ask me never to leave, and the next you try to send me away."

Leron's reply died in his throat as a dull roar came from the harbor. Gannoc got to his feet, excused himself and hurried out, to return moments later with a baffled look on his face. "A great wave has washed in onto the beach, with wreckage of a ship from Vahn. Can the monster have turned upon its masters?"

"They were never its masters," said Dansen. "They have summoned it, but the Naqra is not to be controlled by men. Perhaps we should go and see what has happened."

On the beach there was a confusion of soldiers and curious onlookers, all gathered round the wreckage on the sands. They fell back before the small group from the palace, and the captain of the guards quickly explained what little they knew. There had been a cracking sound out to sea, followed by a brief silence and then the roar they had heard, as a jet of seawater burst onto the shore, carrying with it pulpy mangled mass they could see. Of the ship from Vahn all that remained clearly recognizable were some shattered timbers and the wadded mass of sail, thick with a black and bloody foul-smelling foam that seemed to carry in it fish, weeds, furnishings and armored fragments of the unfortunate sailors themselves.

Of all there, Dansen seemed the least perturbed, his sleeve edge drawn across his face to ward off the smell. "We can learn a little of the beast's appetite and capacity from this," he said. "One ship a day may satisfy him, or one a week. I doubt it will approach the land while there is easy prey for it on the water."

"Appetite?" said Gannoc.

"Of course," Dansen replied. "Surely it is evident that this is the waste spewed out by the monster after consuming the ship. The Dylalyr told me of certain fish that eat in this way, sucking in objects indiscriminately, to chew them a little and then force the unwanted pulp out through the teeth in a great stream of water."

He ran his eyes over the wreckage once more. "If this was one mouthful, then the accounts of the Naqra do not exaggerate with respect to size."

"I think we can see what your poem meant about the greatest hunger," said Sibyl.

Leron tightened his arm about her. "However great his hunger and capacity," he said, "he may find it harder to pull down the town than to plunder helpless ships."

Dansen mused slowly, "There are some fish that also walk the land. Let us hope the Naqra is not such a one."

That afternoon the air cleared slowly—the fog rolling back from the harbor towards the horizon, revealing first the remaining ships of Vahn huddled uneasily together just out of range of the seawall; and farther back, the Naqra. It was dark in color, irregularly patched white with barnacles, and the armored scales on its body flexed slightly, glittering in the weak yellow sunlight.

Imagining a sea monster, Leron had pictured an angular horse-headed creature like the decorative Naqra on a Castledown board: this was most unlike his imaginings. It was so much larger, and yet so indistinct, a mountainous shape rolling slightly on the breast of the water, much higher in the head than in the tail, a little like a whale though more than ten times larger. The giant tail moved slowly sideways, and a rolling wave broke white across the seawall. It seemed the monster's body was covered with spikes as well as scales, for as it rolled to one side the jagged outline showed dark against the sky. Then the head began to lift out of the water and Leron could not help taking a backwards step, distant though he was. The head was high-domed and framed by large fins like black rigid wings, sharp-edged; the eyes were round and yellow and from each corner of the wide mouth sprang three great muscular feelers, like legs.

Dansen, standing with them on the walls, nodded at the ships. "They are within range, my lord. We can burn them now if you wish." Leron shook his head and Dansen sighed, then brightened. "I can now adjust my range and angle quite well. Perhaps if I were to burn their sails, they would send out boats and surrender."

Sibyl looked at him wryly. "Then what would you have to feed the Naqra?"

Dansen looked shocked but Leron laughed. "We could fill the ships with food and sent them out to placate him, as men did years ago. But even the dragons of the western marshes would hardly make one meal for the Naqra."

He nodded to Dansen. "I think you are right; the Vahnians would surrender if we pressed them. At least most would. The monster summoned by their king will surely kill them before it kills us. Speak with Gannoc. We must prepare more room in the cells for prisoners."

Dansen agreed, than added, "I think we should make room today, but not act until tomorrow. If the Naqra takes another ship, they will more certainly accept our terms."

Next morning nothing appeared to have changed, and as Dansen worked on his barge, a small boat with messages from Leron set out across the harbor towards the Vahnian ships. It was still within the harbor when the Naqra began to move its tail from side to side and lowered its head in the water. The birds that had been settled on its back rose up in thick white noisy clouds, screaming with excitement and anticipation. The water about it began to move and suddenly with a great rush it began to suck in a great rolling green wave that drew along with it the outermost of the Vahnian ships. The vessel heeled over on its side so the sails almost swept the water, and as it was pulled in, one of the Naqra's long feelers settled heavily over it, cracking the hull and guiding it into the mouth. In the brief silence that followed, the water was white with movement, the ships from Vahn rocking wildly and the small boat with Leron's messenger holding grimly on course for the shelter of the wall.

The fins on the Naqra's head spread wide as the feelers splayed out on either side high above the water. Its eyes rolled slowly forwards, then the mouth opened and a great convulsion deep inside its armored body jetted out in a thick bloody froth. This time the mangled remains hit against the seawall, and the great wave following after did not rise so high upon the Tredanan beach. The debris was quickly white under a screaming mass of birds. The small boat sent by Leron was swamped but not capsized, and as the water died down again to calmness, it continued on its way out to sea and the frightened ships.

As Leron had suspected, the answer that came back to him was not from Bodrum. The Master was not yet returned from Inivin. In his absence the First Lord Arleon spoke, and arrogantly. Leron reflected that it would ease his fate a little to know that Arleon had perished in the Naqra's belly; even though they all shortly followed him there. As soon as he received the answer, he sent Dansen the signal to proceed, and within minutes the masts of eight small ships were burning bright as torches, high and straight and brilliant. The other ships signaled to each other, their small flags waving white in the morning sun, and moved away in close formation. Of the four large ships remaining, one was evidently the First Lord's, and he now had only twelve left in his fleet. The sailors from the crippled ships surrendered willingly, and there was no further movement from the Naqra that day.

There were now more than two hundred prisoners in Tredana, and most of these were soon put to work improving the harbor defenses. Little supervision was necessary, since the Naqra was a common enemy. In the first part of the afternoon, when the sun was strongest, Dansen tried his weapon against the monster, but as he had already determined, his lens was too small to send the sun that far. He suggested destroying the partially burned, abandoned ships, being boarded by men from the rest of the Vahnian fleet, but Gannoc disagreed and Leron also. It was evident that the First Lord's strategy was to put the empty ships between his fleet and the monster, and Leron agreed since it would buy time for them all. Dansen looked dubious. "It may only enrage the monster. He may need the taste of blood."

"You do not know this Arleon. If there were any slaves rowing his large ships, be assured that some at least lie chained now in those damaged ones. The monster will have his blood. And that is another reason I do not wish to burn them now. At least the sailors can jump."

In the days that followed, the almost empty ships were taken: two the first day, then one on each of the following two days. Each day the monster came closer. Each day the bloody spume on the beach was piled with wood and torched, but the stench hung heavily nevertheless, the smell of the Naqra itself. The air was constantly filled with the sound of squabbling birds.

After the second day, the First Lord's plan became more clear, for leaving the decoy ships at anchor, he was slowly drawing his shattered fleet away to the south. The Naqra did not seem to notice or care. Now that the Naqra was near, the details of its armored body were clear, and its round eyes hung over the city at night as large and yellow as autumn moons. In the spikes that jutted out along its length were entangled remains of past wreckages and destructions, bones of ships and men bleached white and matted with rope and canvas, overlaid with weeds and barnacles. The day it pulled in the fifth decoy ship, it was close enough to pull down also part of the seawall. The rest of the Vahnian fleet was now out of sight, to the south.

Leron walked the ramparts with Gannoc, as he did now every day, and looked down into the almost deserted streets. Gannoc sighed. "Glisser in Villavac will find our exiles a trial to him."

Leron laughed shortly. "I envy him his problems. And the footsmen will make the journey easier. They are much used to travel, and I would be most surprised if Huffing Dick does not maintain good order. He must be glad to find a use for his talents again."

"I would be happier if a few more had joined him on this journey."

"I also."

Gannoc looked out towards the broken wall and the Naqra.
"That wall stood solidly against the sea for more than two
hundred years."

"It will again and for as long. We do not know that the
Naqra can do any harm on land. I am thankful at least that the
fleet fled south and not north. The Karabdu will welcome them
gladly if they attempt to land. Seeing Arleon's head on a spear
would sweeten any day, even a last one."

"Perhaps they fear the Karabdu more than the Naqra. Is that
one of their ships returning?"

Leron squinted into the distance. "It looks to be, although
it is carrying more canvas than before."

"And sailing the swifter. Look, it is making for shore below
the harbor. With your permission I will send a man on horseback to meet it. It must be carrying a message."

In less than an hour Leron held the message in his hands.

> *The two ships nearest your harbor wall carry oil. It is*
> *up to you whether they help destroy the monster or cast*
> *a black slick on your sands. And along those sands you*
> *may relax your watch, this year at least. We sail to join*
> *the Master in Paradon.*

"I do not think the Master will welcome their news. But
what nonsense is this about oil? It is not a poison or a weapon.
If the ships carried ale we might hope to make the monster
drunk or sick: but oil is harmless."

Sibyl was curled up by the fire seemingly half-asleep, but
at his last words she looked up sharply. "What kind of oil
would a Vahnian ship carry?"

"Black oil from the ground. It is cheaper than what is pressed
from beans and useful to farmers in many ways. They may
have been taking this load to Zan:da. I hear that they use it on
their cattle, to keep their hides soft and healthy despite the
cold."

"And it burns!"

Leron shrugged. "Not readily."

She looked from him to Gannoc in bewilderment, then began
laughing. "Of course, you don't have the heat here for it. Look,
believe me, it will burn if you get it hot enough. If Dansen
burns the ships carrying oil you will have a torch twice the
height of the Naqra."

"Perhaps. But how would it defeat it?"

"If you timed it just right, or if you got him in a slick—"

"In a slick?"

"The oil will burn even on the water—it slides around on top. We could cover the Naqra with fire and fill him with it, too. As long as Mike didn't lie about there being oil."

"It is a common cargo."

"Then he's probably hoping we will succeed. It'll make his flight to Paradon a lot more comfortable."

Dansen looked at Sibyl keenly, his head a little to one side. "Is oil used as a weapon in your world?"

"In a way. It is a very common fuel. It can be very volatile, but it helps to refine it first."

Dansen nodded. "I would like to make some experiments."

Sibyl stood up near the fire for warmth and covered her eyes tiredly with one hand. "I wish you wouldn't. But I guess there's no way to prevent it."

Leron began thinking out loud. "We can send a crew out to free the slaves, if there are any aboard. Perhaps we could lash the wheel in such a way as to run one ship against the monster. Let one crash against it as the other is sucked in, touch them both off, and there is fire within and without. What do you think?" Gannoc did not answer, and Leron put his hands on Sibyl's shoulders. "What have to we lose?" he asked.

She leaned her forehead against the mantel, not looking up as she answered, "Everything."

Early the next morning a small crew bravely boarded one of the Vahnian vessels. They released the slaves, opened all the casks of oil, set the sails, and lashed the wheel firmly in place. Then as the ship began drifting towards the Naqra, they hurried over the sides and into the waiting boats. Three men, the best swimmers in the group, stayed with the vessel and did not jump until the ship was within a few hundred feet of the rank and spiny side of the monster. As they struck out for the boats, the ship gently nudged against the Naqra, and the sails entangled in its jagged spikes. In passing it touched the great pectoral fin, and as the monster sluggishly became aware of the ship, its fins, in their awakening movement, crushed the ship more firmly in among the spikes. The slow seepage of oil from its hold made strange dark shapes on the yellow glitter of morning sunlit sea.

Although the amount of liquid seemed little in comparison to the Naqra's bulk, it continued slowly to spread on the water's surface; and as the Naqra moved, the water sloshing against it began to leave dark streaks on its rough and barnacled sides. As the sun rose higher, the dark spreading out on the water showed more plainly, and the smudges along the Naqra's sides also increased. Some apparently washed its gaping gills, for the pectoral fin began to flutter, and the enormous head lifted a little in the water. The monster turned, and as a result a little more oil washed along its side. The fins rose out stiff and winglike, and the feelers lifted from the water. One fell across the seawall, crumbling the stones with its weight. The wide low mouth began to open, and the birds rose up from off its back in noisy eager crowds. As the Naqra began to draw in the last of the Vahnian ships, the oil covered water washed up against its fin and over its feelers. From his new position on the ramparts, Dansen nervously adjusted his range and uncovered the lens. Leron and the rest withdrew to one side.

The ship had heeled over now and was almost within the monster's mouth. Dansen sighted carefully, and a point of flame arose from the ship's hull while it was still a few feet away from the Naqra's gaping mouth. Dansen's timing was well-judged, for the great tower of flame Sibyl had predicted came after the ship was under the bony ledge of jaw. Already Dansen had turned his lens to the ship half-hidden by the sharp-edged fin, and it broke into flames only seconds later. The flames were bright even against the bright sky, as the oil began to light and sheets of flame rose up along the Naqra's side.

For a moment the Naqra did not move, its mouth open and its wings half-spread, its feelers seemingly relaxed. Dansen turned to the others with a shake of his head. "I have done what I can," he said, "but I fear it was not enough." Then the monster began to roar, a terrible sound that filled the sky and hung in the air like endlessly rolling thunder. As it gathered itself to spew out the flaming ship in its mouth, it apparently sucked in part of a burning ship, through its gills. The wings stood out now, shining red, partially hidden in the thick black smoke. The ship in its mouth was dislodged, still burning, and the Naqra curled to one side trying to free the other from its gill. Around it the water was churning, and the flaming oil broke into small bright spots of glitter, dappling the sea in a widening circle. The Naqra rolled over, submerging the ship,

but it did not extinguish the flame; and as it turned from side
to side, its soft-seamed underbelly was exposed and the flaming
oil seeped into the cracks in its armor plate. Now with the
feelers braced against the seawall it reared up out of the water
and made again its terrible roaring cry. It plunged back into
the water with such force, water was sent onto the beach above
the highest tidal mark, and the sand was black where it drained
away again. As the Naqra lifted its head from the water once
more, the film coated its head and fell streakily down across
the great round eyes. Its tail began to beat the water, and it
clumsily turned around towards the south, jerking and writhing,
black with oil and alive with flame. It turned farther around,
towards the east from which it had come, and the great tail
sweeping sideways pulled down the last of the Tredanan seawall. In passing, it also caught the last lingering ship, the one
that had brought the message to Leron, the vessel of the First
Lord Arleon, setting it afire and pulling it under, unnoticing.

A last time the monster roared, and the sound rumbled across
the city. The sky above the harbor was black, and the air stank
of oil and burning flesh. The Naqra coiled and writhed, spreading its fins and closing them in again, raising its blinded head
then plunging under the surface. The sea was crazily alive with
waves crisscrossing in different directions; momentarily the oil
spread it smooth then broke apart in new formations. The flames
on the water had died now, but the wreckage wedged in the
Naqra's gill still burned despite the plunges underwater.

Soon the creature was far distant from the harbor, though
still large against the sky. It made a sudden deeper plunge and
disappeared in an arcing wave of white spray. Leron slowly
relaxed his grip on Sibyl's arm and smiled shakily at the others.
Dansen was the first to recover his voice. "We have a powerful
weapon, here. If we can turn back the Naqra, what might we
not do against a mortal force?" Sibyl had been leaning on her
forearms, her head slumped wearily forward; at Dansen's words
she straightened up and looked at him sadly.

"Dansen the Learned can think of no wiser comment than
that? Can't you all see how we've played into Michael's hands?"

"Arleon is dead—his ship is gone."

"Whether he's dead or not, he's had the last laugh. He spent
less than a year here, and he lived to see the end of everything."
Leron tried to put his hand on her arm again, but she shook
him off. "We're all fools, all of us. And I'm the worst of all.

At least I knew better. Can't you see yet what this means? Do you think your fires will stay tidily at home for defense only? What about the day when someone else sends fire down on your fleet or on your cities, or burns your people in their beds? Secrets like this are never rehidden, once they're opened up. Already you can kill people you have never even seen and be killed the same way. You saw Michael's message. The rest of the Vahnian fleet will join Bodrum in Paradon. Do you think they're going to drop anchor in some peaceful bay and fish? They know about the glass on Melismala. Someday they may learn about the oil. You can't keep it hidden. Someday this will all come back on us, and worse."

She stopped for breath, one hand pressed instinctively against her belly. "Dansen, with all your reading you must see the truth in what I'm saying. Our children will live to see it, if we don't. And they'll hate us for taking away their chances before they could even get started. It would probably have been better if the Naqra had destroyed Tredana. Eventually it would have left, and we would have come back and we would have rebuilt and life would have gone on as before. But now nothing will ever be that simple again. It's over. Damn it, doesn't anyone understand? This is the end. No more nice little one-to-one sword fights. You're in the big leagues now. Look down there!" She pointed towards the beach, and they looked obediently down, like chastened children. "You're not going to get that black out of the sand. But all those miles of white sand aren't as corrupted as the future."

Gannoc fingered his beard nervously, one hand resting lightly on Mara's arm. "We had no choice."

"Oh yes, we did. But we chose to be clever, and now we won't have any further choices. That's the whole point. Weapon after weapon, and all for defense. That's the punchline of this particular joke. We're all in this together. You, me, the enemy, everybody. The world is going to grow very small. It will be fun at first, until it gets too tight. And then you'll wish there was some empty space to get lost in again, like the old days."

She walked over to Leron and covered his hand with her own. "You'd better hold on to me," she said. "I have a feeling my time may be up pretty soon." She shut her eyes and dropped her head forward against his chest. "Don't forget me when I go," she said, and he shut his arms protectively around her.

"You are not going to go," he said firmly, "and things will

be no worse than before. You will see." His voice trembled slightly though, and he could not control it.

Nor could he forget her words in the days and weeks that followed. Ironically, she seemed to. She prepared for the baby's arrival with Mara's calm assistance, oversaw various projects about the city, advised them on the cleaning of the beaches, and watched with interest as the seawall was rebuilt and the fishing fleet put into the water once more. She swore she had never been in better health and continued to ride every day; and Leron made it a point to join her no matter how busy he was.

Within a week of the Naqra's defeat, Dansen left for Melismala. Not long after, the weather became much milder. The gardens around the castle were filled with yellow and purple blossoms, and the trees unfolded their delicately green leaves. A great peace seemed to settle over the city, and it would have settled in Leron's heart also, except that he could not forget Sibyl's words. The last month of her pregnancy was one of increasing anxiety for him. Each day, the trees grew fuller, the weather hotter, the sky bluer; the gardens filled with pink and red blooms, and the nights were not much cooler than the days.

It was during this month, the first of summer, that they received word from Vahanavat, a message in the name of Varys, Master of Vahn. He declared peace and friendship between their two lands, and also spoke for Treclere, self-declared a free town though subject to Vahn in certain matters. Varys had no news of Odric, except that he had forsworn all his titles and left the town on foot. That same month messages came also from the desert and from Zanida. In the desert there were now five territories, each under its own Mekrif and subject to the Karif, but more independent than formerly. The Karabdin alliance with Tredana bore the seals of each Mekrif as well as that of the Karif.

It was in this month also that Sibyl quietly bore her daughter, one sunny afternoon while Leron was away from the palace. Gannoc met him at the gate with the news, and he rushed upstairs filled with apprehension, sure something must have gone wrong in his absence; but all he found was a quiet, dim room with drawn curtains, Mara sitting by the window with her hands folded, and Sibyl asleep on a newly made bed with her dark-haired daughter asleep on her breast.

Mara smiled at him and put a finger to her lips. "It was easy for both of them," she said, "less than three hours, but still they need their sleep. What do you think of your daughter?"

Leron knelt by the bed and tried to see her face, but she was folded in the curve of her mother's arm and her face was buried against the breast. Her black hair was in thick tight curls that Leron tentatively touched. "She has beautiful hair," he said at last and leaned over to touch his lips to Sibyl's face.

His heart was pounding with excitement and she must have sensed it, for her eyes opened and she smiled, very tired yet very peaceful. "How do you feel?" he asked and she smiled again and closed her eyes.

"Fine. But I know now why they call it labor. I never worked so hard in my life. What do you think of her?"

"I can't tell. Is she pretty?"

Sibly chuckled, and the baby stirred. "Not bad, for a baby. Say hello, sweetheart." She shifted the baby to show its face, and it squirmed its fists into its eyes and began smacking its mouth in an instinctive gesture as she held it up, cradling the limp head with one hand. "She's fat, isn't she?"

Leron stroked the face with one finger, and he had never felt smoother skin in all his life. "No," he said, "she's perfect."

He continued to think she was perfect during the difficult first month when she cried at all hours and had no interests other than food and sleep. During the second month she began to reward his faith by settling down into a predictable routine of set needs and desires. They named her Tamaris at Sibyl's request, and in the third month, as was customary, she was given her name officially in a public ceremony, throughout which she screamed. Dastra's son, born a few weeks after Tamaris, was also a healthy child and as fair as his mother. Leron only saw him twice, but it was enough to convince him that one could not compare a hairless pink baby with no eyebrows to a golden-skinned one with dark curls and blue-black eyes. Mara had explained how the eyes would change to brown later, but as Tamaris grew, only her right eye turned brown, so dark it was hard to see the pupil. The left eye stayed dark blue, and it gave her face an intriguing cast.

Whenever possible, Leron held her. He carried her out for fresh air, and he carried her inside for exercise. She slept in the crook of his arm while he visited the stables or the barracks or the kitchens, and Sibyl laughed and said that she would not mind another if it took so little of her time. She had a sling made so she could carry Tamaris before her when she went out riding; and together, she and Leron chose a pony to be trained for her first lessons when she was a year old. In the third month of her life Tamaris visited Villavac with her parents and then, as summer faded into autumn, they took her to Sundrat as well, to visit before the roads should be closed by winter.

The crowds that welcomed them in Sundrat did not seem to surprise her in the least. Tamaris yawned and closed her eyes again. Leron had a distaste for the palace in Sundrat, which had been in Ddiskeard's family in years past. So for their stay he commissioned the use of the old inn built above the sea. The first morning there, while Tamaris slept inside in her nurse's arms, he went with Sibyl to stand in the innyard overlooking the harbor; it was just a year since he had watched the *Damar* take the departing tide.

"This past year seems more full than the eight years that preceded it."

Sibyl laughed. "It has taken us a full year to be together in Sundrat, as Ginas intended. Did you hear that the Players will be here tonight? They visit Sundrat every autumn. If Ginas is with them, I think I should try to soften a little what I said before."

"You did not say more than the truth."

"It was less than the truth, but I'd like to soften it a little anyway. I've been thinking about it. She made this whole problem by trying to prove her own prophecies. Michael wouldn't have come here if he hadn't followed me, in a sense. And it was because of him that Dastra had that child. Of course, it all could have come about some other way, but it still looks as if Ginas was as much manipulated by fate as any of us. She thought she was a mover, and she was just one of the pieces."

They had planned to visit the Players that evening, but Ginas forestalled them by bringing her wagons into the innyard. Liniris cried with happiness as she greeted Sibyl and hugged the wailing Tamaris to her breast; Ginas was silent and composed, but there was a gleam of satisfaction in her eyes. While Sibyl awkwardly welcomed her, she inclined her head but said nothing.

At this Sibyl's temper burst from under her control and she repeated to Ginas the observations she had made to Leron earlier. It was clear that Ginas had never looked at the events of the past year in that light, and she was whiter than normal as she listened. At the end she lifted her hand slowly so the light flashed from her ring, and let her gaze wander slowly from Leron to Sibyl to the child now sleeping in Liniris's arms. "These matters are beyond us all," she said. "It must suffice that all has worked out happily. Sibyl came to us as she was meant to, whether or not I willed it so: and so she will leave as she is meant to, whether or not she wishes."

At this, Sibyl paled and hastily took Tamaris from Liniris's arms, while Liniris looked at her grandmother reproachfully. Leron tried to make light of Ginas's words, but throughout the rest of the afternoon Sibyl kept looking at him and touching his hand as though to be sure of his presence. Even that night, when they joined the crowds in the torchlit square, Sibyl continued to lean against him, and Leron kept his arm tightly about her waist.

The torches were hardly necessary, for the moon was full and its light flooded the square. First they watched the dancers and the acrobats, and as they watched, Sibyl laid her head on his shoulder. "What were you thinking this morning?" She spoke so suddenly Leron was caught off guard.

"When?"

"When you woke and got up on one elbow and looked at me for so long."

Leron smiled. "I was learning your face. In another year or two I should have you all memorized. I am a slow but thorough student."

She hid her face against him, and soon he could feel the heat of tears through the fabric of his shirt. "I'm glad," she said at last in a muffled voice. "I'm glad that you won't forget me."

On stage the play had begun, but Leron was too busy comforting Sibyl to watch closely. A puppet monster had been added to the story, a Naqra that was destroyed with stage fire and coiled and writhed around the stage. He tried to make her look at it and laugh, but she continued to weep against his shirt, refusing to listen to the mocking declamations with which each character bowed and left the brightly lit stage.

I am the Queen, I wear a gold crown,
I wait for the King to call:
As soon as it's dark, I mask and depart,
and so I make fools of you all.

I am the King, I wear a gold crown,
and everyone comes at my call.
If you complain, I will throw you in chains,
and so I make sure of you all.

I am Clerowan, I carry a sword,
I answer to no man's call:
In at the window, out at the door,
and so I make fools of you all.

The Clerowan figure was last to go, and at the play's end bowed deeply to the crowd, making a flourishing salute with his sword. Still she would not look up. He buried his hand in her soft hair and cradled her head against him. Finally she began sniffing and rubbed the back of her hand across her face. "I'm sorry," she said. "Can we go back to the inn?" As he nodded, she took his hand in hers. "Please don't let go."

Some of the Players were making a procession through the streets, trying to entice more people to the show; and Leron and Sibyl found themselves in thicker crowds than before as they walked. A woman nearby screamed, and Leron jumped, tightening his clasp on Sibyl's hand, but there was no danger. Some of the Players, in masks and costumes, were mingling with the crowds, and the woman had been startled by one of the masks when she turned. Leron laughed and spoke reassuringly to Sibyl, and she smiled nervously. Then Liniris pushed through the crowd to join them, taking Sibyl's free hand. Suddenly the puppet dragon appeared, writhing overhead, carried by dancers, and everyone fell back before it. It was a far prettier monster than the Naqra, with wings spangled silver and ruby glass eyes. They were pushed back again, and Sibyl's hand was pulled from Leron's as she stumbled.

The dragon went by, and the crowd swelled forward and Leron's heart pounded with pointless apprehension until he found Sibyl's hand again. He went on a few paces to where

there was a little space and stopped to look at her. It was
Liniris's hand he held. He dropped it in confusion and looked
around. "Where is Sibyl?" he cried, and she looked at him
blankly.

"She was just here. She will catch up with us." Leron's
stomach tightened as he looked up into the round white moon
and down across the dark moving crowd. One of those faces
should be hers, but was not. He pushed back to where they
had been standing, and the futility of it rose in his throat. It
was full moon in Sundrat, and a full year had elapsed. How
could he have released her hand, when she had begged him
not to? Twice now he had lost her, and there might not be a
third chance.

from
THE CHRONICLES OF MELISMALA
Concerning Paradon

. . . *yet another curiosity of Paradon is that the lords of the
seven provinces take, instead of titles, the names of their pre-
decessors. Thus for five hundred years or more there has been
an Arbab in the East, a Dallal in the North-East, a Mimbash
in the North, a Sahlar in the North-West, a Padeshi in the
West, a Zehar in the South-West and a Mulke in the South. To
the South-East lies* INIVIN.

*Sahlar is keeper of the Oracle and it is to him the others
come in times of petition to Vazdz. He is assisted by Mimbash
and Padeshi, but the words of Vazdz come only from his mouth.
Padeshi controls the fleet and Mimbash the army; to Dallal
and to Arbab are allotted the tasks of taxation and distribution,
to Mulke the management of grain and livestock and to Zehar
the maintenance of records. Twice every year they meet at
Mount Timmor, midwinter and midsummer, and plan those
raids our island knows so well, and many other evils.*

Epilogue

Even at night the infirmary was never dark: the corridors were filled with greenish light, and the room with its open door filled up with the smell and color of the halls. Sibyl's head hurt when she finally came fully awake, and she would have turned over except for the I.V. needle taped in place in the back of her left hand. "Of course," she thought, "I fell. But I don't have to stay here anymore." She woke in a sudden panic, trying to remember where she was. The rapid list of places she might find herself asleep in did not include a green-lit hospital. She tried to sit up, but whatever fogged her memory was also dizzying, and she sank back asleep again.

The nurse who woke her was very understanding. "That's the medication, honey. Nothing to worry about. Just a little concussion. You'll be home in a couple of days, that's what the doctor said. Won't even miss any exams. Always seems there's nothing but trouble when the moon's full." She began untaping the needle from Sibyl's hand. "No need for this, you can have a real breakfast. You know, I swear there's something in all this astrology business. Ask any hospital. Always emergencies during the full moon. You're lucky you only bumped your head. It's a mercy that friend of yours wasn't killed when he drove his bike off Weeks Bridge. And that's not the craziest thing that happened this weekend, not by a longshot. How does an omelet sound? Here, I'll crank up your bed." She continued to talk nonstop while she uncovered the pale, white, cellophane-wrapped breakfast and then moved briskly on to the next room.

Sibyl poked at the rubbery egg with her plastic fork and then gingerly touched her forehead.

Memory was coming back. Something she was supposed to do—she mustn't forget—the play. There was a TV button by the bed, and she poked it on. The big calendar numbers behind the morning program desk were a day too late. Opening night had come and gone. She pushed the tasteless tray away and leaned back against her pillows, shutting her eyes. The light in the ceiling was so bright: it flattened out everything in the room. She turned off the TV and tried to remember what else she wasn't supposed to forget—a ship was it? Something about a horse, too, and a bearded man and a baby. She pressed her head again and frowned in concentration. She was almost asleep when someone gently rapped on her door and stepped in. She blinked and tried to sit up and then smiled as she recognized Michael. He held a big bunch of yellow chrysanthemums in his white bandaged hand and smiled back at her with a strange glitter in his eyes. "Hey," he said, "are we friends?" Sibyl sat up, shook her head to clear it, and then reached for the flowers.

"Of course," she said. "What's all this about Weeks Bridge?"

Michael grinned and sat down on the edge of her bed. "Nothing important. Just proved that bikes don't swim, that's all." He took her hand and patted it. "Baby, you sure had me worried there for a while. But now I think everything's gonna be just fine." Sibyl nodded uncertainly and pressed the bitter-smelling flowers up against her face.

A clipping from the *Boston News*, Sunday Edition, October the 12th.

Mr. and Mrs. William F. Barron, of Boston, Mass. and Palm Beach, Fla. are proud to announce the engagement of their daughter Sibyl Tamara to Michael James Arleon, also of Boston. The couple are in their second year at Harvard University in the Faculty of Arts. No date has been set for the wedding.

Airs, Ancient and Modern

Compiled from various sources,
Vahnian, Trecleran and Tredanan

1. Slaves' A, B + T (Book One, Chapter Four)

2. Odric's Footsmen Song (Book Four, Chapter Two)

3. Ballad of Clerowan (trad.) (Book Three, Chapter One)

4. The Dance at the Crossroad's Inn (Book One, Chapter Four)

Fantasy from Ace
fanciful and fantastic!